The Gift Basket from the Newly Undead Welcoming Committee, Kentucky Branch

- A copy of *The Guide for the Newly Undead*
- SPF 500 sunblock
- Iron supplements
- The numbers of every vamp-friendly blood bank in the area
- A six-pack of Faux Type O
- A bottle of Plasma-Protein
- Floss

Bestselling authors sink their teeth into *NICE GIRLS DON'T HAVE FANGS*

"Move over Sookie Stackhouse—there's a new kid in town."
—Susan Andersen, *New York Times* bestselling author of *Cutting Loose*

"Molly Harper is a gifted storyteller with a hilarious new twist on vampire romance."
—Stephanie Rowe, national bestselling author of *Sex & the Immortal Bad Boy*

NICE GIRLS DON'T HAVE FANGS

MOLLY HARPER

Pocket **Star** Books
New York   London   Sydney   Toronto

Pocket **STAR** Books
A Division of Simon & Schuster, Inc.
1230 Avenue of the Americas
New York, NY 10020

This book is a work of fiction. Names, characters, places, and incidents either are products of the author's imagination or are used fictitiously. Any resemblance to actual events or locales or persons, living or dead, is entirely coincidental.

First Pocket Star Books paperback edition April 2009

POCKET STAR BOOKS and colophon are registered trademarks of Simon & Schuster, Inc.

For information about special discounts for bulk purchases, please contact Simon & Schuster Special Sales at 1-800-456-6798 or business@simonandschuster.com

The Simon & Schuster Speakers Bureau can bring authors to your live event. For more information or to book an event contact the Simon & Schuster Speakers Bureau at 866-248-3049 or visit our website at www.simonspeakers.com

Designed by Davina Mock-Maniscalco

Cover illustration by Gene Mollica. Cover design by John Vairo Jr.

Manufactured in the United States of America

10 9 8 7 6 5 4 3

ISBN-13: 978-1-4165-8942-6
ISBN-10:   1-4165-8942-2

For my family, who are nothing like the characters described herein.
(They made me write that.)

Acknowledgments

Acknowledgments for a first novel are something that you write and rewrite in your head for years, without any assurance that your book will be published and those words will be needed. And now I can't seem to find the right way to thank all the people who have helped me make this a reality. Many thanks to my husband, David—I could not ask for a more loving, supportive man. Thanks to my parents, for allowing me to become the person I was supposed to be, even if that person is a little weird. To the rest of my family, who may not always get me, but always love me. To Brandi Bradley, who, despite being the most honest woman I know, never fails to find something nice to say. To Stephany Evans, the greatest agent a girl could ask for—thank you for tolerating so many e-mails. And to editor extraordinaire Jennifer Heddle, who has been incredibly patient while working with a publishing newbie.

NICE GIRLS DON'T HAVE FANGS

Vampirism: (n) 1. The condition of being a vampire, marked by the need to ingest blood and extreme vulnerability to sunlight. 2. The act of preying upon others for financial or emotional gain. 3. A gigantic pain in the butt.

I've always been a glass-half-full kind of girl.

The irritated look from Gary, the barrel-chested bartender at Shenanigans, told me that, one, I'd said that out loud, and, two, he just didn't care. But at that point, I was the only person sitting at the pseudo-sports bar on a Wednesday afternoon, and I didn't have the cognitive control required to stop talking. So he had no choice but to listen.

I picked up the remnants of my fourth (fifth? sixth?) electric lemonade. It glowed blue against the neon lights of Shenanigans' insistently cheerful decor, casting a green shadow on Gary's yellow-and-white-striped polo shirt. "See this glass? This morning, I would have said this glass isn't half empty. It's half full. And I was used to that. My whole life has been half full. Half-full family, half-full personal life, half-full career. But I settled for it. I was used to it. Did I already say that I was used to it?"

Gary, a gone-to-seed high-school football player with a gut like a deflated balloon, gave me a stern look over the pilsner he was polishing. "Are you done with that?"

I drained the watered-down vodka and blue liqueur from my glass, wincing as the alcohol hit the potato skins in my belly. Both threatened to make an encore appearance.

I steadied myself on the ring-stained maple bar and squinted through the icy remains of the glass. "And now, my career is gone. Gone, gone, gone. Completely empty. Like this glass."

Gary replaced said glass with another drink, pretended to wave at someone in the main dining room, and left me to fend for myself. I pressed my forehead to the cool wood of the bar, cringing as I remembered the smug, cat-that-devoured-the-canary tone Mrs. Stubblefield used to say, "Jane, I need to speak to you privately."

For the rest of my life, those words would echo through my head like something out of *Carrie*.

With a loud "ahem," Mrs. Stubblefield motioned for me to leave my display of Amelia Bedelia books and come into her office. Actually, all she did was quirk her eyebrows. But the woman had a phobia about tweezers. When she was surprised/angry/curious, it looked as if a big gray moth was taking flight. Quirking her brows was practically sign language.

My joyless Hun of a supervisor only spoke to people

privately when they were in serious trouble. Generally, she enjoyed chastising in public in order to (a) show the staff just how badly she could embarrass us if she wanted to and (b) show the public how put-upon she was by her rotten, incompetent employees.

Mrs. Stubblefield had never been a fan of mine. We got off on the wrong foot when I made fun of the Mother Goose hat she wore for Toddler Story Hour. I was four.

She was the type of librarian who has "Reading is supposed to be educational, not fun" tattooed somewhere. She refused to order DVDs or video games that might attract "the wrong crowd." (Translation: teenagers.) She allowed the library to stock "questionable" books such as *The Catcher in the Rye* and the *Harry Potter* series but tracked who read them. She kept those names in a file marked "Potential Troublemakers."

"Close the door, Jane," she said, squeezing into her desk chair. Mrs. Stubblefield was about one cheek too large for it but refused to order another one. A petty part of me enjoyed her discomfort while I prepared for a lecture on appropriate displays for Banned Books Week or why we really don't need to stock audiobooks on CD.

"As you know, Jane, the county commission cut our operating budget by twenty percent for the next fiscal year," Mrs. Stubblefield said. "That leaves us with less money for new selections and new programs."

"I'd be willing to give up Puppet Time Theater on Thursdays," I offered. I secretly hated Cowboy Bob and his puppets.

I have puppet issues.

"I'm afraid it's more serious than that, Jane," Mrs. Stubblefield said, her eyes flitting to the glass door behind me. "We have to reduce our salary expenses as well. I'm afraid we can't afford a director of juvenile services anymore. We're going to have to let you go."

Maybe some of you saw that coming, but I didn't. I got my master's degree in library science knowing I would come back to "my" library, even if it meant working with Mrs. Stubblefield. I'm the one who established the library's book club for new mothers who desperately needed to leave the house on Thursday nights for a little adult conversation. I'm also the reason a small portion of the Hollow's female population now knows that *Sense and Sensibility* was a book before it was a movie. I'm the one who insisted we start doing background checks on our Story Time guests, which is why Jiggles the Clown was no longer welcome on the premises. I'm the one who spent two weeks on my knees ripping out the thirty-three-year-old carpet in the children's reading room. Me. So, after hearing that my services were no longer needed, I had no response other than "Huh?!"

"I'm sorry, Jane, but we have no other choice. We must be careful stewards of the taxpayers' money," Mrs. Stubblefield said, shaking her head in mock regret. She was trying to look sympathetic, but her eyebrows were this close to doing the samba.

"Ida is retiring next month," I said of the ancient returns manager. "Can't we save the money through eliminating her position?"

Clearly, Mrs. Stubblefield had not expected me to argue, which proved that she never paid attention when I spoke. Her eyebrows beat twice, which I took as code for "Just leave quietly."

"I don't understand," I continued. "My performance reviews have been nothing but positive. Juvenile circulation has increased thirty-two percent since I was hired. I work weekends and nights when everyone else is too busy or sick. This place is my whole . . . What the hell are you looking at?"

I turned to see Mrs. Stubblefield's stepdaughter, Posey, standing near the main desk. Posey waved, her bagged lunch bobbing merrily. Something told me she wasn't just early for a picnic with her wicked stepmother. Posey was virtually unemployable since she'd set fire to the Pretty Paws Pet Grooming Salon while blow-drying Bitty Wade's teacup poodle. Apparently, doggie nail polish, heat elements, and long-haired breeds are a cataclysmic combination. This was the third job Posey had lost due to fire, including blazes started with overcooked microwave popcorn at the Video Hut and a boiled-dry coffee pot at the Coffee Spot. When Posey wasn't working, she moved back into her dad's house, which also happened to be Mrs. Stubblefield's house. Clearly, my boss had decided she could share a water cooler with Posey but not a bathroom.

I was being replaced. Replaced by someone who needed flash cards to understand the Dewey decimal system. Replaced with someone I'd hated on principle since the sixth grade, when she penned the following in my honor: "Roses are red, violets are black. Why is your front as flat as your back?" Thanks to middle-school politics, I was labeled "Planed Jane" until my senior-year growth spurt. Regarding the use of "planed," I believe one of Posey's smarter friends showed her how to use a thesaurus.

Posey spotted me and froze mid-wave. I uttered several of the seven words you're not supposed to say in polite company. My soon-to-be-former boss let out an indignant huff. "Honestly, Jane. I can't allow someone who uses that language to work around children."

"You can't fire me," I told her. "I'll appeal to the library board."

"Who do you think signed your termination notice?" Mrs. Stubblefield preened while sliding the paper toward me.

I snatched it off her desk. "Your crony, Mrs. Newsome, signed the termination notice. That's not quite the same thing."

"She got approval from the other board members," Mrs. Stubblefield said. "They were very sorry to see you go, but the truth is, we just can't afford you."

"But you can afford Posey?"

"Posey is starting as a part-time desk clerk. The salaries aren't comparable."

"She starts fires!" I hissed. "Books tend to be kind of flammable!"

Ignoring me, Mrs. Stubblefield reached into a drawer to remove an envelope, which I hoped included a handsome severance and detailed instructions on how to keep health insurance and feed one large, ugly dog without bringing home a paycheck.

The final indignity was Mrs. Stubblefield handing me a banker's box already packed with my "personal effects." I stumbled through the lobby on legs that threatened to buckle under me. I ignored the cheerful greetings from patrons, knowing I would burst into tears at the first face I recognized.

I got into my car, leaned my forehead against the white-hot steering wheel, and began to hyperventilate. After about an hour of that, I mopped my blotchy face on my sleeve and opened what I thought was my severance check. Instead, a bright yellow-and-white-striped slip of paper drifted into my passenger seat, shouting, "Twenty-five dollars! Plus free potato skins!" in huge red letters.

Instead of a severance check, I got a gift certificate to Shenanigans.

This prompted another hour or so of hysterical crying. I finally pulled myself together enough to pull out of the library parking lot and drive toward the mall. Shenanigans was one of the first big chain restaurants to come to Half-Moon Hollow after the county commission finally unclenched its "dry" status. After decades of driving over county lines to Maynard to get liquor by the drink, Half-Moon Hollow residents could finally enjoy cocktails close enough to walk home drunk instead of drive. Personally, I find that comforting.

McClure County was one of the last counties in the state where you could legally smoke in restaurants—

thank you, local tobacco farmers—so the bar was cloaked in several layers of cigarette haze. I made myself comfortable on a bar stool, ordered some potato skins and a *large* electric lemonade. For those unfamiliar with the beverage, picture a glass of Country Time that looks like Windex and makes your face numb. After the gift certificate ran out, I handed my Visa to Gary the bartender and told him to start a tab. I switched to mudslides sometime around happy hour. An "I'm too tired to cook" crowd trickled in after dusk. Unfortunately, this crowd included Adam Morrow, the man whose blond cherubic children I would one day bear . . . if I ever worked up the nerve to talk to him.

I've had a crush on Adam since elementary school, when he sat beside me in homeroom. (Thank you, alphabetical order.) When we were kids, he looked like Joey McIntyre from New Kids on the Block, which is like preteen-girl kryptonite. And Adam was one of the few people who never called me Planed Jane, so double points for him. We moved in different circles in high school. OK, we were barely in the same building. He was the dimpled football hero with a mysterious dash of debate-team participation. I spent lunch breaks shelving library books for extra Key Club points. I didn't see him while we were away at college, but I like to think it means something that we both came home to Half-Moon Hollow. I like to think that he values his roots and wants to give back to his hometown. And that it makes me less of a loser for living less than five miles from my parents' house.

Adam's a veterinarian now. He makes his living curing puppies. I'm a woman of uncomplicated tastes.

Adam smiled at me from across the bar, but he didn't come over. It was just as well, since (a) he probably didn't remember my name, and (b) I might have melted off my bar stool into a puddle of hammered, unemployed hussy. Plus, I have had the same reaction around Adam since our very first elementary-school encounter. Total lockjaw. I cannot speak normal sentences. I can only smile, drool, and burble like an idiot . . . which was pretty much what I was doing at the time.

Had I not suffered enough already?

I considered cutting my losses and scuttling home, but I did not need to add "blackout drunk driver" to my already tattered reputation. Nestled in a crook of the Kentucky-Ohio River border, Half-Moon Hollow is not one of those stereotypical Southern towns where everybody knows everybody, we have one stoplight, and our sole cop carries his bullet around in his pocket. We had the second stoplight installed last year. And don't call it a "holler," or I will personally track you down and hurt you.

Of the ten thousand or so people who live in this town, I am on a first-name basis with or related to about half. And if I don't know you, I know your cousins. Or my parents know you, your parents, or your parents' cousins. So I was caught off guard when a complete stranger materialized on the bar stool next to me.

"Hi," I said. Actually, I think I yelled in a too-loud drunk voice. "That was . . . unexpected."

"It usually is," said Mr. Tall, Dark, and Yummy. He asked the bartender for the Tequila Sunrise Special and was served in record time. As I stared at the maroon cloud swirling in the bottom of his glass, he asked if I would like another drink.

"I'm already drunk," I said, in what I'm sure I thought was a whisper. "I probably need to switch to coffee if I'm going to get home tonight."

His hesitant smile showed perfectly even, almost unnaturally white teeth. *He probably suffers an addiction to tooth whitener,* I mused. He seemed to take pretty good care of his skin as well. Hair: longish, winding in dark, curling locks from a slight widow's peak to his strong, square chin. Eyes: deep gray, almost silver, with a dark charcoal ring around the irises. Clothes: dark, well cut, and out of place in the Shenanigans crowd. Preliminary judgment: definitely a metrosexual, possibly gay, with a spontaneous yen for mozzarella sticks.

"What's your name?" Mr. Yummy asked, signaling the bartender to get me a cup of coffee.

"Jane Jameson," I said, extending my hand. He shook it with hands that were smooth and cool. I thought that he must moisturize like crazy. And then I started to babble. "It's mind-blowingly boring, I know. Why don't I just go completely bland and change my last name to Smith or Blank? Or why not do the mature thing and go by my middle name? Well, you'd have to be crazy to go by my middle name."

"And what is that?" he asked.

"Enid," I said, grimacing. "After a distant relative. My

dad thought it was really original because no one else had a daughter named Enid. I guess it hadn't occurred to him *why* nobody else had a daughter named Enid. I think Mama was still hopped up on the epidural, because she agreed to it."

"Purity," he said. I think I squinted at him, because he repeated himself. " 'Enid' is Welsh in origin. It means 'purity' or 'soul.' "

"It also meant there were a lot of jokes at my expense when our full names were announced at school," I muttered sulkily. The coffee was a bitter black jolt to the system after frothy frozen cocktails. I shuddered. "Graduations were hell."

He paused for a moment and then laughed, a good explosion of honest, barking laughter. It sounded rusty, as if he hadn't done that in a while.

"Jane Enid Jameson, my name is Gabriel Nightengale," he said. "I would very much like to keep you company until you are able to drive home."

I wish I could remember that first conversation with Gabriel, but Mighty Lord Kahlua prevents it. From what I can piece together, I gave him the gory details of my firing. I think I impressed him by explaining that the term *firing* came from ancient Britannic clans. When village elders wanted to get rid of someone, instead of accusing him of witchcraft or shunning him, they would burn down the undesirable's house and force him to move on. I don't know how this stuff sticks in my head, it just does.

We eventually wandered into a discussion of English literature. Gabriel expressed affection for Robert Burns, whom I deemed "too lazy to spell correctly." I would feel bad, but he called my beloved Ms. Austen a "repressed, uptight spinster." I was provoked. We called a truce and decided to discuss a much more neutral subject, religion.

It took several hours, but I sobered up considerably. Still, I was reluctant to leave. Here was a person who didn't know me before my life was turned upside down. He couldn't compare the before and after Jane. He didn't know me well enough to feel sorry for me. He only knew this slightly tipsy girl who seemed to amuse him.

And there was something compelling about my new friend. My nerve endings telegraphed "Run, stupid, run!" messages to my brain, but I ignored them. Even if I ended up chained in his secret basement dungeon . . . well, it's not as if I had to go to work the next day.

When the bartender yelled "Last call," Gabriel walked me to my car. There was an uncomfortable second when I thought (hoped) he might kiss me. He was staring at my mouth with a sort of hunger that made me feel light and giddy. After a few agonizing seconds, he sighed, opened my car door, and wished me good night.

I drove slowly along Route 161, pondering my drinking buddy's apparent indifference. Had I ever been the type of girl who got picked up in bars? Well, no. I am the designated girl buddy. If I had a nickel for every time I heard the words "I don't want to ruin our friendship,"

I wouldn't be driving a car with an ominously flashing "check engine" light.

As I passed High Station Road, the taste of coffee and mudslides bubbled at the back of my throat with threatening velocity. I vurped up essence of Kahlua and mumbled, "Great, I'll finish the night off by vomiting."

Then Big Bertha's engine rattled and died.

"Aw, crap," I moaned, thunking my head against the wheel. I did not relish the idea of walking alone at night on the proverbial dark country road. But Half-Moon Hollow had two towing garages, both of which closed after eight P.M. I didn't have much of a choice. Plus, there was also the tiniest possibility that I still had alcohol in my system, so calling the police or AAA was not a great idea.

So, out of my car I climbed, grumbling about useless machines and blowtorch revenge. I was wearing open-toed sandals, very sensible shoes when one is schlepping toward a hatchet-wielding, woods-dwelling maniac. I spent every other step kicking bits of gravel out of my shoes, knowing that it was forming impenetrable gray cement between my toes. I passed roadside banks of wild day lilies, their orange lips clenched shut against the night, their heavy heads leaving tracks of dew on my jeans. To top off my evening, I was going to have to check myself for ticks when I got home.

The one thing I had going for me was good night vision. I thought so right up until I fell face-first into a ditch.

"Seriously?" I yelled at the sky. "Come on!"

Swiping at the mud on my face and the stones embedded in my knees, I made more creative use of those seven words you don't say in polite company. Lights fanned over me. I spun toward the noise of a moving vehicle, wondering whether it was wise to wave and ask for help. Without warning, I felt a hot punch to my side. My lungs were on fire. I couldn't catch my breath. I pressed a palm against my ribs and felt warm gushes of blood spilling out onto the grass.

"Aw, crap," was all I could manage before falling back into the ditch.

You're probably wondering what happened to me. I certainly did. Even in the darkness that cradled me like warm, wet cotton, I thought, *Was that it? Was that my whole life? I'm born. I have an unfortunate permed-bangs era. I'm fired. I die?*

I remember being so sorry that I wasn't able to say good-bye to my family or at least give Adam Morrow a kiss that would have left him inconsolable at my funeral. I was also very sorry about my choice of last words.

Then the movie started. The whole tunnel-of-light thing is a hallucination, but near-death experience survivors aren't lying when they say your life flashes before your eyes. It's kind of a fast-forwarded highlight reel complete with hokey music. My soundtrack was a Muzak version of "Butterfly Kisses," which is something that I will take to my grave.

The *This Is Your Life* flashbacks allow you to watch yourself being born and dying and all the moments in between. Sitting in church in torturously starched tights, first days of school, sleepovers, camping trips, Christmases, birthdays, final exams, each precious bubble of time slipping from you even as you try to grasp and hold on. Some moments you'd rather forget, such as throwing up on the school bus or the time you skipped your grandpa's funeral to go to the water park with your friends. (I swear, I'll explain that one later.)

Near the end of my reel, I watched myself talking to Gabriel and wished I had more time with him. I saw us leaving the bar and my car crawling toward home. I saw a close-up of Bud "Wiser" McElray driving his beat-up red truck down the highway about two miles behind me, drinking his favored Bud Light. I watched my own masterful use of obscenities as I climbed out of my stalled car, Bud following me. I watched as I face-planted into the ditch—which, I have to admit, even I laughed at. There was a wide shot as Bud caught my hunched, muddied form in his headlights.

"Oh, come on," I murmured at the screen as Bud reached for the rifle behind his seat.

"Could be an eight-pointer," Bud mumbled, rolling down his passenger window. Another close-up of Bud's face as he squinted in concentration. His finger squeezed the trigger. I screamed at the screen as I watched myself fall to my knees, utter my oh-so-auspicious epitaph, and slump back into the ditch. Believing he'd missed his quarry, Bud put his truck in gear and lumbered away.

I screamed. "He thought I was a freaking *deer*?"

So, that's how I died. A drunk was driving along Route

161 and decided to do some from-the-truck deer hunting. Instead of a nice buck to put up on his wall, he shot
a recently fired, far-too-sober-to-die librarian.

In the theater of my dying brain, the highlight reel
came to a close. I was cold and tired. And then I woke up
as one of the undead.

2

Welcome to the fascinating world of the undead! Please use this guidebook as a handy reference as you make your first steps toward eternity. Inside you will find information on vampire nutrition, relationships, and safety. But before learning about your future, a word about our past . . .

—From *The Guide for the Newly Undead*

After thousands of years operating right under mortal noses, the Great Vampire Coming Out of 2000 wasn't the result of a TV exposé, a medical breakthrough, or a chatty vampire interviewee. It was a lawsuit.

Some of the undead choose to hold on to their original lives, continuing to work, pay taxes, and floss. In 1999, a recently turned Milwaukee tax consultant named Arnie Frink wanted to continue working for the firm of Jacobi, Miers and Leptz. But the human-resources rep, as ignorant as the rest of the world about the existence of the undead, refused to allow Arnie to keep evening hours.

Arnie got a fellow vamp with a two-hundred-year-old medical degree to diagnose him with porphyria, a painful allergy to sunlight, but the evil HR rep could not be moved. Even if leaving his condo before sunset left Arnie with second-degree burns and body odor similar to scorched dog hair, he was expected to keep banker's hours. Mr. Jacobi was a bit paranoid about office security. This prevented Arnie from making a living (so to speak) and interfered with his pursuit of happiness. So Arnie did what any red-blooded American would do. He sued.

When the allergy-discrimination argument failed to impress a judge, a sunblock-slathered Arnie flipped out in court and demanded that his lawyer be fired so he could represent himself. As his indignant counsel slunk away, Arnie declared that he was a vampire, with a medical condition that rendered him unable to work during the day, thereby making him subject to the Americans with Disabilities Act.

After Arnie was hauled off by the men in white coats, his vitals were checked, and the doctors noticed that his heart wasn't beating. Plus, he bit a nurse who tried to take his rectal temperature, but I think we can all agree she had that coming. After extensive psych evaluations, the doctors agreed that it was *possible* that Arnie was telling the truth. But they weren't willing to put it in writing.

After several lengthy appeals, Arnie won his lawsuit and got a settlement, evening hours, and an interview with Barbara Walters. The international vampire community was incensed and formally voted to have Arnie staked to an anthill at dawn. But after the media firestorm (and the "I told you so" storm from Internet conspiracy nuts), most vampires realized they should have come out a century ago. If nothing else, maybe we all could have avoided the Goth movement.

A select contingent of ancient vampires from across the globe officially notified the United Nations of their presence on Earth and asked the world's governments to recognize them. They also asked for special leniency in certain medical, legal, and tax issues that were sure to come up. Vampires tend to throw away receipts.

The first year or so was chaos. Mobs, pitchforks, the whole deal. The federal government issued mandatory after-dark curfews. Wal-Mart started selling "Vampire Home Defense Kits," including holy water, crosses, stakes, mallets, and a book of quick blessings to bar vampires from your door. The fact that these kits were generally useless didn't bother me nearly as much as the idea of holy water being sold at Wal-Mart.

Humans didn't seem to understand that they'd lived around vampires all of their lives and never realized it, that they had never been attacked before the Coming Out, never been threatened. And vampires posed even less of a threat now that they had better access to legally marketed blood. Vampires would never get their teenage daughters pregnant or tie up the McDonald's drive-through. Hell, vampires were less of a threat than Bud McElray.

Nevertheless, vampire safe houses were torched in major cities all over the world. The same international contingent of vampires, who called themselves the World Council for the Equal Treatment of the Undead, appealed to the governments for help. Vampires were given certain global rights in terms of self-defense against angry mobs, but no real progress was made in laws prosecuting said angry mobs.

In exchange for vampire public assistance programs, the U.S. federal government demanded a certain amount of information. According to the 2000 national census, there are 1.3 million vampires residing in the United States. Of course, less than half of the vampires in the United States trusted the federal government enough to participate in the census. In fact, the results showed that two percent of census takers mysteriously disappeared in the course of their duties.

The census also showed that 63 percent of American vampires live in groups of threes and fours. This is called "nesting," which vampire behaviorists attribute to their need to bond with other creatures who share their unique needs and abilities. I believe that even after death, we want someone to assure us that our butts don't look big before we leave the house. Single vampires tend to live alone in historic family homes . . . with a lot of cats.

Very few surveyed vampires were willing to disclose where they get their blood. And those who did disclose their food sources gave vague answers such as "Willing private donors." That was less of an issue after companies flooded the market with processed artificial blood, which can also be purchased at Wal-Mart. Synthetic blood was originally designed to counteract dwindling American

Red Cross donations and support military surgical units, but vampires found they could live a violence-free unlife on the stuff. This, combined with vampire blood banks offering thirty dollars a pint for real human blood, was more than enough to promote those first semifriendly human-vampire interactions.

An unexpected side effect of the Great Coming Out was the emergence of all-night industries to cater to the needs of "undead Americans." Electronics stores, delivery services, specialty dentists' offices, window-tinting shops, and, yes, tax firms. There was a new skilled, taxable labor force available to work at night. And there were new companies and products, such as SPF 500 sun block and blood banks that actually allowed withdrawals. The economic development was incredible. The recession the government had told us for years that we haven't been having? Gone. With the realization that the undead population generated more above-the-table disposable income, vampires were grudgingly accepted into the living world.

It took me a while to learn the rules. OK, it took the librarian in me weeks of careful, obsessive research to learn the rules. There was a label maker involved. I'd rather not go into it. Here's what I learned: Forget what you've heard from the vamp PR firms. Vampires are not suffering from a skin condition that makes them anemic, sensitive to sunlight, and slow to age. Vampires are magical beings, creatures of the night, children of darkness. But don't call them that to their faces—it really pisses them off.

The undead are highly sensitive to heat and daylight. Some older vamps can venture out in the day under controlled circumstances with no problem. But since their somewhat unstable molecular structure makes them pretty flammable, you get newbies who spend too much time outdoors and end up as little charcoal briquettes. Every vamp has a different level of reaction. I would find out later that I blister and smell like burnt popcorn, which I hate. That smell never comes out of your clothes.

A vamp's sensitivity to religious symbols is directly related to his or her religious participation and ethnic background B.D. (before death). Vampire legends and lore predate Christianity by thousands of years. Some vampires wouldn't react if you shoved a rosary down their pants, though I wouldn't recommend testing the theory. For others, every mention of Jesus is like being punched in the forehead. The cross reminds them of what they once were, how far they've fallen away from God's favor, the fact that they will never die. I don't know how I will react yet, so I tend to stay away from churches.

As far as I know, vampires still have souls. They have the same capacity for good and evil that humans do. The problem is that the worst can emerge when a person is no longer answering to the "no stealing, no hitting, no bloodletting" constraints of human society. The bottom line is: if you were a jerk in your original life, you're probably going to be a bigger undead jerk. If you were a decent person, say a juvenile-services librarian with a secret collection of unicorn figurines, you're probably going to be a kinder, gentler vampire. There are rare exceptions when a repressed person gets turned and goes buck wild and evil. Generally, they calm down after two hundred or so years. Or they're beheaded by angry townsfolk.

Also, for some reason, vampires tend to wear a lot of leather. Animal-rights issues aside, I don't think that's an indicator of evil. When vampires are turned, they buy leather pants. It's kind of like when human men get divorced, they get a sad apartment and a boat. It's a rite of passage.

The undead are, generally, more attractive after being turned. Even vampires who weren't conventionally attractive in life have a certain sensual sparkle. As long as they keep up with basic hygiene, they will stay that way. In order to hunt and feed, they have to be able to attract prey, yes? Chameleons blend in with their surroundings. Anglerfish have those weird dangly-bait things hanging off their faces. Vampires have bright eyes, glistening white teeth, unnaturally smooth skin, and a certain animal magnetism. If they aren't pretty, they starve. It's sort of like life in Los Angeles.

As for the other legends: Vamps do not turn into swirls of fog or bats. They can see themselves in mirrors but not in water, for some reason. They haven't slept in coffins regularly for almost a hundred years now. Leaving knots untied and scattering seeds to distract them will only work on vampires with OCD. Garlic can't really hurt them, but they tend to stay away from it because, hello, supersensitive noses. Plus, it acts as a coagulant, making drinking from someone who's just had Italian food like swallowing chewy Jell-O.

Like most aspects of vampirism, their highly developed sense of smell is both a blessing and a curse. Think about your physiological responses to anger, fear, or even arousal: sweaty palms, increased body temperature, release of certain pheromones. Well, vamps can smell all of that. So, if you're a jumpy slayer wannabe with plans to stake your first bloodsucker, they can peg you at about fifty paces. The drawback is that layer upon layer of emotions and people can be overwhelming and, if dealing with stinky fear-based feelings, pretty unpleasant.

Vampires are allergic to silver. Touching it feels like a combination of burning, itching, and being forced to lick dry ice. If you want to repel attacking vampires, just tell them you've had recent dental work.

They are not invulnerable. A stake through the heart, decapitation, and setting them on fire will kill them, but that would kill most anybody.

You don't become a vampire just by being bitten. Otherwise, the world would be overrun with bloodsuckers. To make a child, a vampire will feed on a victim until he or she reaches the point of death. This is quite an effort, considering that vampires don't usually drink much more than a pint at a time. The vampire must be careful, as drinking too much can leave the initiate unconscious and unable to drink the blood that will change him or her. I know, it sounds gross. But when faced with death by sudden gunshot wound, it's a tempting offer. The process takes a lot out of the vampire sire and is said to be the closest the undead can come to childbirth. It's why a vampire will only turn a handful of "children" in his or her lifetime.

After taking the sire's blood, the new vampire dies. The heart stops beating, the body shuts down. For three days, he or she is actually dead. In some very unpleasant cases, newbies have been embalmed and buried by mistake. I once asked an older vampire what happens to the embalmed vamps, but he just glowered at me and muttered some undead curse word.

So, in a way, it's a good thing that no one found my body. Right?

After my death, I woke up in a stranger's bedroom.

There were soft, deep blues in the carpet over the polished pine floors, in the thick drapes drawn across the windows. The room was gently lit by an old river-stone fireplace, strange in August. Wood carvings, brass knick-knacks, polished bits of glass—little touches that spoke of years of travel—were scattered around the room with a careless sort of charm.

Despite the sluggish pace my brain was keeping, this was alarming. I probably should have mentioned that at this point, I had not had sex in about three years. That's right, a twenty-seven-year-old almost-virgin librarian.

Take time to absorb the cliché.

It's not that I didn't have opportunities for sex. I had plenty of offers from bad dates, anonymous callers with breathing problems, various construction workers. But beyond a rather regrettable "let's just get it over with" en-

counter with fellow virgin and close friend Dave Chandler my sophomore year of college and an even more
regrettable "my first time was awful, maybe it would be
better with someone with more experience" experiment
with a teaching assistant my senior year, my sexual rep-
ertoire was somewhat limited.

My problem with sex was, along with most of my
problems, rooted in my brain. My head was always
speeding ahead of my libido. I could never relax enough
to let nature take its course. And there was just plain bad
sex. My partner mistaking me yelling when I caught my
hair on his watchband for cries of passion. Having to go
to the emergency room for a broken nose when Justin
Tyler head-butted me. The guy who got a mid-thrust leg
cramp and whined to the point that I walked out of his
apartment half-dressed.

I always hoped for this spark of chemistry and com-
patibility, a flash of clarity to let me know that *this* was
the guy, *this* was the time, so I should let go and enjoy
myself. But it rarely came. And by no small coincidence,
neither did I.

Between these extremely unsatisfying experiences
and my apparent inability to develop that "spark" with
any man on the planet, I just decided sex wasn't worth
the effort. If I wanted to spend an evening half-dressed,
humiliated, and unfulfilled, I'd try amateur night down
at the Booby Hatch. So I channeled my energy into my
work at the library and obsessively collecting obscure
BBC movies on DVD. *The Woman in White* with Justine
Waddell is a life-changer.

So, after years of relative inactivity, the idea that I had participated and possibly been videotaped in some drunken one-night stand with an overdecorating stranger was upsetting. The most print-friendly version of my first undead words was: "What did I do?"

I sat up and found that I was wearing clothes, which was good. But I was wearing striped cotton pajamas that were not my own, which was bad.

My brain, my throat, my mouth, everything above my shoulders felt swollen and detached. Swallowing was an effort. I struggled to get my feet over the edge of the bed. I took some solace in the fact that I had been debauched in a well-appointed bed. I rolled off the marshmallow of a mattress and flopped facedown on the floor. (Ow.)

"Misery, thy name is Mudslide," I groaned.

I braced myself against another tasteful piece, a cherry dresser with a high, narrow mirror. My considerable height allowed my head to rest just below the frame, against the soothing cool of the glass. As my eyes slowly came to focus, I thought it must have been an old mirror or some sort of carnival trick, because I was . . . stunning. My skin was clear, lineless, even iridescent in the low light. I was practically a Noxzema girl. My teeth were straighter, somehow, and a bright, unnatural white. My eyes, usually a muddy hazel, were pure amber. My hair had gone from plain straight-as-a-board brown to long waves of glistening chestnut with undertones of honey and auburn. And if I wasn't mistaken, my butt looked smaller . . . and higher.

"She finally did it!" I screeched, clutching my cotton-covered rear. "Mama tranquilized me and booked me on *Extreme Makeover!*"

I opened my shirt to see if there was any change to my breasts. I'd always secretly hoped for a slightly fuller C cup. "No luck."

"What's *Extreme Makeover*?"

I made a sound not quite human and ended up clinging to the ceiling, my fingernails dug into the plaster like a frightened cartoon cat. And I was looking at an inverted version of Gabriel the Tequila Sunrise drinker.

"You!" I hissed.

"Yes?" Gabriel asked, making himself comfortable in a handsomely upholstered wing-back chair.

"*Date rapist!*" I yelled, wondering how to tumble off the ceiling and find the mace in my purse in less than three strides.

Clearly, this was not the response he was expecting. "I beg your pardon?"

"What the hell did you give me?"

Gabriel arched an eyebrow. "Give you?"

"Must have been some pretty powerful drugs to make me forget an entire night and then cling to the fricking ceiling!" I shouted. Some little voice in the back of my brain wondered exactly how my hands and knees were sticking to the ceiling, but since I was far more interested in whatever illegal substances might be in my system, I demanded, "Now, what did you give me?"

"I think it would be best if you came down from there before I explained that."

"I think I'll stay right where I am, thank you," I said.

"And you, you stay where you are, or I'll . . . I don't know what I'll do, but it will really hurt. You, I mean."

He grinned. It was not a friendly smile, more of a "poor pitiful creature whom I'm about to devour, you amuse me" sort of smile. A very white, very pointy smile, set in an unnaturally pale face. This was when it dawned on me that I was dealing with a member of our less-than-living population.

"You're a vampire!" I exclaimed. Not the most original or astute of observations, I'll admit, but I was hanging *upside down*. I can't emphasize that enough.

Gabriel offered that disturbing grin again. "Yes, and so are you."

I'm not sure how long I hung there, staring at him. Eventually, I found my "talking to preschoolers" voice and drawled, "No, I'm a librarian. Or at least, I used to be, before I got fired today, or yesterday, whatever day it is. You stay right there!" I cried, scrambling back across the ceiling as he leaned forward. I had to admit, despite the weird wooshy feeling in my head, that was pretty cool.

"I wouldn't dream of moving," he said, sitting back again. "Perhaps you'd like to come down?"

"No, I—whaaa!" Whatever tentative grip I had on the plaster failed, and I landed safely on my feet. I straightened my pajama top. "I think I will get down, thank you."

"So glad you could join me." My undead host motioned for me to sit across from him. I plopped down in the seat, pulling anxiously at the pajama top to make sure everything was covered. "You're a very unusual young woman."

"You're not the first person to say that."

"I'm sure that's true." He nodded.

"I was just hanging from the ceiling, right? That wasn't a PCP-induced hallucination?" I asked. He shook his head. "How exactly did I do that?"

"You'll be surprised what you're capable of, particularly when you're startled." He smiled warmly. "You know, your mind is a fascinating instrument. It's jam-packed up there. Even now, in the throes of panic, you're observing, cataloging the information for later. I find that intriguing."

"Well, thank you for noticing," I said, standing up. "I am going home now and pouring every drop of alcohol in my house down the drain."

In a flash of movement, he was at my side. His cool fingers stroked my forehead. I wanted to move, to dodge those long, elegant hands. Instead, I sat transfixed, letting him stream his fingers down my cheeks. His lips hovered near my ear, and he whispered. "Remember."

I was watching movies in my head again. I saw it all, remembered everything in a hot rush of oily color. I watched lights fade away as I lay dying in the ditch. Gabriel was there, cradling me in his arms. I was drifting in that gray, misty world bordering on unconsciousness, but I could hear. I could see. He asked if I wanted to die. I shook my head, so weak, too weak even to manage "Duh."

He pressed his face to my throat. I cried out as his

teeth pierced my skin. I ripped the seams of his shirt-front as my whole body clenched. I dully registered the sound of his buttons plinking against the gravel. There was an insistent pressure as he drew my blood to the wound. After Gabriel took a few long drinks, it didn't hurt anymore. I couldn't even feel the gash in my side. I was floating. I was warm. I was safe.

Gabriel pulled away from me, leaving me cold, exposed. I whimpered, lamely trying to pull him back to my neck. That was embarrassing to watch, and it was also the point where it got weird.

Snarling, Gabriel bit into his wrist and held it over my mouth. Even in memory, I was disgusted. The feeling of his cool, coppery blood dripping past my lips was repulsive, but I couldn't stop it. I knew, at a primal, instinctual level, that I needed it to survive. He whispered encouragements in a watery language I couldn't understand. I swallowed, thinking of what was flowing over my tongue as medicine. And soon I didn't care. I claimed his wrist, pressing it to my mouth and devouring. I was drowning, filling the crushing void that threatened to take me down with it. I couldn't think. I couldn't draw enough breath no matter how hard I tried.

Gently, Gabriel pried me away from his arm. He murmured against my forehead as I writhed, my brain screaming for air. I screamed noiselessly, hot tears streaming down my cheeks. Gabriel's eyes held me, cradling me in their sympathy. In English, he whispered that this part was never easy, but it would be over soon. My heartbeat slowed to nothing. One last shallow gasp rattled in my chest. Everything was dark.

I was ripped out of the vision and into reality. I tumbled to my knees. If there was anything in my stomach, I would have gladly tossed it up onto the carpet.

"What did you do to me?" I whispered, shaking away the memory and wiping at my mouth.

"You know what I am. You know what you are," he said quietly, as if we were talking about being Episcopalian. "I offered you a choice, and you took it."

I shot him what I hoped was a truly scathing glare. "Some choice. I was dying. Some drunk shot me from a pickup. Why couldn't I have just woken up with gonorrhea like every other girl of loose moral fiber?"

He barked out a laugh. "You're very funny."

I chose to accept that as a compliment and move on. "Thanks. Well, I've got to go."

I'd taken about half a step toward the bedroom door. Gabriel was blocking my path. How did he move like that? It was really irritating.

"You can't leave," he said, closing his hands around my wrists. He seemed to enjoy the contact, judging from the way his eyes darkened and flashed. It was an epic struggle to ignore the drool-worthiness of the man currently stroking my cheek. Remembering that he'd just given me what amounted to an eternal hickey helped considerably. "You need to feed, soon. It's been three days since you've taken anything at all."

"I'm not taking anything from you." I shoved him

back even as my mind raced. Three days? He couldn't be serious. No one can sleep for three days. Oh, right, I was dead. New rules.

"You must drink, Jane."

"I won't!"

"This could be much more difficult. I'm trying to make it easy on you," he said, advancing on me.

"I don't think that's possible," I said, pressing my hand against his chest to keep him away. It was like touching a brick wall. Hard, immovable, and lifeless. There was no heartbeat beneath my palm, no breath.

This was not good.

"You have to feed, and there are things we need to discuss," he murmured. He moved closer, running the tip of his nose along my hairline. That worried me, considering the three-day bathing hiatus. But my general odor didn't seem to bother him. Quite the contrary. He pulled my hand low, dragging me against him. I desired nothing more than to lean into him, let him wrap me in those long arms, and drink from him until I couldn't care anymore.

And then my stupid logical brain piped up. I didn't know this guy. I didn't even know where I was, really. For all I knew, I was having some sort of bizarre allergic reaction to the GHB he'd slipped me. And now I was going to let him slobber all over me? Um, no.

"Stay away from me!" I threw him into a wall. Hard. Hard enough to knock some attractive watercolors off the plaster and to the floor.

I grabbed my purse, which was conveniently placed

by the front door. Gabriel was such a considerate abductor/host. He even left the front door unpadlocked.

The sun had just set, leaving a muggy late-summer evening in its wake. The scent of growth, quiet and green, hung heavy in the air. I heard everything. I saw everything. I could count the craters on the moon. I could count every mosquito buzz past, bypassing my tender skin out of respect for a fellow bloodsucker. I heard the rustle of every leaf on every tree. I could feel animals in the woods, scuttling through the grass. Dark things feeding, running, feasting—and I envied them.

"Jane!" Gabriel was framed in the front door. He did not seem happy.

I'm not a "spring into action" sort of girl. And yet I was dashing headlong into the woods like an overcaffeinated gazelle. I bounded through the trees, sensing animals stop and watch me as I sprinted by. I laughed into the wind, amazed at this new freedom. I broke into an easy lope when I could no longer sense Gabriel behind me. I stayed away from the main roads, vaulting over barbed-wire fences and through pastures. I disturbed Hank Yancy's cattle enough to send him running to his front porch with a shotgun.

It took about two miles before it registered that my feet were bare and stinging, but even that felt good. I'd never felt so alive, so aware, so ravenously hungry. I finally understood those crazy people who talked about runner's highs.

I bounded up the front steps of River Oaks, the 147-year-old pre-Civil War farmhouse I inherited from my great-aunt Jettie, and threw myself on the living-room sofa, dazed and laughing. I had to figure out what the hell to do next. First order of business, I was starving. Where did a vampire get her very first breakfast?

I was evaluating the overall ick factor of that statement when Zeb Lavelle, my best friend since first grade, strode into my living room.

"Janie, where the hell have you been?"

3

There are many alternatives to drinking human blood, including synthetic blood and animal blood. Warm-blooded animals, such as pigs or cows, are recommended, as reptilian blood tends to be bitter. In order to make synthetic or animal blood more palatable, we suggest microwaving it for thirty-eight seconds at 75-percent power. Dropping a penny into the blood (after microwaving!) also gives it an authentic coppery taste.

—From *The Guide for the Newly Undead*

"I—"

"Wait," Zeb said, pulling me off the couch and wrapping me in his long, gangly arms. I could smell traces of aftershave on his skin and French Onion Sun Chips on his breath. I could feel the blood coursing through his veins, see the staccato beat of his pulse at his throat.

Zeb was oblivious to these disturbing developments. "I'm really glad you're OK . . . what's with the pajamas?"

"I—"

"Seriously, where have you been?" he demanded. "I

heard about you getting fired on *Wednesday,* and I came here *Wednesday* to see how you were doing, but you weren't here. Did I mention that was on *Wednesday*? I can understand that you needed a self-pity bender, Jane, but you have to let someone know where you are. I've been feeding your psychotic dog for three days. Your mom's been going nuts, and you know that means she's been calling me."

"I—"

"I've been able to hold her off from calling the police for this long, but I'll feel bad if some pajama fetish freak has been keeping you in his basement this whole time."

"Stop!" I thundered, my voice pitching to a deep smoker's tenor. The raspy command seemed to settle Zeb down pretty quickly. He dropped to the couch, waiting for my next command. It was the first time in more than twenty years of friendship that he was completely silent and still.

"I'm fine." I cleared my throat and returned to my normal voice, pushing the words around the strange stretching sensation in my mouth. My teeth felt as if they were growing. "Everything is fine . . . Wait, you already heard I got fired?"

Emerging from his stupor, Zeb shot me a look both pitiful and withering. Coming from Zeb, it wasn't that intimidating. Picture Steve Zahn with big brown eyes and less impulse control. "It's the Hollow, Jane. The whole town knows you got fired."

"Oh, that's not good," I said, sinking next to him.

"Aww, it's OK," he said, putting his arm around me

again. "I've told everybody you were fired because Mrs. Stubblefield was afraid you'd take her job. And that you had proof that she was drinking at her desk." Zeb grinned, clearly thrilled with his own cleverness.

"Thanks, Zeb." I nestled into the curve of his neck. He stiffened. This was not a normal move for me. We were in the strictly no-nookie, personal-space-respecting category of platonic friendship.

Just one little nip, a sly voice told me. *He'll barely feel it. Drink your fill. He might even enjoy it.* I could picture his veins opening to me, pouring his blood over my lips, like drinking straight from a bottle of Hershey's syrup. My tongue reached out to trace the path of his jugular.

"Um, Janie, I know you're upset about your job and everything, but I don't think this is the way to go," he said, prying my hands away. Every muscle burned in the grip of my thirst, jumping under the skin. I clutched his shirt, tearing it as I pulled him to me. "I'm sorry, Zeb. I'm just so hungry."

He laughed, a nervous noise that jangled my nerves. I could smell his fear, a thick tang of adrenaline over the sweat breaking on his lip. My stomach rumbled in response.

Zeb blanched. "How about we order a pizza? My treat?"

I clamped my hands over Zeb's and pressed him back against the cushions. "Zeb, I don't want to hurt you, but I will."

"Jane!"

I whirled and, I am ashamed to say, hissed as Gabriel

threw open my front door. He swept into the room with the slow-motion, flowy-coated elegance you only see in the *Matrix* movies. Zeb gave a girlish shriek as Gabriel threw me off him and across the room.

"Sleep," Gabriel told him. Zeb slumped over, and his face melted from blind twitching terror to blissful slumber.

"What do you think you're doing?" I demanded, righting myself from my tumble into the (cold, dark) fireplace. "This has nothing to do with you."

"It has everything to do with me!" he shouted, so loudly that I felt the echo bouncing around my skull. "I am your sire. I am to guide you through your first days as a vampire. Your first feeding is a rite of passage, a sacrament. It will not be wasted on some hormone-driven frenzy. This is why I wanted you to feed from me."

"I will not drink it in a house, I will not drink it with a mouse. I will not drink it here or there, I will not drink it anywhere," I wheezed, hoping I was able to communicate adequate sarcasm through the crippling belly cramps.

"Did you just quote *Green Eggs and Ham*?"

For future reference, my sire did not appreciate being silently flipped the bird by his panting, twitching protégé.

"Jane," he said, gripping my shoulders so hard I felt my bones buckle. "My sire sent me out into the world with nothing. I was left in a root cellar to rise alone and ignorant. My thirst was maddening, bottomless. I came upon a couple of sharecroppers sitting on their front porch, enjoying the cool of the evening. I didn't know how much I could drink. I didn't realize how fragile they were."

"You killed them?"

Gabriel nodded. "I didn't know any better. I wasn't prepared for what happened. This man is your friend, your closest friend in the entire world. I wouldn't have you start your life as a vampire with such regrets."

"But I'm so hungry," I whined. "I feel like I'm going crazy."

"It's like nothing you've ever felt or will feel again," he said, smiling sadly. "You're being consumed from the inside out; all you can think of is feeding, filling up that emptiness.

"Let me make it easier for you," he said. "I've fed recently. I can nourish you."

"That's what they all say," I said, slumping to my knees. My throat was closing up. I couldn't swallow, couldn't concentrate long enough to remember that I didn't need to breathe. "Go away. This is too—" His hands were at the base of my head, pressing my mouth to his throat. I groaned, repulsed but still drawn as he dragged his nails across his jugular.

I resisted, but the smell of his skin and of the blood dripping from his wound was like freshly baked brownies. It sounds bizarre, but I'm trying to put it into terms of a smell humans can understand. It was as if I'd been sequestered on a fat farm for three days and someone was waving Godiva under my nose. I wanted Gabriel's blood. I needed it with the instinctual urgency I'd felt on the side of the road.

It was revolting and compelling. I reached out, tentatively stretching to catch the first falling drops with the tip of my tongue. My teeth ached; that new stretching sensation I realized was my fangs extending. I scraped them across Gabriel's throat, sinking into the skin. The blood gushed, lukewarm, over my lips. I swear I purred, relaxing into the curve of him. He wrapped my hair around his fist and pulled me closer. I lapped at the wound, lazily nuzzling his cheek. He sighed and rubbed my back, whispering to me.

I had flashes of images. At first, I couldn't tell whether they were from my head or Gabriel's. I think they were a mix of both. Gabriel reaching for my hand in the bar, squeezing it. Gabriel walking me to my car and the sad smile he gave me as I drove away from the restaurant. Big Bertha's taillights in the distance as Gabriel followed me home on that dark stretch of road. Gabriel's lips moving, telling me everything was going to be all right as I took my last breath. Gabriel watching over me as I slept in his house, reading passages from *Emma* aloud as he waited for me to rise.

When my stomach was finally filled, I pulled away. Gabriel grumbled a quiet protest. I let the images slosh pleasantly around in my brain as I watched the wounds on his neck close and purple into faint bruises.

"Did that hurt?" I asked, touching a fingertip to the fading mark.

He cupped my face in his hands and wiped at the corners of my mouth with his thumbs. "That wasn't a pained moan."

"Oh," I said, my voice thick and stupid. "Oh."

"You're a rather messy eater," he commented.

"You should see me around barbecue," I said, yawning. "It gets ugly."

"Well, I'm afraid I won't have that pleasure," he said, resting his chin on the top of my head. I raised my eyebrows, not quite catching the joke.

"Is feeding always like that?" I asked. "So . . . cozy?"

"No." He stopped to pluck a pine needle out of my hair. "You set the tone. You needed to be soothed, so you were soothed. With a willing partner, feeding can be as violent, as sexual, as clinical and cold as the vampire wishes. And with a human, the sensations are much more intense. They're more susceptible to our charms."

Vampire. There was that word again. And suddenly, I was awkward. I couldn't decide where to settle my weight. I wondered if I was crushing Gabriel's arm. I wondered if I had vampire morning breath.

"Is Zeb going to be OK?" I asked, watching my friend snoring happily on my couch. "Before we, um . . . before, when you said that Zeb was my closest friend in the world. How did you know that?"

"Well, as I said earlier, before you ran out of my home like a crazy woman"—he shot me an arch look—"I told you, you have a very organized mind. If I want a piece of information, I can just pluck it out."

I grimaced. "So, you read my mind?"

He grinned sheepishly. "No. You tend to ramble a bit when you've had too much to drink. You told me about Zeb at the restaurant."

"That would be your version of humor, I assume?" I asked dryly.

Gabriel actually looked contrite for a second. It passed in favor of a brighter, intrigued expression. "You're not all that experienced in the sexual arena."

If this was a sitcom, I would have just spit water all over him.

"I told you that?" I gaped at him. I couldn't think of a response rude enough, so I moved away under the pretense of checking on Zeb.

Gabriel relaxed against the wall, watching me prowl the room. "No. But I would be able to tell anyway. You smell different from most people. There's an innocence about you, a freshness. It's like the difference between cracking a good egg and a bad one."

"So, I smell like a good, decent egg. Nice." I stopped in my tracks. "Wait, is this a nice-ish way of telling me we had sex and I was lousy? That's how you can tell I'm inexperienced? Because, if so, that's just rude. And what were you doing at Shenanigans? And how did you find me on the road?"

Gabriel looked wounded. "To answer your questions in order: The only body fluid I exchanged with you is blood—"

"That's very comforting, thank you."

"The bartender at Shenanigans is a vampire pet. He keeps pints of screened donated blood behind the bar. If you know to order the Tequila Sunrise special, he mixes palatable liquor with a healthy dose of blood."

"What's a vampire pet?" I asked, suddenly overwhelmed by a vision of humans on giant hamster wheels.

"A human who is marked and kept by a vampire as a companion and a willing source of blood," he said. "They often serve as daytime protectors and help the vampire stay in contact with the modern world. It's a beneficial relationship for both sides.

"And after you left the restaurant, I was concerned for you," he said, reaching out to touch my hand. "I wanted to make sure you arrived home safely. Unfortunately, I didn't follow you closely enough. I couldn't stop that hunter from taking his shot."

"But why did you turn me?"

He ran a thumb along my brow. "I just couldn't stand the idea of a life like yours being snuffed out in such a tragic, ridiculous way. You deserved a better death."

"Oh, well, thanks," I said. "How do you thank someone for turning you into a vampire? A fruit basket? Blood Type of the Month Club?"

He chuckled. I smiled. I was relaxing, feeling some reconnection to the charming, mysterious guy I'd met at the bar. In my head, I heard glasses clinking. I could smell imitation Calvin Klein cologne and the jalapeño poppers being served to the couple next to us. Through the fog of memory, I saw Gabriel's lips curve into a smile as I compared the relative merits of Elvis Presley and Johnny Cash.

"Johnny Cash had all of the same talents and problems as Elvis—a poor upbringing in the rural South, exposure to gospel music throughout his childhood, a penchant for drug abuse," I heard myself saying against the background of chatter and clinking glasses. "They had the same sort of influencing experiences, but Johnny Cash's problematic relationship was with his father, not his mother. If he'd had the mommy issues that Elvis had instead of a compelling need to prove himself to his father, he wouldn't have been the badass man in black, the guy in Folsom Prison watching the train roll by. Elvis was a lot of things, but even with the karate and the gunplay, he was more unstable than badass."

"But you're forgetting one thing," Gabriel had said, motioning for the bartender to bring me another cup of coffee.

I'd sipped the coffee and added far too much cream and sugar. "What's that?"

"Johnny Cash had June Carter."

I had smiled. "Good point."

"The love of a good woman can save a man," I remembered Gabriel saying. "Or it can drive him to fits of unspeakable madness."

I had stared at him a long moment before bursting out laughing. "Well, now I know how to inscribe my next Valentine's Day card."

Gabriel didn't seem accustomed to a woman laughing at him. It had taken him a few seconds, but then he was laughing, too. Gabriel was a rare find. He was nothing like the men my age who lived in the Hollow. For one thing, he seemed to realize that wearing a baseball cap was not a substitute for combing one's hair. He seemed to enjoy the contents of my brain, instead of looking at it as something that had to be canceled out by the contents of my bra. And I don't think he'd even heard of NASCAR.

"How did we even get on this subject?" I'd asked, squinting at him.

"I honestly don't know," he had said, sipping his drink. "I asked you about your family's church background, you went on a tangent about having to sit through the annual All-Gospel Sing and 'Karen Newton's atonal warbling.' Gospel led to Elvis, Elvis led to Johnny Cash. I don't think I've ever absorbed so much random trivia in one sitting. I do enjoy watching your mind work, though. I can practically see all the little cogs and wheels clicking into place. Tell me more. My knowledge of contemporary music is somewhat limited."

"Contemporary?" I'd laughed. "We're talking about rockabilly music from the 1950s."

Gabriel had raised his hands defensively. "Well, I haven't bought an album in a while."

Looking back, I really should have picked up on that as a clue that I was dealing with a vampire. But I'd been too pleased with ebb and flow of the conversation to pay attention, one subject leading to another and another in lazy concentric circles like smoke rings over our heads.

The memory was like reliving a pleasant dream, one that leaves you disappointed when you wake up and realize it wasn't real. Only Gabriel was real, and it seemed I could pick this dream up again if I wanted. Now I touched Gabriel's shoulder and tried to speak as carefully as possible. "Look, I'm really grateful that you saved my life. I know what would have happened if you hadn't intervened. It's just I've had so much to absorb. And I didn't adjust to change gracefully while I was living."

He was quiet again, studying me intently, looking for rhyme or reason in a brain where I was sure he'd find little of either. I looked away, brushing at the bloodstains at the corners of my mouth with a tissue.

"So, you're inexperienced," Gabriel said, more of a statement than a question.

"Yes, I thought we just covered this."

Gabriel would not be swayed from his line of questioning. "How?"

I blushed, a rush of Gabriel's blood coming to my cheeks. "That's none of your business."

"I only ask because vampires with even the slightest hint of innocence are rare these days. For that matter, humans with the slightest hint of innocence are rare these days. It's rather refreshing."

"Why don't you just put a big red stamp on my forehead?" I grumbled.

"Given your literary proclivities, why not a red letter sewn on your clothing?" he asked, his lips quirked.

I frowned at him. "I think it's time for you to go."

"I think I should stay and look after you," he said. "Your first few days can be a difficult transition. Your senses, your feedings—"

"It's already been a difficult transition." Besides, I wondered, where was Gabriel going to stay? Where would he sleep? Where would I sleep? Where would I get blood? Who would pry Zeb off my couch? "I just need some time to myself. I promise to send up the bat signal if I need you."

"After spending more time with your kind, you will realize that remark was in very poor taste," he said, rising. "I'll take your friend home."

I used some super-speed of my own to block Gabriel's path to the couch. "Wait, you can't just take him. I mean, how do I know you're not going to snack on him on the way home?"

"I give you my word," he said, looking wounded again. He was awfully sensitive for someone who'd lived off the blood of the innocent for more than a century.

"But what, specifically, will you do?" I demanded. "You're not going to leave him in a ditch or anything, are you? You don't even know where he lives."

"I've lived through two world wars and the disco era. I think I can manage." I must have appeared unimpressed. He sighed. "I will look at his driver's license and take him home. I will use his keys to take him into his house. He will remember that you are a vampire, but he will have no memory of your attacking him."

"You can just wipe his memory?" I asked. "Can I do that? Because I'd kind of like to get my uncle Dave to stop telling the story about me flashing my panties at his wedding reception."

Gabriel stared at me.

"I was three," I explained. "Pink panties were a big deal."

He snorted, an intriguing and undignified noise. "Yes, you might develop the talent. And you may be able to replace those memories with new ones of your own design. It's a handy trick when one needs humans to forget how they sustained neck punctures. Every vampire has different abilities, talents. Just as every human cannot carry a tune . . ." He trailed off as he read my horrified expression. He rolled his eyes, exasperated. "I'll give him a good memory, with sports victories and beer drinking."

"Thank you," I said, wondering how my Zeb, my sweet, *Doctor Who*-watching Zeb, would react to memories of touchdowns and Budweiser.

"I will see you soon," Gabriel said, taking a step closer to me. I stepped back. He let a frisson of disappointment pass over his features and hefted Zeb off the couch.

"Wait, I thought you had to be invited before you could go into someone's house," I said as Gabriel moved effortlessly to the door.

He shifted, jiggling Zeb. "It's a common misconception. And under normal circumstances, we wouldn't. It's just rude."

I closed the front door behind Gabriel and locked it. Then I unlocked it. What the hell could an intruder do to me, really? Then again, I didn't want some Buffy wannabe sneaking into my house and staking me. So I turned the lock again. Irritated with myself, I sank to the floor and scrubbed my hand over my face. "Three days ago, I was a law-abiding librarian. I had a dental plan and baking soda in my fridge. Now I'm unemployed, undead, and apparently kind of skanky."

"Rough day, pumpkin?"

"Yeah," I said, pressing the heels of my hands over my eyes to ward off a gathering headache.

My great-aunt Jettie appeared at my left and pushed my hair back from my face. "Don't worry, honey, things will work out. They always do."

"Yeah." I said, willing myself not to cry. Vampires, surely, didn't blubber like little girls.

Aunt Jettie patted my head fondly. "There's my girl." I smiled up at her through watery eyes.

Wait. My great-aunt was dead. The permanent kind of dead.

"Aunt Jettie?" I yelped, sitting up and whacking my head against the wall behind me.

Note to self: Try to stop reacting to surprises like a cartoon character.

"Hey, baby doll," my recently deceased great-aunt murmured, patting me on the leg—or, at least, through my leg. My first skin-to-ectoplasm contact with the non-corporeal dead was an uncomfortable, cold-water sensation that jolted my nerves. *Blargh.* I shuddered as subtly as possible so as not to offend my favorite deceased relative.

Aunt Jettie looked great, vaguely transparent but great. Her luxuriant salt-and-pepper hair was twisted into its usual long braid over one shoulder. She was wearing her favorite UK T-shirt that read, "I Bleed Blue." The sentiment was horribly appropriate, all things considered. It also happened to be the shirt she died in, struck by a massive coronary while fixing a flat on her ten-speed. She looked nothing like the last time I saw her, all primped up in one of my grandmother's castoff suits and a rhine-stone brooch the size of a Buick.

Jettie Belle Early died at age eighty-one, still mowing her own lawn, making her own apple wine, and able to rattle off the stats for every starting Wildcats basketball player since 1975. She took me under her wing around age six, when her sister, my grandma Ruthie, took me to my first Junior League Tiny Tea and then washed her hands of me. There was a regrettable incident with sugar-cube tongs. Grandma Ruthie and I came to an understanding on the drive home from that tea—the understanding that we would never understand each other.

Grandma Ruthie and her sister Jettie hadn't spoken a civil word in about fifteen years. Their last exchange was Ruthie's leaning over Jettie's coffin and whispering, "If you'd married and had children, there would be more people at your funeral." Of course, at the reading of Aunt Jettie's will, Grandma Ruthie was handed an envelope containing a carefully folded high-resolution picture of a baboon's butt. That pretty much summed up their re-lationship.

Aunt Jettie, who never saw the point in getting mar-ried, was all too happy to have me for entire summers at River Oaks. We'd spend all day fishing in the stagnant little pasture pond if we felt like it, or I'd read as she put-tered around her garden. (It was better if I didn't help. I have what's known as a black thumb.) We ate s'mores for dinner if we wanted them. Or we'd spend evenings going through the attic, searching for treasures among the camphor-scented trunks of clothes and broken furniture.

Don't get the wrong idea. My family isn't rich, just able to hold on to real estate for an incredibly long time.

While Daddy took care of my classical education, Jettie introduced me to *Matilda, Nancy Drew,* and *Little Men.* (*Little Women* irritated me. I just wanted to punch Amy in the face.) Jettie took me to museums, UK basketball games, overnight camping trips. Jettie was included in every major event in my life. Jettie was the one who undid some of the damage from my mother's "birds and bees" talk, entitled "Nice Girls Don't Do That. Ever." She helped me move into my first apartment. Anyone can show up for stuff like graduations and birthdays. Only the people who truly love you will help you move.

Despite her age and affection for fried food, I was knocked flat by Jettie's death. It was months before I could move her hairbrush and Oil of Olay from the bathroom. Months before I could admit that as the owner of River Oaks, I should probably move out of my little bedroom with the peppermint-striped wallpaper and into the master suite. So, seeing her, crouching next to me, with that "Tell me your troubles" expression was enough to push me over the mental-health borderline.

"Oh, good, it's psychotic-delusion time," I moaned.

Jettie chuckled. "I'm not delusion, Jane, I'm a ghost."

I squinted as she became less translucent. "I would say that's impossible. But given my evening, why don't you explain it to me in very small words?"

It was good to see that Jettie's deeply etched laugh

lines could not be defeated by death. "I'm a ghost, a spirit, a phantom, a noncorporeal entity. I've been hanging around here since the funeral."

"So you've seen everything?"

She nodded.

I stared at her, considering. "So you know about my disastrous fourteen-minute first date with Jason Brandt."

She looked irritated as she said, " 'Fraid so."

"That's . . . unfortunate." I blinked as my eyes flushed hot and moist. "I can't believe I'm actually sitting here talking to you. I've really missed you, Aunt Jettie. I didn't get to say good-bye before you . . . It was over so fast. I went to the hospital, and you were gone, and then Grandma Ruthie started talking about moving all of your stuff out of the house. I felt so lost, and everybody just seemed to be talking over me—Mama and Grandma Ruthie, they just acted as if my opinion didn't matter, even though I was the closest to you. And then the will was read, and Grandma Ruthie just lost her mind in the middle of the lawyer's office and told me I had no right to the house, and it wasn't supposed to go to me, and she was going to contest the will as invalid because you were obviously mentally incompetent. And I didn't care about any of it, because none of it was going to bring you back—"

"Honey." Aunt Jettie chuckled. "Take a breath."

"I don't need to anymore!" I cried.

In my years with Aunt Jettie, I'd learned to recognize her "trying not to laugh" face. She wasn't even making an attempt at it. She was just rolling around on the ground, braying like a hyena.

"It's not funny!" I cried, swatting through her insubstantial form.

Jettie continued to cackle while I pouted.

"It's a little bit funny," I admitted. "Dang it. Change of subject. Did you get to see your whole life played over instrumental soft rock before you died? What about your funeral? I didn't get one, because no one knows I'm dead. But did you get to see your funeral?"

"Yeah." Jettie grinned. "Great turnout. Shame about the suit, though. Couldn't talk your grandma out of it, huh?"

I shrugged. "She wanted to send you to your grave with some semblance of decorum, or so she said."

"I looked like Barbara Bush in drag," Jettie snorted.

"Barbara Bush is dignified no matter what," I offered. "Hey, if you've been here all along, why can I see you now?"

"Because I wanted you to see me." Jettie seemed pained, brushing her icy fingers along my cheeks. "And because you're different. Your senses have changed. You're more open to what's beyond the senses of normal, living people. I don't know whether to be happy that you can see me or sad about what's happened to you, sugar pie."

I groaned. "See, now I know it's bad, because the last time you called me sugar pie was right before telling me my turtle died."

Awkward pause.

"So, what's it like being dead?" I asked.

"What's it like for you?" she countered.

I sighed, even though I didn't have to, technically. "Unsettling."

"Good word." She nodded.

"What do you do? I mean, is there some sort of unfinished business I need to help you complete in order to move on to the next plane?"

Her voice rose to a Vincent Price octave. "Yes, I'm wandering the earth, seeking revenge on Ben and Jerry for giving me the fat ass and massive coronary. And I give out love advice to the tragically lonely."

"Is that an ironic eternal punishment for the lady who died an eighty-one-year-old spinster?" I grinned.

"Single by choice, you twerp."

"Banshee," I shot back.

"Bloodsucker."

I leaned my head against her insubstantial shoulder. "I missed you, a lot. Did I mention that?"

"A time or two," she said. "I missed you like crazy, too. Even though I saw you every day, not being able to talk to you was just horrible. That's part of the reason I just couldn't let go. I wanted to keep an eye on you."

"Well, good job, Aunt Jettie." I rolled my eyes. "I lost my car keys three times last week, and I got turned into a vampire."

"I know, as a guardian angel I leave much to be desired," she said. "But if it makes you feel any better, the car keys were my doing."

"You hid my car keys?"

"Had to amuse myself somehow," Jettie said, her eyes twinkling with ghostly mischief. "I may be dead, but I'm still me."

"Remind me to have that stitched on a sampler," I

muttered. "Though this certainly explains the vaguely obscene limericks composed with my refrigerator poetry magnets."

Jettie shrugged but seemed pleased to have been noticed. I looked out the window and saw the pink streaks of dawn curling into the clouds. I felt my strength leeching from my bones. I was so tired even yawning seemed like a heroic effort. I couldn't think about how I was going to explain my three-day disappearance to my parents or that I may have started a badly fated relationship with a guy who regularly bites people. I couldn't think about the fact that I couldn't die or get a tan anymore. All I wanted was sleep.

I climbed the stairs, drew the shades tight, and then threw a thick quilt over the curtain rod. I dropped into bed and felt Jettie's clammy hands brush my face as she pulled the quilts up to my chin. In a few minutes, I was, to use a bad pun, dead to the world.

4

Loved ones may be upset by your unexplained three-day absence. If you're not comfortable talking about your newly risen condition, try plausible explanations like a severe stomach flu, emergency dental surgery, or temporary amnesia.

—From *The Guide for the Newly Undead*

When the phone started ringing at around seven A.M., I realized the wisdom of sleeping in a soundproof coffin.

"It's jealousy, sweetheart, nothing but pure jealousy," Mama was saying when I pressed the receiver to my ear. Mama had dispensed with phone greetings years ago, when I started giving her reasons I couldn't stay on the phone as soon as she said hello. "Mavis Stubblefield has had it in for me ever since I beat her in the Miss Half-Moon Hollow Pageant in 1967. She's been waiting for years to get back at me, and now she's gone and fired you. Jealousy."

"Yeah, Mama, I'm sure that's what it's all about," I said, straining to see the clock.

Wait, why wasn't Mama screaming at me for disappearing? Why wasn't she reliving the twenty-six hours of labor she suffered only to birth a child who didn't call her every day? Why wasn't she reminding me that it was seven A.M. and I was still unmarried? In my head, I cobbled together an explanation, which was impressive considering the whopping two hours of sleep.

"Mama, did you get a phone call this morning?" I asked, burrowing under the quilts. "A really early phone call?"

"Oh, yes, honey, from your Gabriel," she chirped, as if she and the sexiest man not-quite-alive were exchanging recipes before dawn. And when did he become "my" Gabriel?

"He explained . . . well, I can't remember what he said exactly, but I understood that you needed some time to yourself after you were so unfairly let go. I'm just happy that you found someone so charming to spend your time with."

"Mmm-kay," I murmured, deeply sorry that I'd cast aspersions on the ethics of mind wiping. I owed Gabriel a fruit basket *and* a membership in the Blood Type of the Month Club.

"Since you're free today, why don't you meet Jenny and me for lunch?" Mama asked.

"I don't think I'll be getting out much today, Mama."

Mama gasped. "Why, honey, are you sick? Broke? Hurt?"

"Mama!" I shouted over the din of loving maternal intrusion. "Just come over, after dinner, and we'll talk."

Mama's (s)mothering instinct could not be denied. "Do you want me to bring anything? I could make a pot pie."

"No food. After dinner. Bring Daddy." I hung up before she could answer.

How was I going to explain this to my parents? I foresaw a good deal of blaming and wailing in my immediate future. I pulled the pillow over my face in a lame attempt to suffocate myself. And then I remembered I didn't need to breathe. Dang it.

"Don't worry, pumpkin, I locked the doors. No one, meaning your mama, is going to barge in," Jettie said, materializing at the foot of my bed. I shrieked, launching the pillow through her.

"Can you knock or put a bell around your neck or something?" I grumped. "Maybe rattle some chains before you walk into a room?"

"It's good to see you're still a morning person," Jettie teased, tossing the pillow back at me. "Don't worry, honey, if your Mama comes over, I'll just give her the usual. Cold chills, goose bumps, a vague feeling of unease, as if she's left the iron on. Nobody sticks around with that stuff going on."

"Thanks, Aunt Jettie," I said, falling asleep before the blankets settled over me.

As the sun set, my eyes snapped open. I felt great. Energized. Refreshed. All of the things those fancy mattresses are supposed to do for you. I bounded out of bed and threw the curtains back to bring in the moonlight. I wondered where I could get some of those fancy black-out shades that hotels use. I made a mental note to look up vampire redecorating Web sites.

I heard a knock at my front door, and my good mood dissipated. Mama was early. Knowing there was no time to get dressed, I trotted down the stairs and prepared for the parental pajama critique.

"Yoo-hoo?"

I skidded to a stop. Mama never said "yoo-hoo."

I opened the front door. There was a pair of shapely legs sticking out from under a ridiculously large pink-wrapped gift basket. My world just kept getting weirder and weirder.

"Hello?"

"Hi!" the legs said. "I'm Missy Houston of the Newly Undead Welcoming Committee, Kentucky division."

My uneasiness at letting a strange vampire into my home battled the manners Mama had pounded into my marrow. Manners, marrow, and Mama won out. "Would you like to put that down?"

"Thanks. Inhuman strength or not, this thang's heavy," she huffed, putting the mega-basket on my foyer table. Missy was wearing a perky petal-pink Chanel knock-off suit with a matching faux-Coach purse and heels. Even the headband in her perfectly flipped champagne-colored hair was pink. It was comforting to know that I didn't have to give up pastels in my afterlife. I looked washed-out in black.

"It's so nice to meet a newcomer," Missy trilled in her melted-sugar twang, more Texas than Kentucky. (We tend to abuse our long *I* sounds as opposed to . . . all the sounds.) Missy shook my hand in a digit-crushing grip. Unsure of whether this was some sort of test, I resisted wincing and squeezed right back.

"Jane Jameson," I said, keeping a bland smile plastered across my face. "How did you know I've been . . ."

"Turned? Vayamped out? Recruited to the legion of soulless bloodsuckers?" She trilled again at my perplexed expression. "Oh, shug, you've got to keep your sense of humor about being undead. Otherwise, you'll just go toppling over the abyss into madness."

Yet another throw-pillow saying to be stitched.

"I can sense the location of other vampires, their energy," Missy explained. "Newbies tend to give off megawaves when they rise. That's why I'm in charge of the welcome wagon."

"Makes sense." I nodded. "Haven't I seen you before?"

"On my billboards, most likely. Up until two years ago, I was one of the top-selling real estate agents in the tricounty area. I went to a convention in Boca Raton. I had one too many margaritas, met a tall, pale, and handsome man in the bar, and woke up a vampire."

"I was mistaken for a deer and got shot," I offered.

"Oh." Finally, she was speechless. It didn't last long. "I have always loved this house. Great upkeep, considering the age. They just don't make them like this anymore. High ceilings. Huge kitchen. Wonderful windows. Great natural light, even though you can't really appreciate that now. Original hardwood floors?"

I nodded, watching Aunt Jettie materialize at her writing desk. I glanced over to Missy, who was still appraising my floors as her needle-thin heels clicked on the polished wood. She didn't notice the dearly departed Wildcats fan scowling in the corner.

"Well, this is just a little welcome gift from the local branch of the council," Missy was saying. "Sort of an orientation in a basket. SPF 500 sunblock, iron supplements, floss, a six-pack of Faux Type O, a bottle of plasma-protein powder, and the numbers of every vamp-friendly blood bank in the tristate area. There's also a copy of *The Guide for the Newly Undead*."

"There's a handbook?" I asked, plucking it from the pink-wrapped cornucopia. "Thank God."

Aunt Jettie cleared her throat and rolled her eyes toward Missy.

"Well, this is very sweet," I said. "I really appreciate it. I'm sure I'll see you at the next pot luck or something."

Missy laughed, swinging her tiny pink bag onto her arm. "You're gonna be a hoot at the meetings, I can tell."

Meetings? I was just kidding.

A few more minutes of polite chitchat, and Missy was firmly ensconced in her black Cadillac. After watching her taillights depart through the window, I turned to Aunt Jettie. "What was with the facial charades?"

"I just can't stand Little Miss Matching Everything." Jettie sneered as I toted the basket into my cheerful yellow kitchen with blue gingham curtains and set it on the white tile counter next to the cookie jar shaped like a cheeky raccoon. Jettie perched next to the sink. "Back when she was living, she tried to talk me into listing this place with her. Said that maybe I needed to go into one of those nice assisted-living places. The little snot."

"Why couldn't she see you? I thought seeing ghosts is one of the benefits of being undead."

"I didn't want her to see me," Jettie said.

"Well, she brought treats, so she's not half bad in my book," I told her, removing the ginormous pink bow. As my stomach rumbled, I read over the label of Faux Type O. From what I had heard, it was the Rolling Rock of artificial bloods. Light and palatable, with a smooth finish and 120 percent of your recommended daily allowance of hemoglobin.

"A stranger drops fake blood on your doorstep, and you're going to drink it?" Jettie asked. "I thought we had a nice long talk about stranger danger when you were seven."

"There's a safety seal." I held it up for her inspection. "It's either this or I go hunting for hitchhikers to feed on."

Jettie covered her eyes, but she was able to see through her hands. I was not exactly thrilled at the prospect of snacking on the blood equivalent of Cheez Whiz, but I needed to get used to it. There was no way I was feeding on live victims on a regular basis. I couldn't stand the thought of hunting when I was living. Obviously, that was some sort of cruelly ambiguous psychic foreshadowing.

What the hell. If it was gross, I had a package of fudge

Pop Tarts that I could rub on the raw hamburger in my fridge.

Faux Type O came in little plastic jugs that reminded me of milk bottles. I popped the top and sniffed. It wasn't bad, vaguely yeasty and salty. Jettie came in for a closer look.

"Do you mind?" I asked as she picked up a pencil and poked at my right upper fang. I brought the bottle to my lips, pinched my nose, and swallowed. It rolled past my lips, thick and smooth. I didn't gag, which I took as a good sign.

"How is it?" Jettie asked.

"Not bad," I said, rolling the remnants off my tongue. "It has a kind of Diet Coke aftertaste, artificial and beefy."

"You make it sound just delightful," Jettie snorted as I drained the bottle. I wiped my mouth and tossed the bottle into the recycling bin.

"So, you're dead," I said. "I wasn't together enough last night to ask, what exactly do you do all day? Besides hide my keys."

"I listen to your phone calls. Make you feel like you're being watched. Move things around. Create cold spots." At this point, I glared at her. Unmoved, she levitated my dish of Hershey Kisses just to show she could. "Sometimes I visit other spirits around town. You wouldn't believe how haunted the Hollow is."

"Oh, I think my mind is opening up to the possibility," I said dryly. "Give me a for instance?"

"Well, the golf course. If people realized how many

dead men in ugly pants are wandering around there, they wouldn't go near it," she said, smirking like the proverbial cat with a canary and/or cream. "Including your grandpa Fred."

"Aw, I loved Grandpa Fred," I said, pouting, which was difficult considering the fangs. "I hate to think of him wandering the earth for eternity in plaid polyester."

"Oh, he's fine, honey." She waved a hand. "Happy as a clam. And even happier now that we've been seeing each other."

"You mean you're seeing him as in dating him? I honestly don't know what to say to that." I shook my head.

"I can't help it if your grandma married all of the good-looking men in town. We were bound to cross paths sometime," Jettie said, shrugging.

She had a point. To recall childhood memories of my grandmother, I didn't need the scent of oatmeal cookies or Ivory soap, just Designer Imposter Chanel No. 5 and hearing the phrase, "Darling, I've met the most wonderful man." My grandma Ruthie, Jettie's sister, had been married four times, so many times that I started calling every old man I saw at the grocery store Grandpa. Mama put a stop to that after Grandpa Number Four, Fred. He was a nice man. Shame about the lightning strike.

All of Grandma Ruthie's husbands had died under weird circumstances. A milk truck hit Grandpa John, my real grandpa, back in the days when milk was actually delivered door-to-door. Grandpa Tom had a heretofore-unknown allergy to rhubarb and had an anaphylactic reaction while Grandma was baking her famous strawberry-rhubarb pie. Grandpa Jimmy died from a brown recluse bite on the *inside* of the throat. His doctor's article on the improbability of such a bite was published in several medical journals. And poor Fred, struck down on the twelfth hole at the Half-Moon Hollow public golf course. It's a wonder Grandma hadn't been questioned by the police or at least gotten a cool nickname like the Black Widow.

Of course, that would probably be in poor taste, given what happened to Grandpa Jimmy.

That was why I was allowed to go to the Wacky Rivers Water Park with Rae Summerall on the day of Jimmy's funeral. Apparently, Mama realized that it wasn't normal for a little girl to have a designated funeral dress. After Fred, she told Grandma it was time to slow her prolonged death march down the aisle. Grandma had been dating a very nice man named Bob for the last five years. They'd been engaged for four and a half.

Bob was proof that medical science could keep pretty much anyone alive. He'd had his gall bladder, one of his lungs, part of his pancreas, and his prostate removed. He spent more time in the hospital than out. Why was this sweet man engaged to my Grandma? I can only imagine that he actually wanted to die, and he saw marriage to her as his only way out.

"As long as Ruthie keeps killing off husbands, I'll have an active social afterlife." Jettie preened.

"That's just gross." I shuddered. "But maybe your committing postmortem infidelity will distract Mama and Daddy from my nifty new nocturnal lifestyle."

Jettie blanched. "Your parents are coming here? Now? Oh, honey, that's not going to go well."

"Thanks, that helps," I told her, stuffing the pink bow and cellophane into the trash. "I bet you ten bucks Mama shows up with a pot pie."

Mama's almost-from-scratch chicken pot pie was my favorite B.D. meal. All crusty and filled with cream-of-chickeny goodness. I already missed it, though I did have seven of them in my freezer. Mama operated under the assumption that I was eight years old and incapable of feeding myself. It was physically impossible for her to cross my threshold without some form of nourishment. She once offered me cheese crackers from her purse while we were standing *in my kitchen.*

Like Grandma Ruthie, Mama attributed Jettie's leaving me River Oaks to senility. Obviously, it would have been much better to leave the family manse to my sister, Jenny, who would be able to care for the house properly. Crafty, thrifty, and the proud owner of an industrial-grade glue gun, Jenny made Martha Stewart look like a bag lady. And she fulfilled each of my mother's daughterly requirements by being (a) elected cheerleading captain in high school, (b) married to a chiropractor right after graduating from paralegal school, (c) the mother of two boys, Andrew and Bradley. They were barely children, really, more like hyper badgers in Abercrombie and Fitch T-shirts.

Nonetheless, Jenny assumed that bearing fruit of her loins meant that all family possessions funneled to her.

After I moved into River Oaks, I found dozens of little preprinted "Jenny" stickers marking a good deal of the antiques. In anticipation of Aunt Jettie dropping dead, Jenny had surreptitiously tattooed furniture, figurines, and family portraits, with the little blue dots to claim dibs on what she saw as her share of the inheritance. Fortunately, Aunt's Jettie's iron-clad, very specific will prevented what I'm sure would have been a posthumous robbery. But I was still finding stickers in strange places. I had no idea how she managed to stick them without me seeing her.

She was like a greedy ninja.

From the front walk, I could hear Mama haranguing my father about this big old place and how a single girl like me couldn't keep up with mowing the lawn or cleaning the gutters. The house didn't actually have gutters, but to point that out would tip them off to my super-hearing.

"Jenny could have turned this into a real showplace," Mama was saying as they climbed the front steps. "And Jane, well, she never had any sense for decorating. And I just worry about her being out here all alone."

"She can take care of herself, Sherry," Daddy said, his tone weary. He seemed more and more weary these days when dealing with Mama.

My father. What can I say about the man who read with me every night from birth? And I'm not talking *Good Night, Moon* or *Pat the Bunny*. I'll bet I'm the only person on earth to hear two Lincoln biographies before my first birthday. Daddy was the head of the history department at the local community college. It colored his parenting techniques.

Daddy was the one who persuaded Mama not to enter me in the Little Miss Half-Moon Hollow pageant. He was the one who declared that it was wrong to put me at another family's table at my sister's wedding. If not for his regrettable taste in middle names, he would be Father of the Century.

"Hi, baby," he said as I opened the door. He kissed my cheek, smelling of old books and Aqua Velva. Before I could answer, Mama was shoving a hot foil-wrapped bundle into my hands and checking my furniture for dust.

"Don't you worry, honey, everything will be fine," she said, bustling through my kitchen to check for dirty dishes.

Setting the pot pie aside, I led Mama into the living room before she could start alphabetizing my spice rack. And then we started our usual passive-aggressive conversational volley.

"Don't you worry about not being able to find another job," Mama said, wiping her fingers down my mantel.

My internal response: *That hadn't occurred to me, Mama, but thank you.*

"Nobody I've talked to thinks being fired was your fault."

Exactly how many people have you talked to?

"I've already talked to DeeDee about you working down at the quilt shop with me."

Oh, good merciful St. Jude on toast.

After Jenny and I hurtled from the nest, Mama took a part-time job at A Stitch in Time, a shop that sold fabric and quilting supplies. In the five years she had worked there, I'd received quilted vests for every birthday and Christmas.

I hope this gives you some idea of what I was dealing with.

I couldn't visit my mother at the shop for more than a few minutes at a time. I had allergic reactions to fabric sizing and old women asking me when I was going to settle down. Working there would be my damnation to whatever circle of hell is dedicated to busybodies and fabric artists.

"Oh, Mama, I don't think that would be possible. Ever."

Aunt Jettie appeared at my right, laughing her phantom butt off. I growled at a decibel level below human hearing.

"Let me help," Jettie whispered. I shook my head imperceptibly. She rolled her eyes and faded out of sight.

"Mama, I think you and Daddy need to sit—"

Mama sighed. "Now, Jane, I don't want you moping around this big old place by yourself. I think, for the time being, you should move back in with Daddy and me."

St. Jude had just jumped from the toaster to the frying pan. I made a sound somewhere between a screech and a wheeze. Sensing my distress, Daddy said, "Oh, Sherry, leave the girl alone. Can't you see she's got something to tell us?"

"Oh, um, thanks, Daddy," I said, motioning for them to sit on the couch. Mama fluffed the pillows and beat unseen dust from the cushions before making herself comfortable.

Jettie popped up behind the sofa. It was so weird that they had no idea she was standing less than a foot behind them. "Tell them you're pregnant with a married minister's baby, then say, 'Just kidding, I'm a vampire,'" she suggested.

"Not helping," I whispered.

"What's that, honey?" Mama asked, buffing finger-prints off my coffee table.

"Well, I have some interesting, exciting news," I said, stalling.

"It's about that Gabriel, isn't it?" Mama squealed. "You're engaged?"

"Mama, I've only known him for three days!" I cried.

Mama made that *tsk*/sigh combination sound only mothers can master. "Well, are you at least seeing him? Have you tried dressing a little more feminine? Making an effort? You know, you're not getting any younger."

I snorted. I wouldn't be getting any older, for that matter. "Mama, I don't think you—"

"You're never going to get married if you don't lower your standards a little bit."

"Mama—"

"Don't you want to be settled? Get married? Have a fami—"

"Mama!" I shouted. "I'm not engaged. I'm not dating anyone. I—I . . ."

Time slowed. I could read every muscle, every pore in my parents' faces. Daddy's eyes were narrowed, considering me carefully. Worry crinkled the lines at the edges of his eyes. Mama's mouth was drawn, clearly expecting some sort of bad news beyond "your daughter was fired in a spectacularly public manner that will be chewed over for months." Their emotions came in stinging slaps of scent. Confusion, disappointment, irritation, sadness, impatience, a sour haze that was making my head ache. And that was just from Mama. My eyes burned with unshed tears. How do you tell someone that their child has died? How do you explain when that child is sitting in front of them, seemingly alive? How do you tell your parents that you've moved beyond them on the evolutionary scale? And that your mama's going to need to serve O negative alongside her Thanksgiving gravy?

Well, I didn't. Because I'm a great big coward.

"I'm not ready to date anybody right now, Mama," I said, swiping at my eyes. "And I'm not going to move back home. I just need some time to focus on finding a new job and figuring out what I'm going to do next. I'll be fine."

"I told you, you're going to come to work at the quilt shop with me," she insisted.

"No. Just no."

Her lip trembled as she heaved a sigh and stared at the ceiling. Oh, crap. She did the same thing when I announced that I was attending college three hundred miles away and finally severing that pesky umbilical cord. That was the Christmas I got my first quilted vest. You have to admire a woman who exacts revenge through handi-crafts. "What's wrong with working at the quilt shop?"

"Nothing!" I cried.

"Do you have something better planned?" she de-manded.

"No," I said. "But I have planned not to work at the quilt shop."

I looked to Daddy for help, but he was staring out the window with a puzzled expression.

"What's this interesting news, then?" Mama de-manded. "You said you had interesting news."

I groped for some plausible fib. Fortunately, this was the moment Daddy noticed the absence of Big Bertha. "Janie, where's your car?"

"Oh, it broke down the other night," I said, a little too quickly. "It's in a shop over in Murphy. That's kind of what kept me held up for the last couple of days."

Daddy scrutinized my face. I made a comprehensive study of the crown molding. I've never been able to lie to my father. I rat myself out before I can be accused of anything. The one time I smoked pot in college, I called Daddy the next morning to confess because the idea that he could find out any other way made me want to throw up. After expressing extreme disappointment and mak-ing me feel two feet tall, he promised not to tell Mama, because she would have made me leave school to enter rehab that very minute. It's not exactly a healthy dy-namic, but it's the only one we have.

I managed to shush the two of them long enough to describe Big Bertha's post-Shenanigans breakdown.

Mama proceeded to skin Daddy for not performing routine maintenance on "that old hunk of junk." Over the din, I gave a heavily edited version of my long walk home that night. I decided to omit the part about being shot or identifying the drunken hunter. I did not like Bud McElray. At the same time, I didn't want my cousins Dwight and Oscar to beat Bud bloody with a sock full of batteries. Is that considered forgiveness?

I also skirted around the "got turned into a vampire" portion of the proceedings. Again, I'm a huge coward. I told them I'd been so caught up in the wounds to my pride I just couldn't face anybody. I had holed up at an undisclosed location to think. Technically, that wasn't a lie. It was stretching the truth to the breaking point, but it wasn't a lie.

"But we're your family," Mama huffed, stretching the word out to "faaaamily" in a way that set my fangs on edge. Being faaaamily justified a lot of things in Mama's book, including signing me up for an online matchmaking service without my consent and attempting to wax my eyebrows while I was napping. "Who are you going to turn to if not your family? That's why you need to come stay with us, Janie. You need someone to take care of you."

"I'm twenty seven years old!" I cried. "I can take care of myself! I don't need you folding my laundry and pouring my Cheerios every morning."

Jettie appeared at my left and whispered. "I can take their car keys if you want me to, pumpkin."

"You think I want to prevent them from leaving?" I whispered back.

"Who are you talking to?" Mama demanded, turning to my father. "John, she's talking to herself."

"I'm not—" I started, then reconsidered the wisdom of reintroducing my parents to dear departed Aunt Jettie, who never liked my mother anyway. "Yes, I am. I'm talking to myself."

"And you won't even think about coming back home?" Mama asked.

"Mama, you remember what it was like when I lived at home. I think one of us would go insane," I said. "And I don't think it would be you."

"Well, if you're going to be that way, I'm not going to stay here and be insulted." She exhaled her "You don't care how much I worry about you" martyr's sigh. She tucked her handbag under her arm in a prim gesture and made her way to the door. "John?"

Daddy shot me a bewildered look and rose. "We'll talk soon, honey."

" 'Bye, Daddy." I kissed his cheek. "Love you."

He squeezed my hand and winked at me. "Love you, too, pumpkin."

"John!" Mama yelled from my front porch. As Daddy walked out, Mama poked her head back inside. "Just pop that pot pie in the oven to reheat at three-fifty for thirty minutes." Then she disappeared, leaving me and Aunt Jettie gaping after her.

I flopped down on the couch. "I'm adopted, right? Or

maybe Dad had some torrid affair with a brilliant but sensible humanities professor. I was the result of their passion, and Dad forced Mama to raise his bastard child as her own?"

"Nope," Jettie said, shaking her translucent head. "She's your mother. I asked. Plus, you do look a bit like her. When you're angry, you both get these tense lines around your mouth . . . Look, there they are."

"You're lucky you're dead already," I said, chucking a throw pillow at her. It went right through her torso and bounced off the TV cabinet.

"So, you didn't tell them," Jettie observed as I stomped into the kitchen, my bare feet slapping loudly on the tile.

"Nothing gets by you," I muttered, whipping the aluminum foil cover off Mama's pot pie. "I just couldn't. Did you see the looks on their faces? They're already freaked out by the whole 'unemployed spinster daughter who lives alone' thing. I don't think I want to add 'dead' and 'drinks blood' to the mix right now."

"You have to tell them, Janie," Jettie said, in a firmer tone than she normally takes with me. " 'Did you hear Jane's a vampire?' is not something you want your parents to overhear at the Coffee Spot."

"I will tell them at some point. I just need to get a better fix on my powers, my schedule . . ."

"Fraidy-cat," Jettie muttered.

"Poltergeist," I shot back. The pie was still warm, the gloriously flaky golden crust buckling under my fingers as I scooped out a bite. But it smelled off, as if the cream of chicken had expired. And the onions were strong enough to make my eyes water.

"Honey, you don't want to do that," Jettie said. "Look, there are strings attached to this pot pie."

"I haven't eaten solid food in three days," I told her.

"I don't know if I can watch this," Jettie said, blanching. "Pot pie is not a finger food."

"Shhh." I shoveled the rich, warm pie into my mouth, expecting the pleasant childhood memories I normally associated with the meal to come flooding back to me. Pot pie was one of the few meals Jenny and I could agree on, so Mama made it often. The meals tended to be tension-free because my mouth was full and I couldn't argue with anybody.

Instead of the homey flavors of my childhood, I tasted dirt. Ash. Dirt. Gym clothes. I spat the casserole out and yelled something along the lines of "Bleh! Blech! Blah!" and ran for the wastebasket. After I'd tossed up whatever was left in my stomach, I wiped my tongue with a blue gingham dishtowel.

"It tastes . . . Bleh, it tastes like disappointment and feet. It tastes like you cooked it." I shuddered.

Jettie frowned. "I don't see why that comment was necessary."

"The truth hurts."

"So, no solid food, then?" she asked brightly. "I guess I'll just empty that box of Hostess Cupcakes into the trash. You can't eat them after all."

"Now, see, that's just mean."

5

~~~

While it's tempting to try to resume your normal
social activities with still-living friends, you must
understand that some people will have difficulty
adjusting to your new condition. Warning signs that
loved ones may be planning to stake you include a
sudden interest in carpentry and staring at your
chest to gauge where your heart is located.

—From *The Guide for the Newly Undead*

My visit with Zeb didn't start out much better than
the pot-pie episode.

Unable to determine where my car might be, I walked
to the 1970s-era brick ranch house Zeb rented on Jefferson Street. Zeb had moved out of his parents' home
as soon as it was legal. He even lived on Jettie's couch
for two months while he saved enough to land this little
piece of shag-carpeted heaven. Zeb's family? Well, let's
just say that they make the Osbournes look like a bunch
of teetotaling Nobel laureates.

Is it any wonder that the one-bedroom-and-semi-
private-bath life appealed to my Zeb? The house was

far from what you would consider homey. He had lived there for five years and was still using orange plastic milk crates as a coffee table. The only sign that someone actually lived in the house was the yard gnome smirking next to an overgrown hosta. We stole the gnome from my neighbor, Mrs. Turnbow, our junior year of high school and dubbed him Goobert McWindershins. There were wine coolers involved. Mama found out about it and made us take Goobert back to Mrs. Turnbow. We reclaimed him the week after Zeb moved to Jefferson Street and left twenty five dollars in her mailbox.

I knocked on the door. No response. I walked around the corner of the house and opened the gate. A vaguely canine shape streaked up and stopped just short of me. My pitifully ugly dog, Fitz, whimpered, circled, and sat, staring at me. A low growl sounded from his throat, and my heart broke. My own dog didn't recognize me. I could handle unemployment, a strict new diet, and Mama's hissy fits. But this had me teetering on the edge of an undead nervous breakdown.

"Fitz, it's me," I said, holding my hand out for him to sniff. He stared at me. This dog freaks out and runs to the door every time a Domino's commercial comes on TV, so his mental processes are not the swiftest. I agonized as he considered, then finally bounded up to lick my face. I screeched with joy and let him knock me to the ground.

"Ohhhh, how's my buddy? How's my Fitz? Did you miss me?" Cooing like an idiot, I rolled him over and scratched his belly.

Fitz was the apparent result of a one-night stand between a Great Dane and a loofah. His coat was the color of that stuff that grows in your shower. He was so big that his paws rested on my shoulders when he stood on his hind legs. Loose folds of skin hung over his eyes, so he viewed most of the world with his head tipped back. Fitz's one claim to distinction is that I named him after Mr. Fitzwilliam Darcy from *Pride and Prejudice*.

I have Jane Austen issues.

"I'm so, so sorry I went away without telling you, but I'll make it up to you, I promise," I said, scrubbing behind his ears. His eyes lolled back as he leaned into the scratch, which meant I was forgiven.

It was then that Zeb, my best friend, the fric to my frac, the Shaggy to my Velma, fumbled through his screen door, swaying under the weight of dozens of crucifixes. "Back!" he shouted. "Back!"

Fitz and I both cocked our heads as I marveled at the sheer number of chains around Zeb's skinny neck. Gold plate, silver, rhinestone, Day-Glo orange plastic. Zeb advanced on me, holding an old rosewood cross his grandma McBride used to keep nailed to her wall. "Back, demon! Out of my sight!"

"Oh, for goodness sake." I rolled my eyes.

Nonplussed, Zeb shook the cross like a shoddy flashlight and waved it at me again. "The power of Christ compels you!"

"Interesting tactics from the guy who hasn't set foot in a church in fifteen yea—uggh!"

It was embarrassing to be stabbed, especially when

one considered my new catlike reflexes. I can only say that I didn't expect it. Zeb passed out when we dissected frogs in junior high. He won one fight in high school, and that was because Steve McGee tripped and fell onto Zeb's fist. But still, there I was, mocking Zeb's overaccessorizing one minute, and the next, the orange plastic hilt of his carving knife was protruding from my gut.

"Ow! It has to be wood, you doorknob. And it has to be in the heart!" I yelled.

My experience with stab wounds was limited, but it was certainly different from being shot. This was a cold sensation, the flimsy steel embedded in my flesh like a splinter. The wound itched as I wiggled the blade out of my stomach, back and forth, a loose wound that annoyed more than pained.

I hissed as I pulled it free, glaring at a thunderstruck Zeb. We watched as my skin knit itself back together, the tendrils of muscle and skin tissue reaching out to restore itself. I smacked Zeb's shoulder.

"Dumbass!" I cried, tossing the knife away.

"I'm—I'm sorry," he sputtered. The shock of what he'd done had apparently broken the violent vigilante spell. "I just panicked."

Fitz loped after the knife to retrieve it. Fascinated, we stared as my idiot dog managed to drag the knife back by its plastic handle and drop it at our feet. Zeb grabbed it and rammed it into my thigh.

"Ow!" I yelped, shoving him hard enough for the weight of the crosses to tip him onto his back. "If you stab me one more time, I'm going to kill you. Not funny ha-ha kill you, literally suck the life out of you. And giving me the chair will obviously do the state no good."

I pulled the knife out *again*. Zeb sat up enough to watch the wound close *again*. My jaw dropped. "Zeb Lavelle, are you stabbing me just to watch me heal up?"

He looked defensive. "No!"

"I'm so going to bite you." I tossed the knife up onto Zeb's roof and glared at the cross-a-palooza. "Would you take those stupid things off?"

"So, you are afraid of the crosses?" he said, holding a neon orange plastic monstrosity up in a protective gesture.

"No, I'm afraid of people who look like Mr. T." I shook my head. "Is there a gumball machine in town left intact?"

"Well, I remembered enough of last night to know I might need some insurance," he said, taking off the necklaces but keeping the rosewood cross in his lap.

I plopped down next to him, wondering what to say next. Does Hallmark make a "Sorry I tried to drink your blood and touched you in a vaguely inappropriate manner" card? I settled for "How much do you remember?"

"It's pretty foggy. I remember you having big front teeth and being really strong, me offering to buy you pizza, and then for some reason, me scoring the winning touchdown in a pickup football with the guys, followed by a round of beers at Eddie Mac's. And I've never been to Eddie Mac's."

"And you don't have any guys," I pointed out, glad

that Gabriel had managed to wipe the least flattering portions of the evening.

"So, you're a vampire," said Zeb, always eager to fill verbal space.

I shrugged. "Yup. Is that going to be a problem for you?"

"I don't know yet. I don't know what you're capable of, which is scary. The whole blood-drinking thing is weird," he said, giving me his honesty face. I hated that face. It usually meant I was getting bad news or the truth. Sometimes they were one and the same, which sucked.

"I would never hurt you, Zeb. I was just kidding about sucking the life out of you, really," I said. I didn't reach out. I couldn't stand the possibility that he would shy away from me. Instead, I countered with hurtful sarcasm. "Besides, my drinking blood's not nearly as weird as that time I caught you shaving your legs."

"I was curious!" he yelled. I burst out laughing. Being Zeb, he made his "I'm not responding in order to spare our friendship" face, which was more agreeable. He said, "Besides, I did that once. You're going to be drinking blood for the next thousand years or something. You'll never die, never eat, never grow old, never have kids."

"Thanks, I hadn't thought of that one," I muttered. Like so many elements of my new nature, the thought of never having children hadn't occurred to me yet. It was still one of those things far off in Somedayland, after I got married and learned how crock pots worked. Now, children weren't possible, which was yet another thing my mother could be pissed at me about.

"I was so scared for you, Janie," he said. "You just disappeared. I thought you were in a car wreck, murdered, or, worse, that you'd finally taken Norman Hughes up on his offer to elope. So you were dead . . . or married to a guy born without sweat glands. And when I found out that you were dead but you weren't, well, I didn't know what to think. I mean, it's kind of cool. I have a friend who's got superpowers. But I feel left behind and, well, terrified."

"It's still me, just different," I said lamely.

"How did it happen?" he asked. "Most of the people you read about being turned meet vamps in clubs or over the Internet . . . Ew, did you . . . ?"

"Yes, I met a vampire on the Internet, went to his evil love den, and let him turn me, because I'm that brainless," I huffed, slapping his shoulder. "Look, I don't want to tell the whole long sordid story, OK? Someday, when I'm very drunk, I'll tell you. The bottom line is, I had no choice. It was either vampirism or lying dead in a ditch. Though over the last day or so, I've been wondering whether I should have gone for door number two."

"Aww, don't say that," Zeb said, tentatively wrapping his arm around me. "I'm glad you're alive. Really, I am. I love you, Jane. Otherwise, I would have sold that ugly mutt to the carnival days ago."

Fitz growled.

"He's stupid, not deaf," I reminded Zeb, who scratched Fitz into a forgiving mood.

"There has to be cool stuff, too," he said. "From what I remember through the beer and fog, you're strong.

And you heal up pretty quickly. And being newly un-employed, that opens up a lot of new job opportunities for you. Crime fighter. Bulletproof-vest tester. Naomi Campbell's personal assistant."

"Funny." I grimaced. Zeb was looking around, scanning the porch for something. "You want to stab me again, don't you?"

He didn't look at all ashamed. "Think of it as testing the limits of your new abilities."

I groaned. "I've created a monster."

"I don't think someone who recently crawled from the grave should be throwing around labels like 'monster,'" he said, making sarcastic little air-quotes fingers.

"It wasn't a grave." I sniffed. "It was a comfy four-poster."

When we were kids, Mama used to ask, "If Zeb wanted to jump off the roof, would you do it, too?" And as it turned out, the answer was yes.

Before you start to judge, I had my reasons, including wanting to keep the one living person who knew about my new after-lifestyle happy. But I also wanted to see what I could do. Despite the assumption that all tall people are great at basketball, volleyball, and other net-related sports, I've never been a particularly athletic person. (See previous episode involving me falling face-down in a ditch.) So, testing my newfound ability to leap cow pastures in a single bound was intriguing. But I did feign reluctance right up until the point where I jumped off the second story of my house. Nothing happened. OK, I got a massive headache. But that was it.

The previous generations who had owned River Oaks refused to sell the now unused farmland surrounding the house, so my nearest neighbor was about five miles down the road and not likely to hear suspicious noises. This turned out to be a fortunate decision, as Zeb screamed like a girl when I hit the lawn headfirst.

As pretentious as it is to live in a house with its own name, River Oaks is just an old family home. Two stories, built in the semi-Colonial style out of gray fieldstone. It's more of an English country cottage than Tara, though a traditional Southern wraparound porch was added sometime in the early 1900s. There's a library, a formal dining room, a formal parlor, a living room, a pantry big enough to store winter rations for a family of ten, and a solarium, which is a fancy way of saying sun porch. We do love our porches in the South.

Jettie inherited the house sometime in the late 1960s from her father, Harold Early, whom she cared for in his old age. This did not sit well with Grandma Ruth, who had already packed up her house after Great-grandpa's funeral in anticipation of moving in.

Beyond steam-cleaning out the old-man smell, Jettie supervised most of the electrical and plumbing modernizations to the house. While Harold preferred the soft glow of a hurricane lamp, Aunt Jettie was a stickler about having access to an automatic dishwasher and a long hot bath. She also repainted and refinished almost every surface in the house, so now it felt like an actual home. But her real legacy was in the garden. Jettie planted seemingly random splashes of pansies, heavily perfumed roses, fat and sassy sunflowers, whatever struck her fancy. If you stared at the blooms long enough, you could almost make sense of it. But as soon as you started grasping the pattern, it slipped out of focus. And because many of the plants were low-maintenance, even my special plant-murdering powers hadn't killed them. Yet.

While the Half-Moon Hollow Historical Society was willing to forgive Aunt Jettie for plumbing updates and paint, she scandalized the lot of them when she took River Oaks off the town's spring tour of Civil War homes. An annual tradition, the tour features little old ladies in hoop skirts leading bored high-school students and overenthusiastic Civil War buffs around the five known authentic antebellum homes in the Hollow.

The historical society isn't so much a club as a hereditary social mafia. There are only fifty active memberships, which are passed down from mother to daughter among the older families in Half-Moon Hollow. When my great-grandmother Lillie Pearl died in 1965, it fell to either Jettie or my grandmother to take the Early family slot. Guess which one took the bait? Grandma Ruthie was right at the front of the hoop-skirt pack, but she had no real control over the house. As soon as River Oaks was in Jettie's name, she told those "corset-wearing imbeciles" to take their tour and shove it.

Considering the community's reaction, you would have thought Jettie had declared kittens the other white meat. Her rusted rural-route mailbox was flooded with hate letters. There were editorials in the *Half-Moon Herald* imploring Jettie to reconsider. Her coupons were refused at the Piggly Wiggly. It was the final nail in the coffin of Grandma Ruthie and Aunt Jettie's relationship and the chief reason Jettie left the farmland, the house, and its contents to me when she died.

As much as it upset certain members of my family, owning River Oaks allowed me to move out of the Garden View Apartments. There was neither a garden nor a view. I had both at River Oaks. In fact, Jettie's rose garden was what broke my fall from the second story during our "What Can Kill Jane?" series of experiments. In retrospect, the roof jump should have been planned more carefully. Seeing my head bent at a 157-degree angle seemed to upset Zeb.

"Uggghhhh, stop with the caterwauling," I groaned as Zeb rushed over. I sat up gingerly, waiting for the gashes and bruises on my forehead to disappear. I rolled my neck, popping the vertebrae back into place. That was the dumbest experiment so far. We tossed a toaster in the bathtub with me. It tickled. Zeb hit me with his car. I left a two-foot dent in the grille. Zeb wanted me to eat Pop Rocks and drink a Coke. But considering the pot-pie episode, I declined, and he suggested the roof jump.

Fitz thought me lying on the grass, groaning, was part of a fun game and ran over to lick my rapidly healing face. Zeb batted the canine tongue bath out of the way and shook me.

"Are you OK? How many fingers?"

"Too many." I squinted.

"What day is it?"

"I honestly don't know," I said. "I find that both sad and liberating."

"What's the dot on an 'i' called?"

"A tittle," I said.

"Dude, how do you know that stuff?"

I shook my abused noggin. "I've read books, several of them. So, to sum up, me jumping off the roof—not your best idea."

"Yeah." Zeb made a noncommittal face. "But you survived, and it looked really cool . . . Hey, let's get the chainsaw."

"Children, this is becoming disturbing," Jettie said, materializing on the porch.

"It's OK," I told her. "We're just trying out all of my new tricks."

"Yeah, I know. Are you sure you're OK?" Zeb asked.

"Um, yeah, I was talking to—" I gestured to the porch. I sighed, rubbing my palms over my newly repaired forehead. "Zeb, I was just talking to my Aunt Jettie."

"Of course you were." Zeb laughed. Clearly, he thought the head wound had knocked something loose. "It's only natural. Of course, you're completely nuts, but that's natural, too."

"I'm nuts because I talk to ghosts?"

"Because I've met your mama." He grinned.

"I'm serious, Zeb, my Aunt Jettie is standing right there on the porch. She's wearing her favorite UK T-shirt and rolling her eyes at our stupid attempts to kill me. Aunt Jettie, could you move the rocking chair or give Zeb goosebumps or something?"

"He's not going to be able to see me or hear me," Jettie said.

"Be creative."

Zeb's eyes darted around as if I'd told him there was a spider in his hair. "Jane, this is kind of creepy."

"Oh, come on, vampires you can handle but not septuagenarian phantoms?" I sneered. "No offense, Aunt Jettie."

"None taken," Aunt Jettie said as she made her way over to Zeb's car. She motioned for me to bring Zeb closer.

In the dust coating the dented red paint, she wrote "Hi Zeb" with her fingertip. Zeb gasped. "What the—" He watched as the words "WASH ME" formed under her greeting.

"Oh, very funny!" Zeb grumbled. Jettie cackled.

"She's laughing at you," I told him. "At least you can't hear it."

6

New vampires are discouraged from trying to return to their normal human routines. Especially if those routines include tanning or working as a fireman. Your day will not end well.

—From *The Guide for the Newly Undead*

Unless wrapped up in a good book, I was usually in bed at ten-thirty. I know, even I have a hard time separating my life from Paris Hilton's.

So, imagine my shock after a very busy vampire day when I was still raring to go at two A.M. and *bored out of my ever-loving skull.* I hadn't been unemployed since I started working at the Dairy Freeze when I was sixteen.

I'd always seen my week as a long hallway, a door opening on every new day. Doors leading to work, doctor's appointments, housework, errands. Now that hallway seemed empty and dark. And since I would probably never die, it was stretching out forever.

In a rather manic effort to prove that I could entertain myself through eternity, I filled that first night by reorganizing the books in my collection, beating Zeb in three Scrabble games, bleaching every surface in my home, and rearranging my furniture. (Moving a couch is much easier when you can lift it with one arm.)

I spent about an hour carefully painting my toenails a glossy candy-apple red. I kept my fingernails short and naked for typing and shelving, but my toes were treated to an ever-changing rainbow of polishes. A woman puts on a new dress, eyeliner, lip gloss to please others. A woman paints her toes to please herself. And if there was one thing I was familiar with, it was pleasing . . . There's no way to finish that sentence without embarrassing myself.

Zeb went home at around one A.M., when he nodded off and I threatened to paint his toes, too. He hates it when I do that. He reminded me that he still had to work in the morning but immediately realized that was a pretty insensitive thing to say. Zeb was a kindergarten teacher—a good one. I always thought it was because he was the same emotional age as his students. Plus, he had always loved working with construction paper and paste.

"Janie, you've got to find a job," he told me as he hovered near the door. I think he was afraid to leave me unchaperoned. "Or one of us is going to go crazy. And it probably won't be you."

"I know," I groaned. "I'll have to find something before my savings and the good graces of Visa run out. But there are some financial advantages to all this. I don't need to pay health or life insurance anymore. My grocery bills and medical expenses are practically nothing, even though my monthly sunscreen budget has increased astronomically." Zeb did not seem convinced. "I'm trying, Zeb, really. I've looked in the want ads, online, and there's nothing around here for me. Everything that I'm qualified for with night hours involves a paper hat or pasties."

"And technically, you're not qualified for the jobs with pasties, either," Zeb said, dodging when I reached out to smack him.

After Zeb went home, the remaining sensible-librarian portion of my brain told me to put on some PJs, hide under the covers, and read the *Guide for the Newly Undead*. But the idea seemed so confining. Surely my night life wasn't supposed to get more boring after becoming a vampire. I knew I would just sit there twitching, unable to concentrate. I didn't want to stay home, but I didn't know where I could go. I wasn't comfortable going to any of the known vamp clubs and bars in our end of the state. I wouldn't have been able to make it home by sunrise, anyway. And besides Gabriel and Missy, I didn't know any vampires. Knowing my luck, I'd offend someone with some archaic undead etiquette issue and end up staked.

So I did what any other rational person does at two A.M. I went to Wal-Mart. If nothing else, I wanted to check out the "special dietary needs" aisle, which translates into vampire products.

There are three things vampires need to know about grocery shopping just after they're turned. One, the smell of freshly cut meat is far more appealing. Two, the ice cream aisle is not fun anymore. And the cheesy glow of fluorescent lights is even more unbearable with super senses.

Even at this hour, I was nervous to be venturing out into public for the first time as a vampire. Despite living there for most of my life, I'd never felt I was part of the Hollow. I was accepted, but I didn't belong. I loved the people there, but I knew I wasn't like them. From high school on, I knew I'd never be happy following in my mama's footsteps, marrying some nice boy she picked for me, hauling our kids to basketball practice after school and church every Sunday, making Velveeta-based casseroles for pot-luck barbecues with his fishing buddies. I was different. Not better, just different. I read books that didn't have Danielle Steele's airbrushed face smiling out from the back cover. I didn't consider Panda Express to be exotic cuisine. I honestly did not care whether the Half-Moon Howlers made it to the regional championships.

I briefly entertained the idea of moving after college, but it seemed wrong somehow. Every time I looked at jobs in other states, I got this weird feeling in the pit of my stomach, as if the planet were tilting off its axis. So I stayed, because this was my place in the world.

My weird tendencies were lovingly tolerated by kith and kin, who—with the exception of Aunt Jettie—figured I'd eventually "grow out of it." And when I didn't, they made a hobby of worrying about me. When would I meet a nice boy and settle down? When would I stop working so much? Why did I seem so uninterested in the things that mattered so much to them? I ended up a permanent fixture on the prayer list of the Half-Moon Hollow Baptist Church, where Mama had simply written "Jane Jameson—Needs guidance." Every time a member of Mama's congregation saw me at the library, she pinched my cheeks and told me she was praying for me.

It was a little vexing, certainly annoying, but I knew it came from a loving place. These were people who saw me play a sheep in the Christmas pageant for five years running. They sent me care packages when I was taking college exams. They stood by me and helped me through Aunt Jettie's funeral. Now, for the first time, I was afraid of seeing my neighbors, my family. It was only a matter of time before they found out about me. I couldn't survive on sunscreen and my wits, such as they were.

In Half-Moon Hollow, vampires still occasionally died in "accidental" fires or falls on handy wooden objects. That's why few local vampires had come out of the coffin, so to speak. People stopped talking when the new vampire's parents walked into the room. Their families were frozen out of their churches, their clubs. Friends stopped calling. And eventually, the vampire either left town or succumbed to injuries sustained during a tragic "drapery malfunction." But I wasn't going to leave the Hollow. I didn't care if Grandma Ruthie got kicked out of her bridge club. I didn't care if I got funny looks at the grocery store. I wasn't leaving my home, the only place I knew. I could only hope my friends and neighbors were rational enough not to go the pitchfork-and-torch route.

But even if they did, I was pretty sure I could outrun them.

I wandered the food aisles out of habit and got a little depressed at all the foods I couldn't eat anymore. I had the store to myself, apart from the lethargic stockers replenishing the shelves. They didn't make eye contact, but I think that was more of an "I'm pissed off at the world because I'm stacking cases of adult diapers at two A.M." thing than anything to do with me.

I forced myself to walk away from the food when I found myself tearing up over a box of Moon Pies. Fixating on delicious regional snack cakes that you can't digest anymore cannot be good for one's mental health.

The "special dietary needs" aisle was hidden in the back, between the health and beauty aids and the gardening section. I turned the corner of the feminine-products aisle, thankful that was something I'd never have to deal with again, and found a teeming hive of vampire activity.

"So, here's where all the customers are," I murmured, watching as a vampire lady compared the labels of Fang-Brite Fluoride Wash versus Strong Bite Enamel Strengthener. Farther down the aisle, a vampire couple argued over whether they'd had Basic Red Synthetic Plasma for dinner too many times in the last few months. An older vampire gentleman invested in some lubricating ointment I didn't want to think about until I was several centuries older.

I'd never ventured down this aisle before, because, frankly, it just had never occurred to me. As a human, my shopping trips usually focused on getting in and out of the store as quickly as possible before Fitz destroyed the house in search of Milk-Bones. Plus, the stigma attached to those who were seen shopping in the vamp aisle made it about as desirable as openly perusing hemorrhoid medications on a busy Saturday afternoon. But no one even took notice of me here. Much like humans, the vampire shoppers seemed to be "in the zone," zeroed in on what they needed so they could get out and get back to their lairs.

The range of choices was overwhelming. Fake blood, protein additives, vitamin solutions, iron supplements. The companies couldn't seem to figure out what sort of packaging would attract undead attention. Skinny Victorian glass bottles with filigreed labels. Round, vaguely Japanese pop-art jars in candy colors. Opaque plastic coffins with cartoon Bela Lugosi faces etched into the front. The combination was jarring and left me a little disoriented.

A vampire female who was turned in her late twenties passed by on my left. She seemed to be moving in slow motion, her long blue-black hair swishing behind her in a shining curtain. She made capri pants and Crocs, a combination which I think should be outlawed in the state of Kentucky, look good. She was so . . . put together. She seemed comfortable as a vampire. Carefree, like someone you'd see in a nonthreatening shampoo commercial.

I found myself following her, tossing one of everything that she chose into my cart. Fang-Brite Fluoride

Wash, Undying Health Vitamin Solution, Basic Red, Razor Wire Floss. I followed her all the way down the aisle until she reached the mega-dose SPF 500 sunscreen. I waited in agony for her to decide between Face Paste and Solar Shield (*"Tested on astronauts, to be used in emergency daylight situations"* versus *"Guaranteed protection against reasonable sun exposure for up to thirty minutes"*) and finally realized I was behaving in a rather creepy manner.

I backed away, narrowly avoiding bumping into the ointment guy. But I did grab some of that sunscreen, because you never know.

As I headed toward the checkout, I was struck by a gnawing anxiety. The cashier was going to see my purchases and know that I was a vampire. It felt like the first (and last) time I bought my own condoms at the drugstore near my dorm. No matter how much other random stuff I threw into the cart to distract her, that cashier knew exactly what I (and the colorful assortment of latex I was purchasing) would be up to later. What if the Wal-Mart cashier knew my mama or recognized me from the library? Any anonymity I had would be shot as soon as the cashier woke up from her postmidnight-shift stupor and started making phone calls to the kitchen-and-beauty-parlor gossip circuit.

Aw, hell. I had to do it sometime. Besides, I was going to get pretty hungry without faux blood at home, and that could put me in a precarious moral position with my whole "no forcible feeding" stance.

Fortunately, I underestimated the apathy of employees forced to work the midnight shift. The cashier didn't bother looking up at me, much less pay any attention to what she was halfheartedly dragging across the scanner. The closest thing to communication I got was when she grunted and pointed to the total on her register screen.

Grocery shopping at two-thirty A.M. is the only way to go.

I lugged my lone bag of groceries up the front steps, only to find a slender redhead in a black sundress sitting on my front porch swing. I stopped in my tracks. I stared at her. She stared back. I tried to cast out my senses to pick up any evil tendencies.

Nothing.

She rose on her mile-long legs and spoke in a voice utterly without accent. "Hello, I'm Andrea."

She smelled human, normal. In fact, she smelled great. Earthy and fresh, like something just baked. She had a face made for another century, for high-waisted lace gowns and hairstyles involving ringlets. Yet, here she was, standing on my porch like a nocturnal Mary Kay lady.

It seemed to be my turn to talk. "Can I help you?"

"Gabriel sent me."

"For . . . ?" If Gabriel sent someone to give me an after-undeath Goth makeover, I was going to be seriously pissed. Andrea stood and unknotted the silk scarf at her throat. Even in the dark, I could make out the healing bite marks, the purpling bruises.

"Wait, are you a pet?"

More important, was she Gabriel's pet?

She laughed, a soft, silky whisper that made me feel frizzled and oafish. "I'm a freelance blood surrogate. I have friends in the vampire community. Friends who enjoy my company and my discretion."

I remained silent. How exactly was that different?

"I'm AB negative, so I'm a popular selection," she added.

"That's a rare blood type. Only one percent of the population has it," I blurted. "Bet you're popular down at the Red Cross."

"Yes, I'm sort of a delicacy," she said, smiling. "How did you know that?"

"The brain may die, but my compulsion for useless trivia lives on," I said, ignoring the frown that marred her alabaster brow.

Andrea was clearly unaccustomed to not being jumped the second a vampire spied her snowy swanlike neck. "Gabriel said you were nervous about feeding from a human. So he sent me over to help you through it. I think he's worried about you, to be honest. It's kind of sweet."

I rattled my keys not so subtly and motioned toward my front door. "I'd really rather not."

Andrea was even less accustomed to being turned down flat. Suddenly awkward, she strode toward me, her gait unsteady. "It's OK, I want you to. I enjoy it."

I heaved my groceries onto the hall table and closed the door. Even without my ghost aunt lurking about, I didn't want this conversation happening anywhere near my home. It was just unseemly. If I could have found a polite way to heave this woman off my porch, I would have. Damn Mama and her hereditary devotion to hospitality. "Look, Andrea, I haven't completely decided where I stand on the feeding-on-humans issue. What's the vampire equivalent of a vegan?"

"There isn't one," she insisted. "What can I do to make this more comfortable for you?"

"Get a tourniquet and a glass, and take your neck out of the equation?"

She laughed and led me to the porch swing, where I sat as she tipped her head back. I opened my mouth, extended my fangs, and leaned toward her. I saw her pulse beating beneath her skin, her living, human skin. Every nerve ending was an opportunity for me to cause her pain. She took a steadying breath when she felt my nose awkwardly brush her ear. It reminded me of how I used to exhale sharply when I was stuck at the annual library blood drive.

"I can't," I said, giving her a helpless, apologetic look. "I'm sorry, I'm just afraid I'm going to hurt you."

"Don't worry about being nervous. A lot of vampires have trouble with this from time to time. It happens to everyone."

"If I was a forty-year-old man suffering from erectile dysfunction, that would be a great comfort to me, thanks," I said, even as the thirst sent my stomach rumbling.

"Think of me as a free-range animal," she offered.

"That's . . . a brilliant idea," I started, until I pictured her being led into a slaughterhouse by vampires wearing black cowboy hats and Dracula capes. "But not helping."

Seeing a chink in my argument, Andrea smiled and crooked her head back, offering her delicately veined throat. "Don't think of me as male or female. Or even human. Think of me as a cheeseburger on legs. That seems to help the newbies with pacifist tendencies."

I waited for icky visuals involving an undead Ronald McDonald, but none came. "Oddly enough, I think that might work."

I leaned toward Andrea, who happily settled into her "feeding position," head tilted back, arms relaxed. She moaned as my lips skimmed her throat.

"Um, if I'm going to do this, you can't do that," I told her. "Vampires do not suddenly become sexually ambiguous the moment they're turned . . . unless, you're Angelina Jolie, and then we can talk."

Andrea silently leaned back and offered her jugular. I found a place on her skin that hadn't been marked and sank in my teeth. Her blood was warm, alive, and electric, flowing freely into me and flooding my senses. True to her word, Andrea was delicious, with a delicate, floral flavor under the hemoglobin. Absently, I wondered if blood types were like wines. Maybe type O negative was full-bodied with undertones of oak. Or if you want something light with hints of tropical fruit, type B positive.

Andrea let loose a comfortable yawn and companionably wrapped her arms around my waist as I swallowed mouthfuls of her blood. It was surprising how quickly my thirst was slaked. Then again, there wasn't much in the way of excitement to stretch the procedure out. It was cordial, efficient—like an ATM transaction.

I pulled back, watching a drop of scarlet run from tiny twin punctures I'd left on her throat. Andrea whimpered and collapsed back on the swing, rolling around like a puppy in high grass.

I lay back, too unsteady to stand. The comfy emotional distance I was enjoying evaporated as Andrea writhed and wriggled. Obviously, she had enjoyed the experience far more than I had. I felt dirty, like some married father of five walking away from an encounter at the Lucky Clover Motel. But at least I knew I hadn't hurt her. At this point, I just hoped I hadn't cultivated myself a dandy new stalker.

Andrea's wounds began to close but didn't heal completely. Just after the Great Coming Out, I'd read something about the proteins in vampire saliva speeding up the healing process in humans. It seemed only right that we helped them heal after drinking from them.

Andrea's breathing had returned to normal. She sat up, stretching in a long, lean line. She pulled a prepacked alcohol wipe out of her purse and wiped at what looked like the mother of all hickeys. She tied the scarf in a jaunty knot at her throat and smiled. She looked like a woman who'd just spent an afternoon with a masseuse or possibly *on* a masseuse.

"Why would you do this?" I asked, wiping at my mouth.

"It's nice to be needed." She rose on wobbly legs. "And if you understood what it feels like to be on the giving end, you wouldn't ask."

She stood and fished a card out of her purse.

"I'm going to leave my number," she offered, smiling. "If you'd like to see me again, just give me a call."

"I don't think so," I said. "I mean, you seem nice, but I don't know if you're . . ."

"Someone you would spend time with in real life?"

Open fanged mouth, insert foot. "No, I didn't mean . . . This is so strange. I'm sorry."

She smiled, her lips thin. "It's going to be a little strange for a while. I'll leave it here for you."

She laid the card on the porch railing and walked away without as much as a look back. Humiliated, I flipped Andrea's card between my fingers. She seemed so nice. And I hurt her feelings. I made her feel cheap. This was the sort of thing that was going to keep me cringing for days and then strike me at odd intervals over the next year.

Yep, I'm that kind of social neurotic.

If Gabriel would just leave me alone instead of treating me like some undead child, I could find my footing. I would stop making these weird vampire social gaffes. Who asked him to send take-out on legs to my house? Why couldn't he just let me take care of myself? Smothering, overinvolved, toxically incapable of butting out. He was like Mama with fangs.

Please, Lord, let that be the only time I compare Gabriel to my mother.

I was running before the idea of confronting Gabriel

was even fully formed. Still enjoying my newfound inner track star, I sprinted over to Silver Ridge Road at full speed. It was so much better with shoes. I passed a couple of cars, but if they noticed a woman running at sixty-five miles per hour in the dark, they didn't make a fuss.

I reached Gabriel's driveway just as I was hitting my stride. Even in my foul temper, I could appreciate the sight of Gabriel's house. It was about as stately as houses get in the Hollow. Immaculately whitewashed clapboard, big wraparound porch complete with Corinthian columns, and a front door that covered more square feet than my first apartment. It still amazed me that Gabriel had been able to direct public attention away from this place. My mother and her historical society cronies would probably sacrifice their firstborn just to snoop through the root cellar.

And yes, I do realize that would be me. (Jenny had produced grandchildren, after all.)

I slapped the hood of my old station wagon in a sort of greeting, wondering idly if Big Bertha had behaved herself for Gabriel. It didn't really prick my conscience either way.

Lifting the brass knocker, I was struck by a horrible thought. What if Gabriel wasn't home? Or worse, what if he *was* home and had someone with him? Some vampire groupie/snack or another vampire? What if he was feeding? Ick. Or having weird vampire sex? Ickier.

I had turned on my heel and started to run back to my house when I heard Gabriel ask, "Where are you going?"

7

The bond between sires and the young vampires they create is sacred and should be respected.

—From *The Guide for the Newly Undead*

"Gah! How do you *do* that?" I yelped, turning to find Gabriel standing in all his noir glory just behind me. "Why didn't I sense you or smell you or whatever?"

"I move faster than your young senses can detect," he said, opening the door and welcoming me with a wave of his arm. "You will become more attuned to me in time."

I chose not to respond to that, striding into the slate-blue foyer with my shoulders squared. He followed, hovering on the edge of touching me. His fingers glided millimeters from my arms, leading me through to the den.

"I fixed your car," he said, tossing the keys from a jade dish on the little maple end table.

I palmed them and eyed him speculatively. "You fixed my car?"

"I have walked the earth for more than a century. I managed to pick up some skills along the way," he said, before reluctantly adding, "and one of them is finding skilled mechanics."

I smirked, leaning against the wall. "You almost had me there."

"I supervised," he insisted. He was adorable when he was all flustered and indignant. "That car was a death trap—"

"It's a classic."

"A classic with shot brakes, a fuel line that had been gnawed by rodents, and a carburetor that had been rebuilt using duct tape," he said. "I don't know what any of that means, but my mechanic said he couldn't determine what made your car break down because it would have been much easier to look for what didn't."

"OK, so I've been a little lax in the automotive-repair department," I said defensively. "And I shouldn't have let a high-school student rebuild my carburetor. But that doesn't mean you need to do things like this for me. It makes me feel obligated."

"That wasn't my intention. I liked feeling that I was doing something kind for you, Jane. I haven't felt the urge to do something like that for a woman in a long time. And I thought you would appreciate the restoration of your vehicular independence far more than posies and poetry."

I smiled, and, encouraged, Gabriel took a step toward me.

"Thanks. I mean, it's not exactly a sonnet, but that's really—wait. No," I said, warding him off. "I'm still pissed at you, seriously pissed. That girl at my house, Andrea.

You had no right to do that. Did it even occur to you that you had no right to do that?"

Unimpressed with my outburst, he replied, "You needed someone experienced to help you through your first live feeding."

I jabbed a finger into his chest, backing him into his living room. "So why didn't you just send over a hooker? Hell, why didn't you videotape it? You could have sold it to *Vampire Girls Gone Wild*."

He smiled that "pitiful creature, you amuse me" smile. "Jane, your innocence is one of the many things that make you so interesting. It wounds me that you would even think that."

"First of all, I'm not that innocent. I shoplifted Bonnie Bell lip gloss from the Woolworth's when I was eight. So there. And second, why are you so interested in who and what I eat?" I demanded, again with the jabbing. "And if you use that 'I'm your sire' crap, you will be using your vampire strength to pull a size-nine sneaker out of your ass."

"Though it's an entertaining mental image, that was truly vulgar," he said. "Now, sit, please."

I flopped back on a cozy tooled-leather couch the color of old wine. A toasty fire licked the hearth despite the midsummer heat. Even in my snit, I enjoyed bathing my face in the warm light. I hadn't had a chance to appreciate Gabriel's fine parlor while I was zipping toward freedom. It was just as welcoming and well decorated as the bedroom. Polished, honey-colored wood floors, a thick navy and maroon rug, deep cushy sofas and chairs. This was definitely a wine-and-cheese sort of room.

Watching my mood mellow to just south of truly pissed, Gabriel smiled, his canines gleaming in the firelight. He sat near but not next to me, giving me just enough room to feel comfortable but definitely aware that he could reach out for me at any moment. "So, how was your day?"

"It has been busy," I admitted. "I drank some fake blood for breakfast, talked to my dead aunt, tried—and failed—to come out to my parents, discovered an unfortunate aversion to solid food, got stabbed repeatedly by my best friend, tested the various ways I can't die, went to the grocery store, fed from a human—which was something I said I'd never do. You know, normal, everyday stuff." I laughed far too shrilly. I was starting to sound drunk again. Great.

"Don't worry about your parents," he said. "They sounded very kind when I spoke to them on the phone. You'll find a way to tell them, eventually. I could talk to them for you, if you'd like."

"Thanks, but I don't think that would help," I said. "They don't seem to remember things when you talk to them. But there is the tiny issue of my mother wanting you to come over for Sunday dinner."

"She remembered me?" Gabriel's gray eyes widened.

"You underestimate the mental acuity of the mother of a single woman." I nodded sagely. "She remembers the vague impression of an available man."

"Unusual," he admitted.

"It's a biological imperative." I grinned. "Doing that mind-wipe thing over the phone is pretty impressive, by the way."

"I do what I can. I've never tried it on a mother before. I'll have to concentrate harder next time."

"Exactly how often do you plan on mind-wiping my mother?"

"I suppose that all depends on you." He chuckled, reaching out to wind a coil of my hair around his finger. "I'm glad you came by. I was hoping to see you tonight, but I understood that you probably needed some space. I wanted to call you, but I find myself feeling . . . awkward when it comes to you."

" 'Awkward' is the word du jour," I agreed. "So, I make you nervous?"

"Not quite nervous," he said. "Just unsettled."

I wriggled my eyebrows and inched a little closer to him. "Unsettled, that's even better."

I reached for his hand and pressed it into mine. "Look, the life I had before I met you, it wasn't much, but I could handle it. I could have lived that way forever. And now it turns out that I will live forever, only it's a life I am completely unprepared for. I've never been without a plan, OK? I've never been without a purpose or a goal or a reason to get up in the morning. And now, I don't even get up in the morning. I'm not going to lie, I'm terrified."

Gabriel stared at me with an intensity that was unnerving and, well, mesmerizing. In my compulsive need to fill the verbal void that followed, all of the questions

I'd been dying to ask spilled from my lips. After the whole "you sent a random stranger to my house" thing, I figured I was owed some answers.

"What do you do all day—night? Do you have a job? How is it that I've lived in the Hollow all of my life and I've never even heard of you? Do you feed from live—do we call them 'victims'? Do you feed from Andrea? Or do you drink artificial blood? And where do we get those blackout curtains?"

He mulled over my diatribe(s) and at long last said, "I know you have questions."

I smiled, thrilled to be the smug one for a change. "Yes, that's why I just asked them."

He made a noise I can only describe as a nasal reminder to watch the snarking. "All right, then, I do not have a job. I live off the profits of various investments I've made over the years. I devote my time to my own interests. As a vampire, I've made an effort to stay out of the public eye. I've taken extensive measures with local officials to make sure traffic and public interest are steered away from my property. But it seems wise for vampires to reconnect now that humans are adjusting to our presence. And there are certain things I miss about human society."

"Appletinis?"

He scowled, but there was no real heat in it.

"Well, you were at Shenanigans." I shrugged.

He snickered. "You are not a dull girl."

"Thank you."

He was smiling at me, so I thought it would be a good

time to ask. "Is your relationship with Andrea part of
your 'reconnection' with human society?"

"I do not have a relationship with Andrea," he said. "I
met her a little more than a year after she moved to Half-
Moon Hollow. I introduced her to some acquaintances
of mine. I admire and respect Andrea. She's a friend. But
we agreed that I would no longer feed from her in order
to prevent . . . confusion."

It was like *Melrose Place,* with fangs.

"I do occasionally feed from consenting donors," he
said. "I also drink the occasional bottle of artificial or
donated blood. I prefer donated blood. And you can get
blackout curtains at Bed, Bath and Beyond."

I could have stopped there, but I was enjoying my
power trip.

"Who made you into a vampire?" I asked.

His expression was as bland as bread pudding. "That's
a discussion for another time."

"How many vampires have you made?"

"Three, including you," he said.

"What happened to the other two?"

"That's a discussion for another time."

I scowled. "Do you practice being enigmatic, or does
it come naturally?"

"It comes naturally," he said. He sprang from his seat,
offering his outstretched hand. "Come with me."

He led me outside onto the porch, where we stood,
soaking in the night sounds. He stood behind me, cupping his fingers over my eyes. His lips hovered near my
ear. "You are the night."

"I am the night," I repeated.

"You are the night."

I cocked my head, sending him a questioning look. "I am the night?"

"Jane!"

"Why is it that when you say my name, it sounds like a curse word?" I asked, turning toward him.

He sighed and pushed me back to face the yard. "Please stop talking."

I giggled, bumping the back of my head into his chin. He was doing that hair-smelling thing again, which I didn't dignify with a response. I turned to face him, finding myself nose-to-nose with my sire. He had that irritated look Mrs. Truman used to get when I passed notes in third-grade math. I giggled again, which was becoming an annoying habit.

"I'm sorry, I have a hard time with this vampire Yoda routine. I don't sit around listening to one hand clapping for my inner-selfness. I have never read a single *Chicken Soup for the Soul* book, and, God willing, I'll never have to. I look at the big picture. If I don't like it, I change it, or I'm paralyzed by the fear of change, which is more often than not. It's the one area where I'm sort of complicated."

"I wouldn't say that," he said, turning me back to his darkened yard. "You're more and more complicated with every word that comes out of your mouth. It's time to see the picture in small pieces, Jane. Every blade of grass. The croaking of every frog. The scent of honeysuckle. Let each of these elements wash over you until you can

see the whole of the landscape before you without opening your eyes. Feel the heartbeat of every animal that
skitters across the dirt. Focus on the flow of its blood,
the pulse of it through its veins. Don't settle for the prey
that's closest to you or the easiest to catch, find the right
animal. The size and speed you need. Focus every fiber
of your considerable musculature on that creature, and
throw your body into action."

I felt this was not the moment to tell Gabriel that
was exactly what Yoda would have said (in a slightly less
grammatically sound manner), so I focused on the night
sounds. It was like a combination of night vision and a
thermal camera, all shifting colors and pulsing warmth. I
shut out the coldblooded creatures, the frogs and snakes,
because my culinary courage does not run that far. I
could feel coyotes, and deep in the trees I saw a deer, an
eight-pointer. But given my recent steps in his hooves, I
wasn't planning to hunt him anytime soon.

As if he sensed my interest, the buck raised his head
and met my gaze. It felt as if I could reach out and stroke
his coat. I raised my hand, and the buck started, disappearing with a flash of white tail through the trees.

"All of my life, I've wanted to be more interesting than
I am, special," I said, turning to Gabriel and, I'm sure,
grinning like an idiot. "And now it seems I've got 'special'
out the ying-yang. I don't know if I can handle it."

He made his inscrutable face. "I've been a vampire for
a long time, and I've never heard it described it quite
like that."

"I do have a way with words," I admitted. "Why did this happen to me? How is this possible? Where do we come from?"

"I would never have thought of you as an existentialist, Jane," he said.

I arched an eyebrow at him. "No one likes a smart-ass, Gabriel."

"For your sake, I hope that's not true," he said, to which I responded with a smack on the arm. "No one knows where we come from. The ancient Greeks, Middle Eastern cultures, the earliest people of Malaysia, they all wrote of creatures that stole the blood from humans as they slept. The romantic theory seems to be that Lilith, the first wife that God created for Adam, refused to submit to her husband, particularly in their . . . evening activities. So, as punishment, she was sent away from the garden to live in darkness. She became the first vampire and had her revenge by feeding off Adam's children and turning his descendants into creatures like her. Vampirism is thought to be her vengeance passed down through the generations."

"Trivia monologue. You are so the man for me," I marveled.

"Pardon?"

"Nothing," I said, smiling insipidly and thanking the perverse vampire gods that his super hearing hadn't picked that up. "Do you believe that?"

The twist in his lips showed that he might have heard what I said but was choosing to ignore it. "The truth is, there may be no single origin of vampires. The way we change may have evolved, over time, like humans but never with them."

I crossed my arms. "OK, lightning round. Real or fake: Werewolves?"

"Real."

"Demons?"

"Very real."

"Sasquatch?"

"Real, but he's actually a were-ape."

I decided to explore that later. "Aliens?"

"I don't know."

"Witches?"

"Real." He shrugged. "Some work real magic, and others are deluded children in black makeup and ill-fitting clothes."

"Good to know," I said soberly. "Wait, what about zombies? I couldn't even get through the preview for *Dawn of the Dead* without covering my eyes."

"You don't want to know."

I made a small distressed sound. He chuckled, something I noticed was becoming more frequent.

"I know Dracula was a real person, but is he still, you know, around?" I asked.

"No one knows for sure. He's a bit like our Elvis. Lots of vampires have claimed to see him, but there's never been documented proof. You ask a lot of questions."

"I'm a librarian. The learning curve is steep," I said, ever so sassily jutting my chin forward.

"You're going to be an interesting person to know,

Jane Jameson," he said, leaning forward and brushing his mouth across mine.

Sparks. Hell, fireworks. The Fourth of July was exploding in my head as he slipped his hands under my jaw and pinned me with his mouth. When he pulled away from me, my hands were wound in his hair, my lips bruised and tingling pleasantly.

"I enjoy your height," he said, pressing me against the porch railing. With my butt precariously balanced on the rail, I had to wind my feet around his calves to keep from tumbling over. "Back in my day, I never courted an exceptionally tall woman. But it makes for some interesting possibilities."

"There's that word again, 'interesting,'" I said before kissing him again. I tangled my fingers in his pullover. He tasted like the best share of my trick-or-treating candy, the mini Three Musketeers and Almond Joys. And for most of my life, I'd been gnawing on those stupid orange-wrapped peanut taffy things.

I sighed and wrapped my arms around his neck, enjoying the sensation of Gabriel planting a few more soft, nibbling kisses along the edge of my jaw. Feeling bold, I traced the line of his bottom lip with my tongue and bit down on it gently.

He pulled away and grinned down at me. "Very interesting."

8

Indoctrinated by years of secrecy, many older vampires have histories they may not want to share right away. It's best to respect their privacy.
—From *The Guide for the Newly Undead*

I am not the kind of girl who trusts a man to tell her everything she needs to know in his own due time, so I did some research on my sire. You can take the girl out of the library, but you can't take the neurotic, compulsively curious librarian out of the girl.

Oddly enough, the limited information I could find on Gabriel Nightengale, (yes, that really was his name) started with a passage from my father's self-published textbook on local history. I'd read that thing at least ten times, and I never paid attention to the well-bred boy born in 1858. Gabriel was around to see the Civil War transform Half-Moon Hollow from a grimy little river outpost to a major point of trade along the Ohio. His family owned a sizable tobacco farm on Silver Ridge Road. The family eventually amassed enough money to build a proper antebellum home they called Fairhaven.

The Nightengales were abolitionists, which I found oddly comforting. Beyond considerable wealth, the Nightengale family was utterly normal until Gabriel disappeared at age twenty one. He was healthy, hale, the pride of his family, and then suddenly he wasn't. His parents told their neighbors that they had sent Gabriel abroad for a tour of the Continent. The sole reason for Gabriel's inclusion in Daddy's book was his rumored mauling at the hands—well, flippers—of a sea lion off the coast of Portugal. That was, and is, an unusual cause of death for rural Kentucky residents.

But it's amazing what you can find out with the right Web browser. VampireArchive.com turned out to be deliciously gossipy, the *Us Weekly* of the underworld. According to the archives, Gabriel was a strapping young lad living a privileged, unremarkable life, until he took a strange girl out for a walk after a barn dance. I guess following strange women home is a bit of a habit with him. I couldn't find any information about Gabriel's sire, which was surprising, as I'd heard that vampire historians tended to be incredibly detail-oriented. They have this whole thing about preserving the vampire "family tree."

The unnamed woman who turned him left Gabriel to rise in a cellar about a mile from his farm. Without guidance from his sire, Gabriel returned home after his traumatic first kill and hoped to return to his former life. Considering the times, his family took his being turned well. His brothers tied him to a tree, naked, to wait for sunrise. Gabriel broke free and ran away. When he didn't descend on them in a fit of bloody vampire vengeance, his parents told everyone he was traveling. A year later, they cooked up the story about the sea lion. Apparently, sea lions were thought to be much more vicious back then. And people believed they lived in Portugal.

But Gabriel was traveling, seeking out European vampires to learn how to control his hunger and use his powers. His studies continued until his brothers died in a duel (with each other) a few years later. Having never fully recovered from Gabriel's turning and her husband's ensuing heart attack, his mother, Margaret, died of what my father called "shock and heartache." According to the vampire archives, the undigested Gabriel returned to the Hollow with little fanfare, showing up at his family attorney's office in the dead of night to claim his birthright: the house, the land, and the income. As soon as the papers were signed and sealed, he dropped off the radar again and faded from local memory.

For more than a century, Gabriel bounced between various vampire hot spots and the Hollow. He lived under an assumed name, pretended to die periodically, and then willed the house to himself under the name of a recently deceased young man. I would accuse him of stealing the trick from the *Highlander* movie, but he didn't seem to take my pop-culture references very well. And he did predate the *Highlander* movie by about a hundred years.

Maintaining his faux inheritance technique, he rented his land to sharecroppers and developed a hand at real estate. As more local people began giving up their farms, he bought them. Before he knew it, Gabriel owned a good portion of what used to be the township. He sold it at an obscenely high profit during the Hollow's strip-mall boom and now lived like a sort of vampire gentle-man of leisure, without the smoking jacket.

Gabriel returned to the Hollow in late 1999, though it's unclear whether it was because of the Coming Out or that he just missed his ancestral homeland—his strange, somewhat backward ancestral homeland—where he eventually vamped out yours truly. I'm sure there was more stuff in the middle there, but Gabriel was good at hiding it, which was just driving me nuts.

Aunt Jettie, who practiced moving dining-room chairs while I was elbow-deep in cyberspace, informed me that for as long as anyone in the Hollow could remember, the only people allowed on Nightengale property were the tenant farmers. And even they never met their land-lord, who was reported to travel frequently. Less and less was said about the Nightengales and their farm over the years, until no one could remember ever actually meet-ing a member of the family or seeing the house. It was as if a significant historical property had just faded out of the local consciousness, a difficult feat in a town full of rabid Civil War buffs.

While I was in research mode, I looked up the com-panion Web site for the *Guide for the Newly Undead.* The features were impressive, with links for buying artifi-cial blood online, a virtual global map to help track the sun at all times, and a handy translator to help newbies understand the Language of the Dead. It's a language beyond the realm of human comprehension. It predates living speech, even humanity. It was whispered in the darkness before God said, "Let there be light," and one of the few true ties between vampires and demons. And sadly, it sounds a good deal like Pig Latin.

For instance, *Ihbiensay thethsay carthax vortho inxnay tuathua* means "I believe I left my rapid infuser at the last pot luck." I'm still learning. Vampires use the language to communicate under the human radar . . . and to say rude things about living people without their realizing it. There are some things that you just don't outgrow, no matter how evolved you are as a life form.

The best part of the site was the quiz to help determine your special vampiric gifts, although it didn't tell me much I didn't already know. My abilities included being able to see my elderly phantom roommate and, of course, superhuman speed, strength, and agility. It was a nice turn of events for someone who used to get traded from kickball teams. I had influence over certain people, though I hadn't figured out the formula for *which* people. Dang it. And according to my "human-vampire relations" score, I might eventually develop some-mind reading skills. There was something to look forward to.

I couldn't shape-shift, like some of the ancient vamps. I couldn't fly. And I envied the vamps with off-the-wall powers, such as finding lost objects or being able to tell when people are lying. Then again, some poor suckers were stuck with being able to feel the pain of every living thing around them or communicating with squirrels, so I felt relatively fortunate.

The site also included a listing of vampire-friendly businesses in and around my zip code, the types of places that didn't exactly advertise in the Yellow Pages. You had to know they were there in the first place to find them, apparently. There were the expected clubs and bars but also an occult-focused hobby store called the Stitchin' Witch and a salon that catered to our special grooming needs. You wouldn't believe how hard it is to file down vampire nails.

I was eager to make my debut in vampire society, because surely, shopping stealthily at Wal-Mart didn't count. Knowing only one other vampire couldn't be healthy, especially when he could turn out to be the vampiric version of my mother. Gah, I had to stop thinking that.

I needed someone who knew their way around, someone who was not Gabriel. I would have taken Zeb, purely for entertainment value, but he had an actual date, with a real girl. That hadn't happened in a while, so I was a good friend and put my own needs second to the possibility of him having actual sex with a real girl.

"Aunt Jettie, feel like dusting off your dancing shoes and hanging out with some people who can see you?" I asked, looking up in time to watch my dead aunt try to levitate the china hutch.

That did not bode well.

* * *

"Are you sure I'm dressed OK?" I asked, fidgeting with the plain navy T-shirt and jeans I'd been wearing when Andrea, who was even more pale and elegant than I remembered, arrived at my door an hour early. She'd insisted I was fine, though she was wearing a cashmere sweater and beautifully cut gray slacks. I was starting to wonder if this was some sort of attempt to humiliate me for hurting her feelings. She'd probably take me to the club and all of the other vamps would be in black tie. And then she'd dump a bucket of pig's blood on me.

"You look great," she said, stopping just outside the door of the Cellar, a respectable looking cement-block building in an unassuming corner of Euclid Avenue. "You know that nobody's going to be wearing black leather and dog collars, right?"

I shrugged. "I've never done this before. I didn't go to human bars. Mudslides aside, I'm not much of a drinker. Club people are not my people. Now, book-club people—"

"These are your people, Jane, more than I am," she said, her voice thinning as she pulled me toward the door.

"Is there a secret handshake?" I whispered.

She shook her head. "I stay two paces behind you, because I am but a lowly human. You walk into the room as if you know that you belong, that you're one of them. Make eye contact with as many as possible. Keep your body language aggressive and rigid. You're an aloof, indomitable warrior queen who could fend off attacks from anyone in the room."

She reached for the stainless-steel door, repeating, "Aloof, indomitable warrior queen."

I tensed every muscle in my arms as if I were going to punch the first person I saw, undead or otherwise. Of course, that person was a cuddly, sixty-five-year-old bartender, ironically named Norm, who was clearing pilsners off shiny bar tables.

It was a sports bar, a smoky, noisy, all-American sports bar with dart boards and neon beer signs on the walls. Nobody looked remotely interested in kicking my ass. In fact, nobody even noticed when I came in. They were too busy watching the Cardinals game on an obscenely large plasma screen.

I whirled on Andrea. "You suck."

"No, technically, you do," she said, giggling. "I'm sorry, it was just so easy. You should have seen the look on your face."

"Just for that, I'm not biting you later."

She sighed heavily. "Spoilsport."

We sat, and Andrea ordered a dry martini and a "special" for me. I didn't know what that was, but Norm seemed to know her and didn't seem like someone who was going to slip garlic (or Rohypnol) into my cocktail. I scanned the room, making a game of separating the vamps from the nonvamps.

Norm was definitely human. He was familiar in an "I think I've seen you at church before" way. And he seemed happy and comfortable slinging doctored beers to vampires. Somehow that made me relax. There were two human men mixed in with the crowd watching the baseball game. The vampires were your typical enthusiastic sports fans, cheering, hooting, and sloshing their drinks. The occasional splash of synthetic blood on their shirts was the only sign that something was amiss—besides the vampire Cubs fan sulking in the corner.

A dishwater-blond male vamp wearing faded jeans and a "Virginia Is for Lovers" T-shirt sipped dark lager at the bar, ignoring the hullabaloo behind him. The rest of the tables seated groups of vampire women, immersed in pastel drinks and naughty conversations. Maybe these were vampire housewives?

Seriously, the scariest thing about this place was the sign advertising "Karaoke Tuesdays." The idea of a drunk vampire belting "I Will Survive" off-key was somehow both compelling and terrifying.

I was calm, comfortable, and ready for a good time when Norm returned with a martini, which he declared "dry as dust" with a fond pat on Andrea's head. I got something frothy and the color of ripe cantaloupe.

"Um, what is this?" I asked Andrea, waiting for Norm to pass out of hearing distance.

"It's a smoothie." Andrea watched as I took a tentative sip. It was good, fruity with just enough coppery after-taste. Andrea continued, "A special smoothie. Fruit juice, vitamins, minerals, protein powder, and a little bit of . . . um, pig's blood."

"Pig's blood!" I yelped, spitting the smoothie back into the glass. Andrea shushed me. "You let me *drink* pig's blood?"

Well, at least she didn't dump it on me.

"Shh," Andrea hissed. "Look, Norm uses pig's blood because the artificial blood doesn't mix well with the fruit juice. The enzymes make it go brown. And Norm has some ethical issues with serving human blood. Just try it. You'll like it. It's like a zinfandel, light and sweet. At least, that's what I'm told."

"I'm not loving you right now," I growled at her, swallowing a mouthful. It wasn't bad, but I just couldn't get the visions of a pleading Porky Pig out of my head. This attitude was pretty hypocritical given my before-death enthusiasm for bacon.

"See?" Andrea asked brightly as I took another sip. "Good girl."

"Kiss my ass," I grumbled.

Andrea ignored my grumpiness and gestured to the smoky barroom. "So, what do you think?"

"It's OK," I admitted. "Even with everything I've learned about vampires, I still expected moody lighting and Goth kids reciting bad poetry. Consider me pleasantly surprised."

A lovely rose blush tinted Andrea's cheeks. If she weren't such a nice person, it would really piss me off that she looked like a redheaded Grace Kelly. Andrea was as out of place here as, well, me in a gym. Andrea was probably not the type of person I would have spent time with when I was living. She was too put together, for one thing. She made my sister seem rumpled. But she was the safest person I knew who could navigate her way through the vampire underground. And I really wanted to make up for making her feel like a hooker.

I'd already decided that if I was going to develop a healthy friendship with Andrea—whose last name was Byrne, by the way—I needed to know more than her deliciously rare blood type. I was not going to be able to feed from her again. It was far too intimate an experience, like making out with someone at the office Christmas party and spending New Year's week pretending that person hasn't felt you up. Not that I know what that's like.

"What I want is some answers," I said, picking a pretzel from the bowl on the table. Then, remembering the pot pie, I dropped it. "You know, basic stuff. Who you are, where you're from, how you got into this line of work. You owe me, lady. Let's start with why you can pronounce all your vowels separately, oh ye of little accent."

I dutifully sipped my pig's blood as Andrea told me a sordid tale worthy of her own country song. Andrea was pulled into the vampire world just before the Great Coming Out. She was a sophomore studying information systems at the University of Illinois when she met a vampire professor. Maxwell Norton, age 321, taught history, which was pretty unfair considering he'd been there when most of it happened. Norton, whose real name was Mattias Northon, scented Andrea's rare vintage blood type on the first day of class. He separated her from the class like a wounded gazelle and nurtured her as a pet. She watched over him during the day, fed him, picked up his dry cleaning, graded his papers. And in return, she was introduced to vampire society—like a debutante with really big veins.

Norton taught her how to dress, to speak, to behave in a way that pleased his sophisticated undead friends. Then, seven years later, Norton found a newer, fresher freshman pet and tossed Andrea aside, despite the fact that she'd dropped out of college and given up her life to be with him. Men, even dashing, mysterious vampire men, can be such bastards.

Andrea had suffered from her own overbearing helicopter parents, the kind of people who calculated how every breath Andrea took reflected on them and their family. They accompanied her to job interviews, called her dorm room at least once a day to make sure she was up-to-date on her assignments and her flossing. But as soon as her loving relatives found out she was consorting with vampires, Andrea was unceremoniously pruned from the family tree. Her dad stopped payment on the tuition check, and her mother let Andrea know she was no longer welcome in the Christmas-card picture. This may have been the point of her taking up with Norton in the first place. Vampires may bite you, they may bleed you, but they don't judge you.

Andrea remained in the underground vampire community more out of necessity than anything else. Broke and lacking a degree, she found her rare blood type was the easiest and most lucrative way to make money. She moved to the Hollow to be near a friend she'd met through an online vampire pets' community. She got a job in a boutique downtown that catered to riverboat tourists and the top one percent of Half-Moon Hollow's socioeconomic caste. But her real income came from "protectors" who enjoyed her blood. She'd get a page, go to the client's home, and offer up her veins. She said many of her clients were lonely and often asked her to stick around to talk for a while. They were generous and more than happy to pass her name on to other respectable vampires. Apparently, her line of work was all about referrals. The only occupational hazards were the constant need for turtlenecks and trying to fit enough iron into her diet.

I stuck with smoothies through the night, because after the Kahlua episode, I decided that alcohol and I weren't friends anymore. It was nice just to sit and talk as we discussed childhoods, family dynamics, and men—with the exception of the one man we both wanted to talk about. I deliberately skirted the issue of Gabriel and his relationship with Andrea, whatever that might be. It was cowardly, but Andrea seemed like my first shot at a friend who truly understood this new world I'd been dropped into. I didn't want to run the risk of alienating her.

"So, your experience hasn't made you want to avoid vampires altogether?" I asked. "I'd probably be out burning the undead in effigy. Not that I want to give you any ideas or anything."

"Vampires are just like humans," Andrea said. "You meet good ones and bad ones. Pulse has very little to do with it."

"Have you ever wanted to be turned yourself?"

"You know, I've never had a vampire offer to turn me," she admitted. "They can feed off me if I'm undead, but it's not as much fun, and the nutritional value of my blood drops. I guess they don't want to kill the golden goose, if you know what I mean. But I like living. I'm not afraid of death, which seems to be a problem for people who get turned. No offense."

"None taken," I assured her. "I was afraid. I wasn't ready to die. When I thought of the ways I preferred to die, I wanted to be a hundred years old and surrounded by generations of adoring descendants. Though a hair dryer and an ill-timed fall into a tub was far more likely. I never considered deer or drunk drivers."

"Well, it's certainly a more interesting story than a hair dryer and a bathtub," she said. "What about you? Tell me everything. Do you have a boyfriend or . . ."

"I'm definitely in the 'or' category." I snorted. "Let's see, the last guy I dated—is there a word for someone who's sexually attracted to Muppets?"

Andrea's elegant persona was destroyed as she laughed so hard martini shot out of her nose. That made me feel pretty good. I regaled her with my epic tales of dating men too bizarre to allow past second base—the jobless, the spineless, the one who brought his mama on our first date. By the time I got to Derek, the man with an unnatural interest in Miss Piggy, most of the crowd had drifted out. It was just us, Norm the teddy-bear bartender, and the Virginia-loving lager drinker.

I don't think Andrea had been out on many girls' nights, because she went whole hog on the martinis. Given the late hour, the amount of vodka consumed, and her regular blood donations, it was impressive that she was still upright. But once she started actually watching the Australian competitive darts championship on the big screen, I called for the check. We wandered out just as a gaunt, semimulleted vamp in a faded Whitesnake T-shirt came barreling in. Andrea, already unsteady on her feet, mumbled drowsily as she bumped into me.

"Excuse us," I muttered, retrieving Andrea from her 130-degree lean. I had my droopy new friend tucked into her passenger seat when I realized I'd left my purse behind.

I jogged back into the bar, opening the door on Mr. Whitesnake literally holding Norm upside down by his ankles and shaking him. The lager drinker was nowhere in sight.

"Where's the cash, you useless sack of meat?" Whitesnake snarled, his fangs in full play. Norm, who looked oddly resigned to this treatment, pointed to the wall behind the bar.

"Hey! Put him down!" I yelled, rushing to catch Norm when Whitesnake complied.

"What the hell do you think you're doing?" I demanded, setting Norm on his feet.

"Punching some nosy bitch in the face."

"Wha—?" I managed before Whitesnake's fist collided with the bridge of my nose. Whitesnake stood six feet tall and looked as if he'd been blown out from a straw, and yet the sheer force of the blow threw me back through the bar door and skidding into the gravel of the parking lot.

That did not feel good.

My face felt as if it were located somewhere near the back of my head. I sat up, rolling my neck. My stomach dropped greasily at the sound of my vertebrae snapping back into place. I was shaking off that new entry in the ick files and wondering how the *hell* Andrea was sleeping through this when Norm came flying out the door.

I loved that I was able to spring up and catch Norm's pudgy form before he was a smear on the parking lot. I did not love the look on Whitesnake's face as he came storming out of the bar.

"Run!" I hissed as Whitesnake advanced. Norm, obviously accustomed to this occupational hazard, scurried to his nearby car, found his magnetic Hide-A-Key, and pulled away in less time than it takes to say "Gratuity included."

I turned my attention back to my face-rearranging buddy, who was seconds from slamming me like a rag doll into the hood of an old Mustang. Let me tell you, solid American engineering *hurts*. My legs flailed as I thumped back against the hood, landing a lucky kick to the side of his head. He flinched, letting me land another one, planting the toe of my canvas sneaker in his ear. It also gave me time to shove the heel of my hand under his chin, not to hurt him but to direct his breath away from me. How could someone who didn't eat or, for that matter, need to breathe have breath that smelled like expired Parmesan cheese?

The breath, combined with chapped lips and eyes that were "I just ate special brownies" red, added up to someone I didn't want hovering close to my nose. I gave

Whitesnake another quick punch to the mouth, his teeth scraping deep across my knuckles. I must have hit him hard, because one of his canines clacked to the ground.

I quickly surmised that fangs are the one thing we didn't grow back, because he was really, really pissed about it. I barely got out an "Oh, cr," before I was splayed over the hood, gaining intimate personal knowledge of the hood ornament in a manner I'd rather not discuss again.

With the pummeling, my head snapped back, and I caught a glimpse of Andrea dozing blissfully in the front seat.

"A fat lot of help you are!" I yelled just before Mr. Whitesnake took this lapse of concentration as an opportunity to try to crush my skull with his bare hands.

The popping noise my cranium made was something that would make my skin crawl for the rest of my long, long life. I made an embarrassing girlie squeal as I tried to pry his fingers away from my scalp. Having exhausted my limited fighting skills, I resorted to the one thing that always worked in elementary school.

I kicked Whitesnake in the nuts.

And I was thrilled to find that it worked on men both dead and alive. He crumpled to the ground, howling. I sat up, postponing running and screaming long enough to let my skull knit back together.

A bemused voice sounded from behind the car. "OK, honey, I don't care what he's done to you, you just don't kick a man in his goods. It's just not done."

9

Try to avoid conflicts with other vampires until you can gauge their strength and control your own.

—From *The Guide for the Newly Undead*

The lager drinker had emerged from the bar to watch me get my ass kicked. How gallant.

"I'll keep that in mind while I'm having my panties surgically removed," I griped after snapping my jaw back into its socket.

I followed the sound of his laugh, focusing somewhat bleary eyes on the source of that smoky, smirky voice. It was one of those roguishly handsome faces, the ones that usually got me to do their homework in high school. Deep-set seawater-green eyes, high cheekbones, and a long patrician nose that had obviously been broken at some point. He was in his mid-thirties when he was turned, but the smile and the crinkles around his eyes gave him an impish quality. He was the first vampire I'd met whose smile actually reached his eyes. And he was the only one I'd met who wasn't wearing leather in some form.

"Jane Jameson."

He grinned. "Like the porn star."

I gaped at him. "What? No, *Jane* Jameson."

"Oh, not as fun," he said, making disappointed cluck-ing noises. He grinned and stretched out a long-fingered hand. "I'm Rich—"

The introduction was interrupted when my now-recovered opponent sprang up from the ground and lunged for my throat. I stepped out of the way as "Rich" caught the guy by his collar and jerked him back into a sleeper hold.

"Now, that's not very nice, Walter," Rich said, folding Whitesnake's arm into a painful origami formation. I could hear the bone creak toward breaking.

"That bitch broke my fang!" yelped Whitesnake, whose mystique was somewhat shattered by being named Walter.

"That's no way to talk to a lady. Now, say you're sorry," Rich said, the mock patience in his voice in direct con-trast to the snap-crackle-pop of Walter's ulna.

"Gah!" Walter yelled, which was not the response Rich was expecting, judging from the way he jerked Walter's arm up. I'd never heard a bone break before. It was an experience I'd rather not repeat. Blech. I'd also rather not repeat what Walter screamed at Rich, which would guarantee me box seats in hell, as Aunt Jettie would say.

"That's no way to talk to me, Walter," Rich said, grab-bing Walter by the scruff of his neck as the broken limb dangled. "You've been warned about robbing the Cellar.

Norm's been given permission to dust your hide with silver shot. He just doesn't have the heart to do it, 'cause you don't have the sense to duck."

I protested that all this bone-breaking wasn't necessary. I was fine, no harm done. And thanks to Walter, I was more than alert enough to drive home safely. Walter called me some very creative names and repeated his anatomically impossible instructions to Rich. Rich paused and watched Walter's arm set itself, then he wrenched it again.

"Oh, come on, man," Walter whined.

"I can keep breaking it," Rich told him. "Now, do you have something to say to this lady?"

Even I was disturbed at the display of testosterone. "Really, this is just—oh, come on. What's next? Screaming 'Mercy is for the weak'?"

Rich actually shushed me, saying, "There's a principle here."

Walter mumbled something close to "I'm sorry."

"What was that?" Rich combined the pain of a crooked arm with the indignity of a flicked ear. I could only hope the situation didn't escalate to the dreaded purple nurple.

Walter shrieked, "I'm sorry! I'm sorry!"

Rich smiled brightly at me. "Happy?"

"No!" I shook my head. "This is just wrong."

Rich gave me a look telling me he knew that some small, petty part of me was enjoying this. He released a whining Walter, who rubbed his arm gingerly. "Walter, I want you to go home to your mama's. Have a drink. And whatever you were planning to do with Norm's money, don't do it."

Walter sneered at me, told Rich he hoped an important appendage rotted off, waited a beat, then took off running. Rich nodded to Walter's retreating form. "That was Walter."

Walter had problems, Rich told me. He was a living example that being a vampire made you stronger and faster but not necessarily smarter. Turned behind a bowling alley five years before, he still slept in his mom's basement and made a living selling pirated *Knight Rider* DVDs. It wasn't much of a living, because he robbed the Cellar at least once every few months. Norm didn't even bother locking the safe anymore.

I dusted the parking-lot remnants off my jeans, glaring up at him. "So, I'm supposed to feel sorry for the guy who treats Norm like a human piñata and tried to pulverize my skull?"

He shrugged again. "No, but he's not very bright, so you can't hold it against him."

I winced as several parts of my head fused back together. "And yet I think I will, anyway."

"I like you." Rich grinned and bowed over my hand in a courtly manner. "Richard Cheney."

"Nice to meet you," I said, shaking his hand under his nose, making it much more difficult for him to kiss. "Wait, Richard Cheney, as in Dick Cheney? You're a vampire named Dick Cheney? Somehow, that makes you seem more evil."

"I was Dick Cheney first. I was Dick Cheney before he came along, and I'll be Dick Cheney after he's dead."

"Sore subject?" I asked.

He nodded. I glanced back at the abandoned bar, its neon sign spattering forlornly against the gathering humidity. "What about the bar?"

Dick made a gesture somewhere between a nod and a slouch. "I'll close it up. Norm gave me a key for nights like this."

"How often are you here?"

He laughed. "You'd better get home now, Stretch. Sun's coming up soon."

"Not a hot date for years, and suddenly I'm man bait," I muttered as I opened the car door. Andrea was still napping. I poked her rubbery, inanimate cheek and amused myself by giving her funny faces. "Entrée into the vampire world, my foot."

As dawn pecked at my windows, I tucked a lightly snoring Andrea in on my couch and asked Jettie to wake her in time to change for work. I knew I would wake up bright and early if invisible hands were yanking the pillow out from under my head.

I took a long, hot shower. It was more than a little nauseating when the gravel was forced out of my healing knee wounds and plinked into the enameled metal tub. I also washed a half-pound of grit from my hair and pulled a seven-inch sliver of windshield glass out of my shoulder.

"That can't be good," I muttered, tossing it into the wicker wastebasket. Apathetic about my nudity and the complications it could pose if I were confronted by a ragtag team of stake-wielding teenagers, I hung a thick quilt over the window and collapsed into bed. My last coherent thought was that I'd never retrieved my purse from the Cellar.

According to Jettie, Andrea left for work the next morning wearing an old church outfit of mine, which probably added up to the worst-dressed workday of her life. When I called her cell phone, she was driving two counties over to a client's house. Amused by my tales of parking-lot fisticuffs, she gave me the background on Dick.

Richard Allan Cheney lived in an old Airstream trailer out on Bend Road. Sort of blew those romantic castle-and-cape fantasies out of the water, didn't it? Andrea said the mobile life suited Dick's restless spirit, to know that he could pick up and move any time he wanted. His only fear was a tornado coming along during the day and ripping the house off him.

Dick was an old friend of Gabriel's, and when I say old, I mean 140-plus years. He was the last in a long line of dissolute men who were good with women and bad with fiscal responsibility. Dick's parents died when he was eighteen, leaving him with a perfectly respectable house, a pitiful income, and the one servant the family hadn't had to fire.

He was not exactly what Grandma Ruthie would call a "reputable person." If you needed it, Dick could find it. But you shouldn't ask where he got it. I'm not talking about your typical illegal-fireworks transactions.

A werewolf once tried to stake Dick instead of paying him for a pistol that shot silver bullets. It was rumored that the werewolf was now a fur rug in Dick's badly decorated living room. It's a moot point to ask why the werewolf didn't shoot Dick with the silver-bullet gun. Werewolves are sort of the crazy cousins of the supernatural world, Andrea explained, not great at making decisions.

Eager for a quiet night in, I dutifully read the chapters on finding blood sources and emergency sun protection from *The Guide for the Newly Undead.* The descriptions of spontaneous vampire combustion were going to give me nightmares for weeks. But now I knew not to trust a T-shirt pulled over my head to keep me from bursting into flames. (Coats, heavy-duty trash bags, and high-quality aluminum foil would do in a pinch.)

I nuked a bottle of Faux Type O and pored over my personal library for something that would settle me. As usual, I came back to my dear Jane. Whenever I get restless or stressed, I revisit *Mansfield Park.* Because I know that no matter how rough my life gets, at least I don't have to wear a corset *and* live with a stone-cold witch like Mrs. Norris.

I propped my feet on the arm of my porch swing and settled in. I'd barely begun a proper scratching of Fitz's ears when a set of brass knuckles came flying at me. I caught it a few centimeters from my forehead.

"That's so cool," I marveled. I turned to see Dick Cheney—the vampire, not the former vice president—climbing up onto my front porch. Fitz lifted his head as

Dick sauntered past but dropped back into the scratching position without so much as a bark.

"I figured you might want them the next time you get into a bar fight," he said. "I didn't want to say anything last night, but you hit like a girl, Stretch."

I gave him my best "don't underestimate me" look and muttered, "A vampire girl."

He sauntered over to the swing and made himself comfy, despite my objections when he stretched my legs over his ancient jeans. Not bothering to adjust the "I Know Tricks" T-shirt that rode over some impressive abs, he took particular pleasure in examining my brand-new cotton-candy-pink pedicure. "I do admire a woman who pays attention to her toes. So, what do you have planned for the evening? And where is that tasty friend of yours?"

I tossed the brass knuckles into his lap, drawing a wince from him. "She's not here, and she won't date you."

He grinned, splitting the rugged planes of his face with brilliant white fangs. "She might if she knew me."

"She does know you, and that's why she won't date you."

He gave me his best panty-dropping smile. "I guess I'll have to settle for you, then."

Unable to decide whether that was an insult, I ignored him.

"There's something familiar about you," he said. "I can't quite place it. But you're different."

"It's my shampoo," I said, a smidge too loudly. "It smells like mangoes, very memorable."

"No, that's not it," he said, then squinted at me and gave up. He poked my side, instinctively aiming at my most ticklish places. "How come we haven't met before? How old are you? What do you do when you're not losing fights and quipping me half to death?"

"I grew up around here," I said, slapping his hand away. "I was just turned last week. I'm a librarian."

He stilled, as if I'd just told him I was the inventor of the tube top. "I watched a movie about a librarian once. Well, she was a librarian by day, a call girl by—"

I stopped him with a quick lift of an eyebrow. "If you finish that sentence, we cannot be friends."

"You don't talk like a librarian," he said.

"I know," I admitted. "I'm proof that just enough education can be dangerous. In the right setting, I can argue Faulkner and James Joyce with the best of them. But I think it's going to take a couple of centuries to polish the Hollow off me. My sire's pretty urbane. Maybe he can send me to vampire charm school or something."

"I kind of like it." He smirked and turned his attentions to the gardens. "I knew your family, growing up. Came to a couple of parties here at River Oaks. I was, uh, friendly with your several-times-great-aunt Cessie."

I glared at him. Dick glossed over the subject. "The gardens were never this pretty, though. My mother used to have a garden like this. She liked to leave it kind of wild, but you could see the thought she put into it. She loved her roses."

"So did my aunt Jettie," I said. "I'm barely keeping them alive. I'm better at reading about gardening than the actual gardening itself. But Jettie liked it when I would tell her what the roses meant. You know, white roses mean purity. Red roses mean passionate love. Oddly enough, blue roses signify mystery, the real mystery being that there is no such thing as a naturally blue rose. Roses can't produce a chemical called delphinidin, which makes flowers blue. So florists have to dip them in chemicals to turn them blue."

Even as I was talking, a voice inside my head was yelling, "Shut up! Shut up! Shut up!"

Dick seemed impressed but a little frightened. "You must really like flowers."

"I like finding symbolic meanings in everyday things," I said. "You know, the meanings in some Victorian floral guides conflicted, so sometimes couples sent each other mixed messages. I like the idea of some proper English lady breaking her parasol over a suitor's head because he sent her yellow carnations, thinking it meant affection, but in her book it meant rejection and disdain."

Dick stared at me a long time before saying, "You're—"

"Jane?"

My head snapped up. Gabriel closed the fifty yards to my front door in a few strides. He did not look happy. And he was carrying my purse. My feet dropped to the porch. Fitz lifted his head and let out a huff but didn't move. Dick remained in his casual, cozy pose, a smug grin spreading like molasses.

"Well, if it isn't my good friend Gabriel. How are you, son?"

"What are you doing here?" Gabriel demanded.

Dick squeezed my shoulder in a chummy gesture. "We're writing a vampire children's book, *See Dick and Jane Bite.* What do you think?"

If looks could kill . . . well, Dick was already dead, so nothing would happen. But Gabriel was not laughing.

"See Dick," Dick said, pointing at his chest. He then swept his hand dangerously close to mine. "Jane. Dick and Jane. Come on, you humorless jackass. That's funny."

"Do all vampires know one another?" I asked, fending off Dick's languidly resting hand on my knee. It was obviously for Gabriel's benefit. The last thing I needed was to be caught up in some bizarre undead-male pissing contest.

"Only vampires who were best friends from the cradle," Dick replied. "But Gabriel here likes to pretend that we've always been archenemies. How do you two know each other? You didn't lose a fight with him, too, did you?"

My response was not ladylike at all, which pleased Dick beyond an appropriate measure. After a beat, Dick scowled, leaned close, and sniffed my hair.

"You're her sire?" Dick frowned. "Should have picked up on that. She's not your type at all, Gabe. She can string a sentence together. And she's not evil."

"Thanks," I said, ducking my head away. What was with vampires and hair smelling? Did that mean Gabriel had scented my hair? Like a cat? Note to self: Buy clarifying shampoo immediately.

Gabriel ignored Dick, focusing on me. "Jane, where did you go last night?"

"Not in love with your tone right now," I told him.

"I'll use a more cheerful tone when I have more cheerful news," he said. "Where did you go last night?"

"The Cellar."

He shot Dick the icy glare of death. "With whom?"

"With me," Dick offered. "We had a very memorable encounter in the parking lot."

"That's not what it sounds like," I said, elbowing Dick in the ribs.

"Jane, did you get into a fight with a vampire named Walter?"

I gave him my own lukewarm glare of malaise. "A low-life, scum-sucking, old-man shaker named Walter, yes."

"He's dead," Gabriel said.

Dick snorted. "Yeah, he's dead. You're dead. I'm dead. We're all dead. I thought you knew this stuff."

At this point, I think Gabriel was blocking out Dick's mere presence with some sort of meditation exercise. "No, Jane, Walter is permanently dead. He was locked in the trunk of his car, and the car was set on fire."

"He could have done that to himself!" I exclaimed.

Dick considered that for a moment and nodded.

Gabriel gave me the stern face. "This isn't funny."

I held up my fingers, measuring "this much" humor. "It's a little bit funny. I thought we turned to ashes and dust when we're permanently killed. How do they even know that it's Walter in the trunk?"

"His wallet and other personal effects were found

with him," Gabriel said. "Your purse was found near the car."

"I left it at the bar last night! What's going on? Are the police going to come knocking on my door?"

"Suspicious vampire deaths are not investigated by the living authorities," Gabriel said in a professorial tone that made me want to nibble on his earlobes until one of us lost consciousness.

Gabriel was still talking. "The victims are officially dead, anyway, so the humans figure why bother? Anytime a human kills a vampire, human law enforcement considers it self-defense, something the World Council has been trying to change for years. Either way, the undead are strongly discouraged from killing one another without good reason. Losing a back-alley fight is not considered sufficient cause to set someone on fire."

"Why would I set fire to someone I barely know? And then leave my purse next to the car so the authorities could be sure to track me down? And I didn't *lose* the back-alley fight, I just didn't win it," I corrected. Gabriel stared. "Fine, I lost. But Dick came along and helped settle the disagreement. Walter walked away. I took Andrea home with me and went to bed . . . alone," I added when Dick opened his mouth. "Dick can vouch for the fact that when I left that parking lot, Walter was alive."

"I don't think using Dick as a character witness is going to help you." Gabriel said.

Dick considered that for a moment and nodded.

"She didn't do anything, Gabe," Dick said. "She was

just trying to keep Norm from getting hurt. Even the Council will be able to see that."

"Council?" I squeaked. But neither of them noticed, what with all the seething and male posturing.

"As your sire, I have to take you before the local council to answer some questions," Gabriel told me. "I would suggest you put on some more suitable clothes."

I looked down at my clothes. Apparently, pajama pants imprinted with little cupcakes were not suitable.

I ran inside to change into khakis and a respectable blouse, reluctant to leave Dick and Gabriel alone for fear they might say something interesting in my absence. When I came back out, it appeared that they hadn't said anything at all. Gabriel was leaning against the porch railing, arms crossed and eyes narrowed at his old friend. Dick was stretched out on my swing, scratching my adoring dog. Fitz had roused himself enough to sit up and place his head on Dick's knee.

"You'll be fine, Stretch," Dick assured me with a wink. "See you later."

Gabriel glowered at Dick as he opened the door to his car, a rather sedate Volvo sedan. It was disappointing, despite the total destruction of every preconceived vampire notion I'd had in the last week. The car smelled of old leather and not much else. It was a refreshing change from my car, which smelled faintly of bacon cheeseburgers.

Dick didn't bother leaving before we pulled away. He stayed stretched across my porch swing with my dog's head on his knee. He even blew me a little kiss as I left.

I'm sure it was meant to make Gabriel wonder whether he would still be there when I returned. I bounced between being annoyed and being somewhat flattered that he was using me to irritate Gabriel. I settled on annoyed.

I had no idea what awaited me at the council hearing. After the initial Coming Out chaos subsided, the World Council for the Equal Treatment of the Undead appointed national and state-level commissions to look into suspicious vampire deaths and record the newly turned. Those state councils had local representatives to settle minor squabbles and determine what matters were worth the higher-ups' attention. They were also granted authority to carry out sentences for the Council.

Gabriel drove in seething silence until we reached the edge of town. As we pulled to a stop on Gates Street, he tightened his fingers around the steering wheel and spat. "I can smell him on you."

"Who?"

"You know who," he snarled.

"Is this about Dick?" I finally asked.

He growled.

I crossed my arms, as much to put a barrier between our bodies as to communicate my exasperation. "So, it's about Dick."

Not to be obvious, but wasn't it always?

He pulled me to face him in my seat, his face dangerously close to mine. "I need to make something very clear. I'm not your friend, Jane. I'm not Zeb. I can't spend time with you if you're going to be with someone else."

"I want you to really, really listen to me, because I say

this with all sincerity," I whispered, pressing his hands between mine. "You are not a well man."

"Don't make a joke out of this," he growled.

"I'm not kidding," I growled back. "What the hell do you mean, you're not my friend? And I haven't been with anyone, thank you very much. You'd know that if you really paid attention with that nose of yours.

"Look, Dick was actually really helpful last night. He probably kept Walter from cracking my skull. And he came over tonight to make sure I was OK," I told him. "That's it. Nothing happened. I mean, he touched me, but not in the way you're thinking. And smelling me to determine whom I have and haven't been around is not an appropriate use of vampire powers. In fact, it's kind of pathetic. Your light's green."

Gabriel finally noticed the changed traffic signal and punched the gas. He smoldered for a few beats before he burst out with, "You know he lost his family's house in a card game, yes?"

"Dick lost his house to *you* in a card game." I sighed.

Andrea had acquainted me with this interesting tidbit. Before they were turned, Gabriel and Dick spent much of their time bouncing between the card table (Dick's hobby) and the horse auctions (Gabriel's hobby). One night after several hands of poker and too much of Dick's brandy, Dick wagered his family home against Gabriel's prize stallion. Dick was too drunk to realize he was holding two eights, a seven, a jack, and a two, not a straight. Though Gabriel tried to give the house back, Dick was too proud to take it. This was fortuitous, as the

Cheney manse was where Gabriel ran when his brothers staked him out.

Between the humiliation of Dick's loss and Gabriel's new "nights only" policy, let's just say they were no longer BFFs. Petty grievances and snarky exchanges compiled until they went from not being able to stand each other to open hostility. Dick's propensity for penis-related quips and juvenile pranks didn't help. In the late 1960s, he peppered Gabriel's entire house with silver filings. For more than a decade, Gabriel couldn't sit without minor burns to his behind.

So, despite living within a ten-mile radius of each other for more than a century, they didn't speak unless they had to. By the way, before you start making assumptions, Dick was not turned by the same woman who turned Gabriel. According to Andrea, Dick was turned ten years after Gabriel, after a particularly bad card game. The winner, a vampire from New Orleans named Scat, wanted to make sure Dick's debt was paid off and figured giving him an extra few hundred years would help. Notice a gambling pattern here?

"You—you should not spend time with Dick Cheney."

I nodded. "Especially if he's holding a hunting rifle."

He tipped his head back and roared in "I'm seriously reconsidering my 'I don't hit girls' policy" frustration.

"Feel better now?" I asked.

"No!" Gabriel yelled as he turned into the Hollow's mall area. Most of the city's large-chain restaurants and businesses were clustered here, circling the wagons against cranky local merchants and customers who didn't understand why any store would have a returns policy that required a receipt instead of just trusting the customer's word. The neon signs seemed so bright it hurt to look directly at them, their aggressive reds and greens leaving little spots against my closed eyelids. We passed the full parking lot at Shenanigans, and I was struck by how different I was since the last time I'd driven down this road. The Jane who mourned a lost job and a half-lived life at that bar seemed happier, even in her misery, because she didn't have to deal with angry sires and blood and a murder rap.

"How much trouble am I in?" I asked, finally breaking the quiet.

"I don't know," he admitted quietly. "I've never heard of one vampire killing another so soon after rising."

"Do you honestly believe that I could do something like this? Why would I set fire to someone I hardly knew?"

"As opposed to someone you know well?" He snorted.

"I'll take care of the sarcasm here, thank you," I told him. "Honestly, do you believe I could do something like this?"

He waited for a distressing amount of time before saying "No."

"Then why are you hauling me into court?" I demanded, ashamed of the whine that was creeping into my voice. "I thought vampires had this whole lawless-unholy-rebel thing going."

"Some feel that way," he said. "Others, like me, believe that if you're going to assimilate into the modern world, you have to have some accountability for what you do."

Well, that made me feel horrible.

He stared at the parking lot ahead, unable even to glance in my direction. "Just be respectful. Don't talk back. Don't volunteer any extra information. Don't demonstrate your unique brand of humor."

"Basically, don't be me," I grumbled. "If I wasn't paralyzed by fear, I'd be offended by that."

10

The World Council for the Equal Treatment of the Undead was created to protect the rights and interests of vampires of all ages. If you are summoned by a council official, it is in your best interest to respond promptly and answer all questions honestly. Hiding from the council will only work against you.

—From *The Guide for the Newly Undead*

I expected the local council to be a cross between the Lions Club and a Scorsese-esque panel of mafiosi. How mafiosi would end up in Kentucky, well, I hadn't really thought that through.

Any self-respecting mafioso wouldn't be caught dead at Cracker Barrel at nine on a weeknight. Yes, the council, the grand overseers of justice and decorum among the vampires of Region 813, held their secret meetings under an old metal sign advertising Lux soap. Generally, you don't find vampires in well-lit places surrounded by unpleasant human food smells and an aggressively homey atmosphere. Gabriel explained that meeting in such a neutral, crowded environment was the only way to ensure that nothing would be overheard. Humans tend to be pretty focused when it comes to comfort food. The panel ordered Mama's Pancake Breakfasts and pushed the food around their plates. They were no different from any other customers, except for leaving healthy tips.

Gabriel found the council members at their usual table. The panel consisted of:

Peter Crown, pale, gaunt, dyspeptic. It was clearly communicated that he did not like me. Or Gabriel, or the other panel members, or the people eating pecan waffles at the next table. I think someone turned him into a vampire as a punitive measure. They wanted him to be pissy for all eternity.

A Colonel Sanders lookalike improbably named Waco Marchand. He didn't speak to Gabriel but greeted me with a polite kiss just over my wrist. My hand smelled like peppermint and hair tonic for the rest of the night.

A blond lady with a slight British accent, who went by Sophie. Just Sophie. That was as close to Cher as we got in the Hollow. She was turned in her mid-forties. Her face was unlined and unpainted, leaving a plastic sheen to her skin that was beguiling and disquieting at the same time. She was confident enough not to wear any accessories with her rather fabulous black pantsuit.

Ophelia Lambert, a willowy brunette, was wearing jeans, a T-shirt, and a locket that was probably three hundred years old. Ophelia could have been three hundred years old, but she appeared to be about sixteen. Her dewy, youthful looks conflicted with the imposing presence, a sort of "Yes, I look as if I read *Tiger Beat,* but I can remove your spleen without blinking" attitude. She was almost as scary as some of the girls from my high school.

Council members were assigned to their precincts regardless of origin, so Ophelia and Sophie's "Continental" presence wasn't all that strange. I did, however, believe I recognized Mr. Marchand from a Confederate memorial statue downtown.

Ophelia, who was apparently the head of the panel, motioned for us to sit at the crayon-scarred round table. A brown-aproned waitress named Betty arrived promptly to take our orders—Mama's Pancake Breakfasts all around—and we wouldn't see her for another forty-five minutes.

Despite the gravity of the situation, I couldn't concentrate on the members of the council. Sitting in a crowded human environment was an assault on the senses. Conversation from other tables hovered around us in needling mosquito clouds. And the bacon, which I had loved so much in life, kind of smelled like baby vomit. I concentrated on my silverware, shredding the paper napkin ring into tiny strips and twisting them into long coils.

"Do you know why you're here?" Ophelia finally asked, her eyes as flat and still as a shark's as she spoke to me.

I hesitated. If there was ever a time for me to cure my chronic babbling, this was it. "I was told that you have some questions for me."

Gabriel inclined his head slightly, as if to tell me I was off to a good start. We'd agreed that if I was being inappropriate or started to jabber, he would tap me with his foot under the table. Head nodding was a sign that I'd said or done something appropriate. It was demeaning, but I didn't want to dwell on it. The council stared me down, clearly expecting more.

"I'm told that a vampire was killed last night," I said.

"A vampire you attacked just hours before he was locked in his trunk and set on fire," Sophie pointed out.

"I contend that it's possible Walter did that to himself."

No response from the panel beyond quirked lips from Ophelia. Gabriel kicked me under the table.

"Now, why was a nice young lady like you tussling with some no-account like that?" Mr. Marchand asked, shaking his head in fatherly distaste.

"I objected to the way he was holding Norm, the human bartender, upside down and shaking him like a piggy bank," I said with as little irritation as possible. "Walter and I disagreed. Dick Cheney intervened. Walter drove away. I drove home. Andrea Byrne, whom I believe is well known in the vampire community, stayed on my couch, and . . . she can't tell you much because she was essentially passed out drunk during the fight.

"I need to find a new way to tell stories," I added lamely.

"Listening to the words in your head before you say them might help," Sophie suggested kindly. She stretched out her hand. I felt compelled to take it. As soon as I was within range, she clutched my wrist and dragged me close, wrenching me against the table.

"Hey—" I grunted. Something was wrong. My hand itched. Sophie's fingers were burning into my skin. I gasped, frantically trying to jerk away from her grip. Gabriel's fingers slid under the table and clutched my other hand. His head shook. I was supposed to accept this treatment quietly.

"Don't interfere, Gabriel," Ophelia warned. Gabriel's hand slipped away, leaving me adrift.

"Look into my eyes," Sophie commanded, her voice stripped of the charm she was slathering on just a few seconds before. Hoping that I could still glower effectively through the pain, I met her gaze. Her irises flared to black, and then I was plummeting, dropping through bottomless space. My head seemed so heavy, too heavy to lift. Images of people and tables whizzed past without form or focus.

"What are you doing?" I mumbled, my tongue thick and heavy. My voice sounded far away. I wanted to open my eyes, but the lids wouldn't budge. My stomach pitched. *Oh, please, please, don't let me throw up in the middle of a Cracker Barrel.*

"Sophie is what you might call a walking lie detector," Ophelia said, her tone cheerful. "Her gift allows her to search through your thoughts, sift the truth from what you want us to believe. It will be a difficult, painful procedure if you resist. Now, I want you tell us again. What happened to Walter?"

The sting from Sophie's grip was wildfire, scorching

from my arm to my chest. Hot iron claws were digging into my throat, scraping out words. I don't remember what I said. I just know I said it quietly. Overall, I'd have to rank the experience just under "unanesthetized root canal." That settled it. Gabriel was officially my worst date ever.

On the upside, I was able to relocate my tongue as Sophie's grasp loosened.

"Let go of me," I wheezed. My mouth tasted odd, like rusty nails. I smacked my dry lips and stared angry holes through Gabriel.

"Oh, don't make a fuss," Sophie said lightly. "I'm going to let you go now. You did well."

I wish I could have pulled enough words together to respond with appropriate scorn, but I think I was better off silent and nauseated. Gabriel tried to rub a hand across my shoulders, but I growled at him. If the humans at the next table noticed, they didn't look up from their waffles.

Sophie said, "She's telling the truth, or at least what she believes is the truth. She's so young. Sometimes it's hard for them to tell the difference."

Crown smiled at me, more nasty mockery than friendly gesture. That pissed me off. And I had just gained enough control over my limbs to jerk my hand away from Sophie.

"This is not how people behave in a Cracker Barrel!" I hissed. I snarled at my sire, who had turned the gentle pressure on my foot into an all-out toe stomping.

"We did tell you that the process can be unpleasant,"

Sophie said with a small smile of apology. "It could have been much more painful."

"We have already spoken to Andrea Byrne," Ophelia said in a tone perfect for pronouncing judgment. "She is one of the few humans whose word could sway our opinion. We are willing to believe your account for now, but you should be aware that we will continue to investigate Walter's death. If the attack was justified or we find that you are innocent, you will have our deepest apologies. However, if we learn that you have lied to this council, you will be severely punished. Andrea will be punished along with you."

"If you don't mind my asking," I croaked, "if you were going to use Ms. Polygraph over there, why did you ask me to tell my side of things before?"

Ophelia offered the barest of shrugs. "To see if you would tell us the truth without assistance—if your version of events is, in fact, the truth. Also, we enjoy scaling the punishment to fit the depth of your deception."

"If I may be so bold as to question the council further, what could 'punishment' mean?" I asked.

If I didn't know that my toe bones would regenerate, I would have been very upset about the crushing pressure Gabriel was applying to my foot.

Ophelia smirked. "You could have a choice of being locked in a coffin full of bees or having a red-hot silver poker shoved up your—"

"Ophelia." With an apologetic glance my way, Mr. Marchand interrupted her. "That's enough."

"She's only joking," Sophia assured me. "The silver

poker is actually at room temperature. Ancient vampires called it the Trial."

I asked, "Why?"

"Because it sounds incredibly scary." Sophie nodded.

I was dismissed before my pancakes were served, which was better in the long run. I probably would have found uneaten pancakes singularly depressing. Gabriel escorted me to the car before I could say anything else incriminating. And by escorting, I mean he dragged me across the parking lot like a caveman and ushered me none too gently into the front seat.

"What the hell was that?" I yelled. Having fully recovered the use of my arms and legs, I seized the opportunity to swing at him as he slid behind the wheel. "Did you know they were going to do that to me? And a coffin full of bees? What the hell?"

"Calm down, just calm down," he said, catching my wrists. I thought he meant to stop the hitting, but he was examining my reddened skin, poring over the marks left by Sophie's truth-seeking expedition into my brain. I remained quiet long enough to watch them evaporate away. I had a feeling it would sting for a while longer.

"What is wrong with you people?" I demanded. "Why didn't you tell me they were going to go digging around in my brain? You know, I was raised to believe the contents of someone's brain are that person's own business! And have you noticed how often I yell at you?"

"Jane, I know you were frightened—"

"I was terrified, you ass!"

He was across the front seat with my face between

his palms before I knew what hit me. Despite being extremely pissed, I'm not going to say I didn't like kissing him. Or that I didn't kiss back. Because, damn. I mean, damn, he was some kisser. If our first kiss was sparklers and fireworks, this was a full-scale nuclear detonation. My whole body was involved—face, lips, hands, thighs, legs. I don't think he was actually touching all of those parts. I just know they were involved.

The sweep of his tongue across my lip was subtle at first, then increasingly demanding, until I couldn't tell where his mouth started and mine ended. He pulled me onto his lap, anchoring my ankles on either side of his thighs with his hands, stroking exposed skin with his thumbs. I tugged at his hair, pulling his head back so I could kiss that little thumb-shaped depression in the middle of his chin. Gabriel grunted, protesting my mouth leaving his. He brought me back to his lips, one hand cradling my head as the other kept my hips pinned to his.

A minivan pulled into the spot next to ours. I could hear the gasps and then giggles of the three teens who were piling out with their parents.

One of the kids yelled, "Jeez, get a room!"

I broke away from Gabriel, moving across the seat, ignoring the snickers of the kids as they walked away. I stared at him for what I'm sure was an alarming amount of time. I hadn't had a kiss like that in, well, ever. I'd finally found something simple and natural about my relationship with Gabriel: making out with him.

Yay for me.

Just as I'd managed to produce that coherent thought, he was back on my side of the car again and giving me a repeat performance. It caught me off guard, and I accidentally bit down on his bottom lip hard enough to draw blood. The good news was he liked that, so I came off as provocative, not inept.

"If that was an attempt to shut me up, screw you," I panted after he'd let me go a second time.

Through my hair, where his face was buried, he muttered, "I did it because I wanted to. Shutting you up was an added side benefit."

I shoved at his shoulders. "Ass."

"You said that already," he said, his fingers tracing the lines of my jaw.

"Meant it this time, too."

"Jane, I know you were frightened. I know their methods of questioning can be a bit brutal, but that was necessary," he said, pulling me tighter against his chest. I rested my forehead against the hollow of his throat, happy to find comfort even for a few moments. Having your brain scoured is an emotionally unsettling experience.

"I know you're angry with me for bringing you here," he murmured. "But failing to answer the council would have caused far more problems. And as your sire, I'm responsible for presenting you to the panel. I'm responsible for watching over you in these first weeks. Obviously, I haven't been doing a very good job."

"That's pretty insulting," I said, poking his ribs.

Gabriel finally said, "I'm sorry."

"Excuse me?" I said, cupping my hand around my ear. "What was that?"

"I'm sorry," he said again. "I'm sorry for being so abrupt with you at your house. I'm sorry for blowing up at you over spending time with Dick. I'm sorry for being so . . . unsettled around you. I've never spent time with a childe I've made. There are complications I didn't expect. I have this overwhelming need to protect you, and you're making it very difficult."

"Why haven't you ever spent time with a childe?"

"It hasn't been possible," he said in a voice that brooked no further questions. "And even if you weren't my childe, I would feel this way. We're connected, you and I. That's why seeing you with Dick tonight was so unnerving. He's always had a way with the ladies, and you're exactly the kind of woman he enjoys corrupting. The idea of some other man touching you, kissing you, smelling him on your clothes, your skin. I couldn't take it. Between that and the council summons, I overreacted."

"So, it's not that you like me, it's that a biological function is making you jealous," I muttered.

"Yes, wait—no!" he howled. "Why do you always reduce me to a blithering idiot?"

"This is blithering?" I grinned.

"For me," he admitted.

I had to concede that one.

"You smell him on me?" I asked, sniffing my shirt. "What does he smell like to you? To me, it's all lust and bergamot."

"Uselessness," he grumbled. He tipped his forehead

to mine and kissed my temple, my forehead, the bridge of my nose. He buried his face in the crook of my neck, inhaling deeply. "I do enjoy your scent, though, and I like you. Very much. I want to protect you. If anything happened to you, I don't know what I would do."

I lifted my head to eye him warily. "You're not going to do something weird with my dryer lint, are you?"

"I never know what is going to come out of your mouth," he said, staring at me. "I enjoy that, in a morbid way. I am saying that even before I turned you, your scent was part of what kept me close to you."

"What did I smell like?"

"Mine," he said, kissing the hollow of my throat, the tip of my nose, and finally my mouth. "You smelled like you were mine."

"Can you take me home now?"

"Are you tired?" he asked. "Sophie's methods can take a lot out of you."

"No, I don't want more people to see me making out with some random guy in the Cracker Barrel parking lot."

"I'm hardly random," he said, sliding into the driver's seat. "I'm your sire."

"Well, people don't know that, because they don't know I'm a vampire," I said, rubbing my wrists. "I've already got 'jobless' and 'publicly drunk' going. I don't need to add 'parking-lot ho' to the list."

"One day, you will explain to me what that means, and I don't think it will make me happy," he muttered, turning the ignition.

* * *

Just when I thought our "date" couldn't possibly get worse, we arrived at my house to find my Daddy waiting on my porch swing with a Meat Lover's Pizza. I hadn't had fatherly approval for a "gentleman caller" since I was a senior in college. This was not going to go well.

Gabriel nodded to the porch. "Do you know this man?"

"That's my dad," I said. "I still haven't told him."

"I know," he said. "I can leave now."

"No, the two most influential men in my life are going to have to meet sometime."

"Hi, baby," Daddy said, kissing my cheek between bites of pizza. "Your mama had a sales party thing tonight. Makeup or lotion or home decor or some such thing. I never can keep them straight. I don't object until they try to talk her into hosting the things herself. I thought I'd surprise you, but it seems you had plans for the evening."

"That was sweet. Gabriel Nightengale, this is my father, John Jameson," I said, waving him and Gabriel in through the front door and leading them to the kitchen. "Daddy, Gabriel is my—"

Sire? Interfering pseudo-mentor? Guy most likely to be my first ugly undead breakup? I settled for "Friend."

"Pizza?" Daddy asked, opening the box to display his cholesterol-laden treat on my counter.

"Oh, no, thanks, I couldn't," I said.

Daddy arched a brow as I pulled out a counter-height

barstool for him. I never turned down pizza. Ever. "You're not going on some crazy diet, are you?"

For a brief, wonderful instant, Gabriel looked stricken. I laughed. "No, we already ate, smart alec."

"If you'll excuse me for a moment," Gabriel said, disappearing out the kitchen door.

"Gabriel Nightengale, that name sounds familiar," Daddy mused, chewing on a pepperoni. I could tell from the look on his face that he was searching his massive but not quite reliable memory banks for information.

"Um, he has a lot of family around here," I said, not bothering to add that most of them were in the cemetery. "They've been in the Hollow a really, really long time."

Daddy returned to chewing. Leaning against the counter, I asked, "So, what's new with you?"

"Same old, same old." He grinned, snagging a second piece. "Summer classes. Started writing another textbook I won't finish. Your mama's already getting ready for next year's historical tour."

"I'm not putting River Oaks back on the tour," I said. "Aunt Jettie wouldn't have wanted that."

"Mama's not going to ask," he said. "To be honest, she wouldn't know how. Your mother is at a loss for how to handle this job thing, pumpkin. She's upset and scared for you, but she's embarrassed, too. She worried about you being single and living on your own, but she's never had to worry about you on the job front. She never thought you'd be in this . . . position. She wants to help, but you're refusing to let her just swoop in and take care of everything. She feels as if she's lost her . . . bargaining power with you."

I snorted. "Subtly put, Daddy. Try using fewer pauses. They imply you're searching for the word that will hurt me less than the ones she actually used."

"Your mother is a complicated woman," he said simply.

"And by 'complicated,' do you mean 'manipulative' and 'emotionally crippling'?" I asked.

"Air-quote fingers aren't attractive on anyone, honey," he said, using his authoritative teacher voice. "She may be a little high-strung, but she's still your mama."

Daddy wrapped his arm around me. My head fell to his shoulder, in that hollow made just for me. "You know she loves you," he said quietly.

I sighed. "Yes, I feel the crushing weight of her love from here."

He cleared his throat, which I could tell meant he was trying not to laugh. "She doesn't know how to handle a situation unless she's in charge. Just don't expect me to pick a side between the two of you."

"Even though you know I'm right?"

"Janie." There was the authoritative voice again.

I looked up at him, making the doe eyes. "It was worth a shot."

So, we talked. Eager for normalcy, I savored the mundane details of the life that I'd been missing. None of the freshmen in Daddy's summer class could write a complete sentence, which was nothing new. My second cousin Teeny's face-lift had gone wrong, which just went to prove that plastic surgery is one area where you shouldn't bargain-shop. My future grandpa Bob, Grandma Ruthie's fiancé, was in the hospital having his hip worked on—which meant it was time for his monthly weeklong hospital stay. Why was this sweet man engaged to my grandma? I could only imagine that after surviving gall-bladder removal, knee replacement, dialysis, and chemo, Bob actually wanted to die, and he saw marriage to her as a legal form of assisted suicide.

While Daddy described Grandma Ruthie's legendary surgical-ward histrionics, Gabriel returned to my kitchen door lugging a ratty cardboard box. I sincerely hoped vampires didn't substitute pig pieces for flowers and chocolates. But I couldn't smell anything bloody, just the musty scent of old cigarettes and B.O. With his amazing vampire speed, Gabriel managed to shove the box into a nearby coat closet without Daddy's realizing it existed.

Daddy went into suspicious-father mode, managing to question Gabriel without making it look as if he was interrogating him. And Gabriel, far more accustomed to lying than I, performed beautifully. He deflected all possible vampire giveaways without an iota of irony. He complimented my father on raising such a "fascinating" daughter. He even praised Daddy's textbook.

"I see now where Jane gets her inquisitive nature," Gabriel said. I suppose I should have thanked him for saying "inquisitive" and not "nosy and spastic."

Stuffed to the gills with imitation Italian-style meat products, Daddy rolled out the door sometime later.

I only had to drop seven "Wow, it's really late" hints. I think the phone call from my mom was the only thing that could have pried him away from cross-examining my new "friend." Daddy hadn't had the opportunity in a long, long . . . long time.

"I think Daddy likes you," I squealed to Gabriel in mock giddiness. "I only hope you ask for my hand before my skanky younger sister runs off with a scoundrel and ruins my reputation and hopes for happiness."

Gabriel grimaced. "That's not funny."

"*Pride and Prejudice* references are always hilarious. What's with the box full of funk?" I nodded toward the closet. Gabriel retrieved the box and opened it with a flourish.

A heretofore unknown and disturbing factoid: When you best a vampire in battle (no matter how sad and circumstantial the evidence of that battle may be), you take all of his stuff. No matter how icky that stuff may be. I was the unhappy recipient of the personal effects of Walter the Whitesnake fan: a silver-plate lighter engraved with "Screw Communism," several concert T-shirts with discolored armpits, forty-two copies of *Knight Rider,* season two, and the complete works of Def Leppard on cassette tape.

"Walter's mother was eager to have her basement back," Gabriel explained. "She was glad to be rid of this. She brought it down to the council office this morning. No one else will want it, so Ophelia wanted you to have it. I believe it's a reminder to stay on your best behavior."

I tossed the cassette single of "Pour Some Sugar on

Me" back into the box. "If you beat somebody up, you take their stuff? Wait, what's to keep someone from challenging another vampire to a duel just because they like their car?"

"Nothing," he admitted. "As long as the vampire can find some reason for the duel, even if it's a contrived reason. Some petty perceived slight. The restrictions loosen a bit as you get older. The goal is to keep newly risen vampires from developing a taste for random killing, which is the only reason the council is taking such an interest in Walter's death. They're trying to make an example of you."

I must have made my "that sucks" face, because Gabriel assured me, "There's always been a pecking order, a demand for reason. Even more so now that we're trying to appear civilized for the humans."

"This is a stupid system."

"Yes, so much less civilized than your corporate take-overs and mega-chains," he said, hefting the box. "Where would you like this?"

"Not in my house," I said. "Take it to the mudroom, and I'll burn it later."

Once again displaying that amazing vampire dexterity, Gabriel shifted the box to one arm and reached for the nearest doorknob. It would have been impressive had he not opened the door to the wrong room.

"No, don't go in there!" I cried as Gabriel stepped into my library.

"You have a lot of unicorns," he said, his voice shadowed in both awe and horror.

One of the few things I'd done to make the house my own was installing my collection of unicorn figurines on the library shelves. My late grandma Pat, who had been the oatmeal-cookies-and-Ivory-soap type, bought me a unicorn music box when I was six. I played that thing until the little motor wouldn't tinkle "You Light Up My Life" anymore. So, unicorn figurines, music boxes, and stuffed animals became the gift for unimaginative relatives to get me for birthdays, Christmases, Valentine's Days, graduations, Arbor Days. In fact, I'd just received two ceramic unicorn bookends the previous Christmas from my uncle.

For reasons even I couldn't explain, I could not throw the little suckers away. The majestic sweep of their horns, their imperious painted eyes, held some sort of strange, unholy thrall over me. So, I stashed them in the library, where nobody goes but me. Except, of course, for the one person I really didn't want to see them.

"A *lot* of unicorns," Gabriel repeated.

I tried to close the door, but he stuck his foot in the jamb—most likely to get a better look at my ten-inch ceramic unicorn lamp with the revolving-color, fiber-optic tail. "Fine, fine. You know my secret. I have a unicorn collection."

"That's a very sad secret," he said as he allowed me to shove his foot from the door.

"Strong words coming from someone who was 'devoured' by a sea lion." I snatched the box out of his hands and tossed it into the laundry/utility room. Then I locked both doors with a decisive *snick*.

"I like your father," Gabriel said. "I actually enjoyed speaking to him, very much. In my courting days, meeting a woman's father could be an unpleasant experience. There was male posturing, vague threats to my manhood. Sometimes a shotgun would be cleaned in front of me."

"You didn't by chance meet these girls' fathers in a hayloft while wearing no pants, did you?" I asked.

"I believe it's in my best interest not to answer that."

I snickered. "My dad's not much of a gun guy, so I think you're safe. Besides, with today's fathers, it's more of a background check and pray-for-the-best sort of thing."

"Duly noted," he said, smiling and leaning against the wall across from me. "However, I am glad to have established a friendly relationship with your father, since I have plans for his daughter. Those plans include kissing you again," he said, crossing his arms. The statement seemed as much a challenge as information. "I enjoy kissing you."

"Immediately or eventually?" I asked. "And thank you."

"I haven't decided."

I was proud that I managed not to giggle. "Well, I appreciate the warning—mmmph." The rest of that no doubt brilliant response was muffled as Gabriel decided to pursue the more immediate option.

Again, I say, woo and hoo.

Gabriel pressed me against the wall, grinning as he nipped my bottom lip with his fangs. He traced the lines of my throat with his canines, pressing ever so slightly against my collarbone with his tongue. His fingers slid slowly up my ribcage, stroking the sides of my bra. He drew circles over my shirt, touching every part of my breast except the nipple, teasing me. Since we were being cheeky, I slid my hand down to his zipper and squeezed lightly. I grinned when he jumped.

"Aren't you full of surprises?" He chuckled, toying with a strand of my hair.

"Inexperienced but willing to learn," I said, and was disappointed when his face didn't change expression. "No response?"

"Besides yay?" he asked. I smacked his shoulder.

I was laughing when he kissed me again, lips molding to the curve of my smile. Gabriel's hand at the small of my back led me down the hall toward the stairs. Were we going upstairs? I wondered. As he cupped my jaw in his hands, I found my feet willingly backing up the first step toward my bedroom.

He pulled away and ran a hand down my cheek. "It's been a long night. Time for you to be in bed."

I waited for the little voice in my head to start making excuses, such as I couldn't have sex with Gabriel, I barely knew him. My room was a wreck. I was caught up in a murder investigation. I hadn't shaved my legs. And I found I didn't care about any of it.

I tilted my head and asked, "Will I be going there alone?"

"Tonight," he said. "You're not ready. I've seen inside your head, Jane. In the jumble of lovely and complicated and, dare I hope, creative thoughts, you're afraid we'll have bad sex and then you'll never see me again. And if you think that way, even with my considerable skill"—he paused for me to finish laughing—"it will be bad."

"Look, Dave Chandler left me on the ninth floor of our university's research library without my panties after we lost our virginity together. He never called me again and actually turned on his heel and walked in the opposite direction whenever he saw me on campus. Unless you think you're going to do that, I don't think we're going to have a problem."

Gabriel's face went blank. I waved my hand in front of his vacant, staring eyes. "Gabriel?"

He shook himself back into the present. "Sorry, something strange happened inside my head when you said the word 'panties'—the overwhelming urge to kill Dave Chandler combined with a simultaneous loss of blood to the brain."

I laughed. And yes, I lost my virginity in a library. It seemed like a good idea at the time. Dave and I were both student library workers, and we did have a generous forty-five-minute dinner break. It turned out that while the Russian folklore section offered plenty of privacy (seriously, no one ever went up there), the shelves left really weird bruises on your back. Lesson learned.

Gabriel slid into his jacket and pulled me close. "When you're ready, I will be the first to run for the bedroom, stripping out of my clothes and singing 'hallelujah' at the top of my lungs."

"That's an interesting blend of imagery."

Gabriel played with the hem of my blouse, tickling the skin just above the rise of my slacks. "Besides, when I take you to bed, we're going to stay there for a long, long time. I don't want the sun to interrupt us, which it would in just a few hours."

Did he say hours?

Gabriel kissed my slack mouth and asked, "No response?"

"Yay?"

11

While most vampires develop special abilities, some do not. If you run into vampires who do not have gifts, it is not wise to mock them. They still have vampire strength.

—From *The Guide for the Newly Undead*

The Hollow's vampire grapevine works even faster than the human gossip lines. After word of my super-secret council tribunal got out, my nights were suddenly filled with calls and visits from my new underworld buddies.

Dick called, but he just left dirty voice-mail messages. Let's just say if I'm ever in the market for a massage involving canola oil and marabou feathers, I'm covered.

Missy called, but her message was more of the low-down-dirty girl variety, instead of plain old dirty.

"Jane, honey, I'm sorry if I'm breaking up, but I'm in my car, and you know how the Bottoms are. It's the Land That Cell Phone Towers Forgot." Her tinkling laugh rattled my ear through the receiver. Even from across the living room and muffled through the phone, Fitz's head cocked up at the shrill sound.

"You're where?" The Bottoms were low-lying areas of McClure County near the river, mostly swampland and marshy pastures, hardly the kind of property that would interest the Hollow's top vampire real-estate agent.

"The Bottoms, honey, the Bottoms. There's a little farm down here I'm trying to get my hands on. Just between you and me, the owners don't know how much the property's going to be worth in a few years. So it's up to me to talk them into retiring and letting me take the property off their hands so they can move in with their kids in Florida."

That struck me as sort of evil, but in the great spectrum of possible vampire evildoing, probably not that bad.

"The reason I called, honey, other than to check on one of the Hollow's latest undead additions, is to invite you over to my place for my famous Mojito Mixer Monday!"

When my confused silence buzzed over the line, Missy informed me that she hosted this bastion of undead yuppiedom twice a month, featuring imitation Cuban cocktails and real vampire professionals. It was a chance for the local undead to make connections, meet potential pets, and become more established in the Hollow's "night life." Missy had a rotating guest list that included a mix of newbies and long-established vampires. I could only guess that her Rolodex was a dark, scary place.

"Everybody's going to love you! We've never had a librarian in the mix before. It will be so interesting. And Dick Cheney's going to be there. He's a close personal friend. He mentioned that he met you the other night. He says you have a great personality!"

"Isn't that like saying I'm stump-ugly in man language?"

"Come on, shug, we have to get you out there. You've got to network!" She wheedled in her syrupy voice.

Considering that my social interactions with other vampires so far had amounted to a beating and a cranial route canal, I did my best to decline politely. "I really appreciate the invitation, but cocktail parties aren't my thing, Missy. Also, I don't have a job at the moment, so networking with me would probably be a waste of time."

"Are you enjoying the gift basket?" Missy asked sweetly.

"Loved it. I've been meaning to write a thank you note," I said, gritting my teeth at the rather obvious social strong-arming tactic. Missy was not so subtly reminding me that she'd done something nice for me, and here I was being rude, when all she was asking me to do was attend a nice party. This was the way Southern women worked—all peaches and cream laced with arsenic.

"Oh, honey, don't worry about it. I know you haven't had time," she said. "The first few weeks are so hectic. Working out your feeding schedule, sleeping arrangements. I'm surprised you're as together as you are."

Grr.

"Are you suuuuure you couldn't make it on Monday?" Missy asked. "It's just a little party. I just want to see you make some new friends, that's all."

"I'll think about it," I promised.

"I'll send you an e-vite. You'll love it, shug. Byeeee!" She giggled before hanging up.

I looked down at Fitz, who was lying on his back, flipping his ears back and forth over his eyes. Not for the first time, I envied the simplicity of his life. "How exactly did she get my e-mail address?" I asked.

Andrea broke our contact embargo and called. Her council questioning was far friendlier than my own, by the way. Ophelia even paid for Andrea's pancakes. When someone is a link in your food chain, you tend to be more polite to them. Sensing my boredom and distress, Andrea offered to brave the wrath of the council and bring over some dessert blood and her favorite girlie movie. But I had only sat through *The Divine Secrets of the Ya-Ya Sisterhood* once in my prevampire days. I considered it a sort of afterlife resolution never to suffer through that again. We settled for ice cream (for her) and *Queen of the Damned* (for me).

We'd gotten as far as the concert scene when one of Andrea's clients texted her. He'd been attacked by several quarrelsome "business associates" outside a Dairy Queen and needed an emergency transfusion. As she slid into her strappy black sandals and downed some iron supplements, Andrea admitted a stunted social life was an occupational hazard for blood surrogates.

And my excuse was what, exactly?

I made good use of my free time. I made a strong effort to read every page of the *Guide for the Newly Undead*, twice. I made arrangements with a company that sold and delivered synthetic blood in bulk, so I wouldn't have to run out to Wal-Mart every week. I experimented with various fake-blood concoctions that would add some variety to my diet. There were a few bright spots, but it was generally a progression of entertaining and spectacular failures. Let's just say that tomato juice, Tabasco, and blood should not be mixed. Bleh.

I even looked up meditation exercises to try to find ways to focus my energy and harness my chi and all that stuff. All right, so I probably didn't take it as seriously as I should have. But I found out I can stand on my head for extended periods of time.

I spent a lot of time with Aunt Jettie or dodging Aunt Jettie. Now that I was aware of her presence, she felt free to move objects at will and follow me anywhere in the house. Undead senses or not, I still got startled when someone suddenly appeared behind me in the shower. We had a long chat about boundaries and the ready availability of exorcism rites on the Internet.

On a more menacing note, it was very subtle, but a few times, I thought I felt someone watching the house. If I stayed still enough, I could sense someone standing at the edge of the woods, and the presence was downright jarring. But by the time I got to the backyard, whoever it was had vanished.

One night, I was reading, and I thought I saw a dark shape move outside my parlor window. I immediately reverted to frightened-single-woman instincts and ran for my phone. I had dialed nine and one when I realized, *Hey, I have superpowers,* and ran out the back door. The scent was faint, bitter, and somehow vegetable, like bad asparagus. This is going to sound crazy, but it smelled like greed. I filed that away under "Weird New Jane Thoughts" while I searched my garden for the covetous intruder. I followed the scent to the edge of the trees that lined my yard. Whoever was there was long gone. I had to start running faster. This was embarrassing.

I spent the rest of the night on the porch with an antique hunting rifle from Grandpa Early's collection, just hoping that whoever it was would show up again. Did I know how to shoot? No, but there was always the chance I could club the intruder with the rifle or maybe throw a bullet at him. Besides, it was much safer than letting Fitz run loose to patrol for trespassers. I couldn't risk my mysterious visitor hurting him. Also, the last time I did that, I lost Fitz for about two weeks.

Zeb finally came by for a visit while I was installing my spanking-new security lights. He watched in awe as I deftly balanced on one foot on a wobbly ladder, handing me the wrong tools and cracking jokes about the probability of me electrocuting myself again. (His guess: 97 percent. He wanted to leave some room for the possibility of me falling off the ladder *while* electrocuting myself.) But he was very evasive and made vague excuses for not seeing me over the last few weeks. He didn't tell me about the new girl he was dating, and considering how long it had been since Zeb's last date, this was worth a mention . . . or possibly a billboard. I had to extract the information from his brain.

A startling development in my fabulous vampire

powers was being able to put together mental pictures while Zeb was talking to me. The signal was patchy at best, like trying to watch scrambled pay-per-view. There was a tingly buzzing right behind my ear, then an image would spring into my mind. Zeb told me he spent Friday night reading the Bible to his grandma. I saw him at an Italian restaurant with an unbelievably pretty girl with sleek auburn hair and almond-shaped green eyes. She was laughing, actually laughing, at what Zeb was saying. And I could detect no drunkenness or mental defect on her part, so I could only assume she knew she was dating him. In my vision, he reached for her hand and knocked over a water glass. Then the picture faded out.

"So." I sat on top of the ladder, crossed my arms, and gave him a smirk. "How is your grandma?"

"Fine." Zeb sighed. "Driving my grandpa slowly insane gives her a reason to live. My mom, on the other hand, is focusing on driving me insane . . . which is not as fun."

"Still wants to know when we're getting married, huh?" I asked. Zeb made a miserable face. Ginger Lavelle had never quite shaken those images of Zeb and me playing house when we were little. OK, me forcing Zeb to play house when we were little. She convinced herself long ago that no matter how much we protested or dated other people, we would eventually see things her way and give her the daughter-in-law and grandbabies she'd always wanted.

"Actually, she's decided she's mad at you for not following her professional advice."

"She gave me poufy bangs. I looked like a TV evangelist," I cried, hopping down from my perch and giving the newly installed lights a testing flick. Zeb winced at the sudden flood of light.

"Well, since you so coldly and callously tossed her aside as your personal cosmetologist, she has decided that you are not worthy of the Lavelle name, and I should instead marry Hannah Jo Butler. Hannah Jo gladly lets Mama give her perms that make her look like an electrocuted poodle."

"Well, thank God you have someone to make these decisions for you," I deadpanned as I sat down on a porch step.

"I begged God for a brother, a sister with a lazy eye, anything to distract her, but no. I had to be the only child to the heat-seeking missile of motherhood. Hannah Jo keeps showing up at my house with pies, saying my mother sent her over. She's been at Sunday dinner every weekend for the last two months. Mamaw is making a Christmas stocking with her name on it."

"What happened to my stocking?" I demanded.

"She ripped your name tag off and is hot-gluing Hannah Jo's on in its place," Zeb admitted.

"Well, good luck to the both of you," I grumbled.

"I'm sorry I didn't call over the last couple of days. I lost my cell phone."

I arched an eyebrow. "And you haven't been able to find your land line, either?"

"Um, nope." He laughed nervously. "I guess that means it's time for spring cleaning."

"It's September, Zeb."

Zeb looked down and to the left, a sure sign of lying, and another image came up. Zeb was walking this girl to the door of a neatly kept trailer. He obviously wanted to kiss her and leaned about twenty degrees in but hesitated and pulled back. So, the girl grabbed him and pressed him into a full-on lip-lock.

I couldn't help but feel a twinge of jealousy. I do not have warm, squishy feelings for Zeb. But I am used to being the only woman under fifty in his life. Also, here were two young, vital people, starting what could be a bright future together. They could get married, have children, grow old together. I couldn't do any of those things. I was wallowing in the depths of self-pity and general melancholy when the picture changed again. In the midst of his (fictitious) description of a Sunday spent hanging out with his parents, I saw Zeb trying to round to second base.

"Ew!" I yelled, vainly attempting to wipe the image through my forehead.

"It's not that bad," he insisted. "Better since my dad stopped drinking homemade persimmon wine."

"No, you big liar, ew to the image of your over-the-sweater action!" I cried. "You were out with a girl this weekend. I saw the whole thing in my head."

"You read my mind?" he exclaimed. "That's just . . . well, it's extremely cool. But I don't think I'm comfortable with you knowing what's going on inside my head."

"No one's comfortable with knowing what's going on inside your head." I snorted. "I didn't mean to invade your mental privacy. Really. I'm sorry. But why'd you lie to me, Zeb? I'm glad you're going out with someone. Seriously. Is she nice? What's her name? Where's she from? What's she like? Are you going to answer my questions, or do I have to whack you with a stick until delicious candy surprises fall out?"

Zeb sighed, rubbing his temples. "I don't want this to be weird."

"I can't make any guarantees, but let's give it a shot."

"Janie, I've been going to meetings, and they've been really helpful."

"All right, then." That was out of left field. Beyond the occasional overindulgence in wine coolers, Zeb had never had what I would see as a drinking problem. And after seeing what running a backyard meth lab did to his cousins, he never touched drugs. "Do you mean, like, therapy?"

"It's more of a support group for people who are dealing with alternative lifestyles."

"Oh." I thought for about a second before it struck me. "Ohhhh."

How could I have been so blind? I'd been friends with Zeb for twenty years. Why hadn't I noticed the lifelong lack of a serious girlfriend? His conflicted feelings about his father? His strange obsession with Russell Crowe? He was the only person in the state of Kentucky who actually saw *A Good Year*.

I threw my arms around Zeb and hugged him tight. It was the first time I'd touched him since turning that he hadn't stiffened his spine and gotten all awkward. "Oh, Zeb, why didn't you tell me?"

Weird pause amid the hugging. "I just did."

"You could have told me years ago. I would have accepted you, not matter what. It wouldn't have changed anything. I love you."

Weirder pause. "Accepted what?"

"You being, you know—" I said, trying to find the most sensitive way to handle this life change without hanging umpteen million crosses around my neck and stabbing him. I tried to learn from our mistakes. "But what about the redhead? Wait, is she a he? Because, if so, she's pretty convincing."

Zeb made a sound somewhere along the lines of "Wrok!" Then, "What? No."

Well, now I was confused. "You mean, you're not gay?"

"No! Why would you think that?" he cried.

"You said alternative lifestyles."

"No, *your* alternative lifestyle, you tool," he grunted, waving in the general direction of my head, which I guess meant my fangs. Or maybe my brain; sometimes it interfered with the way I was supposed to live my life. "Jane, I've joined a group called Friends and Family of the Undead. It's a support group for people whose loved ones have been turned into vampires. We meet every week and talk about how to deal with our feelings about your new lives. You know, being unsure of our safety around you. Making you feel welcome in our lives and our homes. Stuff like that."

I stared at him. "Why didn't you just tell me that?"

"I didn't want you to feel like I was so upset about your

change I had to seek psychological help, even though, well, I did," he said. "But it's been great. There aren't a lot of people who understand what going through this is like. It helps to talk about it. I think you should come with me sometime. It might help you talk to your parents."

"Umm, I don't know if I'm ready for something that public."

"It's anonymous," he insisted. "It's a lot like AA, without the drinking. One of the rules is that you can't talk about what's said at the meetings or who's there."

"This is the Hollow, Zeb. Twelve steps of confidentiality mean nothing. Remember that time Flossie Beecher started a Sex Addicts Anonymous group and ended up having to change her phone number?"

"No one will know you're there because you're a vampire," he said. "You could just be there because someone you know has been turned into a vampire."

"If I come to one of these meetings, can I meet the mysterious redhead?" I asked.

"As a matter of fact, that's where I met the mysterious redhead," he said, grinning. "She belongs to the group. Her name's Jolene."

There was a tone in his voice I hadn't heard before—fondness, pride. Zeb was talking like a man in love. This did not bode well. Women do not usually respond favorably to their boyfriends having female best friends. Pretty soon, Zeb would break our movie nights to hang out with Jolene and their other "couple friends." Our code of inside jokes would be broken by a woman who insisted on knowing what the hell we were talking about. I would slowly be phased out until I was that girl Zeb used to hang out with before he "grew up."

I smiled brightly. "Well, now I guess I have to go."

12

Trying to blend groups of friends from the living and undead worlds can be difficult. It's better if social events involving both the living and the nonliving do not center around food. Some more comfortable themes include poker games, bowling nights, and historical reenactments.

—From *The Guide for the Newly Undead*

From the outside, Greenfield Studios looked like a respectable family photography business in one of the newer buildings of the Hollow's riverfront business district. I didn't know anyone who'd had their pictures done there, but the company had only set up shop a few months before, and it was difficult to get Hollow residents out of the Sears Christmas-card-photos habit.

I'd parked Big Bertha almost two blocks away and around a corner, trying to give myself some "pep talk and walk" time. If I'd needed to breathe, I probably would have been hyperventilating with my head against the steering wheel. I hadn't been on a job interview since just after college. And if the head of the library board hadn't been one of my favorite high-school English teachers, Mrs. Stubblefield probably would have launched me out of the room with some sort of spring-loaded chair.

I reread the want ad. Greenfield was advertising for an appointment secretary with a pleasant phone voice, good communication skills, and a "people-pleasing personality." Having two out of three wasn't bad.

One. One out of three wasn't bad.

This was the first ad I'd come across that actually sounded somewhat appealing. I could handle an office job. I could handle pleasing people, to a certain extent, as long as it didn't inconvenience me too much. It seemed sort of odd for a photography studio to be open all night, but the supervisor, Sandy, who was supposed to interview me said clients made their photo appointments after they got home from work.

I climbed out of Big Bertha and straightened what I hoped was an appropriately secretarial outfit—a red cardigan and a black pencil skirt that Andrea had helped me pick out. I had also accepted her ridiculously high black heels with the ankle straps because she said they made me look sophisticated yet sensible. On the walk to the office, I felt well dressed yet nauseated.

I rang the bell outside the brick front entrance and nervously fingered the manila envelope that contained my résumé. Sandy turned out to be a tiny, birdlike woman in her sixties. She reeked of Virginia Slims and had a voice like scraping the bottom of a whiskey barrel, but she looked like the poster woman for clean senior living, with fluffed curls of pure white and a face that was carefully made up. She was wearing a rose-colored track suit, a white golf visor, and a rhinestone pin shaped like a kitten at her shoulder.

"Come in, come in!" she said, smiling as she led me to an all-beige reception area. The lobby was clean, newly painted, and quiet as a church. "It's so nice to meet you."

Sandy gestured for me to sit, and I handed her my résumé. She crossed her leg primly as she sat in the over-stuffed armchair to my left. She looked over my qualifications while I filled out the surprisingly scant job application. Greenfield Studios didn't seem to want to know much about me beyond my name and social security number. However, one of the boxes asked for my "life status," and I was supposed to check whether I was living or undead. While it was illegal to ask an applicant about race, age, or marital status, it was still perfectly legal to ask whether he or she was a vampire. Congressional lobbyists fighting against undead rights claimed it was a public-safety issue, saying that employers had the right to protect their workplaces from "dangerous predators." I left the space blank and hoped Sandy wouldn't notice until after I'd gauged the office's general attitude toward vampires.

I handed her the application, and she smiled brightly. "Well, it seems that you are more than qualified. You have a solid employment history, which is always nice to see in someone your age. Could you do me a favor, honey, and read this out loud for me?"

Sandy handed me a badly copied sheet of paper with several paragraphs in all caps:

> *HELLO, MY NAME IS (BLANK),*
> *AND I'M CALLING THIS EVENING ON*
> *BEHALF OF GREENFIELD STUDIOS.*
> *OUR RECORDS SHOW THAT YOU HAVE*
> *INDICATED AN INTEREST IN HAVING*
> *YOUR FAMILY PORTRAIT TAKEN WITH*
> *GREENFIELD. I'M CALLING TO HELP*
> *YOU SCHEDULE AN APPOINTMENT*
> *AND TO TELL YOU ABOUT AN*
> *EXCITING NEW PRODUCT—*

"That's very nice," she said, pulling the script from my hand. "So, when would you like to start?"

This seemed rather quick. Why wasn't she asking me more questions? Why wasn't she asking me to tell her about myself? Why was my potential supervisor wearing a track suit? And why exactly did the script appear to have me calling people at home to schedule appointments instead of the other way around? And what was the exciting new product?

"Um, the ad said you were looking for a receptionist?"

"An appointment secretary," she said, nodding. "You would call people who have willingly and legally given us their contact information and book appointments for them to have their family portraits taken."

Why were the words "willingly" and "legally" neces-

sary? Wait a minute. Pleasant phone voice, good communication skills, and people-pleasing personality? This
was not secretarial work, this was telemarketing.

"I don't think this is going to work for me," I said,
hesitantly rising to my feet.

"Oh, honey, please, just give it a try!" she cried. "You've
got the voice. And you're well educated, articulate. People
who are lonely, just waiting by the phone hoping someone will call, they'll love talking to someone like you. You
could make a lot of money doing this."

OK, we were talking about telemarketing, *not* phone
sex. Right?

"But I've never done telemarketing before," I said,
clutching my purse like a lifeline and taking a step toward the door.

"Oh, we don't like to use that word around here. We
prefer telecommunications-based sales."

"And the difference is . . ."

Sandy ignored my question. "You said you needed a
night job, and you won't find many nice, safe sales jobs
with hours available this late. We call the West Coast
until eight P.M. Pacific time. You'll get on-the-job training. And you won't find a sweeter group of girls to work
with. We're just a big, happy family here."

I chewed my lip and cast a longing glance at the reception desk, which I now noticed was brand new and
looked as if it had never been touched. I could not afford to be proud or picky. I had bills to pay and a dog
who expected to be fed occasionally. Besides, they probably weren't going to ask me to do anything grosser than

scraping chewing gum off the bottom of tables or de-gunking a grease trap, both of which I'd done regularly while working at the Dairy Freeze in my teens. Hell, I was the one who ran for the "vomit dust" whenever a kid got sick at the library. Nothing could be worse than that. Right now, something was better than nothing. And this was something.

"When can I start?"

As I rounded the corner, I couldn't help but think I'd just made a rather large mistake. I was not a salesperson. I was definitely not a telecommunications-based salesperson. But I'd already given Sandy my social security number, and I think that's the point of no return in terms of employment etiquette. Sandy had even given me an information packet on Greenfield Studios and how the company was bringing affordable family memories to *you*. I was supposed to review the materials before Friday, my first night on the job.

As I turned toward the block where Big Bertha was parked, the breeze carried the scent of blood. I looked around for an injured person, some source of the smell. But the scent was old, the blood long cold and dead.

The closer I walked to the car, the stronger the smell. I could make out splashes of red across the hood. I jogged closer to see that some ambitious soul had scrawled "BLOODSUCKING WHORE" in huge, dripping, bloody letters across Big Bertha's paint.

"What the hell?" I gaped. "What—"

I slid my fingers through the crook of the U. The

blood smeared sticky and cold across my fingers. It was animal blood, something gamey, deer blood. Cringing, I swiped my fingers across my skirt, too shocked to worry about the stains it would leave. I scanned the street for any sign of the vandal. There might as well have been tumbleweeds blowing across the asphalt.

Shock gave way to fear, fear to anger, then anger to shame. And when I realized that I was actually tearing up because someone wrote mean things about me on my car, I rolled right back to anger again. This was a nasty girl trick. This was high school stuff. My hands were shaking so badly it took several passes to try to pull my keys from my pocket.

And now I was driving around town in a car declaring that I was a bloodsucking whore. No one would notice that. I slumped low behind the wheel and drove on as many side streets as I could. Fortunately, there were very few people who needed to wash slanderous graffiti off their cars after ten P.M., so I had the Auto Spa all to myself.

As the remnants swirled red around the drain of the car-wash bay, I pondered the list of people who might have victimized Big Bertha. Unless Sandy had some sort of senior-citizen ninja skills, I doubted she'd be able to beat me back to my car, bloody it, and then get out of sight before I got there. Could it have been a friend of Walter's? A human who guessed my secret and was determined to out me whether I liked it or not?

The more I thought about it, the more pissed off I got. I was a grown woman, a vampire. People weren't supposed to be able to pull crap like this on me. By the time I turned the newly bathed Bertha onto my driveway, I'd gripped the steering wheel so tightly I'd warped it. Big Bertha now aimed slightly to the right no matter how I steered.

That was kind of an improvement.

I couldn't burn Walter's festering grab bag of personal effects. It seemed mean and petty, especially when you considered his fiery end. I decided to give the box to Dick. He was the only person I knew who had some sort of history with Walter and the only person I could think of who could unload so many *Knight Rider* DVDs.

I made absolutely no effort to look nice. Plain white T-shirt, fat jeans, no makeup. I was planning to go to one of Zeb's FFOTU meetings afterward, so I wanted to stand out as little as possible, anyway.

I knocked tentatively on the door, half hoping he wouldn't be home. I wasn't in the mood for dirty charades. The door swung open, and out stepped a familiar, barely dressed blonde.

"Missy! Wow, you're mostly naked," I exclaimed.

"Hi, shug!" she said cheerfully. You'd think that someone with a "public sales persona" like Missy would be embarrassed to be caught in a position like this. But she soldiered through the situation as if she weren't just wearing an old Lynyrd Skynyrd T-shirt and a smile.

"Hi. So, I guess the other night on the phone, when you mentioned you knew Dick, you meant that you *knew* Dick. Wow. Awkward."

"Jane?" Dick came up behind Missy, barefoot and buttoning ragged Levi's. He looked mildly embarrassed but not embarrassed enough to go put on a shirt. I just stared, unsure of what to say or where to look.

"Hi," I said, settling for a long glance at the pull-tab wind chime dangling from Dick's porch light. I intentionally hoisted a mental brick wall between my brain/senses and whatever was going on in Dick's and Missy's heads. I did not need those visuals haunting me for the rest of my immortal life.

"What brings you over, Jane?" Missy cooed, smooching Dick's neck. "Do I have competition for my sweet Dickie?"

"No!" I said, too emphatically. Dick was too occupied by Missy's full-on oral assault to look offended.

I tried to hand the box over, but Missy wound herself around Dick like a strangling vine. A strangling vine with a butt you could bounce a quarter off. "I just wanted to drop this off for you. It's Walter's stuff—"

"Oh, honey, I heard about that awful mess," Missy said, pulling herself away from nipping Dick's Adam's apple. "You just let me know if there's anything I can do for you."

Pulling her tongue out of Dick's ear would have been a nice start.

"Don't you have a meeting to go to, baby?" he asked, untangling himself.

"Why, yes, the Undead Realtors Association is meeting tonight. I'm the chapter president," Missy told me. She laughed, tweaking Dick's nipple. "Wait, are you trying to get rid of me so you can get to your next appointment? You'd better watch yourself, Jane, we may have a little catfight over my Dickie."

Missy laughed and disappeared into the trailer. Dick caught my apparently horrified expression and said, "She's just messing with you. We're not dating or anything. It's not even what you would call a relationship. We're just . . ." He looked away, avoiding eye contact. "You know, sometimes you just need a lukewarm body."

"And there's the Dick I know and . . . barely tolerate," I said, as Missy opened the door. She was wearing another slick pink dress suit and fluffing her blond curls back into their "Junior League gone slightly slutty" style.

"Well, I'm off, shug," she said, then leaned in for another tongue bath. She winked at me. "Jane, don't forget. Monday. Mojitos at my place. You promised you'd try. Y'all be good now."

Did I use the word "promise"?

"I should be going, too," I said, as Missy slid into her sporty little car. "I hope you find some use for that stuff."

He smiled, opening the door to show me his rumpled fold-out couch. "You know, you could stick around—"

"Again, I'm going to have to ask you not to finish that sentence."

"What's the matter, Stretch? We could have a lot of fun, you and me." Dick leaned in far too close and made preliminary moves to kiss me. I leaned out of it until I was bent back at a spine-breaking angle. Spicy man treat though he may be, Dick was not boyfriend material. He was just barely respectable acquaintance material.

"Dick," I said, "I'm really flattered, but I'm not going to let you use me to piss off Gabriel."

"But I do want you. I want to hear you whisper, pant, scream my name. I want to know what kind of panties an out-of-work librarian wears," he said, grinning lazily. "Pissing off Gabriel would be an added side bonus."

I laughed, hoping it would cover up the involuntary shivers Dick was giving me. I hadn't lived a sheltered life where attractive men didn't say that sort of thing to me, but I hadn't had sex in three years. Do the math. "You two have no idea how alike you are. Dick, I like you. But don't make me choose between being friends with you and doing whatever the hell I'm doing with Gabriel. My choice wouldn't make you happy."

Instead of taking my rejection at face value, Dick smirked. "You like me?"

"You're mildly amusing and remotely charming, when you're not giving me the full-on Pat O'Brien routine." I sighed, rolling my eyes. "Plus, you're one of the few people who actually tell me what they're thinking, even when I don't want to know. I appreciate that."

"And you want to be friends?" he asked, scratching his head. "I don't know if I've ever been friends with someone with breasts, particularly breasts like yours. Can I still make inappropriate remarks about you and your person?"

Suddenly self-conscious, I crossed my arms over my chest. "I don't think I could stop you if I tried."

* * *

The Friends and Family of the Undead met at the Traveler's Bowl, a restaurant featuring healthy cuisine. It was known locally as "that place where they sell hippie food." Zeb said the FFOTU meetings were the only thing keeping the restaurant going, besides the "glass sculptures" they sold at the gift shop. (I hadn't spent a lot of time in head shops, but I recognized a bong when I saw one.)

I bought a large mineral water and some hummus, even though I wouldn't be able to eat it. Most chick-pea consumption is based on misplaced politeness. But I wanted to do my part for the proprietors, a nice-looking artsy couple who had sunk their life savings into over-estimating Half-Moon Hollow's palate. It was hard to get local residents to eat anything involving wheatgrass, sprouts, or lentils. If you mashed all those things together into balls and deep-fried them, you might have something going.

The FFOTU, which, given the surroundings, I kept calling TOFU, consisted of twenty or so people of all races, ages, and socioeconomic classes. They were individuals who never would have spoken in "real life" but seemed to share a strong bond within the walls of the Traveler's Bowl. There was Carol, a cook at the Coffee Spot, whose brother, Junior, had been turned by an angry ex-girlfriend. The family had no idea what had happened until Junior flipped out in the middle of a Sunday dinner and tried to bite their uncle. Daisy's banker husband turned in the midst of a midlife crisis. Instead of buying

a sports car and nailing his receptionist to avoid thinking about death, Daisy's husband chose to stop the aging
the process altogether. Daisy was pretty angry at first,
but now she was confused about whether she should let
him turn her, too. She felt pressured to make a decision
soon, as she aged a little every day, but he was forever
forty-seven. George's daughter was turned on a bad date,
and now she refused to speak to anyone in the family. He
couldn't understand why she just cut off contact with
them. He and his wife were left mourning someone they
still occasionally saw at Wal-Mart.

Each of them hurt. Each of them offered understanding and sympathy to the other members. Each tried to
keep a sense of humor. Carol pointed out that had she
been thinking clearly, she would have aimed her brother's fangs at her aunt Cecile, whom no one liked.

Every meeting started with the Pledge, a collection of
five truths the group promised to remember:

"I will remember that a newly turned vampire is the
same person with new needs.

"I will remember that a loved one's being turned into
a vampire does not reflect on me.

"I will remember to offer my vampire loved ones
acceptance and love, while maintaining healthy boundaries.

"I will remember that vampirism is not contagious
unless blood is exchanged.

"I will remember that I am not alone."

Seeing my vampirism from my parents' or even from
Zeb's perspective was sobering. A loved one had died,

but there was no funeral, no chance to grieve, no chance to adjust to their complete change in lifestyle. Plus, there was the embarrassment of telling friends and family that your son/sister/friend had become "infected" with vampirism. And worrying that the new vampire would go all evil and hurt you, as in the case of Carol's brother. It all convinced me that I was not ready to come out to my parents yet, if for nothing else than to spare them those feelings as long as possible.

Fine, it was a rationalization, but that didn't make it any less binding.

I didn't know if anyone in the group could tell I was a vampire. No one asked, which I found refreshing. I was the only one in the room that night, but Zeb said they had a few local vamps who attended off and on. Based on the group's commitment to confidentiality, he refused to tell me who they were.

After discussing changes in vampire legislation, the members traded stories and tips. For instance, I learned about a company in Colorado that made SPF 500 window tinting for cars, allowing vampires to drive in full sunlight. Carol announced that she'd come up with several recipes to help make vampires feel more welcome at family meals. Even as a vampire, I had to say that Plasma Pop Jell-O Molds sounded gross. Eventually, the group broke up to socialize, which was obviously their favorite part of the meeting.

With Zeb distracted by a funny story from Carol involving her brother, a silver platter, and a confused pawn broker, Zeb's new girlfriend bounded up to me and almost knocked me flat. Jolene was just as I had pictured her in my visions, gorgeous in an exotic way that added up to strike one against me liking her. A perfectly oval face with high cheekbones and a lush pink mouth that tilted at the corners. Extremely long, even white teeth that glinted in the low light of the restaurant. Wild curls that shifted from auburn to fiery red to strawberry blond depending on how she tilted her magnificent head. Long-lidded emerald eyes fringed with sable lashes. There was something not quite right, a fierceness to the features that unsettled as much as it staggered. I imagined that males of any species would be willing to overlook that.

I consoled myself with the fact that the nasal back-woods twang that fell from those bee-stung lips stran-gled dead any sort of *Tomb Raider* fantasies Zeb might harbor. The twang was the second thing I noticed, after the weird body odor. It wasn't an unpleasant smell, just an organic punch to the system, like fresh-cut grass and apple skins. Maybe beautiful people smelled different from most?

"It's so nice to meet you!" she squealed. She swiped at my shirt, which was now covered in crumbs from the bran muffin she'd been eating. "Zeb's told me all about you! We're so glad you could join us."

"Well, Zeb said the group has been really helpful, and everyone seems so nice," I said. "He said you've been coming here for a while?"

She shrugged those smooth, tanned shoulders. "Well, my best friend since high school was turned a few years back. It took her a year to come out to me. I felt like an idiot for not seeing the signs. It was hard. My family . . . well, they just don't trust vampires. Never have. And it took me a while to adjust to her being undead. I'm havin' to overcome a lot of built-in prejudice."

"Good for you, though, for trying," I said. "So, do you and your friend still hang out?"

Jolene's lip trembled. Her eyes flashed, an electric glow under the green. I looked around to see if anyone else had noticed, but they were too involved in their kale rolls. "No. Tessie—that was her name, Tessie—um, she got dusted about six months ago. Her family said it was an accident. But she was always so careful. She wouldn't have gone out so early, with the sun still up. I miss her."

"I'm sorry," I said, squeezing her arm.

She tilted her head and smiled. "Well, the group's been really sweet with me. I'm sort of dealin' with a whole 'nother round of grief. My family doesn't really understand what I'm going through."

"I'm glad," I said, meaning it. I hated to think of how Zeb would feel if I'd died and he had no one to turn to for support.

"Good!" She nuzzled and kissed my cheek and bounded away to snatch some of Daisy's pita crisps. Seriously, the woman never stopped eating. She'd gone through an entire one-pound bag of peanut butter M&M's during the meeting and was now trying to sweet-talk a kale roll out of George. The burly trucker was happy to hand over the high-fiber treat.

Zeb wrapped an arm around me. "What do you think?"

"She's gorgeous," I assured him. "Charming. Very affectionate. But, um, did she just quit smoking or something?"

"No, why?" he asked.

"Well, she hasn't stopped eating the whole time we've been here. And she's not exactly a stocky gal."

"OK, you have to promise that you're not going to freak out," Zeb said, pulling me away from the rest of the group.

"You've pretty much guaranteed that I'm going to now, but go ahead."

"The thing is that . . . well, Jolene's a werewolf," Zeb said, his voice lowered.

"Oh, ha ha, Zeb. Halloween's not for a few more weeks." I laughed, mugging spookily. "Ooh, Jolene's a werewolf. You brought me to a vampire-support-group meeting to introduce me to a werewolf. I guess that explains the long teeth and the flashing green eyes and the nuzzling . . . Oh, crap, you're serious, aren't you?"

"Yep." Zeb nodded. "Her whole family is made up of hereditary werewolves. It's not a curse or anything. She was born like this. I was sort of surprised you didn't guess, to be honest. I thought you creatures of the night could sense each other or something."

"How would I possibly guess werewolf? Swimsuit model, maybe. But it makes sense. If vampires are real, then I guess werewolves, the Mummy, the Creature from the Black Lagoon, and the rest of the Universal horror-movie standards must be real, too. Wait, does that mean she already knows I'm a vampire?" I whispered.

Jolene came up behind me, tapping my back and making me jump. "Zeb told me on our first date."

It took me a few seconds to register the different emotions I was experiencing: hurt, a little betrayal, the sting of being excluded. I finally landed on the ability to produce sarcasm, which was far more useful.

"Well, thanks for telling me," I said, rolling my eyes. "I've faked eating hummus all night for nothing!"

Jolene squeezed my shoulder. Ouch. She had some very strong hands. "I wasn't lying when I said my family is antivampire. But it's because they're werewolves, not rednecks. Actually, they're a little bit of both.

"I came to the FFOTU meetings to try to get a better grip on how to deal with Tessie's being a vampire. I wanted to stay friends with her, and I knew my family, my clan, wouldn't be happy about it. And after she died, the group members were the only people I knew who were nice about it, who could understand why I was so upset. So I kept comin' because I wanted to help other people who were going through the same thing."

"And then I met Zeb, and—I'm in love with your friend," Jolene blurted out. "I know y'all have been close forever, and I want us to get along. I really do."

"OK," I said, at a loss to drum up any other response.

"You're not upset?" Zeb asked, sounding suspicious.

"Why would I be upset?" I asked. "I mean, I haven't had much time to process the information, but it's not as if Jolene can help being what she is, any more than I can help being a vampire. In fact, you were born this way, right? You had even less of a choice than I did. It would be hypocritical of me to go all crazy just because my friend is dating a—"

"Werewolf," Jolene said for me.

"Right." Of course, that probably wouldn't keep me from going all crazy later, but I had to give myself some credit for being able to string that many words together through the shock.

"I'm so glad you feel that way!" Jolene squealed, throwing her arms around me. "We're going to be really good friends, I can just tell."

As Jolene gave me a neck-cracking hug, I narrowed my eyes at Zeb, who smiled and shrugged. Great. My best friend was dating a werewolf, who also happened to be a hugger.

13

Vampirism can lead to a wealth of new and exciting career opportunities, including overnight-delivery driver, stunt person, and custom perfume blender.

—From *The Guide for the Newly Undead*

I may be the only person in history to have a telemarketing career lasting a total of three hours. Apparently, vampire powers do not translate to phone sales.

I'd reviewed the promotional material on Greenfield Studios. Despite its claims that the company brought quality family photography to the people without the high overhead or "high-pressure sales tactics" of in-store studios, I was just as uncomfortable with the prospect of shilling for them. But I'd filled out an application and given my word. And if my Anglo-Saxon Protestant heritage had blessed me with anything, it was a profound guilt-based work ethic.

Since I wasn't going to be seen by the public, I abstained from my gal Friday look and wore jeans and my lucky blue sweater. ("Lucky" in that it was my one sweater that had never been stained.) Now sporting a lemon-yellow track suit, Sandy met me at the front entrance and led me through the lobby to a shiny pine door. It was a lot like *Charlie and the Chocolate Factory,* only instead of a magical room where everything is made of chocolate, I got a backroom filled with headset-wearing chain-smokers. The clamor of desperately pleasant conversation was deafening. The room was as dingy and chaotic as the lobby had been spotless. Green contest entry slips exploded out from in-boxes in each cubicle. Poster-size performance charts were layered on top of each other on the wall, listing who'd made sales that night and who hadn't. The stained floor was littered with old entry slips, crumbs, and cigarette butts. And casting an evil eye over it all was a banner that read in huge red letters, "If you don't sell, you go home."

Inspiring.

"Greenfield Studios is a national operation with call centers across the country," Sandy chirped. "Half-Moon Hollow is our latest branch to open. Our field representatives pass out these entry slips at community events, school fairs, fundraisers. And if people are interested, they fill out their personal information. The slip clearly states that even if they don't win the cruise, we reserve the right to contact them for future promotions." Sandy handed me a neon green slip that screamed, "Win a cruise for two to the Bahamas from Greenfield Studios!" where some poor sap named Aaron Miller had traded his phone number and an evening's worth of peace for a shot at a vacation.

"Each shift, you receive seventy five slips. You call the numbers, remind the customers that they willingly gave us their entry information, and let them know that our traveling studio is coming to their hometown."

"Traveling studio?" I said, my heart sinking just a degree further.

"Yes, our photographers travel to mid-price hotels, where they set up a portrait studio in a conference room or suite and take family pictures by appointment. Your job is to arrange the appointments and persuade the customer to preorder one of these." Sandy rifled through a pile of papers on a nearby desk and found what looked like a normal wall clock until she turned it so that I saw the face. Some poor family with stiff, uncomfortable smiles was frozen in time there, forever pinned beneath a minute hand that seemed to be sprouting from the mother's chest like a grotesquely ornate spear.

"Wow." At least I knew what the exciting new product was: the scariest freaking clock I had ever seen.

"It's a beauty, isn't it?" Sandy sighed. "Every year, the company comes up with a new promotional item. Last year, it was throw pillows with the family photo silk-screened on. This year, it's kitchen clocks.

"You're paid minimum wage plus a two-dollar commission per appointment booked. You book an average of three appointments in an hour, or you will be sent home. If less than fifty percent of your bookings follow through with their appointments, your commission will be reduced. You pay for use of your headset, phone line, and office supplies."

My head spun as I realized the level of sleaziness I'd let myself slip to. Eyes closed, I said, "Let me get this straight. My job is to call these people at home, remind them of a contest entry they made months before, not to inform them that they've won but that I'm now using that information to try to talk them into bringing their family to a motel room to have their picture taken by a total stranger? In a temporary studio that will disappear in a few days?"

"And push the clocks," Sandy reminded me. "We like to call them a 'memory that will last through time.'"

"Is there an actual cruise?" I asked, holding up a contest entry slip.

"Yes, the CEO takes one every year," Sandy said with a conspiratorial wink.

I looked around the room at the sadly desperate women, shuffling through their entry slips, joylessly logging their bookings on the progress charts. Each had a pleasant, cheerful voice and a face that looked like ten miles of bad road. And they all seemed to be wearing track suits in varying stages of shabbiness. Any time between calls was spent bent over their cubicles in a racking cough. Their endless streams of smoke had already stained the walls a lovely shade of nicotine gray. And if I wasn't mistaken, one of them appeared to be taking a sponge bath in the ladies' room with the door open.

What had I gotten myself into? In terms of looking back at how your life went horribly awry, it was possible that accepting this job was worse than stumbling into vampirism.

Waving at the tendrils of smoke curling around my head, I cast a sidelong glance at the little plaque on the wall that declared the office a "smoke-free workplace." Sandy laughed and threaded an arm companionably through mine. "I know, it's not really all that legal to let them smoke inside like this, but they just couldn't work without a smoke every once in a while. And the breaks would kill our productivity. So, we just let them enjoy a nice cigarette while they work. It saves so much time, and everybody's happy."

"What about the nonsmokers?"

She smiled. "You know, everybody who has come to work here eventually started smoking, so it's never come up."

Well, there was something to look forward to. At least I knew I couldn't get lung cancer.

Sandy led me to an empty cubicle. The ladies on either side of me never broke their stride in their pitches to acknowledge my presence. Sandy didn't make any effort to introduce me, and I assumed that was intentional. Sandy strapped a freshly disinfected headset over my ears and handed me the script, a tip sheet titled "Never Take 'No' for an Answer: How to Battle Common Excuses" and a green slip containing the name and phone number of Susan Greer of Portland, Oregon. "Shouldn't I get some sort of training before I start making calls?"

"Oh, there's no better training than jumping right in," she said. "And you're a quick study, I can tell. Just take a few seconds to go over your script, and dial the number."

I stared at the script long enough to realize that the

words weren't making any sense in my head. No matter how long I sat there reading this thing, I would never be able to translate it into a tempting sales pitch. With Sandy sitting at my side listening to every word, I dialed the number and prayed that Susan Greer wasn't home. No such luck.

"Hello!" I shouted into the receiver when a female voice answered. "Is Susan Greer available?"

"This is Susan Greer," the woman said, a weary note of suspicion creeping into her voice.

"My name is Jane, and I'm calling this evening on behalf of Greenfield Studios. Our records show that you have indicated an interest in having your family portrait—"

"Not interested," Susan grumbled, and hung up.

I shot a guilty look at Sandy. "It happens all the time," she assured me. "Just try again."

This time, I dialed Jamie Hurley of Portland, who was not much more receptive than Susan Greer. "Did you really interrupt my dinner to call me about this?" she demanded.

I closed my eyes and tried to pick back up on a spot in the script I remembered. "Our records show that you have indicated an interest in—"

"How did you even get my number, anyway? I'm supposed to be on a no-call list!"

When I stopped reading the script, I had time to process exactly how small and guilty I felt calling this poor woman. I scanned the excuses list for "How did you get my number?"

"Oh, um, well, you entered a contest to win a Caribbean crui—"

"I don't have time for this," she fumed. "I can't believe you harass people at home like this. How do you live with yourself? How do losers like you even get jobs? If you call me again, I'm going to file harassment charges!"

At the sound of the phone slamming in my ear, I turned to Sandy, my jaw slack. She patted my hand. "All right, honey, that wasn't a great call, but you get those sometimes. And it takes everyone a few calls to develop a rhythm. When someone is rude, the best thing to do is to take a deep breath and make another call."

So I made another call, and another. I was hung up on, had an air horn blown directly into my ear, and was called a bitch in three languages. Every time I dialed a number, I prayed the phone would ring unanswered. After four hours, when Chester Zimmerman of Piedmont, North Dakota, told me to commit unspeakable acts upon my own person with a cheese grater, I turned to Sandy, defeated.

"I don't think I'm comfortable with this."

"And they can tell, honey," Sandy said, patting my hand again. "You just need to relax your voice and speak in a more natural, confident tone."

I reached for my headset and realized I would rather attempt strangling myself with the phone cord than dial another number. "I just don't think this is going to work for me."

Sandy smiled, despite the tension pulling at the corners of her mouth. "Well, we have other sales divisions you can try."

"I don't—"

"Oh, come on, Jane, nobody likes a quitter! I want to find a place for you here." She pulled me out of my seat and motioned for me to follow her to another door, where we found another smoke-filled cubicle farm. "Greenfield Studios is just one sales arm of Greenfield Enterprises. Our sales force also sells Revita-Water, the new miracle cure that 'they' don't want you know about. Revita-Water's scientifically calibrated balance of electrolytes and nutrients, plus a selection of health supplements and ephedra-free diet aids, will prevent almost any illness, from cancer to fibromyalgia to Lyme disease. But the main benefit is this amazing product's ability to reverse vampirism! Studies show that people who drink Revita-Water as part of their daily health regimen will not turn if they're bitten. Just between you and me, police departments and emergency services are buying Revita-Water in huge batches for protection when the vampires finally launch their antihuman campaign. It practically sells itself."

I stared at her. Apparently, Sandy had not yet noticed that I'd left the life-status box blank on my application. But now I knew where the company policy stood on vampires. "Beg pardon?"

"All right, so it doesn't actually cure vampirism," Sandy whispered. "But there's nothing to prove that it won't help people get healthy enough to outrun the filthy bastards. You know, I never thought, at my age, I'd have to worry about being attacked by vicious, blood-sucking monsters in my own home, but that's the state of the world today. People are looking for protection, for assurance. And Greenfield Enterprises is here to fill that need."

Sandy wasn't saying anything in the way of antivampire ranting that I hadn't heard before. Heck, my grandmother had said worse over Christmas dinner. But I'd never heard it as a vampire, and I found it hurt more than I thought it would. Being in such a small, crowded room, I'd been keeping my mind "clenched," for lack of a better word, to keep the other women's thoughts from bouncing around in my skull. But I imagined a little window in her head sliding open and was given a psychic slapping for my efforts. The fears and worries of every sad-eyed woman in the room came pouring into my head from all sides. Unpaid bills, cars with shoddy brakes, kids suspended from school, husbands who wouldn't get off the couch and earn a paycheck, the soul-sucking drudgery of having to show up for this job every night and not having any other choice.

I shook the buzzing sensation out of my head and concentrated on Sandy. She may have hated vampires with a frantic and paranoid passion, but she sure liked me. She saw me doing well at Greenfield Enterprises. In fact, she saw me wearing the headset with pride, becoming a star employee, moving up in the ranks, and taking over the damned office so someone named Rico would finally let her retire. She had no idea I was a vampire; in fact, the thought never occurred to her.

I'd never been part of any minority before, unless you counted those who thought Timothy Dalton made a decent James Bond, and I didn't particularly like people assuming that they could make rude comments about said minority because they thought I was "safe." It was humiliating, and, worse, it really pissed me off.

"Or if you prefer something more tropical," Sandy said, reaching toward a door labeled Greenfield Coastal Time Share Sales.

"Sandy, I'm going to have to stop you right there," I said. "I am not going to be a good fit here. I'm sorry to have taken up your time. This has been a very enlightening experience. Please don't call me, ever."

"But we need a girl like you, Jane. You have the voice. With some practice, you could clear one hundred dollars, two hundred dollars a night," she said. "We have girls quit without notice all the time because they can't stand the work or they just decide they don't want to come in that night. Someone like you isn't going to do that. You're one of those nice, responsible girls. You're going to show up on time and ready to work. You won't call ten minutes before your shift and tell me you can't come in because you've been arrested. And you won't try to live in your van out in the parking lot. You'll serve as a good example to the other girls."

"So, you need me to class up the joint?" I asked, my eyebrow arched. "That's new."

"Exactly." Sandy sighed.

"Thanks, but I'm still going to say no," I said, hustling toward the nearest fire exit. "After all, working here might interfere with my participation in the antihuman campaign."

Sandy stared at me in bewilderment, so I flashed my fangs, rolled my eyes, and stalked out of the building. The words "bloodsucking monsters" and "filthy bastards" rang in my skull, and my cheeks burned as I stomped back to Big Bertha. I swore that if I found blood on her, I was going to go back to River Oaks, pack up, and move to Tibet.

I had one of those out-of-body automatic driving experiences, where I put the keys in the ignition, and the next thing I knew, I was turning Big Bertha around the corner to Gabriel's road. I pulled into his driveway, climbed the stairs, and stared at the house. My hand froze in midair as I started to knock on his door.

This was nothing new. I'd been to Gabriel's house before. Of course, I'd behaved like a screaming harridan when I was there before . . . and here I was, coming to his door with problems again.

I chewed my lip and considered running back to my car. Then again, Gabriel was always going on about his responsibility in leading me through my vampire growing pains. Oh, let's be honest, I was there to get a few sympathy kisses and maybe an elder-vampire platitude or two. Something like "It's always darkest before the dawn . . . and we never really see that, so why worry?" Before I could knock, the door swung open, and Gabriel was there.

"Jane!" Gabriel exclaimed with a grin that faltered at the sight of my expression. "What's wrong?"

I tilted my head and have him a long, appraising look. "I know this is a long shot, but did you ever read a book called *Alexander and the Terrible, Horrible, No Good, Very Bad Day*?"

"No, but the title does lend itself to inference." Gabriel nodded.

"Well, whatever you're inferring, add cigarette smoke and desperation."

"That explains the smell," he said, sniffing my hair. "Where have you been?"

"Working."

"You found a job? That's—"

"As a telemarketer."

He made the "ouch" face. "Oh."

"For a company that sold, among other sleazy and dubious products, a vitamin tonic they claimed would reverse vampirism."

Gabriel scoffed. "Well, that's ridiculous. No one's ever been able to accomplish that."

"Not the point."

"Sorry."

"I agreed to sell this crap. Well, actually, I agreed to try to ensnare innocent families into booking appointments in questionable locations with complete strangers wielding cameras. But I was just terrible at it, because the customers could apparently smell my fear through the phone and just hung up on me, or they told me to drop dead, and we both know that horse is already out of the barn. It was hell, OK? I took a job in the stinkiest pit of minimum-wage hell."

Gabriel gave me a blank look. "Why didn't you ask more questions about the job before you took it?"

"I was just tired of not working. I wanted a job. Any job. Anything to make me feel useful and productive . . . and not doomed to move back in with my parents."

"Jane, if it's a question of money, I could—"

I touched a finger to his lips. "Don't. Don't make an offer that will change our relationship. I appreciate the thought, but I'm not comfortable when you blur that daddy/boyfriend line."

"The offer, which you wouldn't let me make, still stands."

"Thank you. Anyway, when I could not lure people into these said appointments, my new boss told me all about the other stuff I could sell, including this antivampire snake oil. And then she told me that vampires are filthy, vicious creatures who are going to overthrow the human government in some bloody coup we've been planning for years."

"I take it she didn't know you were a vampire?" he said as I shook my head.

"Not only was I subjected to the general abuse that telemarketers receive—and, I now realize, deserve just the tiniest bit—but I got treated to my very first hate speech."

"Oh, you'll hear much worse over the years," he said, wrapping an arm around my shoulders and pressing me to his side. "I once had a drunk in a tavern tell me a delightful joke about two vampires, a priest, and a—"

"I don't need to hear it," I assured him. "Also, I'm

pretty sure this is one of those stories that ends in 'and then I ate him.'"

Gabriel shrugged but didn't deny it. I laughed.

"You're laughing. That's always a good thing. Of course, you're laughing at me, but I'm getting used to that," he said.

I leaned my forehead against his. "You really need to."

Gabriel pulled me onto his lap like a child woken by a nightmare. "Humans fear what they don't understand. And I don't believe that they will ever truly understand us. You will come across the stupid, the ignorant, the misinformed."

"And I'm related to most of them," I said, leaning my head against his shoulder.

"You will meet these people. And they will insult you. They may try to hurt you. You managed to escape the situation without lashing out or hurting anyone, despite your anger. You did escape without hurting anyone, right?"

"Yes," I grumbled. "I may have made a rude gesture or two behind a closed door, though."

"See? You left with your dignity intact, which is far better than I would have done at your age. I'm proud of you. Try not to take the things humans do so personally, Jane. You have to take the good with the bad."

"And enjoy snacking on the bad?"

"Sometimes, yes." He chuckled, playing with the buttons of my sweater. "Can I offer you the use of my shower?"

I rolled my eyes at him. "That is the most abrupt pickup line I've ever heard."

Gabriel's lips twisted into a half-smile, half-grimace that somehow communicated that he wasn't just being playful and bantery.

"The smoke smell is that bad?" I cried. "I was only there for a few hours!"

"It is pungent," he admitted. "But my nose is much more sensitive than the average man's. And to make up for this insult, I will take you upstairs and wash you from head to toe."

"Will there be bubbles?" I asked.

"Bubbles can be arranged." He nodded solemnly, parting the buttons to toy with the Chinese finger trap that was my front-enclosure bra.

Gabriel peeled away my sweater. I was enjoying the novelty of being both topless and outdoors when an expression of revulsion skittered across his features. I looked down, checking my torso for any sort of disfiguring scars or moles I may have missed in the last two decades. "What?"

"It's actually worse now," he said, his nose wrinkling.

I choked out a shocked laugh. "Nice!"

"I can work around it," he promised quickly, realizing he'd hurt my feelings. "I don't need to breathe."

"Thank you for your commitment to the task at hand."

Gabriel went back to work with a determined air, stroking my skin as he pressed kisses along my throat. I tipped my head back. My bones seemed to become liquid as he rubbed slow circles over my spine. I looked down and saw him hesitating as he pressed his lips to my skin, as if the contact would sting. He was forcing himself to continue his path from my throat to my collarbone.

"You really shouldn't have to try this hard," I told him, pushing his hair back from his face. "But it's very sweet."

"I'm sorry. It seems to have taken up residence in your pores," Gabriel said kindly.

"This is not the night to do this. Stinky is definitely not the note I want to start out on," I said, sniffing my once-lucky-now-destined-for-burning sweater. "I'm going home and bathing in tomato juice. It worked when Fitz used a skunk as a chew toy last summer."

"Stay a few moments," he said, stroking my knees as I slipped the sweater back on. "I think I can tolerate your aromatic presence a while longer."

"Gee, thanks," I muttered. He kissed me softly, tracing the line of my mouth with his tongue before withdrawing and doing his best to hide his instinct to recoil.

"It was a valiant attempt," I told him.

"It's rather like licking an ashtray," he said apologetically. "You don't breathe. How did you get that much second-hand smoke in your mouth?"

"I talked constantly for four hours."

"Tell me again why this job didn't suit you?" he asked, making an undignified *uhhff* sound when I poked his stomach. "I'm sorry you had a terrible, horrible, no good, very bad day. Still, knowing you, you'll turn it into some sort of learning experience."

"Yes, I've learned I'm going to be a lot nicer to telemarketers from now on." I sniffed as I snuggled into his chest.

"See? There's a silver lining after all."

We sat in silence and listened to frogs chirping on his front lawn. Gabriel was slowly but surely leaning his head away from me. After a minute or so, his face was as far away from me as his neck would allow.

"All right, all right," I grumbled, getting to my feet. "I'll go home and shower."

"I'm sorry," he assured me as he followed me to my car. "Otherwise, I find you irresistible."

I glared at him halfheartedly as he leaned in for a kiss. Thinking twice when he was hit with my aura of nicotine, he reached out and shook my hand. I laughed.

"You're laughing. That's always a good sign," he said again as I climbed into Big Bertha.

I kept laughing until I stopped at the end of Gabriel's road. I looked into the rearview mirror and saw a girl with a glint in her eye and a goofy grin on her face.

"Oh, Jane. You've got it baaaad."

14

Vampires can be territorial and possessive creatures. While it makes them passionate and exciting lovers, it can also make them terrifying ex-lovers.

—From *The Guide for the Newly Undead*

You know how people complain that Christmas has become too crass and commercial? Well, boo-hoo. Have you seen what humans have done to Halloween? It's all "excuse to dress slutty" witch costumes, chainsaw serial-killer movie marathons, and life-size electronic dancing mummies. And let's not even talk about how culturally insensitive the whole dang holiday is toward the undead. How would humans feel if we put inflatable versions of them on our lawns?

I didn't take this all so personally until my first undead Halloween. Believe it or not, vampires tend to hole up on All Hallows Eve and refuse to come out until the last candy corn has been consumed. Part of it is the commercial resentment, but mostly, it's the hope to avoid a bunch of drunk idiots doing their worst Transylvanian accent.

While explaining the various holiday pitfalls, Gabriel said he usually spent Halloween watching old movies, an incurable Hitchcock fan. And then he invited himself over to my house.

This may sound juvenile, but I was nervous. Then again, our first date involved me being interrogated, so I didn't feel this was unwarranted. We were going to have the place to ourselves. Aunt Jettie had a date to go out with Grandpa Fred, walking the earth when the veil between the spirit world and reality was at its thinnest and all that.

It had taken some work, but I'd finally exorcised the offensive eau de Marlboro Man scent that clung to my skin for days after I left Greenfield Studios. I bathed in tomato juice, used four different types of clarifying shampoo, and invested in the economy pack of Listerine. I also took more care with my appearance than usual that night. I wore a gauzy green blouse and my "good" jeans. I'd actually bothered with earrings, a rare thing for me. And I was wearing makeup. Yes, I did own makeup, blush and powder and Chapstick. But not eyeliner. There was an incident in college. I had to wear an eye patch for two weeks.

I wanted my sire to see that when I wasn't drunk or freaking out, I wasn't a total gorgon. And I even wore cute black underwear, because you never knew.

The only real problem was entertainment. I didn't think building an evening around "Come over and make out with me" was a good way to start a relationship. Then again, "Come over and play canasta" is just lame.

My DVD collection did not include the old-fashioned thrillers Gabriel liked but rather an alarming number of romantic comedies that I didn't want Gabriel to know I had seen, much less owned. And I never realized what a minefield Halloween television could be. Imagine my horror to find the channels crowded with the *Blade* trilogy and *The Lost Boys*. In terms of entertainment value, *Lost Boys* is a great movie. But it involves the unholy trinity that is Corey Feldman, Corey Haim, and Joel Schumacher, and therefore I cannot claim it as a suitable model for my lifestyle.

We finally settled on Francis Ford Coppola's version of *Dracula*, which, unfortunately, Gabriel seemed to think was a comedy. I think it was the combination of Keanu Reeves's British accent and Gary Oldman's elderly Count Dracula hairstyle. They're just misleading.

"Why would he arrange his hair into buttocks on top of his head?" Gabriel laughed.

"You're not the first person to ask that," I told him.

He was just so darn cute when he laughed. The skin around his eyes crinkled. His face relaxed. It made him seem so alive, so normal, which in itself seemed weird.

"I never realized how funny *Dracula* could be," he said. "Most vampires resent Stoker for the public-relations nightmare he visited on us all, but we secretly enjoy the story. It was the first time vampires were portrayed as sensual creatures, as opposed to mindless, reeking ghouls."

"Mmmm, you know what book talk does to me," I growled, stopping when I noticed how prim he looked, sitting in the exact center of my sofa with his back ram-rod straight. He was sitting almost a foot away from me, with his hands at his sides. "Why are you sitting like that?"

"I know you have a problem with this on occasion, but I was talking just then."

"Seriously, why are you sitting like that?" I asked, ignoring his grimace at being interrupted again.

"Because the furniture designers didn't intend for us to sit on the back of the sofa?" he suggested.

"You are blatantly violating the rules of the couch date," I said.

"Couch date?"

"When you spend an entire evening on the couch with an attractive person of the opposite sex, it's called a couch date," I said.

"I've never been on a couch date," he admitted.

"Well, let me introduce you to the protocol." I nudged him into the corner and laid his arm across the back of the sofa. "You sit here. I sit here. As the movie progresses, I will lean closer and closer. Eventually, I will be in this position." I curled against his side with my head leaned against his shoulder. "You can use this to your advantage."

"How?" he asked, clearly intrigued.

"You'll figure it out," I said, bringing his arm around me.

Did you know there at least nineteen different types of kissing? Open-mouthed and soft kisses that make your toes curl. Tiny, dry kisses peppering your jaw.

Tongue. No tongue. And Gabriel knew all of them. Sometimes it paid to date a really old guy. He had a lot of experience. And the best part was that I didn't have a thought in my head the entire time. OK, yeah, I did, but most of them were along the lines of "Mmmmm." "Ohhhh." And "Thank God I wore the black panties."

"Is this a violation of couch-date protocol?" he asked when I opened my eyes, half-dazed.

"No, this is, in fact, exactly in keeping with couch-date protocol," I murmured.

"I'm so glad," he said, toying with the hem of my blouse before dragging it over my head and tossing it into a pile on the other side of the couch.

I enjoyed the skim of his hands against my bare arms, my stomach against his chest, as I slid onto his lap. He bent his head to run his lips along the contours of my ribs, flexing his fingers around my hips when it made me jump. His hands slid up my back, dragging me down to meet his mouth.

He glided his fingers across my belly, brushing them over my aforementioned panties and the little strawberry-shaped damp spot I'd left on them. I jumped again, forcing his hand harder against me in a way that wasn't entirely unpleasant. I made a breathy little noise that had Gabriel grinning. His clever hand rubbed slow circles over the fabric. I felt his mouth close over my nipple, through the lace of my bra, as he pushed the fabric aside.

And then the doorbell rang.

"Seriously?" I gasped as Gabriel bit gently at the place where my neck and shoulder joined.

"Ignore it," Gabriel whispered. He undid my bra completely and tossed it across the room. "Please."

I nodded in mute agreement as my mouth closed over his again. I was fully prepared to ignore anything less than an alien invasion on the front lawn, when the bell gave three more quick peals. Apparently, whoever it was refused to go away, which would have been the reasonable response of any reasonable person harassing a girl who hadn't had sex in three years.

"Whoever it is, I'm going to kill them," I vowed as the doorbell chimed again.

"What if it's trick-or-treaters?" he asked as I disentangled myself and straightened my clothes.

"Anyone over five feet tall is fair game," I conceded as I struggled into my blouse. "Where is my bra?" Gabriel looked around the room and shrugged. "Well, whoever it is will have to deal with free-swinging Jane," I said. "And let that be a lesson to them."

I opened the door to find Jack and Rose from *Titanic* standing on my porch. Or, at least, Zeb and Jolene dressed as Jack and Rose in their "jump scene" clothes. Because I needed Gabriel to meet Jolene while she was wearing a gorgeous Edwardian rental gown. I wouldn't pale by comparison or anything.

"What are you guys doing here?" I asked, my tone not exactly welcoming.

"Well, we just finished up at a costume party, and we thought you might not have plans tonight," he said.

"Zeb, honey, I think she has somebody here," Jolene said, pulling him back as she took in the tousled hair, the general state of me. I would have blushed if I still had circulation. Even I could smell the coppery scent of arousal in the room, and with Jolene's senses . . . At that moment, Jolene motioned down to my shirt, which was inside out. I groaned. With my vampire senses and agility, you'd think putting on a blouse wouldn't be that difficult.

"Yeah." I looked back toward my parlor. I really hoped Gabriel still had pants on, because, otherwise, this could be awkward. "Actually, there is someone here whom I want you to meet, in a way that you remember."

"OK, that's not cryptic," Zeb said, hauling a duffel bag and some carry-out sacks from Smoky Bones BBQ into the house.

"You are going to change clothes before you eat the barbecue, right? If not, she can kiss that costume deposit good-bye," I asked. I'd seen Jolene around ribs.

"I heard that!" Jolene called as she went into the kitchen to search for plates.

Sensing that Seminaked Happy Fun Time was over, Gabriel, pants intact, came out of the parlor just as Jolene came back in to claim her share of the ribs.

"Hi! I'm Jolene. It's real nice to meet you." Jolene crossed to him and shook his hand.

"Gabriel Nightengale," he said, tapping his teeth. "McClaine clan?"

"Very good," she said, grinning. "Not a lot of people pick up on canine patterns."

"Behavior patterns?" I asked.

"No, the actual pattern of her canine teeth," Gabriel said. "Werewolves have strong and specific genetic markers, even for something as simple as dental configuration. Different clans have different bite patterns. Jolene has the classic McClaine arrangement, a slight overbite with nicely spaced bottom incisors."

"You know an alarming amount of information about regional teeth," I told him.

Jolene giggled, a sound that was followed by a long conversational pause.

"Well." Zeb rubbed his hands together. "This is really awkward."

Zeb and Jolene busied themselves with unwrapping enough barbecued ribs, potato salad, and cole slaw to feed about ten people.

"So much food." Gabriel marveled at my coffee table, groaning under the weight of the spread.

"Um, you know we don't eat, right?" I asked.

Jolene laughed, a throaty sound that was equal parts growl and giggle. She wiped a smear of sauce from her chin. "Oh, this is just a snack." She rolled her eyes. "I'll probably have to eat a pork shoulder or somethin' before bed."

"On our first date, she ate a whole lasagna and still had room for tiramisu. Who's my bottomless pit? Who's my little bottomless pit?" Zeb said proudly, snuffling behind Jolene's ears.

"Down, boy." Jolene giggled. "We didn't forget about y'all, though. We brought bottled blood, and we got wine. It's strawberry."

She held up an obscenely red bottle with dancing berries on the label.

Gabriel shuddered, an imperceptible movement caught only by my vampire eyes. "I don't drink . . . wine."

I shot a look at Gabriel. I hoped he could see me thinking, *I know you stole that line from* Dracula!

Undeterred, Jolene offered the bottle to me. "Jane?"

"No, thanks."

Handing Gabriel and me each a warmed bottle of an imported, upmarket synthetic blood called Sangre, Zeb gave me a sly look. "Jane never drinks, anyway. Not since the 'incident' her sophomore year."

"Zeb," I growled.

"Having seen Jane drink, I think I'd like to hear this story," Gabriel said, cheerfully passing the wine to Zeb.

"Like I'm the only person who's ever vomited while drunk," I grumbled.

Zeb grinned. "You were the only person I know who's done it on an occupied police car."

I glared at him. "If you want to start trading stories, we can start trading stories. As a former member of the Richard Marx Fan Club, you don't want to start this arms race."

Zeb smiled meekly around a rib. "Agreed."

"Richard Marx?" Jolene asked.

"He went through an obnoxiously cheerful pop phase. Don't ask."

Over the course of the evening, I saw again how besotted Jolene was with Zeb, and vice versa. He hung on every word that spilled from her perfect pout. If they would just have stopped smooching and slobbering all over each other, I could have stood being in the same county with them.

As predicted, Jolene and Zeb plowed through the food. I used Aunt Jettie's favorite glasses to serve the wine and a delicious dessert version of synthetic blood, Café Transylvania by General Foods International Coffees. There was that awkward moment when everyone runs out of food and drink to occupy themselves, and we were all left looking at each other with nothing to say. Well, Jolene was still engrossed in her barbecue, but Zeb, Gabriel, and I were at a weird conversational impasse.

Fortunately, Gabriel had a full century's worth of experience with uncomfortable social situations, so he was able to break the ice. "Zeb, Jane says you're a kindergarten teacher."

"Yep," Zeb said, bracing for the inevitable "Isn't babysitting a bunch of kids sort of a weird job for a grown man?" questions that inevitably followed. Since entering the classroom, Zeb had found that male teachers were welcome at the high-school level but that men who wanted to spend their time with small children were immediately suspected of being lazy or creepy.

"I admire people who can work with small children," Gabriel said. "I have always found them to be . . . unsettling little creatures."

Zeb grinned. "Well, they are, but I'd rather spend time with them than most of their parents. Yesterday, I had a mother try to tell me that her son shoving another kid off the top of the jungle gym was a form of creative expression, and then she launched into a lecture on why

I should only serve gluten-free carob cookies for snack time. Between the helicopter parents and the parents who drop their kids off without a word except to tell me that their kids are 'my problem now,' I will take nose picking and toy grabbing anytime. Also, I just really like taking a nap after lunch every day."

Gabriel chuckled and poured Zeb another glass of wine.

"So, Gabriel, Jane says you saved her life with this whole vampire thing," Zeb said. "I appreciate that. She's been my best friend since we were kids, and I'm glad she didn't die in a deer-hunting mishap. For me to win the pool, her death had to involve a tragic waterskiing accident."

"Touching, Zeb," I muttered.

"But Jane also said you played shake-the-Etch-a-Sketch with my memory. I would prefer you not do that again. Even if you think I can't handle some part of your world, let me decide whether I want to remember it or not."

"Same goes," Jolene said, raising her hand, her voice muffled by a rib. "Hey, Jane, Zeb told me about the tele-marketin' thing."

I tamped down the urge to be annoyed with Zeb for sharing my humiliation with his girlfriend. Of course, he told Jolene about my disastrous one-night stand with phone sales. I needed to accept that my life was now their "And how was your day?" fodder.

"Don't feel bad," Jolene told me. "My uncle Lonnie

gave me a job in his bait shop one summer, and I let a whole cooler's worth of crickets loose. One of the customers started screamin' that it was a biblical plague and started havin' chest pains. We had to call nine-one-one. For the rest of the summer, all my cousins called me Cricket, and Uncle Lonnie sent me to work at the sandwich shop. It was a much better fit for me. That's all you have to do, Jane, just find your fit."

"Or I can follow your lead and unleash a plague of locusts like this town has never seen," I said, rubbing my chin with an evil-genius glare.

Jolene snorted, clapping her hand over her mouth to keep from spewing potato salad over my coffee table. "No more jokes while I'm chewin'!"

The good news was that Jolene and Zeb really seemed to like spending time with me and Gabriel. The bad news is that meant they stayed, and stayed, and stayed . . . and stayed. Gabriel and I were cuddled under a throw at one corner of the couch, barely able to cover that we were desperately trying to touch each other without being noticed. We watched the rest of *Dracula,* moved on to *From Dusk till Dawn,* and resorted to *Fright Night* before Gabriel finally gave up and decided to take his leave for the evening. I walked him out as Jolene popped her fourth bag of Super Butter Lovers' Popcorn in my microwave.

"I think they've moved in with you and just haven't told you," Gabriel whispered as I closed the door behind us. He clutched my face in his hands and seized my mouth in a fierce kiss. "What are they trying to do to us?"

"I don't know!" I giggled as Gabriel pulled me with him on his trek to the car. "Zeb is usually much better at taking hints, but I think he's doing some sort of weird brotherly protection thing. It's either very sweet or just this side of cruel and unusual."

"Did I just pass some sort of test?" he asked. "The test to determine whether your friends think I'm good enough for you?"

"Test." I sputtered, giving a raspberried laugh. "That's just crazy talk. There was no—yes. Yes, you did. I wasn't intentionally testing you, but you did beautifully. Jolene was eating out of the palm of your suave and charming hand. Zeb obviously both fears and admires you. But you did turn his best friend into a vampire. He still rants about a guy who borrowed my iPod after a second date and didn't return it. It could take some time for him to adjust to us double-dating."

"I like Zeb," Gabriel said. "He's odd."

"That he is."

"He suits you. And he loves you, that much is obvious. You're very lucky to have such a friend."

"That's very progressive of you. Some guys are uncomfortable with the whole male-best-friend thing."

"Well, if I thought he had romantic designs on you, I would have to make him forget he'd ever met you and give him a sudden urge to relocate to Guadalajara," he said solemnly.

"Aww, that's so sweet." I chuckled, kissing him. "You know, this counts as our third date since you made your 'I'll know when you're ready for sex' declaration. In human terms, that's very significant."

"Third date?"

"Yeah, there was an actual meal served while we were at Cracker Barrel, so I'm counting it. And the smoke-filled porch coziness and then tonight. In human dating terms, that's three, which is like a sexual green light. So, next time, yes?"

"If the universe was fair, we would have finished what we started on the couch," he agreed. "Next time."

I gave him one more smacking kiss before he started his car. "And if Zeb shows up, he's bound for Guadala-jara."

"Agreed."

15

When you encounter unpleasantness from the human population, try to keep in mind that you will be able to dance on their graves long after they're dead. It's a cheering thought.

—From *The Guide for the Newly Undead*

As I headed toward my three-month undead anniversary, I got twitchy. Not "espresso marathon" twitchy but certainly not the sort of person you'd want to get stuck in an elevator with. My nerves were crawling under my skin. I couldn't sit still. I couldn't find anything I wanted to drink, but I still drank every drop of fake blood in the house—which I was sure would go straight to my thighs.

It took two episodes of an *Intervention* marathon for me to realize I was going through book withdrawal. I hadn't purchased a new one in more than a month. And I hadn't checked anything out of the library since the morning before I was fired . . . which also meant I had four books that were long overdue.

I had late fines.

I had never had late fines in my entire life.

I had to go to the library, right? It was closing in an hour, and there couldn't be that many people there this late on a weeknight. Plus, I needed more information about wolves' mating habits and the probability of accidental friend mauling. I'd done some research online, but I didn't know how reliable it was. According to WerewolvesDebunked.com, werewolves manage to pass as human but they are far more in touch with their natural instincts than most humanoid creatures. It can mean a certain earthy, rugged appeal for the werewolf males who manage to hold on to all their teeth. But it also means they're impulsive, temperamental, fiercely territorial, and not a whole lot of fun one week a month. They had my sympathy on that count.

Werewolf metabolism is so high that they have to scarf down calories all day just to sleep all night, like a mini-hibernation. Thanksgiving in a werewolf clan is like a full-on farm-animal massacre. Multiple turkeys, hams, chickens, sides of beef, legs of venison, and then they fight over the bones in the weirdest touch-football game ever. But constantly thinking and talking about food is what makes werewolves some of the best chefs in the world.

Think about it. Have you ever seen Emeril Lagasse during a full moon?

Contrary to popular myth, werewolves are born, not made. No matter how many times they bite someone, that person will not turn, though they will probably bleed profusely and will definitely be annoyed. Also, were-creatures can change day or night, no matter what phase of the moon. But their change is less controlled, more complete, during the full moon.

Personally, I thought they used it as an excuse. "Oh, I can't remember eating your chickens and peeing on your couch. I was wolfed out last night."

Werewolves are pack animals, led by a patriarchal alpha male. A pack generally lives in close quarters, filling an apartment complex, a subdivision, or a gated community in more affluent clans. In Southern packs, it usually means parking a number of trailers and houses on a farm. This fits nicely into the redneck stereotype of big, dysfunctional, overly close families.

After the chaos of the Coming Out, werewolves were sure that vampires had doomed themselves to extinction. Since many werewolves consider vampires to be stuck-up, pretentious snobs, they didn't consider it a great loss. Most were-creatures watched with interest as vampires integrated into human society, but few were ready to come out into the open. Werewolves share their secrets with few select, trusted humans. Those who betray werewolf clans . . . well, I don't know what happens to them, because they're never heard from again.

While this information was a good start, it didn't do much to convince me of Zeb's safety.

On top of my research problems, I needed Mrs. Stubblefield's signature to file for undead unemployment benefits, a service for new vampires. The 2000 Census showed that 29 percent of newly turned vampires lost their jobs during the unexplained three-day absence while they waited to rise. New vampires who lost their jobs could file for Council-funded benefits for up to six months. Fortunately, you didn't have to prove that losing your job was a result of being turned. And since people expected me actually to pay for my synthetic blood, I was going to need all the help I could get.

Besides, I had to face the library sometime, right?

Well, I couldn't. I got as far as the book drop in the parking lot and had a crisis of spine. I pictured having to make eye contact with my former coworkers, checking books out from the public side of the desk, looking Mrs. Stubblefield in the eye, and watching Posey incorrectly shelve books. I just couldn't do it.

So I shoved the books into the drop and ran away like a girl. It took me a few blocks before I realized I'd forgotten my car, which was becoming a bit of a habit. I slowed on a seedier section of Main Street, with its big decaying brick structures from the town's boom days. My parents never ventured through this part of town when I was growing up, and my mother offered dire warnings of what might happen if I did. And now that I was walking down the dark, weed-choked street, I could see why. I passed several pawn shops, liquor stores, a shop with cardboard sign over the windows that simply said "Videos." And on the corner, I noticed a little blue sign that read "Specialty Books," in peeling gold paint.

Half-Moon Hollow's literary outlets were limited to an ailing Waldenbooks and the library. How could there be a bookstore in this town that I was unaware of? Of course, this place didn't look as if it was a member of the local chamber of commerce.

Sure that I was about to enter a cleverly disguised adult bookstore, I pushed the door open. An old cowbell tinkled above the door as I walked in. It was an Ali Baba's cave of literary treasures, their cracked spines winking out at my superhuman eyes through the incredibly bad lighting. I loved old books as much as the next bibliophile, but these were crumbling, suffering. I wandered the shelves, running my fingers over the spines. The shop offered everything from sixteenth-century manuscripts hand-copied by monks to old *Tales from the Crypt* comics, but finding either on purpose would be a small miracle.

Hanks of herbs hanging from the ceiling, candles of all colors and shapes, and scattered crystal geodes only added to the air of committed disorganization. There was no effort to let the customer know what subjects were located where. Plus, there didn't appear to be a division of subjects, anyway. Books on astral projection were mixed in with books on herb gardening. Books on postdeath tax issues were mixed in with guides on the proper care and feeding of Yeti.

I picked up an orange soft-cover book, titled *The Idiot's Guide to Vampirism.*

"It is official. Vampires are now uncool," I muttered to no one, as there didn't appear to be anyone else in the building.

I shuffled through the books. There were some useful selections, but it took a keen eye to find them.

Werewolves: A Vampire's Best Friend or Foe?

A Compendium of Self-Defense Spells.

From Fangs to Fairy Folk: Unusual Creatures of Mid-western North America.

50 Ways to Add Variety to Your Undead Diet.

Living with the Dead: How to Happily Occupy a Haunted House.

And perhaps the most bizarre title: *Tuesdays with Morrie.*

I was so engrossed in my task, I didn't detect the presence over my shoulder that asked, "Oh, hello, what are you doing?"

I turned to see a skinny old man, wizened to the point of cuteness. He was dressed in a gray cardigan with skipped buttons and brown corduroy pants held up with a black leather belt and bright red suspenders. There was a Mont Blanc pen stuck behind his ear, practically lost in the frizzled gray nest of hair. A pair of bifocals, repaired with white tape and a paper clip, sat perched on his balding crown.

I looked down and saw I was balancing stacks of books in my hands. I hadn't even realized that I'd spent about a half hour sorting the books by fiction, nonfiction, author, then subject. It was as if I were in some sort of alphabetically induced trance.

I dropped the books to the floor. "I'm so sorry. I'm a complete freak. I used to work at the library, and it—it just drives me crazy to see books so out of order."

"It's a pretty habit. There are more shelves in the back, you know." He grinned. Following Gabriel's advice, I cast out my senses, feeling for anything out of the ordinary. There was nothing. He was 100-percent human, just a funny old man who loved weird stuff.

"I must be the rudest customer you've ever had," I moaned, shelving the books.

He chuckled. "No, that would be Edwina Myers, a horrible woman who tries to close me down every few years. Claims I'm a bad influence. Though whom I'm influencing I have no idea." He nodded to the empty store.

"I've lived in the Hollow for my whole life. How did I not know about this place?" I asked.

"Well, I don't advertise in the Yellow Pages. And there's a limited interest in occult books in the Hollow. We don't have walk-in business. I like to think of the store as one of those mystical places you pass right by unless you already know it's there."

"But I found it."

"Yes, you did. Gilbert Wainwright, by the way," he said, extending his hand.

"Jane Jameson." I reached out to shake it, then shrieked as my fingers brushed the silver band he wore around his middle finger. I yowled, and my fangs extended. A defense mechanism, I suppose, kind of like cursing when you touch a hot iron. I drew back my hand and watched the dirty gray streak across my palm fade away.

"How interesting," he said, his voice tinged with awe as he stared at his ring. "It's still thrilling to meet one of your kind, you know. The Great Coming Out was a dream come true for me. As a boy, I used to pretend I was a vampire hunter on a mission to kill Dracula. Or

I would pretend I was the vampire, stalking the foggy streets of London for a tasty lady of ill repute."

"You must have had a very interesting childhood," I said, suppressing a smirk.

I don't think he heard me, because he continued, "It came as absolutely no surprise to me that vampires lived among us, so to speak. I've devoted my entire life to studying the paranormal. Ghosts, demons, the living dead, the undead, were-creatures. I've always found it all fascinating. But still, it gives me a zing whenever I see that." He nodded at my healing palm.

"Gave me a zing, too," I said, my fangs snagging my lip when I smiled.

He took a moment to get the joke and laughed uproariously. "Yes, yes, in the future, I suppose it would be more polite to offer vampires my left hand."

"Or you could take the ring off," I suggested.

"Oh, no," he said, absently stroking the worn band. "I never take it off."

"OK, then. Not cryptic at all." I chuckled. "You have an interesting selection here, Mr. Wainwright. How much of this was added after the Coming Out?"

He gave me a curious look.

"You had books on vampire diets and after-death tax issues before you knew for sure that we existed?" I asked. He nodded. "Do you have any books on ancient vampire laws? Because I'm pretty sure I'm getting hosed on a murder rap."

"Actually, no, but I can probably find something if you give me a few days," Mr. Wainright said, apparently unimpressed by my mentioning the murder thing. This made me wonder about his clientele. "So much of my business is handled online now, I just don't have time to keep things up here at the store."

"You sell online?"

"Eighty percent of my sales are online. My Web site registers fifty thousand hits per month." A smirk lifted the wrinkles at his mouth. "Loyal customers and eBay are enough to keep me going. Just last week, I sent three volumes on were-monkeys to Sri Lanka."

"Were-monkeys?" I repeated, unsure if he was joking.

Obviously upset by my lack of familiarity with were-monkeys, Mr. Wainwright gave me a copy of *A Geographical Study of Were-Creatures.* He explained that he became familiar with the more exotic weres while he served in World War II. After that, he continued to pursue his interests abroad. There are some things you just can't study in the Hollow. He'd returned home thirty years earlier to tend to his ailing mother, who had died only the previous year.

I scanned the shop. It had so much potential. And now, with the emerging vampire population, there was an emerging market. And I'd be able to work around books again. The schedule would be flexible, and the boss seemed to understand, nay, embrace, my special needs. Sure, there wouldn't be a lot of kids in an occult bookshop, but you can't ask for everything.

"I don't suppose you'd be looking for a shop assistant, would you?" I asked. "I could box and ship orders, do some shelving, maybe a little light cleaning. I could start off part-time, night hours, obviously, on a trial basis to see whether it works out."

Mr. Wainwright chewed his lip thoughtfully and patted his pockets. It looked as if he was searching for his glasses, which were perched on top of his head. I plucked them from his crown and pressed them gently into his hands. He smiled.

"I've worked in the public library for six years. I have a master's in library science. I have experience helping people finding the right books for their needs."

"It sounds like you might be overqualified, dear."

"I'm not, really. I just want to work around books again."

At the rear of the store, a bookcase collapsed, sending several leather-bound books skittering across the floor. He lifted a scraggly white eyebrow. "Perhaps you could start off with some reorganization," he said, looking at the neat stacks of books I'd arranged around us. "You seem to have a steady hand at that."

I had learned my lesson from Greenfield Studios, so we sat down to discuss schedules, pay scale, distribution of responsibilities, and the fact that at some point, he was going to want to see a copy of my résumé. I left the shop feeling considerably lighter than before. I believe happy people call this emotion hope.

I got as far as the parking lot before I ducked my head back through the door, thanked my new boss, and said, "Mr. Wainwright, do me a favor, if you meet a woman named Ruthie Early, don't marry her."

* * *

I emerged from my first night shift at Specialty Books covered in dirt and suffering several injuries that would have probably resulted in tetanus before I was turned. But I was happier than I'd been in weeks. It was like being given a glimpse into my life before my firing.

My first order of business was cleaning. I chased several generations of spiders from the storage closet with a very large broom. I scrubbed the windows until you could actually see outside. (I remained undecided about whether that was a good thing.) I hauled away the broken shelves and organized the stock into piles by subject. I had not found Mr. Wainwright's office or computer, but I did find what could have been a blueberry muffin petrifying in the back of the cash-register drawer. Also a small vial of dirt, a mummified paw of some sort, a pack of Bazooka, and currency issued by twelve governments, three of which had collapsed.

And at the end of the day, you could not tell I'd done anything. But still, Mr. Wainwright was thrilled to have that paw back. He'd been looking for it for twelve years.

We didn't have a single customer all night, but Mr. Wainwright assured me this was normal. He shooed me away just after one A.M. The shop was closed for the next few days, he reminded me, because he was about to leave town on a purchasing trip in deepest, darkest Tennessee.

"But I look forward to seeing you on Monday. It's been so refreshing having someone else to talk to. I mutter to myself, of course, and to the plants, but I rarely answer back."

I looked over the shriveled remains of a spider plant. "And the plants don't seem to be on speaking terms with you, either."

Mr. Wainwright was still hooting at that one as he bustled me out of the shop.

Euphoric about my newfound and respectable employment, I took my dog for a very long walk on the old farm property to celebrate. As happy as I was to have a job, I knew it meant Fitz would have to readjust to my schedule, just after getting used to me being nocturnal. Plus, even with Aunt Jettie's "hanging around," he would be alone more often after weeks of constant attention. I imagined this was what mothers felt when heading back to work after maternity leave . . . only with more slobbering and shedding.

Sensing my guilt-based permissiveness, Fitz decided to push at the usual walk rules: no running away where I couldn't see him, no rolling in substances I couldn't identify, and no chasing woodland creatures that can fight back.

We explored areas of River Oaks we'd never seen at night: the creek where I'd showed Jenny how to swing on wild grapevines on one of her rare visits to Aunt Jettie's, the path where I had to carry Jenny when she fell off the grapevine and broke her leg, post holes left by a fence I'd had to tear down as penance for letting Jenny break her leg. Fitz chased irate bullfrogs on the normally peaceful shore of the cow pond and gave a possum the chance at an Oscar-winning death scene.

I found a sturdy-looking oak and climbed catlike,

leaping from branch to branch until I could see the house, the road beyond, the faint-twinkling lights of town in the distance. It still seemed strange that all of this had been passed to me. River Oaks had always seemed like its own little kingdom when I was a kid. And I couldn't honestly say that I'd seen every inch of it. It seemed right that I would be able to look after it for generations to come. Maybe if Jenny's children's children's children managed to outgrow their genetic predisposition to jackassery, I would pass it along to them one day.

From the base of the tree, Fitz barked and spun in circles. He apparently didn't care for my Tarzan routine. I jumped, careful to avoid smacking into branches on the way down. I landed on my feet with a soft *thwump*. Fitz, who was used to me landing on other parts of my body, sat on his rump and cocked his head.

"I know, it's new for me, too, buddy," I told him, scrubbing behind his ears. "You'll get used to it, I promise. Do you want to race back home? Huh, boy? Want to race?"

At the word "race," Fitz broke into a run, streaking across the field in a blur of dirty brown-gray. I gave him a few seconds' head-start before running after him. When I loped past him, Fitz gave a confused bark, nipping at my heels as if to say, "This is not how we do things! You chase me! Not the other way around!"

I jogged up the porch steps, Fitz close at my heels. With long strings of thirsty doggie drool hanging from his jowls, he made a beeline for the water bowl I kept in the corner of the porch. As he did, some organic alarm crawled up my spine. Something smelled weird, which was normal where Fitz was concerned. But this scent was chemical, sweet, familiar. It was a garage smell, something I can remember my dad keeping on the shelf with wiper fluid and car-wash supplies. It seemed to be coming from the end of the porch.

Using all the speed I could muster, I leaped over my dog and slapped the water bowl out of his reach. I landed on my side with a thud. Water splashed across my chest, and the bowl skittered down to the lawn. Fitz cocked his head and stared at me with a "What the hell?" expression—which, frankly, was becoming far too familiar.

I swiped at the water soaking my shirt and sniffed. I remembered the smell. Antifreeze. There was antifreeze in Fitz's water dish. If he drank it, he would have died a miserable, painful death, and I probably wouldn't have realized what had happened to him. I wasn't even sure I had antifreeze in my garage. There was no possible way it had accidentally landed in the bowl. Someone had come onto my property, onto my porch, and put it there. Someone had intentionally tried to hurt my dog.

This was not a stupid teenage prank. This was someone who was serious about hurting me through Fitz. What the hell? Who was angry enough at me to do that?

"It's OK," I told Fitz, who was sniffing at my neck. "It's OK. I'm not going to let anything happen to you."

I took the bowl inside and washed it carefully, then threw it away in a fit of compulsive madness, because I knew I'd never feel it was safe again. I fed Fitz a Milk-Bone and gave him fresh water. With shaking hands, I stroked his fur as he gnawed on his treat, blissfully unaware.

If you want to hurt me, fine. Take my books. Burn down my house. Shave my head while I'm sleeping. But nobody, *nobody* screws with my dog.

After the water-bowl incident, I was afraid to leave Fitz at home alone while I was at work. I decided the safest place for him would be at Zeb's. I didn't elaborate on the reasons, because, frankly, I hadn't quite absorbed it all yet and didn't want to have to explain what happened. I just told Zeb that I'd taken a night job and Fitz was having trouble adjusting. I asked Zeb and Jolene to keep an eye on him for a few nights. Jolene was thrilled, as she and Fitz got along famously. And short of a Secret Service detail, I didn't think I could ask for better canine protection than a werewolf escort.

But when I dropped Fitz off for their first sleepover, Zeb looked, well, weird. Dazed and weird, while Jolene was practically jumping out of her skin. "We have something to tell you," he said.

It was curious how quickly they'd become a "we." "We wanted" and "we have." And I used to be a "we." Zeb and I were "the" we. And I was suddenly relegated to being a "you." I would have sulked further if a loopy, stupid grin hadn't split Zeb's face as he said, "We wanted you to be one of the first people to know that—"

"We're gettin' married!" Jolene crowed, waving a ringed hand in front me. "We're engaged!"

"What the hell?"

Jolene's head snapped toward me as I let loose the first words that came to mind. Damn my nonexistent internal filter.

"Not the reaction I expected," Zeb said, putting his arm around a paled Jolene. Clearly, it was not the reaction she expected, either.

"I think I'll just go get a snack," she mumbled as she walked away.

"What is wrong with you?" Zeb demanded as he pulled me outside onto his back deck.

"Me? What is wrong with you? You've known her for two months," I hissed, jerking my head toward the kitchen, where Jolene stood, nervously gnawing on Fritos.

"Could you be more rude?" Zeb demanded.

"I like Jolene, Zeb. She seems nice and everything, but you can't spring 'Hey, my girlfriend's a werewolf' and 'Hey, we're getting married' in the same month. It's just too much. Wolves mate for life. Did you know that? If you want to get a divorce, she could, I don't know, eat you or something. And what about her family? We've already established that they don't like vampires. How pleased are they going to be that she's marrying outside her species?"

He rolled his eyes. "Humans marry werewolves all the time. Sure, there are some old-school packs who pride themselves on their pure old blood and refuse to breed with outsiders. They're the ones who turn out cross-eyed cubs with extra toes.

"Progressive packs, like Jolene's, they're actually grateful to have fresh genes stirred into the pool," he said. "All right, fine, some of her cousins are kind of pissed about it. But her parents are really nice, much nicer than mine. Our children would be half werewolf, giving them fifty-fifty chance of being able to turn. Personally, I kind of hope they can, because that would be cool."

I ignored the second abdominal twinge at the thought of Zeb having children. "But what if you're not safe? What if she hurts you while she's all, you know, *grrr*?"

"Funny coming from the girl who tried to make me her first vampire meal," he said, ignoring the face I made at him. "Look, I didn't think of you as any less human after you changed."

"You *stabbed* me."

"After my initial shock, I got over it, and I still saw you as the same Janie," he said. "You're the same person you always were, which, of course, means you're a giant pain in my ass. But you would never let anything happen to me. And neither would Jolene." He held up his hand to shush me when my mouth popped open to protest. "Don't ask me how I know, I just do."

He huffed out a breath. "She could be suspicious of me having a best friend who's a woman, but she's not. And trust me when I say that being territorial is her nature. I would hope that you'd show her the same, I don't know, courtesy."

Well, that made me feel awful.

"Yeah, but Zeb . . ." I whispered. "Werewolf."

"Vampire," he said, pointing at me.

"Noted," I muttered.

"I know, I don't know everything about her, but I want

to spend the rest of my life learning." He sighed. "I love her. This is a woman I look forward to seeing every day, Janie, and I've never felt that way about anyone, except maybe you. I always figured, well, that you and I would end up in some nursing home together, fighting over the last pudding. But then you had to screw it up and go all immortal and ageless on me.

"Your change has opened my eyes to a world I never even imagined could be real. I knew vampires were out there, but I never thought I would know one, much less have one for my best friend. And seeing how well you've handled things . . . in your own special ass-backward way . . . I never would have had the courage to marry into Jolene's family."

I snorted.

"You are the wind beneath my wings?" he offered.

"If you start to sing, I will bite you," I growled. "So, when are you planning to do this?"

"As soon as possible. Jolene has been waiting a long time to be, um, married," he said, struggling with the choice of words.

"Last single cousin in her pack?" I asked.

Zeb looked embarrassed. "Well, wolves mate for life, so . . ."

"So she's never . . . wow," I marveled.

"Yeah."

I wanted this for Zeb. A nice woman who, after lots of time, and possibly medication, I would able to share Zeb with. Not in a gross way. Jolene was someone who was dealing with her own "special circumstances." Some-

one who would be able to understand my special circumstances and embrace them instead of making Zeb
find new "normal" friends and join a progressive dinner
club.

So, why was I being a jerk about this?

"We were sort of hoping you would be the maid of
honor," Zeb said. His expression made it clear that he
knew how I felt about wearing another bridesmaid's
dress. "We both know you'd be the best man for me,
anyway. And Jolene has too many cousins to choose one
without causing a blood feud."

I made a distressed little noise. On the other side of
the window, Jolene's million-watt smile beamed. I would
worry about the fact that she had heard our entire conversation later. "But I barely know her."

"She likes you. And this would be a great way to get to
know her," Zeb said in his special "I'm making a point"
voice. "By the way, her colors are peach and cornflower
blue."

Dizzied by thoughts of giant butt bows and matching
shawls, I stammered, "But—but I can't do this again—"

Zeb tipped his head, all smiles and Precious Moments
eyes. "I love you."

"Dang it, Zeb. That's not fair."

16

Because vampires tend not to trust perceived bias in human media sources, they depend largely on "word of mouth" to stay informed of current events. This can lead to a localized and somewhat limited world view.

—From *The Guide for the Newly Undead*

With Fitz safe and sound, I threw myself into my work. It had taken me just a few nights for Mr. Wainwright to leave me unsupervised. I think once someone returns your wallet to you, cash intact, four times, it tends to cement your faith in that person's character. I wasn't returning the same wallet repeatedly. It was various wallets from over the years that I found misplaced all over the shop. Mr. Wainwright had to be public enemy number one on the credit-card companies' frequent-card-loser watch list.

Mr. Wainwright never had to worry about my productivity in his absence, though I did take frequent breaks to study the books. I had missed that smell, old paper and starched cover canvas. Cozied between the crowded shelves, my feet propped up on a stack of *Encyclopedia Demonica,* and my nose buried in a first edition of Mary Shelley's *Frankenstein,* it was like returning home after a long exile. Mr. Wainwright, who lived in a little apartment above the shop, had a hard time getting me to leave in the mornings. I wanted to wallow in the old volumes, some priceless, some cheap reproductions, all housed together in a mishmash. I had a purpose here. I belonged. The books *needed* me.

The cowbell on the shop door rang, jolting me out of Geneva circa 1818. I dashed for the door, eager to help a live customer . . . or, really, any customer. A pulse wasn't necessary.

I found Ophelia the Teen Vampire Queen perched on the counter, wearing a black velvet minidress and silver go-go boots, flipping through a copy of *From Caesar to Kennedy: Vampires and Their Clandestine Political Influence throughout History.*

"Ophelia?"

She snapped the book shut and gave me what I'm sure passed for one of her warm smiles. "Jane, nice to see you. I was pleased to learn that you'd found another job. From what I hear, you need some constructive ways to fill your time."

Suddenly aware that I was surrounded by literary chaos and covered in an inch-thick layer of shop grime, I wiped my hands on my jeans. "How did you know I work here?"

She hopped off the counter and gave me a wry look. "We know everything, Jane."

The way she said that was unsettling, implying not only that the council seemed to know every detail of my life but that they knew things that I was trying to conceal. And so far, I wasn't trying to conceal anything from them, so this was distressing.

I cleared my throat and tried casually to sort through some remaindered ritual candles. "Can I find something for you, or are you just browsing?"

"I thought I made the reason for my visit clear with that comment about constructive use of your time," she said pointedly.

"I know, I was trying to gloss over it." I sighed, turning to her and crossing my arms. "Would you mind just asking me the questions this time instead of yanking the answers out of my cortex?"

"I didn't bring Sophie along, because she assures me that you are a terrible liar," Ophelia said, stretching her lips into a thin smile. "Don't mistake this as a compliment. I merely came by to let you know that the investigation into Walter's death continues. In fact, it has become far more interesting in the last few weeks as rumors of your behavior just after your turning have come to our attention."

I thought back to the night I rose, running through what I did and what could be construed as a vampire faux pas. "OK, so it was a mistake to try to feed from my friend, but Gabriel stopped me. Zeb wasn't hurt. In fact, he has no memory of that night, so no harm done."

"I don't know who this Zeb person is, and I don't particularly care. I am referring to the widely circulating public opinion that you and Walter were involved in a passionate affair," she said, the hint of a smirk giving her youthful features a cruel, unnatural twist. "That he broke it off because you were too possessive and 'clingy.' And that you attacked him at the Cellar and set him on fire in a jealous rage."

"Why—why—why would anybody say that?" I stammered. "Why would I get involved in a passionate affair with anybody right after turning, much less a passionate affair with Walter? And what do you mean by circulating public opinion? Does that mean a bunch of vampires are sitting around gossiping about me?"

"Our social circles tend to be rather limited but close-knit. We do enjoy it when a little excitement spices up an otherwise dull conversation," she admitted. "And once you are the subject of a story our community enjoys repeating, it's difficult to convince the tellers that it's less than the absolute truth. It's a fault of our species."

"You all sound like my mama and her friends." I leaned heavily against the counter. "I don't know which part is worse, that people think I set Walter on fire or that they think I dated that mung bean."

"As you know, if these stories were true, the council would be far less sympathetic to your case. We can support self-defense or a legitimate battle to the death. But we can't just let vampires run around throwing matches at each other because of lovers' spats."

"Trust me, it's not true," I told her. "I'd never met Walter until that night, and he's the one who attacked me, not the other way around."

"I'd hoped as much," Ophelia said. "You seem to have better taste. On that note, you should also know that there are certain stories circulating about you and Dick Cheney, stories that were told with a bit more zeal."

"Stories about our being bosom companions with no hint of sexual tension whatsoever?"

There was the nasty little smile again. "Stories about the two of you committing indecent acts in the bathroom at Denny's."

"What?"

"And the photo booth at the mall. And the Sanderson crypt at Oak View Cemetery."

"Well, that's just in poor taste," I complained. "None of those stories is true, either."

"You wouldn't be the first young vampiress that Dick Cheney has . . . charmed," she said, her smile fading.

"I haven't been charmed," I insisted. "My relationship with Dick is nothing more than a budding friendship based on ridiculously inappropriate banter. Where is all this stuff coming from? Why am I suddenly the Lindsay Lohan of the vampire set?"

Ophelia shrugged. "If they behave themselves, new vampires slip unnoticed from one group to the other, quietly accepted by the vampire community. But you seem to have an enemy. Someone is trying to keep you alienated from other vampires, to keep them suspicious of you. I can't track the rumors back to a specific source; it's always something heard from a friend of a friend of a friend, which is typical for the Hollow. Did stories like this follow you around when you were living?"

"No. I mean, other than the typical mean girl stuff in school. Mary Rose Davis accused me of pleasuring our school football team with the aid of Jell-O products, but she was just angry that I beat her for Beta Club treasurer." Ophelia obviously was not prepared for this mental image and did not respond. "Oh, and Craig Arnold told everybody he 'made me a woman' in the back of his pickup after Homecoming. The truth was he was finished before he could get my panty hose down, and then he threw up on my dress. But he told everybody in our grade he'd given me the ride of my life . . . oh, and that I was frigid and lay there like a dead fish."

Ophelia glared, tilting her head at me. "I'm sorry, was that an attempt at bonding with me because I appear to be a teenager?"

I sighed. "Generally, I was well liked when I was alive. Not exactly popular but certainly not the target of slander and possible public execution. And I haven't had any run-ins with anybody since I was turned, except, of course, Walter."

"Until you can figure out who might wish you harm, I would advise you to keep a low profile. Avoid situations that can be misconstrued. Don't give us a reason to question your actions further."

"But if you know I can lie to you, if you don't believe any of this, why am I still being investigated?" I asked.

"Because the council answers to higher authorities in the vampire community. Even if we cannot supply real justice, we have to give the impression that we're trying. Otherwise, the delicate balance of power we have built since the Coming Out will topple down on our heads."

"So I'm a cautionary tale?"

"In a word, yes."

"I'll be good," I promised.

"Excellent. Good night," she said, pinching my cheek in an extremely patronizing manner. She turned on her high heel and walked toward the door.

"Can I ask one more question?"

"Good night." She continued out the door without looking back.

"Well, that was cryptic and unhelpful," I muttered, walking around the counter to the mini-fridge where Mr. Wainwright happily stocked a supply of Faux Type O for me. I drank it cold, which gave it a sort of rusty aftertaste, but I was too distracted to try to find the microwave.

My genetic propensity toward denial was just keen enough to allow me to put off connecting the nighttime visitors to my house, the car vandalism, the attempted dog poisoning, and now these unholy rumors about me being the sluttiest vampire since Elvira, Mistress of the Dark. And sitting there, propped against the counter, drinking my frigid fake dinner, I finally allowed myself to mull over the circumstances that had led me here.

Fact: Bud McElray was still out there somewhere.

I didn't know if Bud was aware that he'd shot me, and even if he was, I doubted he would march into the sheriff's department to confess to driving drunk (again) and shooting some poor roadside bystander. But maybe he remembered just enough through his drunken haze, doubled back to find my car the next day, and figured out whom he'd shot.

From what I knew of Bud, he would have no qualms about poisoning an innocent dog or using blood to paint antifeminist slurs on a car. Maybe he'd recognized that I was a vampire since I survived and I was not showing up in the daytime anymore. Maybe he was trying to intimidate me so I wouldn't go to the police.

That was an awful lot of maybes. And I doubted that Bud had that many gossipy contacts to spread vicious lies within the vampire world.

Moving on.

Fact: This could be some elaborate plot on Jenny's part to get rid of me and move into River Oaks.

Far-fetched? Sure. Jenny didn't have any contacts in the vampire world, as far as I knew. But she was always doing that sales-party/social-networking stuff. There was no telling whom she'd come into contact with. And the woman idolized Martha Stewart. God only knew what she was capable of.

But if she was going to paint "BLOODSUCKING WHORE" on my car, Jenny would have probably used a whimsical font and subdued matte craft paint.

Fact: I didn't know anything about Andrea Byrne beyond what she had told me.

As much as I hated to suspect a new friend, it was Andrea who suggested going to the Cellar in the first place. Did I really keep track of how much she drank that night? Was the snuggly-drunk routine an act? Gabriel said vampires kept pets. Could Andrea be an operative planted by a vampire to torment me? If I could control my stupid mind-reading powers, I would know.

The question was what vampire would want to torment me.

Fact: Gabriel could have turned me just so he could play creepy James Spader mind-games with me.

I chose not to explore that last one.

Mama was master of the "psychological reset." It went something like this: We'd have an argument. I'd hurt her feelings (or I'd disobey a direct order, pretty much the same thing). She'd sulk for a while and refuse to speak to me until I apologized. Eventually, she'd realize that I was not going to apologize. Then she'd just breeze back into my life as if the disagreement never happened. And we'd be right back where we started.

It was infuriating. It was toxic. It was evil. But damned if it wasn't extremely effective. How do you continue an argument with someone who claims to have no memory of the argument ever happening? That was why I could not comfortably watch *Gaslight*.

So, I wasn't exactly surprised the next Monday night when Mama breezed into my kitchen just before dusk, all smiles and sweetness. She didn't bother to knock, but why would she? It was only my house. She and Grandma Ruthie had this whole thing about the "doors of River Oaks never being closed to an Early."

I had to get some thicker doors.

Fortunately, I had woken up insanely early when

Fitz howled at the approach of some Jehovah's Witnesses. That avoided the "Why are you sleeping through the afternoon?" questions. In the unfortunate column, I was experimenting with a synthetic-blood breakfast smoothie. I had a combination of Faux Type O, protein powder, Undying Health vitamin solution, iron supplements, a frozen pink-lemonade mixer, and orange juice in my blender. I was putting the blood back into the fridge when she walked in. I snapped the door shut and dropped a dish towel over my copy of the *Guide for the Newly Undead*.

"Hi, Mama. What—what are you doing here?"

"Do I need a reason to drop by?" Mama asked, peering into the blender. "What are you making?"

"It's a health shake," I said, hitting the frappe button before she noticed the streaks of red. The resulting mixture was a garish vermillion that practically screamed, "There's fake blood in here!"

Mama pinched my cheek as the blender whirred. "Honey, you might want to think about a new shade of makeup. This one makes you look awfully pale. You know, your cousin Junie just started doing Mary Kay. She could come over and show you how to make yourself up properly. She's been looking for someone to practice her at-home demonstrations on."

"I don't think I want makeup tips from a day-shift dancer at the Booby Hatch." I shook my head as I let the blender grind to halt. "But thanks."

Mama ignored me in her special way as I poured some smoothie into a glass. "Your daddy mentioned you turned down pizza the other night. You're not going on some weird vegetarian diet, are you? I don't want you going anemic on me. It would explain why you're so pasty."

I laughed. "No, I'm definitely not a vegetarian. This is very good for me. Lots of vitamins, minerals, see?" I took a big sip. "Mmmm."

Mama arched a brow and took the glass and sniffed.

"Mama, I wouldn't—"

Before I could stop her, she'd brought the glass to her lips and taken a sip. All right, I probably could have stopped her with my lightning-fast reflexes. But I kind of wanted to see if she would actually do it. There was nothing in there that could hurt her.

Fine, fine, I let my mother drink fake blood. I was going to hell.

"Oh, my, that's awful!" she said, gagging as she swallowed.

"There's a lot of iron in it," I said, taking the glass back and draining its contents. "It takes a while to get used to it."

"Well, I'll just dump it out while you're getting dressed," she said, pouring the contents of the blender into the sink.

"What would I get dressed for?"

"I thought we could all go out for a nice dinner," she said brightly, pushing me toward the den.

"We all?" I arched an eyebrow at her.

Mama marched me into the den, where my older sister and Grandma Ruthie where checking over the contents of my china cabinet.

"Oh, boy." I sighed, prompting Grandma to bobble the little china cow she was holding. Jenny's lip curled instinctively at the sight of me and my sloppy PJs. She was wearing pressed white linen slacks and a peach scoop-neck sweater paired with Grandma's heirloom pearls. Pearls that had been Aunt Jettie's until I foolishly left Grandma unsupervised during Jettie's funeral luncheon at River Oaks.

I declined to sit across from them as they made themselves comfortable on my couch. Frankly, it was a better defensive position to have them looking up at me.

"Jane." Grandma Ruthie sniffed, toying with her purse strap. "I haven't seen you in so long I hardly recognize you. Have you put on a few pounds?"

Was that two or three insults in one shot? Sometimes I lost track. I offered a thin-lipped smile but said nothing. I think we can all agree this was the wisest course of action.

"Now, Mama," my own mother warned in a tone that would ultimately do nothing to stop Grandma Ruthie.

Mama had her moments, but she was a rank amateur in terms of good old-fashioned offspring manipulation compared with my Grandma Ruthie. Guilt and passive-aggression were Grandma Ruthie's weapons of choice, all wrapped up in pastel dress suits and a cloud of White Shoulders. Miss a Sunday dinner at her house, she developed a debilitating migraine. Go to the movies with a boy she didn't approve of, and she ended up in the hospital with chest pains. Announce you were planning to study library science instead of elementary education, as she had planned for you, she checked herself in for exploratory surgery. All the while, she moaned from underneath her soothing gel eye mask that she "doesn't want to be a burden" with all of her demands, but "who knows how long I have left?"

Jettie appeared near the window, surveying the little tableau we presented and grinning from ear to ear. "And it's not even my birthday."

Aunt Jettie danced over to the china cabinet a few feet behind Jenny and Grandma and began levitating various bric-a-brac over their heads. Fortunately, Mama was rearranging the photos on my mantel to keep hers at the forefront, so she didn't notice. I clenched my jaw and shook my head at my ghostly great-aunt, who was making spooky "Ooooooo" noises that nobody else could hear.

Jenny, who had obviously been waiting patiently for this opportunity, was unaware of the candlestick floating over her head. She quirked her carefully painted lips (which matched her twin set) and said, "So, Mama says you haven't gotten another job yet."

If I corrected her and said anything about my new job, it would only prolong their visit, so I shrugged it off. "Daddy says you repainted your kitchen."

"How are you going to pay the bills? You know, the taxes on River Oaks are coming up soon," she said, trying her hardest to be nonchalant. "If you can't pay them, you can always come to Kent and me for a loan."

I narrowed my eyes at my sister. Same old Jenny. The same Jenny who refused to let me touch her pep-squad pom-poms because I'd "mess them up." The same Jenny who picked our second cousin to be a bridesmaid over me because everyone else in her wedding party was thin and blond, and she didn't want me to "stick out." Well, screw the same old Jenny.

"I'd rather roll naked over broken glass and dive into a pool full of lemon juice, but thanks," I said, smiling back. "Besides, Junie said there are some shifts opening up at the Booby Hatch. I thought I'd give that a try."

Mama gasped and turned, prompting Jettie to drop the candlestick behind the couch with a thud.

No one noticed, because Grandma Ruthie loudly demanded, "You know what your problem is, Jane?"

"No, but if I had a couple of hours, I'm sure you'd tell me."

"You're too full of yourself." She sniffed. "Always have been. I've never understood what you thought was so special about you—"

"Why don't you just go get dressed, honey, and we'll wait down here?" Mama asked, her voice desperately cheerful.

"I wasn't finished, Sherry," Grandma Ruthie said.

Behind her back, Aunt Jettie muttered, "The minute she's finally 'finished,' that's when we'll know to call the undertaker."

"Well, what about selling the house?" Jenny asked, irked that the conversation had strayed from her agenda. "You don't need all the space to yourself. I have two growing boys. We need the room. And it's just impractical for you to have all this room now that you're broke."

"I'm not selling you the house so you can raise those two wolverines you call children here." I rolled my eyes. "Honestly, Jenny, you're about as subtle as a sack of hammers. And I'm not broke. So just back off."

"Jane, how about getting dressed?" Mama asked again. Her voice was desperate now. "We'll need to hurry if we're going to get a table."

"Mama, I can't. Really, I can't."

"And why not?" Mama cried, eyeing my pajamas, which were decorated with little goldfish. "What could be so important that you can't drag yourself away to spend a little time with family? I haven't seen you in weeks. And it's not like you have a busy schedule without working."

"I am working! OK?" I exclaimed. "I've had a job for almost a week now."

Oh, crap.

"What?" Mama demanded, her face paling. "How could you not tell me you have a new job? You know how worried I am about you! How could you not do something as simple as pick up the phone to tell me you got a job? And where, if I'm allowed to ask, are you working?"

"It's a little book boutique, very specialized, in the old downtown area. You probably haven't seen it before."

Mama scoffed. "Well, excuse me for not having the sophisticated tastes in books that you do."

Jettie circled Mama, shaking her head. "You really shouldn't have told her, Jane. It's going to make them stay longer."

"I know," I ground out through clenched teeth.

"Jane! What a hurtful thing to say!" Mama exclaimed.

For a moment, I lost track of the various conversations. "Wait, what?"

"Now, I think you need to just go upstairs and get dressed." Mama sighed, plucking at my pajama top. "I don't think it's too much to ask for you to join your family for a simple meal. You know, your Grandma Ruthie only has so much time left."

"Mama, I can't go out with you tonight."

"Why not?" she demanded.

"Because I—" I looked up, in the hopes that a plausible excuse would be written on the ceiling, I suppose. Monday night—what could I be doing on a Monday night? If I said I had plans with Zeb, Mama would tell me I could see him anytime. I couldn't say, "Date with Gabriel," because Mama would demand to see him.

"Um, a party!" I cried, peering through the kitchen door and spotting Missy's card stuck to my fridge. "I've been invited to a cocktail party tonight."

"Who would invite you to a cocktail party?" Jenny asked, eyeing me suspiciously. Even without telepathy, I could tell what she was thinking: Who would invite me to a cocktail party but not her?

"It's just a networking thing." I smiled and winked at Jenny. "You know, all of the Hollow's best and brightest young professionals, getting together, making connections, swapping numbers."

OK, it sort of sounded like a swingers' cocktail party when I put it like that. Jenny's lips disappeared as if she'd eaten a persimmon, though, so it was worth it.

"Well, I'm so glad!" Mama cried, patting my back. "It's wonderful that your new job has you socializing."

"You know what they say about jobs that involve socializing," Grandma Ruthie said under her breath. From behind her, Aunt Jettie slapped the back of her head. Grandma cried out and turned to look for what had hit her. I snickered. Jenny shot me an annoyed look.

This wasn't turning out to be such a bad visit after all.

Mama turned on me, hands on hips, asking, "So, what are you going to wear?"

Oh, crap.

17

Never leave a vampire social gathering without thanking your host. A faux pas like this can lead to feuds lasting hundreds of years.

—From *The Guide for the Newly Undead*

It took another hour and fourteen outfits before I could get everyone out the door and get ready for the party. I'd decided to actually attend, since (a) it would get Missy off my back, and (b) Mama was likely to swing back by the house to see if I really left or not.

I knew that Ophelia had told me to stay home, keep a low profile, but if nothing else, attending the party would prevent further "Oh, come on, shug!" calls from Missy. Also, I kind of wanted to see what the gossipy undead would say about me to my face.

Besides, Jenny and Grandma had a wonderful time "helping me," perched on my bed, picking each and every outfit apart. The pink dress made my ankles look chunky. The yellow sweater made me look sallow. The green jacket made my shoulders look like a linebacker's.

I finally agreed to Mama's chosen outfit—a navy-blue

dress I'd had since high school, complete with a white sailor's collar—just to get them out of the house. And then I ran back upstairs to put on black slacks and a soft blue cashmere sweater that Aunt Jettie had bought for me on my last birthday. Touched by the gesture, Jettie agreed to stick around the house that night, just in case Jenny and Grandma returned to help themselves to the silver.

Missy lived in a brand-new subdivision called Deer Haven, in an unassuming little two-story ranch house that looked exactly like the twenty-seven unassuming little two-story ranch houses on the same street, most of which were empty. It was easy to find the party, as Missy's place was surrounded by cars. From the front door, I could hear smooth jazz piano and people chattering and laughing. Before I died, my idea of a good party had involved an ice cream cake. Somehow, I doubted that would be offered at this soiree.

Before I could register someone coming to the door, Missy had it open and was squealing in greeting. "Jane, I'm so glad you could make it!"

I just said, "Here I am."

I'd brought a bottle of merlot that a library patron had given me for Christmas as a hostess gift, because I figured Missy would be into that sort of thing. Fortunately, I'd remembered to remove the gift tag. As I handed it over, Missy cooed, "Oh, shug, you didn't need to do that. Come on in."

Missy hooked her arm through mine and steered me into the foyer. The walls were sponged a subtle beige.

There was a maple table with a bowl full of business cards and a votive of roses. Beyond the living room was a huge, airy, and empty kitchen decorated in a rustic Tuscan motif. It was obvious the kitchen was never used and, given Missy's dietary habits, never would be. About thirty vampires were circulating pleasantly in the living room, admiring Missy's collection of blown-glass sculptures, all of which looked vaguely anatomical to me.

These were definitely newer vampires. There was no mystery here, no mystique. They were all cheerful and shiny and clean-cut. Some of the guys were wearing polo shirts, for goodness sake. They still seemed remotely human, as if they were clinging to remnants of their former lives. I kind of liked them.

"Now, y'all know the rules!" Missy lectured in a preschool teacher's tone, dragging me through the crowd. I bumped into several people, sloshing their drinks. Missy seemed oblivious to this. "A few minutes of chat, exchange business cards, and move on! We want to meet as many people as possible, don't we?"

Missy handed me a frosty cocktail glass, glittering with ice and mint, led me around the room, and forced me into several introductions. Everyone else was prefaced by their profession—Joan the vampire party planner or Ben the vampire tax attorney—or the brilliant things they were doing with radio advertising or blood brokering. I was introduced as "Jane Jameson, she used to be a librarian." Or "You must know Jane, she's Gabriel Nightengale's childe." It felt like the time Mama dragged me around the Girl Scout campout, determined that I would have the most signatures in my friendship book. The words "Stay sweet, have a great summer" still make my stomach turn.

And much as at that third-grade campout, I was not a hit at the cocktail party. At first, the undead movers and shakers were thrilled to meet me, but as soon as my name was mentioned, their lips twisted into snide little grins. They'd smirk and ask me about the price of a Grand Slam or tell me they'd heard the tombs over at St. Joseph's offered great leverage. As soon as Missy pulled me away from one group, they'd snicker and bend their heads together to talk about me as if I couldn't hear them. Some of the female vampires seemed downright hostile when Missy told them who I was.

I could only guess that they were former "acquaintances" of Dick's and had heard the Denny's bathroom story.

If Missy noticed the insults, she certainly didn't show it. That bright "success" smile stayed plastered on her face, even as one particularly snarky vampire HR manager told me he was surprised to see me socializing with Missy, since he'd heard I didn't get along very well with Dick Cheney.

"No, we're actually good friends. I really like Dick."

"Yes, dear, I'm sure you do—like dick." He snickered.

"Well, I walked right into that one, didn't I?" I muttered as Missy gave a tinkling laugh and introduced me to her good friend, the vampire dental hygienist.

And so it continued for almost an hour. I got past the point of embarrassment or even irritation and merely thanked the stars that Ophelia wasn't there to do an "I told you so" dance. It was clear that I would not be welcome in polite vampire society—or even this vampire society—for some time. And from what I had seen tonight, I wasn't missing much. I just wanted to go home, take off my uncomfortable shoes, and burn the business cards that had been stuffed into my hand.

By the time I met a sharply dressed antiques dealer named Hadley Wexler, I had prepared myself for the worst, when Missy said, "You must get to know Jane Jameson. She lives in River Oaks, that fabulous house out off County Line Road."

"Oh, really?" Hadley smiled, showing perfect, even white fangs in a smile that was actually friendly. "I'd love to get a look inside that place. I've always thought it's a shame it's not on the historical tour. Anytime you're interested in selling some of the family dust collectors, you just let me know."

"I'll keep it in mind," I promised, thinking of the hair ball Jenny would cough up if I sold so much as a thimble from our great-great-aunt's sewing basket. It might be worth it.

Hadley and I chatted pleasantly for a minute on the difficulties of sorting through old family collections. Then she sipped her mojito and spluttered a little. "Wait, Jane Jameson? Oh, yes, I've heard of you." Her nose wrinkled in distaste. "Shouldn't you be off somewhere striking matches?"

I gave an awkward little laugh. "Excuse me?"

"You know, creatures like you give vampires a bad

name. Some of us are just trying to live our unlives here. But then you go and start killing your own kind because you think, 'Oh, I'm a vampire, I guess I have to do something evil today.'"

Missy giggled gaily and quickly led me away. "You have to watch Hadley. She gets a bit snippy when her iron gets low."

"I think I just need to go, Missy. It was really nice of you to invite me, but between the Walter thing and the Dick stories, I'm just not going to be able to connect in the way I think you want me to. By the way, Dick and I are just friends."

"Oh, honey, don't say another word." She clucked, holding both of my arms in a sisterly clench. She shot me a sympathetic look and shook her head. "And don't worry, I don't believe a word of it. I mean, you're hardly his type."

It took me a second to realize I'd been insulted.

"It's just going to take a little longer to fit in with the new crowd, that's all," she assured me. "You know, it might help if you were a little more closely connected to the community. I have a lot of places here in Deer Haven still available. It's a very vamp-friendly neighborhood, close to the shopping district. I'd be happy to show you something in your price range. A lot of the vampires here tonight are going to be moving in soon, so you'd already know some of your neighbors. Besides, it must be awfully lonely rattling around that old house by yourself. We don't want you to become some undead cliché, now, do we, honey?"

I surveyed the room in all of its prefab splendor and realized I'd rather set *myself* on fire than live near any of these vampires. And the house creeped me out. It was sterile, artificial, like silk flowers on a grave. Missy had technically never "lived" there, and it showed. River Oaks might have the occasional roof leak and mold issues, but at least I was comfortable there. I knew the history of every room. I had memories there, a legacy. I couldn't just give it up to live in a perfectly decorated little box.

"Wow, you can take the Realtor to a party—"

"But she'll still be a Realtor." Missy giggled and took another sip of her drink. She gave a cheery little wave to a guest who passed by.

"I'm really happy at River Oaks. It's sort of a family-responsibility thing. I couldn't just give it up. But thanks."

She gave an apologetic little shrug. "Well, you can't blame me for trying. Your aunt Jettie felt the same way. But if you ever change your mind, you let me know, OK? I could find a really nice place for you, something more suited to your needs. Now, I should probably see to some of the other guests. Just stay a little while longer, please? I want to see you mixing and mingling, all right? Good girl."

Missy wandered into the crowd and left me staring at an orange glass sculpture that looked like a foot. God, I hoped it was a foot. Without the social buffer Missy provided, I was left standing in the middle of the room, looking at other vampires' backs. I wandered into the kitchen and appreciated the enormous decorative bottles of vegetables preserved in olive oil. I finished off my drink and calculated the amount of time I had to stay before I could politely catapult myself out the front door.

Through the sliding glass door, on the back deck, I saw a tall, lanky vampire in blue jeans and a plaid cowboy shirt leaning against the railing. Dick looked terminally bored. Whom Missy thought he was going to "network with" at this shindig, I had no idea. The fact that he was probably enjoying himself less than I was was some consolation, considering it was possible that he was telling people he'd done dirty *bendy* things to me. Since no one was paying any attention to me, I didn't think it would hurt my reputation further if I talked to him.

Dick turned away from the moonlit, perfectly manicured lawn and took a long pull from his beer bottle as I slid the glass door open. "Hey there, Stretch."

"Do you mind telling me why there are stories circulating about you and me committing indecent acts in the photo booth at the mall?"

Dick snickered. "That's funny. I heard it was the bathroom at Denny's."

"You knew?" I smacked his arm, using the closed-fist "frogging" technique Jenny used to use on me.

"Ow!" he yelled. "Yes, I knew. Missy told me she's heard it from a bunch of people! And then some ass-hat tax attorney in there asked if it was true that you had 'exotic piercings.'" As my face contorted in alternate waves of disbelief and nausea, he assured me, "I told him no!"

"You knew people were saying those things about me,

and you didn't do anything?" I cried. "You couldn't have told me that your girlfriend knew?"

"They were saying those things about me, too!" he exclaimed, laughing as he halfheartedly fended off my blows. "You don't hear me complaining."

"People say those things about you all the time." I grunted, hitting him again.

"Well, yes, but I'm used to getting credit for the bad things I've actually done, not just things I've thought about."

"Do you have any idea who would say stuff like this?"

"You mean, besides me, because it would really piss off Gabriel?"

"It's not you, though, right? Because I *would* have to hurt you."

Dick reached into a little blue Coleman cooler and pulled out a beer for me. "It's not me, but only because I hadn't thought of it. I wouldn't get all worked up about it, Stretch. I mean, all of these vampires don't have anything better to do than sit around gossiping like a bunch of old fishwives. It'll blow over as soon as someone else lands on their radar. Just ignore it."

I used the deck railing to pop off the cap and clink the bottle against his. "This has been an extremely crappy week."

"Well, tell your good friend Dick all about it," he said, patting a spot on the railing. "It'll keep me from having to talk to any of those yuppie freaks in there."

"What are you even doing here?" I asked. "I thought

you and Missy had one of those 'no strings' friends-with-benefits things going."

"Me, too," he said, pursing his lips. "I don't know what happened. She called and told me about our spin on the rumor mill. And she started pouting and fussing, and before I knew it, I was apologizing. For things I hadn't even done! And then, to make it up to her, she made me promise I'd come to this thing tonight. She talked in circles until I don't even remember most of the conversation. She is a hell of a salesman."

"Saleswoman," I corrected.

"Whatever. All I know is, I'm not allowed to take my beer into the house because Missy says it doesn't match the theme. Which is just fine with me. And now you're here, so the evening's not a total waste."

"Well, thanks."

"So, how are you and Captain Gloom and Doom getting along?"

"If you're referring to Gabriel, we're getting along just fine, thank you."

"Haven't done the deed yet, huh?"

"Wh-what kind of question is that?" I gasped. "Oh, is this one of those smell things again? Because that's just gross."

"No, it's not a smell issue, even though you downright reek of his manly sobriety. I can tell because you're still capable of humor. What's wrong? Is Gabriel too prim and proper to get beyond a good-night handshake?"

"I am not going to talk about this with you!" I exclaimed.

"Why not? If you're not going to let me see you naked, we might as well be girlfriends."

"You're a twisted little man."

"Come on, Stretch, share with the class."

"No!" I laughed.

"Prude."

"Perv."

"Schoolmarm."

"Some other word that essentially means perv."

We were laughing when Missy decided to join us out on the porch. "I figured I'd find you two out here together," she said brightly. "Jane, you have to promise you're going to come to my next mixer. Everybody wants to know if you're coming. You're like the vampire Jessica Simpson! They can't understand why they're interested in you, but they can't stand not knowing what you are going to do next. You have some serious buzz going in there. I bet you start getting all kinds of business at your little shop."

"Well, on that note, I think I'm going to call it a night."

Missy grabbed my arm. "Are you sure, shug? We're going to start playing Jenga pretty soon!"

"Well, as much as I love games that combine alcohol with fine-motor skills, I think I'll pass." I shot a wink at Dick, who was standing behind Missy, giving me a pleading look. "Dick, enjoy the Jenga."

I slid the glass door open and was met with silence over jazz. Ever walk into a room and realize that someone has suddenly stopped talking because they were saying something bad about you? Ever had it happen in a roomful of vampires? Most of the guests pretended to be absorbed in their drinks or played with their cocktail napkins as they tried to contain their snickers. Others, including Hadley Wexler, just stared at me as if they hoped I would spontaneously combust as some sort of party trick.

"Well, good night, all," I said, smiling pleasantly and winding my way through silent, motionless bodies. I closed the front door behind me and heard conversation rumble back to life.

I walked quickly toward Big Bertha, eager to put as much distance between myself and Missy's snotty vampire friends as possible. As soon as I reached for the door handle, the driver's-side window exploded in front of me. I stood, dumbfounded, as little slivers of glass rained at my feet. A few seconds later, I heard several faint hiss-pops and felt hot, stabbing agony in my left shoulder, my lower back, my ribs. I fell to the ground as another bullet shattered Big Bertha's rear window. Blood slowly trickled down my arms, soaking my clothes as I scanned the silent row of houses.

Even with my night vision, I couldn't tell where the shots were coming from. While the pain of the wounds faded quickly, I experienced some residual panic, leftover sensations from the night I was turned. My hands shook, and my mind wouldn't clear. I couldn't focus enough to figure out how to open the car door. My thoughts spooled on a loop through my head—had to flee, get to safety, get home.

If anyone inside Missy's house heard anything amiss, they weren't making any move to come outside and help me. Against the yellow light of the closed window shades, I saw silhouettes of people talking, laughing. The music played on. Somehow I didn't think I would find help if I ran back inside.

Whoever was pulling the trigger had stopped shooting. When my legs steadied, I jumped over Big Bertha's hood, using her massive body as cover as I frantically searched with numb, clumsy fingers. I climbed into the front seat and slumped down as I started the ignition. As calmly as possible, I sped down the street toward home.

18

Sexual relationships can prove difficult after turning but no more difficult than they are for the living.

—From *The Guide for the Newly Undead*

Note to self: Bullet wounds tend to itch when you're conscious during the healing process.

With Aunt Jettie floating helplessly by the tub, wringing her hands, I washed away the dried blood and inspected the wounds. If she'd been living, I probably would have scared ten years off her life when I stumbled, bloodied and cursing, through the front door. Unsure of how to help me, she disappeared upstairs and ran a bath, while I staggered toward the fridge and glugged down three bottles of synthetic blood. As the thick, sweetened plasma rolled down my throat, the nausea and dizziness faded away. I was able to crawl up the stairs.

I'd been shot in the shoulder, near my right kidney, and a few inches left of the base of my spine. It stung considerably, especially when the healing tissue forced the small-caliber bullets out of my wounds. But at least

I knew I didn't have Bud McElray's rifle shot floating around in my gut.

I'd given Bud quite a bit of thought during the drive home from Missy's. Now, as I sat in lukewarm pink water, draining another blood bottle of its contents, I kicked myself for not at least checking on Bud's whereabouts since the *first* shooting. I'd been far too passive through the whole ordeal, waiting for it to just go away, hoping it would stop if I ignored it. As the only person who'd ever shot at me, he was now the prime suspect in every weird incident over the last couple of months. And now I wanted to give him the whuppin' he thoroughly deserved. I wasn't entirely sure if (a) I could find him, and (b) I could get away with it.

I changed the water in the tub twice and still didn't feel clean. I could still smell blood on every inch of my skin, sending the synthetic stuff in my stomach roiling. At the sound of a fist pounding on my front door, I ran to my room without bothering to towel off and threw on a bra and underwear. If Bud McElray was going to take another shot at me, I wasn't going to be naked when he did it.

"Jane?" Gabriel called from my porch. "Are you home?"

Relieved, I threw on my robe and padded down the stairs. I was about to throw my arms around him and tell him the whole sorry tale when he barged through the door. "Why am I hearing rumors that you and Dick have had an intimate knowledge of each other in the dressing rooms at Wal-Mart?"

I groaned, pulling at the soaked robe as it clung clammily to my skin. "So, we're at the Wal-Mart now?"

Gabriel blanched. "What?"

"Don't worry about it. None of it's true."

"No, I do believe I—" He sniffed the air. "Why do I smell blood? Your blood?"

Given the way Gabriel's fists were clenching and unclenching, I wasn't sure I should tell him. Sensing my hesitation, Gabriel took my chin in his palm and made me meet his gaze.

I sighed, turned my back, and dropped the robe. "Someone shot at me as I was leaving a party earlier."

"Why would someone shoot at you?" he demanded, roughly pulling me closer to inspect my healing skin. "Normal bullets wouldn't be enough to kill you."

"No, but it annoyed the bejesus out of me," I grumbled, yanking my robe back together. "I haven't been entirely honest with you about some things that have happened around here lately. Someone's been hanging around outside my house at night. Someone used deer blood to paint insults on my car. They tried to poison Fitz with antifreeze. And then, obviously, tonight someone shot me. Again."

"Why didn't you tell me?" he asked, his voice dangerously soft. "Jane, if anything happened to you . . ."

"I hoped it would just go away. I thought maybe it was some weirdo antivamp crazy who wanted to make me uncomfortable. But now, this combined with Walter's being set on fire, I think the guy who shot me the first time, Bud McElray, is trying to scare me or finish the job or something. I don't know what to do. Can I complain to the human authorities? Do I go to Ophelia and tell on him—" I saw Gabriel's face grow tense at the mention of Bud's name. "What?"

Gabriel grimaced. "You haven't read your paper lately, have you?"

"Besides want ads? Not really," I admitted. "Why?"

He went into my kitchen and shuffled through the old *Half-Moon Herald*s in my recycling bin until he found what he wanted. He handed the news section to me.

"Half-Moon Resident Killed in Hunting Mishap," I read aloud from a front page dated two weeks before. "Half-Moon Hollow native Bud McElray died Tuesday when the deer stand he was climbing collapsed, bringing a thirty-two-foot oak tree down on top of him. Coroner Don Purdue described the cause of death as multiple blunt-trauma injuries, including a broken spine, fractured skull, and massive internal bleeding. Purdue added that several empty beer bottles were found around the fallen tree. He said it would take several weeks for toxicology tests to determine whether there were drugs or alcohol present in McElray's system."

Let's see, the man who mortally wounded me with a hunting rifle while drunk was killed in a freak accident on a deer stand that he was too drunk to climb. That wasn't suspicious.

"Jane, Bud McElray can't be the person who shot you, and he's not the one who's been harassing you. He's been dead for weeks."

"I swear I didn't do it," I said, dropping the paper. "It wasn't me."

"Of course, it wasn't you. Trees fall. Mr. McElray had the bad luck of standing under it at the time."

"And that doesn't strike you as . . . convenient?" I asked.

"No." He snorted. "It was a terrible inconvenience to push a very heavy tree on top of Mr. McElray."

I gaped at him, the salty-sweet gorge of faux blood rising in my throat. "You killed him," I whispered.

He sat there, still as stone, as he stared at me. Looking back, this may have been Gabriel's way of saying, "Duh!"

"*Say* something!" I yelled. "You can't just tell me how *inconvenient* it was to shove a tree on top of a living human being and then not say anything. Please tell me—just say something."

"He hurt you," Gabriel said, his eyes flashing silver even in the dim light. "He left you to die like some animal and just went on living his life."

"He thought I *was* an animal! How could you do that? You weren't trying to feed or to defend yourself." I whimpered, shrinking away. "You murdered him."

"And you would have let him live?" He followed me into the living room, clearly irked that I didn't appreciate what was probably considered a romantic gesture in the vampire world. "You would have let him go unpunished for what he did? Let him hurt other innocent people?"

"I will not pretend that I'm sad to see Bud McElray

dead," I admitted. "A part of me hates him for what he did to me. I'm glad that he will never be able to hurt anyone else. But I wouldn't have had any human die that way. It's cruel and vicious, and it's beneath you, Gabriel, with all your noble-creature-of-the-night bullshit. Don't you dare think you did this for me. Plus, I'm already suspected of setting other vampires on fire. I don't need a human murder charge on my head. Did you even think about that?"

"No one will connect it to you, because no one knows McElray was responsible for shooting you," he said. "There was never any report, any evidence."

Damned if he didn't have a point there. So, instead of following logic, I demanded, "Why wait until now?"

"I gave him time to forget what had happened, if he even remembered it in the first place. I watched him. I let him settle back into his drunken useless wasted life and when he least expected anything, I extinguished it."

His voice, the absence of passion or any sort of feeling about the fact that he had snuffed out a human life, chilled me to my marrow. My hands began to shake. I bunched them into fists, flexing the fingers to try to pump warmth into the joints. "What about me makes you think I would be OK with that? What makes you think I would find that acceptable? What happened to not taking the things humans do personally, taking the good with the bad?"

"This is different."

"How is it different?" I demanded.

"He hurt you!" Gabriel shouted, stepping closer to

me. I backed away, but he pursued me, backing me up against the edge of my writing desk. "He left you to die. What about me makes you think I would find that acceptable?"

"Back off." I shoved him away. Well, I tried. He was pretty much unmovable. "He didn't *know* he'd shot me, Gabriel. He wasn't an evil man, just a stupid drunk who didn't know any better. No matter what kind of person he was, he was still human. And you've made me responsible for his death. You said you didn't want to give me experiences to regret, but this is a big fricking regret."

"I know you're upset. But I hope that someday you will understand why I did this. You will understand what you mean to me. I will do anything to keep you safe, anything."

He reached for me. For the first time since I'd known him, he looked unsure, unsteady—probably because I slapped his hands away. "Don't touch me. Just get away from me."

He seemed vaguely amused by this. "You haven't minded me touching you in the past. In fact—"

Even as I punched him in the mouth, I couldn't believe I'd done it. For one, the deep scrape of Gabriel's fangs against my knuckles was excruciating. And two, I'd never really hit anyone before and meant it, besides the usual sibling brawls and the unfortunate Walter encounter.

Gabriel sprawled across the floor, sliding across the polished wood until he hit a wall. I was this close to helping him up and apologizing profusely when he snarled up at me. Which just made me hit him again. I think I had some anger issues I needed to work out.

My fangs extended, nicking my lip. The taste of my own blood only stoked my temper, tingeing the edges of my vision a hot, glossy crimson.

The shock of his spastic childe being coordinated enough to land a blow had plainly disoriented Gabriel. As he stumbled to his feet, I flew at him and knocked him back down. I kicked him again, but he swept an arm out and knocked my legs from under me. From my position on the floor, I kicked at him as he rose, pushing him against the wall. But as I tried to gain advantage, he used my momentum to slam me against the wall instead.

"Good. Good." He hissed, pinning my wrists. "This is what we are, Jane. This isn't some fairy story. It's not one of your books. You could pretend you didn't know this was in your nature, but you'd be lying to yourself and to me. You've known ever since the night you rose. You've sensed it under the surface. We're predators, Jane. We hunt, and we feed, and we kill."

I strained against his grip, but he was too strong, slapping my useless hands against the plaster. He smirked as he drew in for a kiss, then seemed to think better of it, unsure whether I would chew on him—in the bad way.

"You talk too much," I grumbled, seizing his mouth.

There was a pleased purring sound in his chest as his fingers slipped up my wrists and intertwined with mine. He let me shove away from the wall, and we stumbled backward, tripping over my leaded-glass coffee table and sending shards of glass exploding over the floor as we fell.

Gabriel rolled, trapping me between the solid weight of his body and the unyielding floor. His stare pinned me as much as the knees pressed against my thighs. I wanted him without thinking. I didn't care that I had crazy wet hair or that I was wearing underwear featuring cartoon ladybugs. I didn't care if I was kissing him the right way. I didn't care if the sex might be bad. I just wanted.

Still wrapped around him, I used all of the strength in my legs to roll over him, pin him to the floor. His eyes flashed as I strained to keep him held there. He was enjoying this, watching me struggle. My hair curled in wild, damp ropes over my face as I crouched over him, scraping my fingers along the edges of his bared torso.

His palm curled around my chin, forcing me to look him in the eyes. He grinned. He wanted me. He wanted me to touch him, finally to take control. He took my hand in his and pressed it against his chest. He was so smooth. Pale, hairless, and cool as marble, sculpted from years of whatever manual labor a nineteenth-century planter's son performed. I ran my fingertips along the lines of his chest to his sides, giving in to the urge to kiss the skin just below his belly button. The muscles of his abdomen bunched. He was ticklish. That had possibilities.

I chuckled as my hand snaked down his body and wrapped tight around the length of him. His hips bucked, and his eyes widened as he looked down at me. Sensing his shock, I grinned back at him.

Gabriel moaned and pulled me into another kiss

that had me reeling. In the tussle, my robe had come completely off, though somehow the belt was still tied in a tight, damp knot that refused to give. I pulled at it frantically. Gabriel laughed and ripped the material away easily.

He dragged my bra down to my waist, making me shriek when he gently bit the curve of my breast, drawing blood into his mouth the way human men might worship a nipple. He threw me back to the floor, and I cried out as shards of glass sliced into my back. Then Gabriel's good, strong hands found the round weight of my cotton-clad rear and rocked me against him, showing me just how much he wanted me.

Gabriel's lips skimmed my hip bones (my personal Achilles heel), and I let loose a very girlie squeal. I could feel the bow of his smile against my skin as he peeled away my panties. His hands explored lower, and I moaned gibberish as he slipped testing fingers into my warmth.

Gabriel slid between my knees, holding them firmly apart while he played me, stroking and coaxing while I chased his movements with my hips. It had been so long since I'd been touched, and I was shamefully ready. Within moments, I was throwing my head back and screaming his name as I shattered from the inside out. Later, I would take the time to be embarrassed at my hair-trigger response and the fact that I actually whined when he moved his hand away from me. I wrapped my legs around his waist, terrified of losing the sensations he was giving me.

Gabriel chuckled, and, kissing me with a gentleness that seemed impossible given our foreplay activities, he moved into me, testing how much I could take. I grabbed at his hips, needing more. He reared back and sank his fangs into my throat, thrusting up until he was completely inside me.

He drank from my throat as he moved slowly, timing each thrust to draw out the pleasant ache I felt every time he came back to me. I brought his wrist to my lips and sank my teeth into the spot just under his palm, all the while staring him down. It was a dark starburst on the tongue, singing to my senses in a way bottled blood never could. It was the sensation of his blood flooding my system that pushed me over the edge. My fingernails bit into his shoulders as I convulsed around him.

"Mine," he whispered to my skin. "Mine. Mine."

I lay there, boneless and sated, while he began moving in earnest, reaching for his own climax. Each stroke was more forceful, driving me into the floor. Using what strength I had, I pushed back, forcing him to work harder, fight for control. Eyes lit with some awful pride, he finally shook under me. He leaned his forehead against mine as his body stilled.

For a minute, it was almost normal. We lay there, wound around each other, my face resting on his chin. My head was empty, drained of all worries. I didn't care what came next, as long as I was able to feel this way every once in a while. Then I wondered how much it would scare a man to tell him he'd given you your first-ever orgasm achieved with the help of another person. Then I realized we were lying on the broken shards of what used to be my coffee table.

I was stunned by what I'd done. I was a big undead skank. My feelings for Gabriel were a dirty gray miasma of lust, resentment, and the psychotic devotion of a teen-age crush. Add to that the fact that I was still angry with him about his ironic vigilante routine. I couldn't stand what he'd done. He'd killed a man in cold blood. And I'd responded by having sex with him. What sort of degenerate did that make me?

I lay there, the broken glass slicing into my skin, wondering what to do. Did we cuddle? Was I supposed to offer him breakfast? I wasn't exactly well versed in the postcoital ritual of the living, much less that of the undead. I tried to reach out to his mind, pick up any emotion Gabriel might be feeling. Nothing. Stupid inconsistent powers. So I stared at the ceiling and prayed to the good Lord that Gabriel would say something, *anything,* to keep me from having to bridge the uncomfortable silence.

Maybe I could fake going to sleep? Sure, it was 2:34 A.M., the vampire equivalent of midday. But a sexual effort like that deserved a catnap, right? Plus, I'd lost a lot of blood earlier in the evening—

"If you don't get up off the glass, your skin's going to heal over it. It will itch for decades."

That was . . . not what I expected.

He shifted to his feet, shaking debris out of his hair. His skin was ruddier, suffused with my blood. He looked almost tan. That must have been what he looked like in life, minus the splinters of table sticking out of his back.

Gabriel made a hesitant grab for his pants and slid them on. "Are you all right?"

"Don't go all prom date on me, Gabriel," I said, my voice harder than I intended. I got up, leaving a wake of glass tinkling to the floor. I grabbed my robe and yanked it over my back. "My father isn't going to show up on your doorstep with a shotgun and a preacher."

He touched my arm and made me turn to face him. "In light of what's happened, I think you should come stay with me for a while."

"I don't think moving in together is the answer to our problems."

"We don't have problems," Gabriel insisted.

"You killed someone!"

"I killed someone for you!"

"Well, pardon me if I don't think that's going to make it into the next collection of Hallmark cards!" I cried. "And don't think that this changes anything," I growled, fangs creaking to full length. I closed my eyes, tamping my temper down. "We are not back to normal, whatever normal is for us. I'm still—I just don't want to be around you right now. I think you'd better go."

Well, if punching him in the face didn't hurt him, that certainly did. His lips parted, but he pressed them back together, reconsidering saying something that would probably piss me off even more.

"Jane, please, we can talk about this," he said, stepping toward me. When he saw the anguish on my face, he stopped. "I'll call you."

"Please don't."

The door clicked shut behind him.

"Well, at least that wasn't weird." I scrubbed a hand over my face and surveyed the damage to my living room: chipped bric-a-brac, a shattered table, and a scrambled brain. And I didn't know where my underwear was.

19

Remember, you're much more flammable now than you were in life. So live every day as if you're soaked in gasoline.

—From *The Guide for the Newly Undead*

Sometime between my sustaining multiple gunshot wounds and losing my panties, Dick had called my cell phone to leave me a cryptic voice-mail message.

"Hey, Jane, it's Dick," he said, his voice unusually quiet and subdued. "Do you think you could stop by my place sometime tonight? I need to talk to you."

It was almost four by the time I heard the voice mail. And Dick wasn't answering his phone, so I risked some early-morning exposure to drive to his trailer. Because if I was at home, I would be cleaning up broken glass and thinking about what I had decided to call "the incident."

My phone rang as I jogged up the steps to Dick's trailer. The caller ID said it was Gabriel. I debated picking it up but finally hit the ignore button. I knocked on the door and—

WHHHOOOOOMMMMMMPPFFF

Red and gold stars exploded at the base of my skull as I was blown off Dick's porch and onto the hood of my car. My frustration at being thrown through yet another windshield was superseded by the fact that my sleeves were on fire. It seemed to be a more pressing concern. I slapped them out just before a secondary explosion knocked me back again. The blast threw me off the car, thwacking the back of my head against the cement blocks supporting a nearby El Camino. The flames burned orange behind my eyelids. I slipped into a soft black place where the burns on my arms didn't leave me screaming.

I was still able to be knocked unconscious. That was comforting. What was not comfortable was the cot I was currently chained to. I was lying in a dimly lit room that smelled of bleach and cement dust. Someone had taken the time to remove my smoldering clothes and put me in blue hospital scrubs. I jerked at the handcuffs binding my wrists and shrieked. Though healing, the burns on my arms were the color and texture of barely cooked hamburger.

"Agh, I am fortune's bitch," I moaned. Not exactly Shakespeare, I'm aware, but I was operating with a concussion. I sniffed at the chains. Under the tang of steel, I smelled something stronger.

"They're reinforced with titanium," a smooth, young female voice informed me from the darkness.

"Fortune's bitch," I said again.

Ophelia was sitting in a folding chair in the corner.

Her fangs glinted as she offered a thin smile. "You do have a way with words."

"What is going on?" I asked, trying to sit up. My very sensitive equilibrium told me this was a bad idea. "Who let the mariachi band loose in my head?"

Ophelia, who I could now see was wearing an obscenely short plaid skirt and a schoolgirl blouse, crossed to the foot of my bed. "I told you to behave yourself. I told you to stay under the radar."

"I did," I protested, the slightest hint of a whine creeping into my voice.

"Then how do you explain your being found unconscious outside a burning trailer belonging to one of the oldest vampires in the region?"

Not that again. "Look, for the last time, I didn't do anything. I walked up to the door, and the trailer exploded. Wait! Was Dick inside? Is he dead?"

There were the shark eyes again, which were even scarier when they were flashing at me from the dark. "Considering the hour, we're assuming he was inside. Of course, we wouldn't find him if he was inside. The fire would reduce him to dust. The question is why you were stupid enough to knock yourself out before you were able to leave the scene of the crime."

The terror was giving way to anger, which I assumed was a good sign. I demanded, "Why would I set Dick on fire?"

"Why would you set Walter on fire?" she asked.

"I didn't set Walter on fire!" I shouted.

"Give me an explanation, Jane. Give me something

to take back to the other council members, to the vampires who will demand justice. Give me some plausible reason for two men you are rumored to be involved with—whether that involvement is real or imagined, it won't matter to the community—having both been set on fire. Explain why you were found outside Dick's burning trailer after you were recently seen having a lovers'quarrel with him at a party."

"That wasn't a lovers' quarrel! That was a friendly conversation!"

"You were seen hitting him repeatedly."

"It was a friendly conversation that involved me hitting him repeatedly."

Ophelia did not look convinced.

I sighed. "What's going to happen to me? Is a vampire detective going to come in here and question me with a phone book and a rubber hose?"

I could see the amusement reach her eyes, but she refused to smile. "A tribunal has been called to discuss your case. Depending on the outcome of that discussion, you may have a trial tomorrow."

"A trial," I repeated before realization dawned. "*The* trial? Wait, don't I get a lawyer or a phone call or something?"

"No," she said, uncuffing me. I sat up slowly. She was across the room and out of my reach in a glimmer of movement. Where was the trust? "You're accused of immolating two of your own kind. The Bill of Rights no longer applies to you."

She turned toward the door, then whirled back on

me. She stood by the cot, peering down at me with those glowing black eyes.

"I regret this. You seem to be an interesting vampire."

"Then don't do this!" I yelled. "Stop making an example of me for other young vampires. I'm a terrible example. More weird stuff happens to me in a week than is foisted upon the average person in an entire lifetime."

"I regret this," she repeated. "But I also regret the loss of Dick Cheney. Once upon a time, we were . . . close acquaintances."

"Am I the only person in the Hollow who hasn't slept with Dick Cheney?"

"Possibly," she admitted.

"Sorry," I said. Shrugging my shoulders was a painful gesture that let me know there were bits of glass embedded somewhere near my shoulder blade. Gabriel was right, it itched.

Gabriel.

"My sire, Gabriel Nightengale, does he know I'm here?" I asked as she opened my cell door.

She nodded. "You're not allowed visitors," she said, shutting the very solid door behind her.

And for the first time since being shot and left for dead, I was truly frightened.

Whenever those horrible "women in prison" movies were played on Lifetime, I thought, what's the big deal about prison? I could handle solitary. Even if I couldn't read, I could daydream. I could write. I would take naps.

Well, like many of my predeath preconceived notions, that one was destroyed. There was no window, so I couldn't tell whether it was night or day. There was no clock, so I never knew what time it was. I couldn't sleep, because the healing burns on my arms itched like crazy. And my daydreams were interrupted by pesky questions such as, "Where is Gabriel?" "Why does this keep happening to me?" "Am I going to die for real this time?"

I spent half my time trying to figure out where the hell I was. When I pressed my ear against the wall, I could hear traffic. I heard voices at least twenty feet above my head, but I couldn't make out any actual words. And there was a rat somewhere in the plumbing.

The only good thing I could say about the clink was that the blood (served in a paper cup shoved through a slot in my door) was fresh and tasty. It was also of an indeterminate origin, but I decided not to ask questions.

I was halfway to drawing "LOVE" and "HATE" on my knuckles, when Ophelia returned. She was wearing black silk pants and a top that may, at one point, have been a handkerchief. I stood up, grateful for any sort of interaction, even if it could mean I was facing a spookily titled punishment.

"Are you comfortable?" she asked, not sounding as if she actually cared.

"Bored, mostly. How long have I been in here?" I asked. "Two days, three days?"

"Nine hours," she said, looking as if she were suppressing a giggle.

"Well, that's embarrassing," I muttered, scratching at my arms.

We sat there and stared at each other. It was like a staring contest with a really hot statue.

Finally, she said, "The tribunal has voted against a trial."

I sat up, feeling something like hope rising. "Really? That's good news."

"They voted against it because Missy has challenged you to trial by battle, which is her right as Dick's consort."

"You guys are just making this up as you go along!" I cried. "Dick and Missy weren't even in a real relationship. Hell, if everyone he slept with could challenge me to a duel, I'd be fighting half the county. You could challenge—"

She crossed her arms and glared at me. Probably not good to give her ideas.

"Never mind," I said. "Is it going to be pistols at dawn? Swords at sundown? How does this trial-by-battle thing work?"

"The last battle was fought with sharpened snow shovels," she told me.

"Now I know you're screwing with me." I snorted. Her expression didn't change. "Oh, come on!"

"Missy will choose the weapon," Ophelia informed me.

"She's going to accessorize me to death?"

"Or she can choose hand-to-hand combat." Ophelia nodded.

"I stand by my statement," I deadpanned.

My arms finally healed up about an hour after Ophelia left me. She said she would come back an hour before my appointment with Missy the grieving ex to let me feed and update me on the duel arrangements. She even promised to serve as my second. How did I get to a point in my life where I needed a second?

Semierotic fisticuffs with Gabriel aside, I didn't have any faith in my fighting skills. Walter had nearly splintered my skull with his bare hands, and from what I heard, he'd spent most of his time watching *Battlestar Galactica* in his mother's basement.

After pacing, humming, yoga, and playing Six Degrees of Kevin Bacon with the entire cast of *Good Times,* exhaustion finally got to me, and I managed to fall asleep. I dreamed that I was walking along that long, dark country road and felt the pain of Bud McElray's bullet all over again. Only instead of finding me and turning me, Gabriel drove by in a big black Cadillac. He laughed and pelted me with cigars and drove away. Anyone care to interpret that?

I jolted awake, yelling, "Freud!" Dick was sitting in the corner of my cell, smirking at me. "I can't leave you alone for two seconds, can I?"

"Dick?" I said, wiping an alarming amount of sleep drool from my cheek. "Wait, are you a ghost?"

He sat on the cot and grasped my knee, so I could feel he was substantial. "Nope, still as undead as ever."

I removed his hand and put it back on his own knee. He gave me a blithe grin, which, Lord help me, made me hug him. He was clearly caught off guard by this and, after hesitating, gave me a completely innocent squeeze.

"Hey, you're not trailer dust!" I exclaimed. "And your hand is on my knee again."

"Sorry," he said, not looking the least bit so. "And no, I'm not dust. I had a fireproof sleeping compartment built under the trailer a few years ago. I smelled the gas and jumped into it just in time."

"Your sleeping compartment is fireproof?"

"I have my reasons," he said, feigning indignation. "I just figured my place got torched by one of my less than civically minded associates. I laid low for a while. I didn't know you'd been blamed for the whole thing until this evening when I heard about the duel. I couldn't leave you locked up. With the public showers and the shackles—"

"Shh," I said, holding a finger to his lips. "I'm glad you're OK. Let's not ruin that."

He kissed the fingertip, which I then used to tweak his nose. He caught my hand and smelled my skin. He cocked an eyebrow and smirked, then rolled his eyes. If he could smell Gabriel on my hair *before* we had sex . . .

"If you say what is in your head right now, I will rescind my previous statement and kill you. For real this time," I told him.

"Speaking of that, how about I give you a ride home?" he said. "There's some stuff we need to talk about in private."

"The stuff you cryptically referred to during your call? How did you get my cell-phone number, anyway?"

"We'll talk about it later," he said, dragging me to the door.

"Dick, they're not going to just let me walk out of here. They think I tried to kill you. It's apparently one of the big no-nos."

"And obviously, I'm not dead. No harm, no foul," Dick said.

"That doesn't change the fact that someone tried to kill you and I'm still a prime suspect. I'm actually the only suspect, which I find insulting and surprising."

"Look, I vouched for you, OK? I said there was no way you could have done this. It took some convincing, but Ophelia has agreed to release you into my custody. They figure if you really did try to kill me and somehow you end up mysteriously disappearing, it's a wash."

"I don't want to know what you did to convince Ophelia, do I?"

Dick smirked.

Ophelia, Sophie, and Mr. Marchand were waiting in the hall, ready to offer me an apology on behalf of the council. Well, Sophie and Mr. Marchand were apologizing. I didn't need telepathy to know Ophelia would not bother with a "trial/no trial" vote the next time I got into trouble.

Dick managed to speed the process along and practically launched me through the entrance to the council office—which was actually a Kinko's. I felt silly walking through a weeknight crowd of people copying their tax records in hospital scrubs and bare feet. But the patrons seemed used to this sort of thing.

Dick threw me into the front seat of his car, an old beat-up El Camino, and pulled out of town as quickly as our two stoplights would allow.

I crossed my arms and spoke with overly sweet clarity. "OK, I'm getting tired of being thrown in and out of shitty situations because people withhold information from me. What were you calling to tell me about? And why couldn't you talk about it at the council gulag?"

"I couldn't talk about it before because I didn't know who was listening," he said, turning toward my house. "Look, Missy has it out for you. I found these papers in her briefcase. I was looking for a light while she was in the shower. She's got these sketches for a planned community thing out near your place. She's got a clubhouse smack in the middle of your backyard."

My head swam. "Use smaller sentences, please?"

"She wants to get her hands on River Oaks."

I grabbed the door handle, not sure if I could manage a *Charlie's Angels* roll on gravel. "Stop the car."

"Why?"

"Stop the car!" I yelled. "It took me a while, but I finally caught on. You call me over to your trailer to give me mysterious information. The trailer blows up. I'm framed for your murder. Missy challenges me to a duel and stands to inherit my property. Do the math, Dick."

He stared at me and nearly ran the car off the road. Somewhere in Dick's brain, ten thousand chimpanzees had just typed the opening act of *Hamlet*. "Missy set fire to my trailer?"

"There you go." I resisted the urge to pat his head.

He huffed. "Missy's determined, but she's not crazy."

"She matches her cell-phone case to her shoes!" I

yelled. "That's one stop short of Hannibal Lecter territory in my book." And as I realized the true depth of my stupidity, I sputtered, "Oh, for God's sake, there's no such thing as the new-arrivals welcoming committee, is there?"

"No, actually, there is," Dick said. "I think she just does this other stuff as a side project."

"OK, say Missy is the big bad blond evil force behind the shooting and the fires and the really hurtful rumors. How do I know that you're not in on all of this?" I yelled. "You could be luring me into some sort of trap. You could be her little henchman. Or you could be under her thrall. Stop the car, Dick!"

"Let go of the door now," he said in a soothing "talking down the crazy lady" tone. "I'm not a little anything. I haven't been under anyone's thrall since an unfortunate incident in 1923 involving a succubus from Baton Rouge without a sense of humor. The gravel would take a chunk of your hide and your pride. Just let me drive you home. And then you can call Gabriel, and we can all talk about this and decide what you should do."

"I'm not calling Gabriel," I said, far too shrilly. "I just want you to drop me off here, and I'll walk home. Then I'm getting a gun and a much smarter dog."

Dick reached out for my hand. "Oh, come on, don't you trust me, Stretch?"

I stared at him for a long pause. *"No!"*

20

Dueling is a time-honored tradition among vampires and is closely monitored by the council. Do not enter into a battle without first consulting a Council representative.

—From *The Guide for the Newly Undead*

Dick did not stop the car.

Instead, he promised to drive me home, give me his cell phone, and let me call Gabriel the second I felt anything out of the ordinary. He had Gabriel's number saved in his phone book under "Jackass." Dick also offered to let me kick him in the goods if he let anything happen to me. If that wasn't a guarantee of my safety, I didn't know what was.

My parents' car was parked outside the house when we got to River Oaks, but I couldn't find them anywhere. Jettie materialized next to me and started talking at a speed only birds could understand. Thrilled to see someone I knew for sure wasn't trying to kill or frame me, I tried to hug her and fell through her. Fortunately, Dick came in a few seconds later, so Jettie was the only one who saw it. Distracted, Jettie let her guard down enough to allow Dick to see her. He tried to introduce himself but was ignored in favor of more gibbering at me.

My phone rang. I shushed Jettie and picked it up. I could hear someone sobbing softly in the background. I recognized that sound. It was my mother.

"Mama?" I yelled. I checked the caller ID, but the number was blocked. "Mom?"

"Jane, hi, shug, how are you?" Missy cooed from the other end of the line. "I was just talking to your folks!"

"Missy, let me talk to them," I said in as cool a tone as I could manage. "Let me talk to them right now."

"Oh, now, shug, they can't come to the phone, they're a little tied up," she said, chuckling at her own little joke.

"Right now, you crazy bitch."

"Language, Jane, language. You know, maintaining your composure is the first step in any negotiation."

"I'll try to keep that in mind when I'm not dealing with a *freaking sociopath*!" I yelled into the phone. "Now let me talk to my parents!"

"I think you'll want to be more cordial, Jane, honey, or I might not feel quite so hospitable toward your parents," she said, her voice constricting like the coils of a snake. "Now, we're going to meet at my place in an hour. If you don't arrive promptly and in a more cooperative mood, I may have to do something drastic. Some of your daddy's favorite parts may just find themselves removed. Then he might end up being turned and, by horrible coincidence, locked in a concrete box until he goes mad with thirst."

"Please, just let him go."

"That's nothing compared with what I'll do to your mother," she said. "Jane? Are you listening?" she asked when I didn't respond immediately. "Jane!"

"I'm thinking!"

I could hear Mama's squeals of indignation from the other end of the line. If we all survived, I was pretty sure I would never hear the end of this.

So, suddenly, the mysterious deaths and explosions and my poor standing with the council made a lot more sense. It took me thirty-five minutes and a smashed chair or two before Dick and Jettie would let me out of the house. Dick insisted on coming with me, and I couldn't help but be grateful for it. Missy had not, after all, made the clichéd supervillian demand that I come alone. I might have called Gabriel, but I didn't want to have to explain how I managed to stumble into *another* life-threatening situation in such a short time. Every man has his limits.

When I arrived at Missy's, I tried to close the car door as quietly as possible, but Missy still yelled, "We're around back, shug!"

I was starting to hate being called "shug."

Dick had agreed to lurk around the front yard until he heard the sounds of a struggle. I found my parents on Missy's back deck, surrounded by twinkling Christmas lights and Japanese paper lanterns. While they were bound and gagged, Missy had taken the time to set out a nice cheese tray and a chilled chardonnay. And there was a covered presentation easel set up behind them. Maybe this was all an elaborate setup to get me to buy one of her stupid prefab houses.

"Jane!" Missy chirped. "So nice to see you."

My father looked groggy and confused. Mama looked ready to chew through the gag and start screaming at somebody.

"You guys OK?" I asked.

"Have a seat. Can I get you something to drink?" Missy offered sweetly, the picture of Southern charm. I hoped that if we lived through this, it would serve as a lesson to Mama that having fancy cocktail napkins and coordinated clothing did not necessarily make you a well-adjusted person.

"No, thank you." I sat next to my dad and squeezed his taped hands.

Ahem-ing pointedly, Missy motioned to the shackles attached to my chair. I reluctantly snapped them around my wrists and jangled them, hoping Dick could discern the noise—surely he had to recognize it.

"Well, aren't you the tricky one?" Missy said, pouting prettily. "Do you know how much trouble I've gone to just to get your attention? I used my powers to track you, followed you around. I lured that idiot Walter back to the scene of your pathetic fight, killed him to get the council to watch you. I played those stupid pranks on you, watched your house to make you feel uneasy, painted your car, put a little something extra in your doggie's bowl. Hell, I even shot at you."

"Shot me," I corrected her as Mama shrieked under her gag. "You actually shot me, and it hurt, quite a bit."

"Aw, shug, don't take it personally. It's not like I left any permanent scars. I just wanted to make you desperate enough, paranoid enough, to want to leave town. Whether it was to get away from the council or whoever you thought was out to get you, I didn't care. I figured, since you don't like your sister anyway and we're such good girlfriends, you'd sell me the property and leave. But you just wouldn't budge. So I stepped it up, set my precious Dickie's trailer on fire, framing you for his murder so I could challenge you. But then he intervened, and the council let you walk away scot-free. Nothing has worked, Jane. Nothing. Do you have any idea how frustrating that is?"

"I knew it!" I yelled. "I knew all that random stuff couldn't happen to one person!"

"Well, subtlety has never been my strong suit," she said, smirking as she sipped a virulently pink cocktail.

From inside the model home, I heard a voice call, "Missy? Are you out back?"

"It seems our last guest has arrived." Missy smirked. "I believe you two know each other."

"Jenny?" I yelled as my sister stepped out on onto the deck. "Run, Jenny, get out of here!"

"Why?" Jenny asked. "Wait, why are y'all tied up? Missy, what's going on here?"

"You know her?" I demanded.

"Yes, I know her. Missy's in my Thursday night scrapbooking group."

"Oh, of course she is." I groaned.

"This isn't what we talked about, Missy," Jenny said, staring at our bound parents.

"What do you mean, what you talked about?" I demanded. "You do know she's a vampire, right?"

"Oh, sure." Jenny rolled her eyes. "Like I'd spend Thursday nights scrapbooking with a vampire."

In the calmest tone I could muster, I said, "Jenny, I've been waiting for a really long time to say this to you. You're a moron."

Jenny ignored me. "Jane, what exactly have you gotten us into?"

"I'll answer that," Missy said sweetly, just before punching Jenny.

"I'm not going to say that bothered me," I told Missy as she hog-tied my dazed sister.

"I thought as much." Missy offered a vicious grin as she shoved the gag into Jenny's mouth. She turned to me and put on her "sales face." "Jane, have you ever had a vision?"

"I had a reaction to antibiotics when I was five and saw tigers jumping out of the walls," I offered.

"A vision," Missy repeated, obviously annoyed. "The ability to anticipate future events and possibilities. The ambition to better oneself through the pursuit of an ideal, a goal. Vision, honey. So few people have it, living or undead. Even fewer appreciate it. Imagine my irritation when I see someone like you with a beautiful piece of property like River Oaks." She tinkled, her laugh hard-edged. "Did you know that I own every little bit

of property surrounding your acreage? I've been buying it up, a piece at a time, for almost ten years now.
In fact, I own quite a bit of property in this end of the
state. The old-money vampires can't seem to hold on
to it. Of course, that might have something to do with
the fact that I tricked them into selling or killed them
in battle."

Missy bent so we were nose to nose, tilting her head
so she could give me a winning smile.

"Real estate is the one thing you can always count on,
Jane. It's eternal, just like we are. Gold, jewels, stocks,
bonds, they can fail you. But the one thing people can't
live without is land."

"Do you realize you based your whole evil life phi-
losophy on a quote from Lex Luthor?" I asked. "How has
the council not caught on to this?"

"Oh, the council's not nearly as all-seeing as it likes to
believe." She sighed, toying with the tiny umbrella in her
glass. "I have little helpers who claim the property for
me, for a fee, and a few low-level council minions who
turn a blind eye to loose ends, for a fee. I guess subtlety
is my strong suit."

"You want to move into River Oaks?"

"Oh, no, I want to knock River Oaks into the ground,"
she said, standing with some ceremony and whipping
the cover off the easel. "Jane, I give you my vision."

A disturbingly pert sign read, "Half-Moon Meadows,
a gated community for the undead," and showed a pale,
sophisticated-looking couple enjoying a glass of blood
on their front porch. Different graphics showed sketches

of a clubhouse, a trendy bar, a blood bank, a spa, a dentist's office.

"What. The. Hell." I gaped. Jenny made similarly distressed noises.

"Isn't it fabulous?" Missy squealed. "I had planned to start a gated suburb for the living, but then I was turned, and I was struck by the lack of specialized housing for vampires. Realtors just can't resist a hole in the market, Jane. Half-Moon Meadows will be the first community of its kind. Vampires from all over the world will come to our corner of paradise for a community that provides for their every need, every whim. If they never want to venture out into the living world again, they won't have to."

When I didn't applaud her brilliance, Missy continued, "My Deer Haven complex is just the beginning. All I need is your teeny little plot right in the center there," she said, pointing to an aerial view of the planned development. "I tried to talk your aunt Jettie into selling, but the old bat was so stubborn! When she died, I spent months trying to come up with the right way to approach you, to get you to sign it over. And then you were turned. It was a sign, Jane. I had a reason to meet you, the means to follow you, a way to cause . . . complications for you. Hell, I even went to Thursday night scrapbooking parties just to cozy up to your sister. Jenny is not a fan of yours, by the way."

I glared at my sister, who refused to meet my gaze.

Missy sneered. "Get a couple of margaritas in her, and she becomes quite the Chatty Cathy. She's been coming to me for advice on how to whisk that house out from under you, what with my real-estate expertise and all. She came here tonight thinking I'd come up with some way of forcing you into signing it over for tax reasons. You know, she's been feeding me information about you for months. Your schedules, your habits, your friends' names, your favorite foods. Of course, she didn't realize all of that had changed, because she's too damn dumb to figure out you're a vampire, but it was a good start.

"And now, it's time for the final act, Jane. I tried playing nice. I tried playing dirty. And now I'm going to play rough. I'll say you came after me in a jealous rage over Dickie, and I had to kill you in self-defense. And if the council doesn't believe that, I'll just keep talking until I find a story they do believe. You'd be amazed at what I can do to sell a story."

For a long time, I stared at Missy, unable to absorb what she'd said. "Let me get this straight. You tried to kill me so you could build a tacky planned community? That is just *evil*. I'm so going to kick your ass . . . just as soon as I'm untied. And then, maybe, I'm going after Jenny."

"It's not tacky," Missy hissed through clenched fangs. "It's innovative." She gripped her drink until the glass shattered in her hands, but she seemed to recover her composure as she flicked the shards away. "And technically, darling, you're chained."

Missy stepped over to my parents to adjust their bonds. She pinched my father's cheek until I thought blood would well from under her nails and then slapped him lightly. I growled, but she ignored me.

"Here's the deal, Janie. When I dust you, I'll gain control over River Oaks and everything you own. And then I'm going to kill your parents and your sister. And then I'm going after that boring ass of a husband and her imbecile children so there are no living heirs to claim River Oaks. That's the difference between you and me, Jane. I don't sit around whining and waiting for something to happen. I see what I want, and I take it."

"Look, this entire deck is made of wood. Just stake me and get it over with so I don't have to listen to any more evil-overlord speeches." I grumbled under my breath, "Two-bit dyed-blond social-climbing huckster."

Missy whirled on me, her face twisted with rage. "What did you say?"

She took a step toward me. Seeing that, I said, "Bottled blonde."

"No, not that." She snarled and took another step away from my parents.

"Nouveau riche." I smiled nastily, watching her move farther away from my family. If I could distract her long enough, maybe Dick could sneak around the building and release them.

When Missy's fangs glinted, I added, "Pretentious. Megalomaniacal. Two-faced. Cheap. Gigantic skank. About as real as Jenny's tan."

"No, that last part," Missy seethed.

Cheerfully, I said, "Oh, huckster, con artist, snake-oil peddler. If you were any good at sales, you wouldn't be in this position, would you? Aunt Jettie would have packed up for Florida and sold out to you. You'd be sitting pretty in River Oaks, and I would be—"

Missy let loose a guttural scream and kicked me square in the chest with her knockoff Jimmy Choos. Still chained to a lawn chair, I was launched through the deck railing, landing about twenty feet away. I left an ankle-deep rut in the recently sodded yard, my head pillowed on the mound of dirt. Spitting out grass and mud, I felt a grinding throb in my shoulder. I looked down and saw a chunk of the deck jutting through my collarbone.

"That is just gross," I heard Zeb say. I looked up to see him, Dick, and Gabriel standing over me. While this was touching in a "The cavalry is here!" sort of way, it didn't change the fact that my parents were now alone with an over-lip-glossed psychopath who planned on killing them. I looked up to the deck and saw empty chairs. Great, my parents were now hidden from sight by an over-lip-glossed psychopath. That was so much safer.

Dick shook his head. "This is what happens when you roughhouse. It's all fun and games until somebody gets impaled."

Wearing his grim expression, Gabriel knelt next to me. He said, "This is going to hurt."

"What are you doing here?" I asked as Gabriel yanked the offending lumber from my clavicle. "Ow!"

"I told you it was going to hurt," Gabriel said, shrugging.

"I called him," Dick said, looking sheepish. "I thought you could use some help, or at least another witness. I would have called Andrea, too, but you never gave me her number."

"And you?" I asked Zeb as Gabriel yanked my shirt away from the wound and inspected it.

"I called him," Gabriel told me, peering up at Zeb. "Though I remember asking for Jolene."

Zeb's clever reply was interrupted by Missy racing across the lawn, looking to wrap her arms around an unmoving Dick. "Dickie! I'm so glad you're all right. I was so worried."

"Now, why would you worry about me, darlin'?" Dick asked, his smile nasty. "Just because you torched my trailer, with me inside? Why would that make you worry your pretty little head?"

Missy's mouth formed a slick, astonished O. "Now, Dickie, honey, you know I'd never—"

"Missy, we're going to have a little talk, you and I," Dickie growled.

"Now, Dickie, Gabriel, you know you're not allowed to interfere once a challenge has been made," she cooed, toying with the hem of Dick's "Federal Bikini Inspector" T-shirt. "And I issued a legal challenge to Jane at the council office days ago. It doesn't matter that Dick is alive—the challenge stands."

"Suddenly, we're concerned with the rules?" Dick asked in the same saccharine tone.

"Only when they work to my advantage." She smiled.

That meant I still had to fight. Dang it. While Dick had Missy distracted, I had a small panic attack.

"I haven't been a vampire for very long, but I'm pretty

sure I can't toss someone like that," I said, wincing as the wound in my shoulder closed. "I want her tested for steroids."

"She's been drinking the blood of older vampires for years. It makes her the equivalent of an East German gymnast," Dick called over his shoulder. He glared at Missy. "Trust me, I know."

This prompted more indignant chatter from Missy. I groaned, clutching Gabriel's arms. "Gabriel, I don't want this to be the way you remember me. Just leave now, before I get my ass handed to me by a sorority reject from hell. I'm sorry I dragged you into my weird, drama-ridden existence. I'm sorry I screwed things up so badly with you and me. I'm sorry I have the emotional maturity of a grapefruit."

He grinned, his fangs glinting. "You don't have the emotional maturity of a grapefruit. A tangerine, maybe, but I think you've got to work your way up to grapefruit."

I smacked his chest. "You're joking. I'm going to be beaten to death with a hot-pink faux-alligator handbag, and you pick now to develop a sense of humor."

"You're not going to be beaten to death," Gabriel said in a bemused, soothing tone. He held his wrist to my lips. "Drink."

Sensing Gabriel's maneuver, Dick began arguing in a louder, more demanding tone, casting aspersions on Missy's character, business acumen, and sexual prowess. She screamed back that she faked something a lot. I didn't catch what, but I think I can guess.

"I don't think now is the time for naughty blood-swapping fun," I said, shoving Gabriel's arm away. "Besides . . ." I jerked my head toward Zeb. "He's watching."

Zeb waved my concerns away. His eyes were glued to Dick and Missy baring fangs and snarling insults. "I can't tear myself away from the most frightening break-up fight I've ever seen."

Gabriel nudged his wrist toward me again. "You'll absorb some of my strength. It will help you."

"It's just that, drinking your blood, it's kind of what got me into this mess," I said.

"I didn't see you complaining when you were dying along the roadside," he huffed. "Or when we were making love."

"What?" Zeb shouted.

"Zeb, shut it," I warned.

Gabriel ran his hands through his hair, making it stand on end in a wild Beethoven that would have been hilarious under different circumstances. "Would you please just accept help from me and stop being so, so—"

"So Jane?" Zeb suggested.

"Zeb!" Gabriel warned.

"OK, you need to back off," I said, poking Gabriel's chest. "You're suffocating me. You never tell me anything unless it's your 'listen to Daddy' voice, which is incredibly annoying in someone you have feelings for. I never know how you feel about me, about anything, except that you like to see me naked, and you have caveman 'must protect Jane' impulses. I'm not a mind reader."

"Technically, you kind of are," Zeb volunteered.

We both growled at Zeb, our fangs bared.

"Shutting up!" Zeb said, throwing up his hands and backing away.

"I don't write love poems," Gabriel said. "I don't cuddle. I don't spend hours on the phone, cooing, 'No, you hang up first.' I was raised in a time when if you had feelings for a woman, you proposed or you made her your mistress. I think, given the circumstances, you should give me credit for being as evolved as I am."

Damned if he didn't have a point. But I would have to hand over my womanhood membership card if I ever admitted it.

"You're going to make me say it, aren't you?"

I threw my arms up. "I don't even know what *it* is."

He sighed, a short snort of impatience. "I like you. You're unpredictable, and you always say what you think, even if it would be better if you didn't. You get yourself into situations that Moliere couldn't think of."

"OK, OK, so you like me."

"Yes, I think we should see each other on an exclusive basis," he said. I stared at him. "I am your sire, and we've made love."

"I'm familiar with your résumé," I said, shushing him with another furtive look at Zeb. "This is not a good time for this."

"I doubt we'll ever find a good time," he muttered, thrusting his arm against my mouth. "Now, drink, before Missy figures out what we're doing." With nothing else I to say, I chomped on his wrist. Gabriel yelped, prompting a smile against his skin. Unusual for me,

I knew, but I could hear Missy and Dick's argument winding down. Gabriel winced as I drew huge mouthfuls of his blood.

Zeb watched, coming closer and closer. "Is it going to be a Popeye thing? She eats her spinach and has the strength of twenty squinty sailors?"

"How have you survived this long without someone hurting you?" Gabriel asked as I finished feeding. I wiped a drip from my chin and offered Zeb a red-tinged grin. He recoiled, clearly grossed out.

Gabriel pulled a handkerchief from nowhere and dabbed at my mouth.

"I love it when he does that," Zeb said, looking Gabe over for hidden pockets. "Why can't I be a cool sleight-of-hand guy?"

"You've got a huge man crush on him, don't you?" I said, shaking my head.

Zeb measured "this much" sexual confusion with his fingers.

The sudden drop in volume signaled that Missy had finally noticed us.

"Gabriel, I do believe what you just did could be considered cheating," Missy said, her voice teasing and pouting.

"Do not attempt to explain the ancient codes to me," he growled.

Missy ignored the chill in Gabriel's tone. "Then I can count on you to mind your own business and let us girls sort this out."

"You can count on me to keep this farce as close to the

codes as possible. And if by some misfortune you happen to kill my bloodmate, I will make you wish for dawn."

Bloodmate? What was that, exactly? It sounded like something I didn't necessarily want to be. But the term seemed to have an effect on Missy. The supreme Tony Robbins-bred confidence melted away for a second before she flashed a guileless grin. "I'll just let you two say your good-byes."

"She's really good at that intimidating smack-talk stuff," I said, watching her flounce away. "Any advice?"

"Keep your hands up," Gabriel said. "Protect your neck and chest at all times. And don't try any of those fancy women's self-defense tactics. She probably took the same classes when she was alive, and she'll be expecting them."

Before I could retort, Gabriel crushed me close and gave me a bloodless, friendly smack on the lips. He smiled. "For luck."

"Idiot," I said, before grinning broadly and crushing his mouth to mine.

"We need to pick new pet names for each other," he muttered as I hefted myself up from the ground.

Honestly, how did someone who never once got into a fight in school end up getting into so many of them as an adult? Missy was standing in the middle of the yard, in a worn circle of dirt. I felt like that first anonymous fighter who gets killed off in the Jean-Claude Van Damme cage-fighter movies. Missy smiled, and I circled.

"I guess we're going to get to have that little catfight after all," Missy said, rolling her shoulders.

"I'm not worried. If you kill me, my dead great-aunt will fix it so you spend eternity looking for your car keys," I said.

I felt the power of Gabriel's blood coursing through me, warming me, giving me that drunk driver's confidence that maybe I could make it home. The burns on my arms had finally healed over. And the wound in my shoulder was a shiny, slightly sore memory.

"Question. Did you actually wear that Juicy Couture track suit with this in mind?"

Missy scowled. "If we're going to talk fashion, shug, I think we need to start with those Payless specials you wear."

"Ow, I wear cheap shoes, you got me," I deadpanned. "Let's just cut the banter and fight. I feel the need to warn you, I'm a hair puller."

"I feel the need to warn you," Missy said, before simply punching me right in the eye.

I responded by collapsing to the ground. That'd show her.

Can someone punch you in the head so hard that it actually decapitates you? Because Missy came close.

From my position on the ground, I could see the heel of Missy's shoe on a collision course with my throat. I rolled, ramming into her shins and knocking her off balance. She fell on her butt with an outraged *"uhff"* and kicked up, launching me about twenty feet in the air. Giddy from the fall, I landed on my feet but didn't have time to avoid the crushing kick to my solar plexus. I stumbled back, making a sound not found in human language, and struck out, punching her in the eye. She swung blind, dragging her frosted-pink nails down my chest. I swiped my fingers under my shirt and found blood streaked across them.

I grunted and stomped on her foot. She screamed and kicked me in the shin. I had no choice but to pull her hair, which was remotely shameful, even though I'd warned her. But it was surprisingly effective. Missy squealed and snaked her hands against my scalp, yanking hard. And soon we were just rolling around on the ground, cursing and screeching and ripping out handfuls of hair.

Without super hearing, I wouldn't have heard Zeb whisper, "This is the coolest thing I have ever seen."

"Maybe they'll get muddy," Dick said. "Please, Lord, let them get muddy."

Gabriel turned on them. "You two do realize this is a battle to the death, yes?"

Neither seemed particularly embarrassed.

After several ringing blows to the head, Missy tossed me in a limp pile at the feet of Dick, Gabriel, and Zeb. Gabriel helped me to my feet and gave me an encouraging slap on the back. Dick, however, took a hint from Burgess Meredith's performance in *Rocky*.

"Would you kick her ass already?" Dick said, shoving me back toward Missy. "Come on, Stretch, man up. You can do better than this! Get mad."

I nodded, rolling a dislocated shoulder back into place with a grunt and staggering back toward my opponent.

Behind me, Zeb yelled, "She tried to hurt Fitz!" He turned to Gabriel and Dick. "That'll get her mad."

Gabriel rolled his eyes. "She's been framed for murder twice over, shot in the back, her arms were set on fire, and her parents are being held hostage. You think tampered dog water is what's going to make her angry?"

"You tried to hurt my dog!" I wheezed as I lurched toward a grinning Missy.

"Oh, big deal," Missy huffed. "It's the ugliest dog I've ever seen."

"You tried to hurt my dog," I said again.

"I would have been doing you a favor." Missy sneered.

"Nobody. Screws. With. My. Dog." I growled, punctuating each word with a punch to Missy's face. I gave an upper cut to the chin that sent her flying back into a pile on the ground.

Zeb grinned at Dick and Gabriel. "Told you."

I took a running start at Missy, hoping to drive my elbow into her chest. But she rolled out of the way, kicking me in the back of the head when I face-planted into the dirt. Ow.

I pushed up to my knees, but Missy tackled me, throwing me to the ground, cursing, and pulling my hair. I tried every move I'd ever seen on the rare evenings Zeb got me to watch wrestling: head butting, eye gouging, ear pulling. But nothing would get Missy off me.

Still rolling in our cartoon fight ball of flying fists and cat yowls, we knocked into the storage shed, popping the door open. A slew of Missy's old Realtor signs spilled out, their pointy wooden stakes glinting like a dozen golden opportunities.

We glanced at the stakes, looked at each other, and dove. I landed first, with Missy grabbing my ankles to pull me away. I managed to snag one as she dragged me facedown over the grass. Spitting dirt and grass and a couple of foul words, I sprang to my feet. Missy was still on her back, hate and surprise radiating from her eyes as I lunged and drove the sign through her chest. Missy howled, wriggling to free herself from the spike pinning her to the ground.

"The heart, you moron!" she screeched, clutching at the stake. "It has to be the heart!"

"Oh, right, thanks," I said, grabbing another sign. I screamed as I drove it home, aiming more carefully this time.

She looked down at the wood pinning her heart, disbelief flickering over her features before they crumbled away to dust. It happened in a wave, first the skin, then the musculature, then a bare skeleton that exploded in a cloud of particles. The sign swayed once, twice, then fell flat, pushing Missy's smiling photo into the mound of her dust.

"Get the point?" I asked, offering the boys a triumphant smile.

Gabriel, Zeb, and Dick stared at me, aghast.

"What? Sarcastic postkill comeback. Isn't that what you're supposed to do in situations like this?

"Too harsh?"

21

You cannot control your family's reaction to your new lifestyle. You can only control your reaction to your family. It's best if that reaction does not include eating your family.

—From *The Guide for the Newly Undead*

Gabriel offered to wipe my family's memories. It was so tempting to hide for a little bit longer, to let one area of my life stay the same for just a little while. But I'd had enough. The lies took too much energy, and, frankly, I was having a hard time keeping track of to whom I'd told what.

Gabriel wanted to stay and help me explain, which was sweet. But I didn't think it was fair to put him in the line of fire. I wouldn't have been there if I didn't have to be. So, after sending everyone else home, I sat on Missy's deck and stared at the newly unshackled pair. I insisted on leaving Jenny hog-tied and gagged for the duration of this discussion. Mama was too shell-shocked to argue, which I thought was a normal reaction to one's first hostage crisis.

"Um, you probably have some questions for me," I said finally.

Mama was dry-eyed and mad as hell. "Jane, what is going on? We got a call that you needed us at the house. And that awful woman just kidnapped us right off your front porch. Why would she do that? Why was she talking about vampires? Thank God your friends were here to help us, or I just don't know what we would have done. Was that your Gabriel? The tall one with the dark hair? He seems very nice. Lovely manners. I don't think I like the other one, though, the one in the vulgar T-shirt."

"Mama." I ignored the part where Mama negated my share in her rescue and stuck to the matter at hand. "Mama, you probably figured out, from what Missy was saying earlier, that I'm a vampire." My throat tightened around every word. "In fact, if you think back on some of the stuff that's happened in the last couple of months, you'll see that there were some pretty big hints. And I understand why you didn't see it, because you weren't ready yet. And I wasn't ready to tell you. But now I have to. I'm a vampire."

My mother's jaw hung slack. She paled. "You haven't told Gabriel, have you?"

I would have laughed, but it wouldn't have improved the situation. "He's a vampire, too. In fact, he's the one who made me a vampire."

While they sat, stunned silent, I very quickly told them what really happened the night I was fired, my Shenanigans bender. I described Gabriel's following me home to make sure I arrived home safe and my car breaking down. I told them about the shooting, though I omitted the identity of the drunken hunter. It just seemed petty now that Bud was dead. I also glossed over the more erotic aspects of Gabriel's turning me, because I liked being able to look my father in the eyes. I would have to put that off for a while anyway, because looking him in the eyes at the moment made my chest hurt.

I assured them that I hadn't fed on anyone living and planned to stick to bottled blood as much as possible. I judiciously omitted the Andrea episode. Daddy's face contorted in alternating waves of rage, sorrow, and over-whelming curiosity.

Mama's first question was "Have you tried not being a vampire?"

To which I responded, "Yes, for the first twenty-six years of my life."

My father, who had remained silent and thin-lipped until this point, asked, "Why did you lie to us, honey?"

The hurt in his voice made my throat constrict. "To keep you from looking at me like you're looking at me right now. Like I'm some kind of freak. Like you're ashamed of me. Like you're not going to want me to be your daughter anymore. I was scared, and I didn't know how to tell you. And after a while, it seemed really difficult to fit 'Guess what, I'm undead' into a conversation."

"But you didn't just lie once, Jane," Daddy said softly. "You've had months to tell us. You lied over and over."

All I could muster up was a weak "I'm so sorry, Daddy."

"Are you all right?" Daddy asked, tears of his own welling up. "Did—did it hurt?"

"Being shot hurt," I admitted, reaching for his hand. His fingers wrapped around mine without hesitation. The weight that was crushing my chest seemed to wiggle loose. "Getting turned was just like falling asleep. I woke up three days later, and Gabriel took care of me. He saved me. I would have died without his help. Please don't be angry with him or act weird around him. He's a good man, for the most part."

"What can you do?" he asked.

It took me a few seconds to catch up to Daddy's question. He was asking about my snazzy new vampire powers, not expressing helplessness about my being turned by a guy with "shoves trees on people" tendencies.

"Oh, um, a lot of stuff, except, you know, eat solid food and go outside during the day," I said.

"Even my pot pie?" Mama cried.

Yes, because in this situation, pot pie was what we should be focusing on.

I nodded. "But the upside is, I don't have to feed very often. I can lift couches over my head one-handed. I've finally stopped running like a girl. I can smell fear. And you saw that I can hold my own in a fight. You don't have to worry about me anymore."

Daddy's expression brightened. And yes, I intentionally left out the part about the mind-reading, because that tended to weird people out. Plus, it was a hand I didn't want to tip to Mama.

After a long pause, Mama said, "Well, I don't know what to say."

Daddy checked his watch and marked the time. "It took thirty years, but it was bound to happen sometime."

Mama looked horrified. I started giggling, which made Daddy laugh. Then we just kept braying like donkeys until tears were streaming down our cheeks. I was so glad that dying hadn't ruined my sense of humor. Or Daddy's, for that matter.

Mama wasn't as thrilled. "Well, that's fine, just fine!" She cried fat crocodile tears, clumping her carefully feathered Maybelline Great Lash. "You two just sit here and laugh your fool heads off. You have your cozy little meeting of the We're Smarter Than Sherry Club, as usual. I'll just go home and mourn my daughter's death."

"I'm not dead, Mama, I'm undead. There is a difference."

"Well, pardon me for not knowing the right words," Mama huffed. "I've never met a vampire. I don't know any. No one I know does. Oh, my, what are people going to say? What kind of mother am I to let her daughter get turned into a vampire?"

I snorted. "I'm not asking you to march in any pride parades, Mama."

Daddy stood, wedging himself in the crossfire. "Now, let's not say anything we'll regret."

"Oh, I think we're already there." I was fully prepared to vamp out and leap onto the roof just to complete Mama's traumatic-offspring-treachery scenario. She was definitely sending Reverend Neel after me for this one. "You didn't *let* me get turned into a vampire. I didn't let me get turned into a vampire. It just happened. And there's nothing I can do about it."

"Honey, please, we're just trying to understand what's happening," Daddy pleaded.

Mama and I trenched ourselves in a sullen silence. Poor Daddy just looked back and forth between the two of us, like some spectator held prisoner at a tennis match.

"How do you expect to live this way?" Mama finally demanded. "How will you work? Where are you going to live? How will you take care of yourself?"

"I've been taking care of myself for quite some time now," I insisted. "I'm going to keep living at River Oaks, as long as someone doesn't try to kill me for it again. And I've gotten a new night job at a bookstore. I'm going to be fine, Mama. You know, Zeb joined this group, the Friends and Family of the Undead. It's like a support group for people who know newly turned vampires. I think it might help you."

"You told Zeb before you told us?" Mama shouted.

Oh, crap.

"How could you do that?" Mama cried. "We're your family!"

"He found out the night I rose," I said. "But no one else knows. Except for some of the vampires I've met. And Andrea, a girl who hangs out with a lot of vampires. Oh, and Jolene, Zeb's fiancée."

"Zeb's getting married? Before you?"

Double crap.

"We just need to get you over to Dr. Willis and let him take a look at you," Mama said, moving to pat my leg, then stopping, her hand frozen a few inches over me.

She was afraid to touch me. My own mother could not bring herself to lay her hands on me. Something inside me greeted quick, quiet death. "There's not much he can do for me."

"I don't have to listen to this," Mama snarled. "I'm not going to sit here and listen to you talk like this. You can't even try taking it seriously, can you? You died, and you have to make jokes, have to make me feel like an idiot for not understanding."

"Mama, just let me take you home," I said, reaching for her.

She shied away from me. "No, I think we'll stay right here. Why don't you go on home?"

"Well, because it's not safe for you to be here by yourself. Who knows what Missy has here or whether one of her newbie minions is going to show up? You would be easy prey. I need to stay with you. And technically, I think this is my house, anyway. When you kill another vampire, that usually means you get their stuff. Besides, you don't have a car. How are you going to get home?"

"We'll have Jenny drive us." Mama sniffed.

Great, bring up the living daughter. One more thing Jenny had on me—two kids, a husband, and a pulse.

I reluctantly untied my sister. With an indignant squeal, she broke loose from the ropes and pulled her gag away. She was about to scream at me when I clapped a hand over her mouth. "Don't. Whatever you're about to say, whatever excuse you're about to give, don't. I'm not talking to you for a while. Not until the urge to throttle you goes away. Stay away from the house, and stay away from me. Pretend that I don't exist. It should be easy enough considering the practice you've had."

"Jane, get your hands off her!" Mama yelled.

I stared at my mother. "You think I'm going to hurt her, don't you?"

Mama said nothing. Daddy wrapped an arm around her. "Now, Sherry—"

"John, don't!" she snapped, pushing his arm away. "Don't take her side!"

"Stop! Please, just stop," I told her, holding my hands up in my best "I'm not going to attack you" stance. "It's OK, Daddy. I'm leaving."

Daddy shot a bewildered look my way and rose. "We'll talk soon, honey."

" 'Bye, Daddy." I stepped close to kiss his cheek and was grateful when he didn't pull away.

He squeezed my hand and winked at me. "Love you."

"Love you, too," I whispered. "I'm sorry."

Tears finally spilled over my eyelashes and down my cheeks. He hesitated, then kissed my cheek again.

I rounded the house and wiped my eyes on my sleeve. And that's when I learned that vampire tears have blood in them. Bloody tears that my father saw. Great.

I pulled my car away from the house but watched from the end of the street. I watched the taillights of Jenny's SUV fade into the distance as my family drove away.

Well, I'd finally been honest. My parents knew everything, and they'd heard it from me. Whether my family accepted it or not was up to them.

On a positive note, maybe I wouldn't have to go to Christmas dinner that year.

22

Remember that life, or unlife, is what you make of it.

—From *The Guide for the Newly Undead*

I figured that if I could rescue my parents from my super-secret arch-nemesis in a battle to the death, I could face my former coworkers. Besides, I still needed Mrs. Stubblefield's signature for my undead employment benefits.

I was obviously going to have to find another part-time job until the council unclenched and handed over my ill-gotten gains for dusting Missy. Personally, I thought they were withholding the money to teach me a life lesson in self-sufficiency and keeping my nose clean. Or something. Also, I thought it amused Ophelia to watch me squirm.

And Jenny, aware that she might never inherit River Oaks now that I was immortal, had sent me several legal notices demanding certain antiques and valuables. So, now I had legal fees to worry about.

It was a nice, clear evening, just after dusk, no worry

about spontaneous combustion. Vampires live(ish) for sunsets like that. Pressing my hands against the doors, I prayed for strength and the fortitude not to use my stealthy vampire powers to do something bad to Posey . . . or Posey's stupid lunch bag.

The first thing I noticed was that the security system was turned off, meaning anybody could just walk out the library's front door with an unchecked book without setting off the alarm. Posey was sitting behind the front desk, flipping through a copy of *Elle* instead of helping the elderly patron carrying a heavy stack of Agatha Christie mysteries. Despite the fact that I did not punch her in the face on sight, she was not thrilled to see me when I sauntered up to the information desk and asked for Mrs. Stubblefield in my most syrupy-sweet voice.

"She's not available," huffed Posey as she turned her back on me to give the elderly patron some attention finally.

I tapped her on the shoulder.

"Well, could you please let her know that I'll be in the special collections room, and when she has a minute, I would really appreciate just a few minutes of her time?" I cooed.

"I'll see if she has a minute." Posey sighed, rolling her eyes.

"Thank you so much."

I took the long way to the special collections room via the children's department and was greeted by utter bedlam. Outside Mrs. Stubblefield's office, I could hear the mayor's wife complaining about an unwarranted thirty-six-dollar late fee assigned to her account. There was a book cart parked in the middle of the reading room, covered in jumbled books. From the thick layer of dust settled on their spines, it was clear nobody cared whether they needed to be reshelved. In nonfiction, the Golightly sisters were fighting over the last available copy of *The Secret*. I stared in slackjawed horror at a silverfish crawling over the opened pages of the massive dictionary kept near the reference desk.

I'd had postapocalyptic nightmares like this, dreams of walking into the library and finding it ravaged, abandoned to scavengers and, possibly, zombies. Apparently, abandoning the library to Mrs. Stubblefield and her niece was not much better. And none of this bothered me nearly as much as walking into the children's department, which looked like Paris circa 1944. Books were scattered like dead birds across the floor, split open, their spines cracking. The stuffed Mother Goose was in an anatomically correct position with Humpty Dumpty. The bookshelf containing the baby and toddler books had collapsed and was leaning against the wall, broken and discarded. Three little girls were running around the Storytime Carpet, spiking paperback copies of Junie B. Jones like footballs. Ten-year-old twins Jake and Josh Richards sat in the corner, furtively drawing breasts on the women in the *Illustrated History* books.

Seven-year-old Jimmy Tipton, who had been repeatedly warned not to bring juice to the library, was tossing prechewed Gummy Bears through the puppet theater.

His mother, who had been warned not to bring Jimmy to the library, was nowhere in sight. I was prepared to let it go. To walk away. It was someone else's problem. And then I saw Jimmy rip his juice box open and start to pour juice on the carpet. The carpet I'd installed with my own two hands.

"Stop!" I thundered in a voice not my own. It resonated inside my skull, echoing out over the children in waves. I could see everything, every page in every book. Every drop of blood coursing through the children's veins. Every drop of Hawaiian Punch dripping onto the carpet. "Stop what you're doing right now!"

The children froze. Their arms fell to their sides, and they awaited orders. To think of all the time and frustration this could have saved me during Story Hours.

"This is not how I taught you to behave in the library. This is not how I taught you to treat books. I want you to erase every mark. I want you to put everything away," I intoned. "Everything. Even if you didn't touch it, put it in its proper place."

The kids scrambled to do my bidding. Even the kids who didn't know the Dewey Decimal System, or their alphabet, were shelving books. I handed Jimmy a roll of paper towels from behind the counter.

"Blot," I told him, and marched into the special collections room.

I was nose-deep in a rare edition of *History of Hematology* when Mrs. Stubblefield peeked around the corner. I caught her in my peripheral super-vision but deliberately ignored her until she was standing right in front of me. She jumped when I snapped the book shut and offered a sharp, sweet grin.

"Hi, Mrs. Stubblefield!" I chirped, cheerful to the point that it pained me.

She blanched, clearly expecting me to indulge in some sort of Texas Chainsaw Fired Employee Revenge Fantasy.

I stretched out to scan her mind. She put up no resistance, and I was overwhelmed with chaotic images. I saw whimsically tilted stacks of unshelved books left untouched for weeks. Mrs. Stubblefield finding my reminder (written in red Sharpie) on the calendar to call the exterminator for our annual spraying two months *after* the silverfish invaded. Posey sending out a Story Time flyer with the word "public" spelled without an "l." Mrs. Stubblefield fruitlessly trying to reset the server when the online card catalog crashed.

"You asked to see me?" she asked as I enjoyed her memory of the library board standing around her desk, demanding to know how she had lost control of the place so quickly. Before I could speak, Mrs. Stubblefield blurted out, "We were hoping you might come back to your position as director of juvenile services. There would be a decrease in pay, of course, and you would have to take on more evening and weekend hours. I would hope that you would take these inconveniences in stride and recognize this offer for the gesture that it is."

In other words, the library board was telling her to give me my job back, but she wanted my tail tucked between my legs when I returned.

I smirked nastily. "I guess that budget issue cleared itself up, hmm?"

I knew it was mean, but I was sure I'd get a free pass on that one. Mrs. Stubblefield made a sound somewhere between a laugh and a sob.

I looked across the hall to the children's department, a room where I had spent the better part of six years. If you'd asked me as I walked into the library that night whether I wanted my old job back, I probably would have said I'd jump at the chance. But it's true what they say about going home again. Everything about the library seemed so foreign to me now, almost cold. I loved the kids, the patrons, but I didn't belong at the library anymore. There was nothing for me there. Plus, I didn't know whether I could handle rooms full of chattering children with my super hearing.

I smiled. "You know what? No, thanks. I'm doing pretty well. Good luck replacing me, though."

"Jane, please be reasonable," Mrs. Stubblefield begged.

"I am being reasonable. I'm not accepting your sad, hobbled excuse for a job offer. The only reason I came here tonight is that I need a signature here," I said, pushing the form toward her.

Her eyes scanned the top of the form, with "Federal Bureau of Undead Affairs" in huge Arial font. Understanding flicked across her features, and she turned roughly the shade of wallpaper paste. The moth eyebrows shot to her hairline and fluttered there indefinitely. She stared at the canines I was allowing to edge over my bottom lip. My eyes traced the slightly varicose veins along her throat, her collarbone.

I slid a blood-red ink pen across the table for her. "Oh, wait, it says it has to be signed in black. Silly me, what was I thinking?" I gave her a wide smile. "Red just seems to be my favorite color lately."

Now fidgeting with the gold cross she wore at her throat, Mrs. Stubblefield signed the paper. She carefully avoided touching any part of the paper where she'd seen my hands.

"Thank you." I let a low, hungry note creep into my voice as I said, "It's so good to see you, Mrs. Stubblefield. I've been thinking about you a lot lately. I think I may have to come by more often."

I stood, refrained from rolling my eyes when Mrs. Stubblefield flinched, and stuck my book on the correct shelf. I reached the door of the special collections room and turned back to my former boss.

"By the way, I've always wanted to tell you. Eyebrows. There should be two."

Mrs. Stubblefield gasped in indignation as I swaggered out. I made a point to be pleasant to Posey as I checked out several volumes on remedial gardening and creating healthy boundaries in adult relationships. (My hope sprang eternal.) And yes, an Aretha Franklin chorus was ringing in my head as I left the building.

"R-E-S-P-E-C-T, find out what it means to me," I hummed. Gabriel was perched on the Veterans Memorial Fountain across the street, dragging his fingers through the burbling water.

"How did you know I would be here?" I asked when I reached him.

"I made a lucky guess," he said. He nodded toward the library. "What were you doing?"

"Having a truly excellent moment in my life," I said, grinning shamelessly. "One of the best ever, to be honest, before and after you came along."

"I don't know how to take that," he said.

"Doesn't feel too good, does it?"

"How are you?" he asked. He pushed my shirt aside and traced his fingertips along the shiny edges of the scar over my collarbone. "Wood wounds take longer to heal. It will be gone in a few days."

"I kind of like it," I said, not bothering to move his hand away. "My very first war wound."

"So, how are you?" he asked again.

"Recovering," I said, meeting his gaze. "Zeb's still a little weirded out. He watched me kill somebody, which was a horrible new experience. Plus, he had semisexual feelings when he watched me wrestle with Missy. I don't know which was more disturbing for him.

"In another milestone in my emotional development, I sent Jolene a bridal planner specifically written for were-brides," I said, adding flatly, "and in exchange, Jolene sent me a catalog of bridesmaid hair accessories."

"I'm very proud of you," Gabriel told me. "And your parents?"

"Not very proud of me right now," I said. "And my sister is suing me."

"I could still talk to them for you," he offered.

"What would you possibly say? 'Sorry I bit your daughter?' They're just going to have to work it out at their own speed," I said. "I think Daddy's going to be OK. In fact, I think he's kind of leaning toward it being cool to have a vampire daughter. He called yesterday, mentioned that he'd like to talk to you."

Gabriel made an "uh-oh" face.

"No, I think he just wants to ask you some questions about your Civil War days. When I told him how old you are, he kind of started drooling." I laughed.

"It's been a long time since I've had a friendly chat with a special lady friend's father," he said, tugging at his shirt collar. "It will be friendly, won't it?"

"Decidedly," I assured him as he slipped his arm around mine. "He likes you. The fact that you're a living record of everything he's ever wanted to know about the history of the Hollow just gives you that much more of an edge."

"And your mother?" he asked.

"Has taken to her bed and is refusing to come out. I think I have been officially written out of my grandmother's will, but really, my name was in pencil, anyway, so it hardly matters.

"I am allowed to be friends with Andrea again, which is nice. Aunt Jettie says hi, by the way, and that she prefers that you wear pants the next time you're in the house."

"I'm sure you'll explain that, at length, at another time," he said, clearly confused. I'd forgotten that he and Aunt Jettie had never been properly introduced.

"My first battle to the death," I said. "How many of those am I going to have? Because they're not fun."

"They're rare," he assured me. "Maybe we could put you in one of those plastic hamster balls for your protection."

"That's two jokes in two nights. You're on a roll."

"I think you're having a bad influence on me," he said solemnly.

"It's nice to return the favor."

"So, is this purely a social visit, or is there news from the council I should be aware of?" I asked, playing with the lapels of his coat.

"You've been cleared in Missy's death," he said. "Cleared in the sense that the council knows you killed her but feels it was justified. Also, they've ruled that you were not involved in Walter's death."

"Does that mean I have to give the *Knight Rider* DVDs back? Because they were kind of destroyed in the fire at Dick's place. Where is Dick staying, anyway?"

"Not with me," Gabriel muttered. "And that is all that matters."

"You are going to have to come to some sort of truce with the guy," I told him. "Now that I know he wasn't involved in a conspiracy to defame and murder me, I consider Dick a friend. And as my . . ." Gabriel's eyes focused on mine as I searched for an appropriate term. Unfortunately, all I came up with was "another important person in my life, I think it's important that the two of you get along. Oh, come on, I'm not asking you to invite him to move in with you."

Gabriel's lips disappeared as he mulled that over. He finally relaxed enough to say, "Ophelia sends her regards. She also said she would like to *not* see you for several months."

"The feeling is mutual," I told him.

"The good news is you can expect a rather large deposit in your accounts soon," he said. "And you'll inherit the land surrounding your property in addition to Missy's other holdings."

"I don't want to know how they know my account numbers, do I?" I asked.

He shook his head.

"I still have a hard time believing this was all about real estate and money," I murmured as I stared up at the purpling sky.

With the weight of an impending murder trial off my shoulders, the world was a beautiful place again. The stars stretched out forever, and anything seemed possible . . . except maybe getting a tan. For the first time in a long time, I felt comfortable in my own skin.

"I kind of hoped that vampires were above petty greed," I said.

He smiled that maddening Buddha smile. "Well, we were all human once."

"Speak for yourself."

Read on for a sneak peek at Molly Harper's
next hilarious romance,

Nice Girls Don't Date Dead Men,

coming in September 2009!

1

~~~~~

With foot and paw planted in the human and animal worlds, were-creatures mix techniques from both cultures to secure relationships. This can lead to lifelong happiness or very confused potential mates.

—From *Mating Rituals and Love Customs of the Were*

"I can't do this."

"Jane."

"It's just wrong," I whimpered. "It defies the laws of nature, the thin line that separates good and evil, right and wrong."

Zeb rolled his eyes and snapped the bridal binder shut. "It's just a dress, Jane."

"It's a puce dress, Zeb."

"Jolene's getting it in peach." He grunted, clearly at his limit in dealing with whiny undead bridal-party members. "Why are you being so difficult?"

"Why is your fiancée insisting that I dress like Naomi from *Mama's Family*?"

"It's not that bad," Zeb insisted.

"Not that bad?" I opened the binder and pinned the offending picture with my finger. The model's defiantly blank expression could not mask her embarrassment at wearing this sateen nightmare. It was off the shoulder, with a wide ruffle of retina-burning material that gathered at the cleavage with a fabric cabbage rose. The traditional butt bow actually connected to what can only be described as a waist lapel.

Despite not having that many girlfriends, somehow I had been a bridesmaid three times. Apparently, I was tall enough to "match" the rest of the bridal party for Marcy, my college roommate from freshman year. And when a cousin of my sophomore roommate, Carrie, had the nerve to get pregnant, I just happened to fit the abandoned nonmaternity bridesmaid's dress. And I'm pretty sure my junior roommate, Lindsay, only asked me because she wanted "plain" bridesmaids. She said something about not wanting to be outshone on her big day.

I was thankful to get a private room my senior year.

My sister, Jenny, never even considered making me a bridesmaid. Ironically, her reason for not asking me—not liking me—resulted in this inadvertent and certainly unintentional kindness.

I'd suffered butt bows. I'd carried those stupid matching shawls that never stayed on past the ceremony. I'd worn Mint Sorbet, Periwinkle Fizz, and Passionate Pomegranate—all of which translated into "hideous $175 dress with shoes dyed to match, neither of which you will wear again."

And now, Jolene McClaine, the betrothed of my best

friend, wanted me to wear the ugliest dress of them all. Jolene and Zeb had met at the local chapter of the Friends and Family of the Undead, where Zeb had sought help after my new undead condition left him even twitchier than usual. It was your basic love story. Boy meets girl. Boy dates girl. Girl turns out to be a werewolf. Boy and girl get engaged and slowly drive me insane.

In a way, I brought the two of them together—which means I had no one to blame for this hoop-skirted fiasco but myself. I knew the whole point of having bridesmaids was dressing them like the walking dead so you would look better by comparison. But this was beyond the pale. I'd be lucky if angry villagers didn't pelt me with rotten produce.

"This is why I wanted to go shopping with you!" I cried, flopping back on the couch with the boneless petulance of a teenage orthodontia patient.

"Well, the Bridal Barn closes at about three hours before sunset, Jane. So, unless you're willing to risk bursting into flame just to exercise your control issues over a stupid dress, I think we're out of options."

"Hmmph."

I hadn't been a vampire for very long, so sometimes I forgot about the limitations of my condition and the pains Zeb took to avoid throwing said limitations in my face. It didn't mean I was going to wear that monstrosity of a dress, but I would at least stop giving Zeb a hard time. I had developed a nasty habit of needling Zeb since he'd started planning his wedding. Zeb had been my best friend since . . . well, forever. I was used to having his undivided attention. Of course, he was used to me breathing and eating solid foods. We'd both had to make adjustments. He was just much better at them.

It seemed doubly cruel to pick on Zeb now. While some members of Jolene's family were thrilled that she was marrying a nice guy with a stable income and his own home, there were two uncles who declared the union "clan shame"—the werewolf version of a *shandeh*. Uncle Luke and Uncle Gerald, plus a cousin named Vance, who had what could only be deemed unnatural feelings for Jolene, were doing everything in their power to stop the wedding.

In a werewolf pack, you cannot interfere with the mate choice of a clan fellow. You cannot intentionally harm that werewolf's chosen mate. You are not, however, required to help that person should they find themselves in a life-threatening situation. Somehow, Zeb had managed to stumble into several such situations in the few months he'd been engaged to Jolene. He'd had several hunting "accidents" while visiting the McClaine farm— even though he didn't hunt. The brakes on his car had failed while he was driving home from the farm—twice. Also, a running chainsaw mysteriously fell on him from a hay loft.

He would never get that pinkie toe back.

Jolene insisted that her relatives were just being playful. I insisted that Zeb not venture out to the McClaine farm without a vampire escort, which certainly hadn't improved his stance with the future in-laws. Despite the grudging acceptance they offered Zeb, most of the clan was distrustful of vampires. Some, in fact, wore vampire fangs around their necks, next to the gold-plated charms that spelled out their names.

On the other side of the aisle were Zeb's parents, Ginger and Floyd, and they weren't exactly thrilled about the wedding, either. Mama Ginger had been planning my wedding to her son since we were kids. Apparently, the image of Zeb coming home to my pretend kitchen carrying a briefcase made of newspaper was permanently burned into her cortex. She figured that having known me since I was six and seen multiple examples of my being firmly planted under my own mama's thumb, I was the only acceptable candidate for a potential daughter-in-law. For my last living Christmas, she had given me a Precious Moments wedding planner with my and Zeb's names already filled in.

Mama Ginger saw the world as it should be, according to Mama Ginger. And when something didn't conform to that vision, she went to drastic lengths to correct it. I didn't know what made her think she had the right. It may have had something to do with all the chemicals she inhaled at her not-quite-licensed kitchen beauty shop. Just to give you an example, Mama Ginger could not fathom that I would go to senior prom with anyone but Zeb, so she told several of the mothers at her salon that I was being treated for a suspicious rash. This fixed it so no boy at our high school would go anywhere near me with a corsage. With no other eleventh-hour options, Zeb and I ended up going together. Mama Ginger kept the pictures in a place of honor on her mantel.

At least, she did, until an unfortunate incident in which she gave me TV evangelist hair. When I disdained Mama Ginger's professional integrity by going to Super-Cuts, she decided that her favorite new hair client would make a much better daughter-in-law. Mama Ginger even gave the poor girl my spot on the family's annual run to the mega-flea market in Nashville. I didn't mind so much.

As Mama Ginger couldn't have her say in choosing the bride, she'd decided to make planning the wedding as unpleasant as possible. She'd objected to the wedding date, saying it conflicted with her bingo night. Every plan Jolene had was dismissed as alternately "trashy" or "too high-falutin'." Mama Ginger was also incredibly insulted when Jolene politely refused the Precious Moments bride-and-groom cake topper she'd saved for Zeb's wedding. Precious Moments. *Gah.* I could rip a man's spinal column out through his nose, and I still found those things frightening.

Zeb's father, Floyd, had expressed little interest in the wedding after he found out there wouldn't be a Velveeta fountain or access to the scheduled UK game.

So, the reception was going to be fun. As much fun as one could have while dressed as Satan's tea cozy.

The Naomi Harper bridesmaids' dresses were a concession to the McClaine family tradition of renting formal wear from Jolene's aunt Vonnie's dress shop, the Bridal Barn. Vonnie made all of the dresses herself, using three patterns, all of which ended up looking like a Butterick circa 1982, called "Ruffles and Dreams."

"I know, Janie, I know it's ugly," Zeb said, his big doe eyes all guileless and earnest. Dang it, I always buckled under the baby browns. "It is the world's ugliest dress. Of all the dresses you will ever wear, this is the one your body may reject like a faulty organ. As soon as I get back from the honeymoon, I will help you build the bonfire to burn this dress. But I'm asking you as my closest friend in the entire world, will you please just wear the stupid dress for one day? Without whining? Or describing it? Or making Jolene feel bad? Or pissing off Jolene's cousins?"

"Any more conditions?" I asked, my brow arched.

"I reserve the right to make addendums," he said.

Engagement had changed Zeb. He was more aggressive, more mature, partly from defending himself in life-threatening situations. Unfortunately, he was being more aggressive and mature with me, which sucked.

"What kind of kindergarten teacher talks like that?" I asked.

"What kind of children's librarian takes a job at an occult bookstore?"

"Vampire." I pointed to my chest. "And I'm not a librarian anymore. When they fire you, they kind of take the label, too."

Zeb's smile thinned as he blinked owlishly and pressed his fingers to his temples. He took a pill bottle out of his pocket.

"You OK?"

"Yeah." He sighed. "I've just been getting these headaches lately."

My pessimistic brain flashed on possibilities like clots and tumors. Batting down small flares of panic, I asked, "Have you seen a doctor?"

"Yeah, he said they're probably stress-related."

I poked a finger at the wedding binder. "I can't imagine."

"Wedding planning is stressful, even when you're not marrying into a family with mouths full of fangs aimed at you," Zeb muttered as he dry-swallowed two Tylenol. "On a brighter note, where's your ghostly roommate?"

"Out," I said of my great-aunt Jettie, who had died about six months before I was turned and had been pleasantly haunting me ever since. "With my grandpa Fred again. They're becoming quite the hot and heavy couple."

"I didn't realize ghosts roamed around so much," he said. "Where do they go?"

"As long as it keeps me from seeing two deceased old people from getting all touchy on my couch, I do not care."

He grinned. "That's so gross."

"Tell me about it." I grimaced. "I'm working extra shifts at the bookstore, unpaid, just to get out of the house. I keep walking into rooms and finding them . . . *guuuuh*. And speaking of the store, we need to table the dress negotiations for now. My shift starts in about an hour. We're expecting some ancient Babylonian scrolls that Mr. Wainwright found on eBay, so he's really excited. He thinks they may have been used in a summoning rite."

"So, you purchased ancient Babylonian texts, which

may or may not call forth Gozer the Destroyer, on eBay?" Zeb asked. He cocked his head and gave a goofy grin. "You know, a year ago, I would have thought you were kidding."

I shrugged, pushing the dreaded bridesmaid's dress photo from my considerable field of vision. "And yet . . ."

I scooped up the ringing phone, knowing before I pressed it to my ear that it would be my mother. I didn't use my spiffy new mind-reading powers or anything. Mama called every night before my shift to make sure I was careful on the three-step walk from my car to the bookstore. She tended to "forget" that I now had super strength and could twist any prospective mugger into a pretzel.

Mama had responded to my coming out as a vampire with the traditional stages of grief. She just got stuck at denial. She had decided to ignore it completely and pretend it away. She brought two frozen pot pies over to my house each week to "help me out with meals," which was handy, because I needed something around to feed the ever-ravenous Jolene. Mama dropped by during the day, then got upset when the vampire "sleepy-time" instinct kept me from chatting. It was as if she thought I could change my mind about being a vampire and give back my membership card.

"I have some bad news, honey," Mama said as I picked up the phone. She'd long since parted with the niceties of phone greetings. After a dramatic pause, she said, "Grandpa Bob passed last night."

"Awww," I moaned. "Another one?"

This may seem like a strange, even cold, reaction. But you have to understand my grandma Ruthie's marital history. She'd been widowed four times, via milk truck, anaphylactic shock, spider bite, and lightning strike (the lamented, aforementioned Grandpa Fred). I wrote a poem titled "Grandpa's in an Urn" in fifth grade. I had to spend a lot of time in the guidance counselor's office after that.

I loved Bob. Despite not being my actual grandpa or even a step-grandpa yet, Bob had always been nice to me. But he was engaged to Grandma Ruthie for five years and had chronic conditions of the heart, lungs, and liver. He had survived longer than expected.

"Your grandmother says there was some sort of mix-up with his medication." Mama sighed. I could practically hear the cap from her own "nerve pills" rattling loose.

Knowing this would take a while, Zeb got out my blender to begin another batch of experimental "Jane shakes." He'd been trying to find a way to make my synthetic blood more palatable with a combination of herbs, condiments, and dessert toppings. My current favorite was Faux Type O mixed with a little bit of cherry syrup and a lot of Hershey's new Blood Additive Chocolate Syrup: "The pleasant sensation of chocolate without the unpleasant undead side effects!" That was an excellent selling point considering those side effects were the vomiting and agony that came with vampires trying to digest solid foods.

Mama's voice trembled under the weight of Grandma

Ruthie's expectations. "I don't know what I'm going to do. Grandma seems to think we should be hosting the funeral as the next of kin. Bob's children are having a fit. She's already made a scene down at Whitlow's Funeral Home over the release of the body. And now she expects me to help her plan the visitation, the buffet, the service—"

"The full Ruthie Early-Lange-Bodeen-Floss-Whitaker special?" I asked.

"I wish you would stop calling it that," Mama huffed.

"She's held the same funeral service for four husbands. I'll call it what I want." I snorted.

"Jane, I'm really going to need your help with this," Mama said, the faintest wheedling tone creeping into her voice.

"Why can't Jenny help you with this?"

"Jenny's busy with the Charity League Follies, and she's serving as chairwoman of the Women's Club Winter Ball this year." Mama was in a full-blown whine now.

"But good old Jane doesn't have a life, right? So, why not make her chairwoman of the funeral luncheon?"

"Don't start that, Jane," Mama warned. "If you would just talk to Jenny and work out this silly business, you could both help me."

"I think it ceased being silly business when I was deposed," I told her.

Jenny had made good on her promise not to talk to me after I came out to my family. She had, however, sent me a lovely note through the law firm of Hapscombe and Schmidt, stating that Jenny wanted access to the family Bible. The Bible, which contained all of the Early genealogical information, had been willed to me through our great-aunt Jettie as part of the contents of our ancestral home, River Oaks. Jenny's lawyers had stated that as a vampire, I could not touch it and had no use for it. I'd had the local offices of the ACLU and the World Council for the Equal Treatment of the Undead send her a cease-and-desist letter stating that such statements were inflammatory and untrue. She'd responded by sending me a copy of the family tree she'd painstakingly calligraphed onto parchment, with my name burned out with a soldering iron. An ugly flurry of legal correspondence followed, and I ended up drinking Thanksgiving "dinner" with my parents after the rest of my family went home.

"Now, don't expect me to take sides," Mama said. "You girls are going to have to work this out yourselves."

"Most of the funeral stuff is going to be done during daylight hours," I said. "I'm a vampire. I'm not even going to be able to attend the burial."

"But you have all the time in the world to plan Zeb's wedding," Mama grumbled. She always got a little cranky when I brought up the "v word." "Where's the happy couple registered? The Dollar Store?"

"First of all . . . that was really funny," I whispered, glad that Zeb had ducked into the walk-in pantry and hadn't heard it. "But it was a mean thing to say. I'm the only one allowed to make mean jokes about Jolene's family, as I am the one wearing the ugliest dress in the history of bridesmaid-kind."

"What color is it?" Mama demanded. "It's not yellow, is it? Because you know yellow makes you look sallow."

"Mama, focus, please. I will help with the prep work for Bob's funeral as much as I can, during the evening, when I can fit it in around work hours. But I can't do much."

"That's all I'm asking for, honey, a little effort," she said, placated.

"As little as possible," I assured her. "How is Grandma doing?" I asked, trying not to let the resentment in my voice bubble through the phone line. "Should I stop by her house on the way to work?"

"Um, no," Mama said in a sad attempt to be vague. "There's going to be such a crowd there . . ."

"And it would be a shame for me to come by and make things awkward," I finished for her. The heavy silence on Mama's end said I was right, but Mama preferred not to put it into words.

I don't know why Grandma's rejection of me still stung. Elderly relatives were supposed to give you lip-sticky kisses and ask intrusive questions about your love life. They were supposed to brag about your achievements to the point where nonrelatives wanted to gouge their eardrums at the mere mention of your name. They were not supposed to request at least one week's advance notice if you attended family gatherings or insist on wearing a cross the size of a hubcap whenever you walked into a room. My only consolation was that Grandma looked like Flava Flav and usually tipped over under the weight of her bling.

Eager to get back to a subject she could control, Mama listed the dishes she expected me to prepare to perk up the usual funeral pot-luck offerings. Apparently, there was some sort of dessert involving Jell-O, cream cheese, and mandarin oranges in my future. While I saw it as completely unfair that someone who didn't eat should have to cook, these arguments failed to impress Mama. I promised to come by for my assigned shopping list after dark.

"How are things going with that Gabriel?" Mama asked. Mama was happy I was dating someone, particularly someone who literally came from one of the oldest families in town. But she was pretending that Gabriel wasn't a vampire, either. I could only expect so much. "Have you seen him lately?"

"Not for a week or so. He had to go to Nashville for business."

On the other end of the line, Mama sighed. Dang it. I had just extended the conversation by about twenty minutes. Ever since I'd established a semi-sort-of-relationship with Gabriel, Mama's favorite activity had been giving me relationship advice. I thought she saw it as a girlie bonding thing. "Honey, what have I always told you?"

Now, honestly, that could be any number of things, ranging from "Avoid contact with any surface in a public bathroom" to "Men don't buy the cow when you hand them the keys to the dairy." So I took a shot in the dark.

"Um, never trust a man with two first names," I guessed.

"Well, yes, but not what I had in mind."

"Never trust a man with a remote-control fireplace?" I suggested.

"No," she said, her patience audibly thinning.

"Never trust a—"

"Honey." I could almost hear Mama shaking her head in dismay at my lack of man-savvy. "Relationships are fifty-fifty, give and take. You have to make an effort. He's up there all by himself for a whole week. Why couldn't you go up to visit him?"

"I have to work. And isn't that kind of desperate?"

"There's nothing wrong with showing a little interest. You could make a little more of an effort. I could have Sheila take a look at your hair—"

"Mama, I really need to get off the phone if I'm going to make it to work on time," I said. "And Zeb's over here, and we're trying to talk about bridesmaid stuff. I've really got to go."

"Don't let them put you in yellow. You know how washed-out you look in yellow!" Mama was saying as I put the receiver in its cradle.

"Someone has to lock my grandma up. She's single-handedly taking down the Greatest Generation," I moaned.

Zeb smirked at me as I slumped down and smacked my head against the counter. In a granite-muffled voice, I told him, "Shut it, or I'm calling your mama and telling her that your parents' names aren't on the invitations. That'll keep you tied up for months."

"That seems uncalled for," he muttered.